# James Grippando

# BEYOND SUSPICION

HarperTorch
*An Imprint of HarperCollinsPublishers*

This is a work of fiction. Names, characters, places, and incidents are products of the author's imagination or are used fictitiously and are not to be construed as real. Any resemblance to actual events, locales, organizations, or persons, living or dead, is entirely coincidental.

❦

HARPERTORCH
*An Imprint of* HarperCollins*Publishers*
10 East 53rd Street
New York, New York 10022-5299

Copyright © 2002 by James Grippando
Excerpt from *Last to Die* copyright © 2003 by James Grippando
ISBN: 0-06-000554-8

First HarperTorch paperback printing: July 2003
First HarperCollins hardcover printing: September 2002
First HarperCollins special printing: September 2002

HarperCollins®, HarperTorch™, and ❦ ™ are trademarks of HarperCollins Publishers Inc.

Printed in the United States of America

Visit HarperTorch on the World Wide Web at www.harpercollins.com

10  9  8  7  6  5  4  3  2

*To Tiffany, always.*
*And forever.*

# Acknowledgments

•

*Beyond Suspicion* is a sequel to my first published novel, *The Pardon*. That first Jack Swyteck story was a true labor of love that came into being only after I'd spent four years, nights and weekends, writing a big, fat, multigenerational murder mystery that now collects dust on a closet shelf. Six novels later, I have to say that the best part about returning to my debut was the time spent reflecting on a point in my life when I didn't have time to start writing until eleven o'clock at night, and when I wouldn't stop pecking away until long after Tiffany had fallen asleep on the couch with the latest draft pages spilled at her side. Thanks, Tiff, for being there when it all began, and thanks for putting up with me all these years later.

A big thank-you goes to my editor, Carolyn Marino, and my agent, Richard Pine. Both were early fans of *The Pardon*, and both have left their mark on *Beyond Suspicion*. I'm also grateful to my team of first readers who endured some very rough drafts, Dr. Gloria M.

Grippando, Cece Sanford, Eleanor Rayner, and Carlos Sires. Probate attorney Clay Craig lent his usual expertise, Patrick Battle and Joseph N. Belth provided insights on viatical settlements, and the World Federation of Neurology offered a wealth of information on amyotrophic lateral sclerosis.

The people who helped most with my research wish to remain anonymous, which is perfectly understandable in the case of cops who work undercover. Their insights into the growth of Russian organized crime in South Florida were invaluable.

Finally, character names are often a pain to come up with, so I want to thank Mike Campbell and Jerry Chafetz for making my job easier. Through their generous contributions at fund-raising auctions for the benefit of St. Thomas Episcopal Parish School in Coral Gables and for The Gold-Diggers Inc. of Miami, they have lent their names to two of Jack Swyteck's buddies in *Beyond Suspicion*.

# BEYOND
# SUSPICION

# 1
## .

Outside her bedroom window, the blanket of fallen leaves moved—one footstep at a time.

Cindy Swyteck lay quietly in her bed, her sleeping husband at her side. It was a dark winter night, cold by Miami standards. In a city where forty degrees was considered frigid, no more than once or twice a year could she light the fireplace and snuggle up to Jack beneath a fluffy down comforter. She slid closer to his body, drawn by his warmth. A gusty north wind rattled the window, the shrill sound alone conveying a chill. The whistle became a howl, but the steady crunching of leaves was still discernible, the unmistakable sound of an approaching stranger.

Flashing images in her head offered a clear view of the lawn, the patio, and the huge almond leaves scattered all about. She could see the path he'd cut through the leaves. It led straight to her window.

Five years had passed since she'd last laid eyes on her attacker. Everyone from her husband to the police had assured her he was dead, though she knew he'd never really be gone. On nights like these, she could have sworn he was back, in the flesh. His name was Esteban.

Five years, and the horrifying details were still burned into her memory. His calloused hands and jagged nails so rough against her skin. The stale puffs of rum that came with each nauseating breath in her face. The cold, steel blade pressing at her jugular. Even then, she'd refused to kiss him back. Most unforgettable of all were those empty, sharklike eyes—eyes so cold and angry that when he'd opened his disgusting mouth and bit her on the lips she saw her own reflection, witnessed her own terror, in the shiny black irises.

Five years, and those haunting eyes still followed her everywhere, watching her every move. Not even her counselors seemed to understand what she was going through. It was as if the eyes of Esteban had become her second line of sight. When night fell and the wind howled, she could easily slip into the mind of her attacker and see things he'd seen before his own violent death. Stranger still, she seemed to have a window to the things he might be seeing now. Through his eyes, she could even watch herself. Night after night, she had the perfect view of Cindy Swyteck lying in bed, struggling in vain with her incurable fear of the dark.

Outside, the scuffling noise stopped. The wind and leaves were momentarily silent. The digital alarm clock on the nightstand blinked on and off, the way it always did when storms interrupted power. It was stuck on midnight, bathing her pillow with faint pulses of green light.

She heard a knock at the back door. On impulse, she rose and sat at the edge of the bed.

*Don't go,* she told herself, but it was as if she were being summoned.

Another knock followed, exactly like the first one. On the other side of the king-sized bed, Jack was sleeping soundly. She didn't even consider waking him.

*I'll get it.*

Cindy saw herself rise from the mattress and plant her bare feet on the tile floor. Each step felt colder as she continued down the hall and through the kitchen. The house was completely dark, and she relied more on instinct than sight to maneuver her way to the back door. She was sure she'd turned off the outside lights at bedtime, but the yellow porch light was burning. Something had obviously triggered the electronic eye of the motion detector. She inched closer to the door, peered out the little diamond-shaped window, and let her eyes roam from one edge of the backyard to the other. A gust of wind ripped through the big almond tree, tearing the brownest leaves from the branches. They fell to the ground like giant snowflakes, but a few were caught in an upward draft and rose into the night, just beyond the faint glow of the porch light. Cindy lost sight of them, except for one that seemed to hover above the patio. Another blast of wind sent it soaring upward. Then it suddenly changed direction, came straight toward her, and slammed against the door.

The noise startled her, but she didn't back away. She kept looking out the window, as if searching for whatever it was that had sent that lone leaf streaking toward her with so much force. She saw nothing, but in her heart she knew that she was mistaken. Something was definitely out there. She just couldn't see it. Or maybe it was Esteban who couldn't see it.

*Stop using* his *eyes!*

The door swung open. A burst of cold air hit her like an Arctic front. Goose bumps covered her arms and legs. Her silk nightgown shifted in the breeze, rising to midthigh. She somehow knew that she was colder than ever before in her life, though she didn't really feel it. She didn't feel anything. A numbness had washed over her, and though her mind told her to run, her feet wouldn't move. It was suddenly impossible to gauge the passage of time, but in no more than a few moments was she strangely at ease with the silhouette in the doorway.

"Daddy?"

"Hi, sweetheart."

"What are you doing here?"

"It's Tuesday."

"So?"

"Is Jack here?"

"He's sleeping."

"Wake him."

"For what?"

"It's our night to play poker."

"Jack can't play cards with you tonight."

"We play every Tuesday."

"I'm sorry, Daddy. Jack can't play with you anymore."

"Why not?"

"Because you're dead."

With a shrill scream she sat bolt upright in bed. Confused and frightened, she was shivering uncontrollably. A hand caressed her cheek, and she screamed again.

"It's okay," said Jack. He moved closer and tried putting his arms around her.

She pushed him away. "No!"

"It's okay, it's me."

Her heart was pounding, and she was barely able to catch her breath. A lone tear ran down her face. She wiped it away with the back of her hand. It felt as cold as ice water.

"Take a deep breath," said Jack. "Slowly, in and out."

She inhaled, then exhaled, repeating the exercise several times. In a minute or so, the panic subsided and her breathing became less erratic. Jack's touch felt soothing now, and she nestled into his embrace.

He sat up beside her and wrapped his arms around her. "Was it that dream again?"

She nodded.

"The one about your father?"

"Yes."

She was staring into the darkness, not even aware that Jack was gently brushing her hair out of her face. "He's been gone so long. Why am I having these dreams now?"

"Don't let it scare you. There's nothing to be afraid of."

"I know."

She laid her head against his shoulder. Jack surely meant well, but he couldn't possibly understand what truly frightened her. She'd never told him the most disturbing part. What good was there in knowing that her father was coming back—*for him*?

"It's okay," said Jack. "Try to get some sleep."

She met his kiss and then let him go, stroking his forehead as he drifted off to sleep. He was breathing audibly in the darkness, but she still felt utterly alone. She lay with eyes wide open, listening.

She heard that sound again outside her bedroom window, the familiar scuffle of boots cutting through a carpet of dead leaves. Cindy didn't dare close her eyes, didn't even flirt with the idea of sliding back to that place where she'd found the cursed gift of sight. She brought the blanket all the way up to her chin and clutched it for warmth, praying that this time there'd be no knocking at the back door.

In time the noise faded, as if someone were drifting away.

# 2.

Jack Swyteck was in Courtroom 9 of the Miami-Dade courthouse, having a ball. With a decade of experience in criminal courts, both as a prosecutor and a criminal defense lawyer, he didn't take many civil cases. But this one was different. It was a slam-bang winner, the judge had been spitting venom at opposing counsel the entire trial, and Jack's client was an old flame who'd once ripped his heart right out of his chest and stomped that sucker flat.

*Well, two out of three ain't bad.*

"All rise!"

The lunch break was over, and the lawyers and litigants rose as Judge Antonio Garcia approached the bench. The judge glanced their way, as if he couldn't help gathering an eyeful of Jack's client. No surprise there. Jessie Merrill wasn't stunningly beautiful, but she was damn close. She carried herself with a confidence that bespoke intelligence, tempered by intermittent moments of apparent vulnerability that made her simply irresistible to the knuckle-dragging, testosterone-toting half of the population. Judge Garcia was as susceptible as the next guy. Beneath that flowing black robe was, after all, a mere mortal—a man. That aside, Jessie truly was a victim in this case, and it was impossible not to feel sorry for her.

"Good afternoon," said the judge.

"Good afternoon," the lawyers replied, though the judge's nose was buried in paperwork. Rather than immediately call in the jury, it was Judge Garcia's custom to mount the bench and then take a few minutes to read his mail or finish the crossword puzzle—his way of announcing to all who entered his courtroom that he alone had that rare and special power to silence attorneys and make them sit and wait. Judicial power plays of all sorts seemed to be on the rise in Miami courtrooms, ever since hometown hero Marilyn Milian gave up her day job to star on *The People's Court*. Not every south Florida judge wanted to trace her steps to television stardom, but at least one wannabe in criminal court could no longer mete out sentences to convicted murderers without adding, "You *are* the weakest link, good-bye."

Jack glanced to his left and noticed his client's hand shaking. It stopped the moment she'd caught him looking. Typical Jessie, never wanting anyone to know she was nervous.

"We're almost home," Jack whispered.

She gave him a tight smile.

Before this case, it had been a good six years since Jack had seen her. Five months after dumping him, Jessie had called for lunch with the hope of giving it another try. By then Jack was well on his way toward falling hopelessly in love with Cindy Paige, now Mrs. Jack

Swyteck, something he never called her unless he wanted to be introduced at their next cocktail party as Mr. Cindy Paige. Cindy was more beautiful today than she was then, and Jack had to admit the same was true of Jessie. That, of course, was no reason to take her case. But he decided it wasn't a reason to turn it down, either. This had nothing to do with the fact that her long, auburn hair had once splayed across both their pillows. She'd come to him as an old friend in a genuine crisis. Even six months later, her words still echoed in the back of his mind.

•

"The doctor told me I have two years to live. Three, tops."

Jack's mouth fell open, but words came slowly. "Damn, Jessie. I'm so sorry."

She seemed on the verge of tears. He scrambled to find her a tissue. She dug one of her own from her purse. "It's so hard for me to talk about this."

"I understand."

"I was so damn unprepared for that kind of news."

"Who wouldn't be?"

"I take care of myself. I always have."

"It shows." It wasn't intended as a come-on, just a statement of fact that underscored what a waste this was.

"My first thought was, you're crazy, doc. This can't be."

"Of course."

"I mean, I've never faced anything that I couldn't beat. Then suddenly I'm in the office of some doctor who's basically telling me, that's it, game over. No one bothered to tell me the game had even started."

He could hear the anger in her voice. "I'd be mad, too."

"I was furious. And scared. Especially when he told me what I had."

Jack didn't ask. He figured she'd tell him if she wanted him to know.

"He said I had ALS—amyotrophic lateral sclerosis."

"I'm not familiar with that one."

"You probably know it as Lou Gehrig's disease."

"Oh." It was a more ominous-sounding "oh" than intended. She immediately picked up on it.

"So, you know what a horrible illness it is."

"Just from what I heard happened to Lou Gehrig."

"Imagine how it feels to hear that it's going to happen to you. Your mind stays healthy, but your nervous system slowly dies, causing you to lose control of your own body. Eventually you can't swallow anymore, your throat muscles fail, and you either suffocate or choke to death on your own tongue."

She was looking straight at him, but he was the one to blink.

"It's always fatal," she added. "Usually in two to five years."

He wasn't sure what to say. The silence was getting uncomfortable. "I don't know how I can help, but if there's anything I can do, just name it."

"There is."

"Please, don't be afraid to ask."

"I'm being sued."

"For what?"

"A million and a half dollars."

He did a double take. "That's a lot of money."

"It's all the money I have in the world."

"Funny. There was a time when you and I would have thought that *was* all the money in the world."

Her smile was more sad than wistful. "Things change."

"They sure do."

A silence fell between them, a moment to reminisce.

"Anyway, here's my problem. My *legal* problem. I tried to be responsible about my illness. The first thing I did was get my finances in order. Treatment's expensive, and I wanted to do something extravagant for myself in the time I had left. Maybe a trip to Europe, whatever. I didn't have a lot of money, but I did have a three-million-dollar life insurance policy."

"Why so much?"

"When the stock market tanked a couple years ago, a financial planner talked me into believing that whole-life insurance was a good retirement vehicle. Maybe it would have been worth something by the time I reached sixty-five. But at my age, the cash surrender value is practically zilch. Obviously, the death benefit wouldn't kick in until I was dead, which wouldn't do *me* any good. I wanted a pot of money while I was alive and well enough to enjoy myself."

Jack nodded, seeing where this was headed. "You did a viatical settlement?"

"You've heard of them?"

"I had a friend with AIDS who did one before he died."

"That's how they got popular, back in the eighties. But the concept works with any terminal disease."

"Is it a done deal?"

"Yes. It sounded like a win-win situation. I sell my three-million-dollar policy to a group of investors for a million and a half dollars. I get a big check right now, when I can use it. They get the three-million-dollar death benefit when I die. They'd basically double their money in two or three years."

"It's a little ghoulish, but I can see the good in it."

"Absolutely. Everybody was satisfied." The sorrow seemed to drain from her expression as she looked at him and said, "Until my symptoms started to disappear."

"Disappear?"

"Yeah. I started getting better."

"But there's no cure for ALS."

"The doctor ran more tests."

Jack saw a glimmer in her eye. His heart beat faster. "And?"

"They finally figured out I had lead poisoning. It can mimic the symptoms of ALS, but it wasn't nearly enough to kill me."

"You don't have Lou Gehrig's disease?"

"No."

"You're not going to die?"

"I'm completely recovered."

A sense of joy washed over him, though he did feel a little manipulated. "Thank God. But why didn't you tell me from the get-go?"

She smiled wryly, then turned serious. "I thought you should know how I felt, even if it was just for a few minutes. This sense of being on the fast track to such an awful death."

"It worked."

"Good. Because I have quite a battle on my hands, legally speaking."

"You want to sue the quack who got the diagnosis wrong?"

"Like I said, at the moment, I'm the one being sued over this."

"The viatical investors?"

"You got it. They thought they were coming into

three million in at most three years. Turns out they may have to wait another forty or fifty years for their investment to 'mature,' so to speak. They want their million and a half bucks back."

"Them's the breaks."

She smiled. "So you'll take the case?"

"You bet I will."

•

The crack of the gavel stirred Jack from his thoughts. The jury had returned. Judge Garcia had finished perusing his mail, the sports section, or whatever else had caught his attention. Court was back in session.

"Mr. Swyteck, any questions for Dr. Herna?"

Jack glanced toward the witness stand. Dr. Herna was the physician who'd reviewed Jessie's medical history on behalf of the viatical investors and essentially confirmed the misdiagnosis, giving them the green light to invest. He and the investors' lawyer had spent the entire morning trying to convince the jury that, because Jessie didn't actually have ALS, the viatical settlement should be invalidated on the basis of a "mutual mistake." It was Jack's job to prove it was *their* mistake, nothing mutual about it, too bad, so sad.

Jack could hardly wait.

"Yes, Your Honor," he said as he approached the witness with a thin, confident smile. "I promise, this won't take long."

# 3.

The courtroom was silent. It was the pivotal moment in the trial, Jack's cross-examination of the plaintiff's star witness. The jury looked on attentively—whites, blacks, Hispanics, a cross section of Miami. Jack often thought that anyone who wondered if an ethnically diverse community could possibly work together should serve on a jury. The case of *Viatical Solutions, Inc. v. Jessie Merrill* was like dozens of other trials underway in Miami at that very moment—no media, no protestors, no circus ringmaster. Not once in the course of the trial had he been forced to drop a book to the floor or cough his lungs out to wake the jurors. It was quietly reassuring to know that the administration of justice in Florida wasn't always the joke people saw on television.

Reassuring for Jack, anyway. Staring out from the witness stand, Dr. Felix Herna looked anything but calm. Jack's opposing counsel seemed to sense the doctor's anxiety. Parker Aimes was a savvy enough plaintiffs' attorney to sprint to his feet and do something about it.

"Judge, could we have a five-minute break, please?"

"We just got back from lunch," he said, snarling.

"I know, but—"

"But nothing," the judge said, peering out over the top of his wire-rimmed reading glasses. "Counselor, I just checked my horoscope, and it says there's loads of leisure time in my near future. So, Mr. Swyteck, if you please."

With the judge talking astrology, Jack was beginning to rethink his reavowed faith in the justice system. "Thank you, Your Honor."

All eyes of the jurors followed him as he approached the witness. He planted himself firmly, using his height and body language to convey a trial lawyer's greatest tool: control.

"Dr. Herna, you'll agree with me that ALS is a serious disease, won't you?"

The witness shifted in his seat, as if distrustful of even the most innocuous question. "Of course."

"It attacks the nervous system, breaks down the tissues, kills the motor neurons?"

"That's correct."

"Victims eventually lose the ability to control their legs?"

"Yes."

"Their hands and arms as well?"

"Yes."

"Their abdominal muscles?"

"That's correct, yes. It destroys the neurons that control the body's voluntary muscles. Muscles controlled by conscious thought."

"Speech becomes unclear? Eating and swallowing becomes difficult?"

"Yes."

"Breathing may become impossible?"

"It does affect the tongue and pharyngeal muscles. Eventually, all victims must choose between prolonging their life on a ventilator or asphyxiation."

"Suffocation," said Jack. "Not a very pleasant way to die."

"Death is rarely pleasant, Mr. Swyteck."

"Unless you're a viatical investor."

"Objection."

"Sustained."

A juror nodded with agreement. Jack moved on, knowing he'd tweaked the opposition. "Is it fair to say that once ALS starts, there's no way to stop it?"

"Miracles may happen, but the basic assumption in the medical community is that the disease is fatal, its progression relentless. Fifty percent of people die within two years. Eighty percent within five."

"Sounds like an ideal scenario for a viatical settlement."

"Objection."

"I'll rephrase it. True or false, Doctor: The basic assumption of viatical investors is that the patient will die soon."

He looked at Jack as if the question were ridiculous. "Of course that's true. That's how they make their money."

"You'd agree, then, that a proper diagnosis is a key component of the investment decision?"

"True again."

"That's why the investors hired you, isn't it? They relied on *you* to confirm that Ms. Merrill had ALS."

"They hired me to review her doctor's diagnosis."

"How many times did you physically examine her?"

"None."

"How many times did you meet with her?"

"None."

"How many times did you speak with her?"

"None," he said, his tone defensive. "You're making this sound worse than it really was. The reviewing physician in a viatical settlement rarely if ever reexamines the patient. It was my job to review Ms. Merrill's medical history as presented to me by her treating physician. I then made a determination as to whether the diagnosis was based on sound medical judgment."

"So, you were fully aware that Dr. Marsh's diagnosis was 'clinically possible ALS.' "

"Yes."

"*Possible* ALS," Jack repeated, making sure the judge and jury caught it. "Which means that it could possibly have been something else."

"Her symptoms, though minor, were entirely consistent with the early stages of the disease."

"But the very diagnosis—possible ALS—made it clear that it could've been something other than ALS. And you knew that."

"You have to understand that there's no magic bullet, no single test to determine whether a patient has ALS. The diagnosis is in many ways a process of elimination. A series of tests are run over a period of months to rule out other possible illnesses. In the early stages, a seemingly healthy woman like Jessie Merrill could have ALS and have no idea that anything's seriously wrong with her body, apart from the fact that maybe her foot falls asleep, or she fumbles with her car keys, or is having difficulty swallowing."

"You're not suggesting that your investors plunked down a million and a half dollars based solely on the fact that Ms. Merrill was dropping her car keys."

"No."

"In fact, your investors rejected the investment proposal at first, didn't they?"

"An investment based on a diagnosis of clinically possible ALS was deemed too risky."

"They decided to invest only *after* you spoke with Dr. Marsh, correct?"

"I did speak with him."

"Would you share with the court Dr. Marsh's exact words, please?"

The judge looked up, his interest sufficiently piqued. Dr. Herna shifted his weight again, obviously reluctant.

"Let me say at the outset that Dr. Marsh is one of the most respected neurologists in Florida. I knew that his diagnosis of clinically possible ALS was based upon strict adherence to the diagnostic criteria established by the World Federation of Neurology. But I also knew that he was an experienced physician who had seen more cases of ALS than just about any other doctor in Miami. So I asked him to put the strict criteria aside. I asked him to talk to me straight but off the record: Did he think Jessie Merrill had ALS?"

"I'll ask the question again: What did Dr. Marsh tell you?"

Herna looked at his lawyer, then at Jack. He lowered his eyes and said, "He told me that if he were a betting man, he'd bet on ALS."

"As it turns out, Ms. Merrill didn't have ALS, did she?"

"Obviously not. Dr. Marsh was dead wrong."

"Excuse me, doctor. He wasn't wrong. Dr. Marsh's diagnosis was clinically *possible* ALS. You knew that he was still monitoring the patient, still conducting tests."

"I also know what he told me. He told me to bet on ALS."

"Only after you pushed him to speculate prematurely."

"As a colleague with the utmost respect for the man, I asked for his honest opinion."

"You urged him to *guess*. You pushed for an answer because Ms. Merrill was a tempting investment opportunity."

"That's not true."

"You were afraid that if you waited for a conclusive diagnosis, she'd be snatched up by another group of viatical investors."

"All I know is that Dr. Marsh said he'd bet on ALS. That was good enough for me."

Jack moved closer, tightening his figurative grip. "It wasn't Ms. Merrill who made the wrong diagnosis, was it?"

"No."

"As far as she knew, a horrible death was just two or three years away."

"I don't know what she was thinking."

"Yes, you do," Jack said sharply. "When you reviewed her medical file and coughed up a million and a half dollars to buy her life insurance policy, you became her second opinion. You convinced her that she was going to die."

Dr. Herna fell stone silent, as if suddenly he realized the grief he'd caused her—as if finally he understood Jack's animosity.

Jack continued, "Ms. Merrill never told you she had a confirmed case of ALS, did she?"

"No."

"She never guaranteed you that she'd die in two years."

"No."

"All she did was give you her medical records."

"That's all I saw."

"And you made a professional judgment as to whether she was going to live or die."

"I did."

"And you bet on death."

"In a manner of speaking."

"You bet on ALS."

"Yes."

"And you lost."

The witness didn't answer.

"Doctor, you and your investors rolled the dice and lost. Isn't that what really happened here?"

He hesitated, then answered. "It didn't turn out the way we thought it would."

"Great reason to file a lawsuit."

"Objection."

"Sustained."

Jack didn't push it, but his sarcasm had telegraphed to the jury the question he most wanted answered: *Don't you think this woman's been through enough without you suing her, asshole?*

"Are you finished, Mr. Swyteck?" asked Judge Garcia.

"Yes, Your Honor. I think that wraps things up." He turned away from the witness and headed back to his chair. He could see the gratitude in Jessie's eyes, but far more palpable was the dagger in his back that was Dr. Herna's angry glare.

Jessie leaned toward her lawyer and whispered, "Nice work."

"Yeah," Jack said, fixing on the word she'd chosen. "I was entirely too *nice*."

# 4
## .

Jack and Jessie were seated side by side on the courthouse steps, casting cookie crumbs to pigeons as they awaited notification that the jury had reached a verdict.

"What do you think they'll do?" she asked.

Jack paused. The tiers of granite outside the Miami-Dade courthouse were the judicial equivalent of the Oracle of Delphi, where lawyers were called upon daily to hazard a wild-ass guess about a process that was ultimately unpredictable. Jack would have liked to tell her there was nothing to worry about, that in twenty minutes they'd be cruising toward Miami Beach, the top down on his beloved Mustang convertible, the CD player totally cranked with an obnoxiously loud version of the old hit song from the rock band Queen, "We Are the Champions."

But his career had brought too many surprises to be that unequivocal.

"I have a good feeling," he said. "But with a jury you never know."

He savored the last bit of cream from the better half of an Oreo, then tossed the rest of the cookie to the steps below. A chorus of gray wings fluttered as hungry pigeons scurried after the treat. In seconds it was in a hundred pieces. The victors flew off into the warm, crystal-blue skies that marked February in Miami.

Jessie said, "Either way, I guess this is it."

"We might have an appeal, if we lose."

"I was speaking more on a personal level." She laid her hand on his forearm and said, "You did a really great thing for me, taking my case. But in a few minutes it will all be over. And then, I guess, I'll never see you again."

"That's actually a good thing. In my experience, reuniting with an old client usually means they've been sued or indicted all over again."

"I've had my fill of that, thank you."

"I know you have."

Jack glanced toward the hot-dog vendor on the crowded sidewalk along Flagler Street, then back at Jessie. She hadn't taken her eyes off him, and her hand was still resting on his forearm. *A little too touchy-feely today.* He rose and buried his hands in his pockets.

"Jack, there's something I want to tell you."

The conversation seemed to be drifting beyond the attorney-client relationship, and he didn't want to go there. He was her lawyer, nothing more, never mind the past. "Before you say anything, there's something I should tell you."

"Really?"

He sat on the step beside her. "I noticed that Dr. Marsh was back in the courtroom today. He's obviously concerned."

His abrupt return to law-talk seemed to confuse her. "Concerned about me, you mean?"

"I'd say his exact concern is whether you plan to sue him. We haven't talked much about this, but you probably do have a case against him."

"Sue him? For what?"

"Malpractice, of course. He eventually got your diagnosis right, but he should have targeted lead poisoning as the cause of your neurological problems much earlier than he did. Especially after you told him about the renovations to your condo. The dust that comes with sanding off old, lead-based paint in houses built before 1978 is a pretty common source of lead poisoning."

"But he's the top expert in Miami."

"He's still capable of making mistakes. He is human, after all."

She looked off to the middle distance. "That's the perfect word for him. He was *so* human. He took such special care of me."

"How do you mean?"

"Some doctors are ice-cold, no bedside manner at all. Dr. Marsh was very sympathetic, very compassionate. It's not that common for someone under the age of forty to get ALS, and he took a genuine interest in me."

"In what way?"

"Not in the way you're thinking," she said, giving him a playful kick in the shin.

"I'm not thinking anything."

"I'll give you a perfect example. One of the most important tests I had was the EMG. That's the one where they hook you up to the electrodes to see if there's any nerve damage."

"I know. I saw the report."

"Yeah, but *all* you saw was the report. The actual test can be pretty scary, especially when you're worried that you might have something as awful as Lou

Gehrig's disease. Most neurologists have a technician do the test. But Dr. Marsh knew how freaked out I was about this. I didn't want some technician to conduct the test, and then I'd have to wait another week for the doctor to interpret the results, and then wait another two weeks for a follow-up appointment where the results would finally be explained to me. So he ran the test himself, immediately. There aren't a lot of doctors who would do that for their patients in this world of mismanaged care."

"You're right about that."

"I could give you a dozen other examples. He's a great doctor and a real gentleman. I don't need to sue Dr. Marsh. A million and a half dollars is plenty for me."

Jack couldn't disagree. It was one more pleasant reminder that she was no longer the self-centered twentysomething-year-old of another decade. And neither was he.

"You're making the right decision."

"I've made a few good ones in my lifetime," she said, her smile fading. "And a few bad ones, too."

He was at a loss for the right response, preferred to let it go. But she followed up. "Have you ever wondered what would have happened if we hadn't broken up?"

"No."

"Liar."

"Let's not talk about that."

"Why not? Isn't that just a teensy-weensy part of the reason you took my case?"

"No."

"Liar."

"Stop calling me a liar."

"Stop lying."

"What do you want me to say?"

"Just answer one question for me. I want you to be completely honest. And if you are, I'll totally drop this, okay?"

"All right. One."

"Six months we've been working this case together. Are you surprised nothing happened between us?"

"No."

"Why not?"

"That's two questions."

"Why do you think nothing happened?"

"Because I'm married."

She flashed a thin smile, nodding knowingly. "Interesting answer."

"What's so interesting about it? That's the answer."

"Yes, but you could have said something a little different, like 'Because I love my wife.' Instead, you said, 'Because I'm married.' "

"It comes down to the same thing."

"No. One comes from the heart. The other is just a matter of playing by the rules."

Jack didn't answer. Jessie had always been a smart girl, but that was perhaps the most perceptive thing he'd ever heard her say.

The digital pager vibrated on his belt. He checked it eagerly, then looked at Jessie and said, "Jury's back."

She didn't move, still waiting for him to say something. Jack just gathered himself up and said, "Can't keep the judge waiting."

Without another word, she rose and followed him up the courthouse steps.

## 5
### .

In minutes they were back in Courtroom 9, and Jack could feel the butterflies swirling in his belly. This wasn't the most complicated case he'd ever handled, but he wanted to win it for Jessie. It had nothing to do with the fact that his client was a woman who'd once rejected him and that this was his chance to prove what a great lawyer he was. Jessie deserved to win. Period. It was that simple.

*Right. Is anything ever that simple?*

Jack and his client stood impassively at their place behind the mahogany table for the defense. Plaintiff's counsel stood alone on the other side of the courtroom, at the table closest to the jury box. His client, a corporation, hadn't bothered to send a representative for the rendering of the verdict. Perhaps they'd expected the worst, a prospect that seemed to have stimulated some public interest. A reporter from the local paper was seated in the front row, and behind her in the public gallery were other folks Jack didn't recognize. One face, however, was entirely familiar: Joseph Marsh, Jessie's neurologist, was standing in the rear of the courtroom.

A paddle fan wobbled directly over Jack's head as the decision makers returned to the jury box in single file. Each of them looked straight ahead, sharing not a glance with either the plaintiff or the defendant. Professional jury consultants could have argued for days as to the significance of their body language—whether it was good or bad if they made eye contact with the plaintiff, the defendant, the lawyers, the judge, or no one at all. To Jack, it was all pop psychology, unreliable even when the foreman winked at your client and mouthed the words, "It's in the bag, baby."

"Has the jury reached a verdict?" asked the judge.

"We have, Your Honor," announced the forewoman. The all-important slip of paper went from the jury box to the bailiff and finally to the judge. He inspected it for less than a second, showing no reaction. "Please announce the verdict."

Jack felt his client's long fingernails digging into his bicep.

"In the case of Viatical Solutions Incorporated versus Jessie Merrill, we the jury find in favor of the defendant."

Jack suddenly found himself locked in what felt like a full body embrace, his client trembling in his arms. Had he not been there to hold her, she would have fallen to the floor. A tear trickled down her cheek as she looked him in the eye and whispered, "Thank you."

"You're welcome." He released her, but she held him a moment longer—a little too long and too publicly, perhaps, to suit a married man. Then again, plenty of overjoyed clients had hugged him in the past, even big burly men who were homophobic to the core. Like them, Jessie had simply gotten carried away with the moment.

*I think.*

"Your Honor, we have a motion." The lawyer for Viatical Solutions, Inc. was standing at the podium. He seemed on the verge of an explosion, which was understandable. One and a half million dollars had just slipped through his fingers. Six months earlier he'd written an arrogant letter to Jessie telling her that her viatical settlement wasn't worth the paper it was written on. Now Jessie was cool, and he was the fool.

*God, I love winning.*

"What's your motion?" the judge asked.

"We ask that the court enter judgment for the plaintiff notwithstanding the verdict. The evidence does not support—"

"Save it," said the judge.

"Excuse me?"

"You heard me." With that, Judge Garcia unleashed a veritable tongue-lashing. From the first day of trial he'd seemed taken with Jessie, and this final harangue only confirmed that Jack should have tried the case to the judge alone and never even asked for a jury. At least a half-dozen times in the span of two minutes he derided the suit against Jessie as "frivolous and mean-spirited." He not only denied the plaintiff's post-trial motion, but he so completely clobbered them that Jack was beginning to wish he'd invited Cindy downtown to watch.

On second thought, it was just as well that she'd missed that big hug Jessie had given him in her excitement over the verdict.

"Ladies and gentlemen of the jury, thank you for

your service. We are adjourned." With a bang of the judge's gavel, it was all over.

Jessie was a millionaire.

"Time to celebrate," she said.

"You go right ahead. You've earned it."

"You're coming too, buster. Drinks are on me."

He checked his watch. "All right. It's early for me, but maybe a beer."

"One beer? Wimp."

"Lush."

"*Lawyer.*"

"Now you're hitting way below the belt."

They shared a smile, then headed for the exit. The courtroom had already cleared, but a small crowd was gathering at the elevator. Most had emerged from another courtroom, but Jack recognized a few spectators from Jessie's trial. Among them was Dr. Marsh.

The elevator doors opened, and Jack said, "Let's wait for the next one."

"There's room," said Jessie.

A dozen people packed into the crowded car. In all the jostling for position, a janitor and his bucket came between Jack and Jessie. The doors closed and, as if it were an immutable precept of universal elevator etiquette, all conversation ceased. The lighted numbers overhead marked their silent descent. The doors opened two floors down. Three passengers got off, four more got in. Jack kept his eyes forward but noticed that, in the shuffle, Dr. Marsh had wended his way from the back of the car to a spot directly beside Jessie.

The elevator stopped again. Another exchange of passengers, two exiting, two more getting on. Jack kept his place in front near the control panel. As the doors closed, Jessie moved all the way to the far corner. Dr. Marsh managed to find an opening right beside her.

*Is he pursuing her?*

It was too crowded for Jack to turn his body around completely, but he could see Jessie and her former physician in the convex mirror in the opposite corner of the elevator. Discreetly, he kept an eye on both of them. Marsh had blown the diagnosis of ALS, but he was a smart guy. Surely he'd anticipated that Jessie would speak to her lawyer about suing him for malpractice. If it was his intention to corner Jessie in the elevator and breathe a few threatening words into her ear, Jack would be all over him.

No more stops. The elevator was on the express route to the lobby. Jack glanced at the lighted numbers above the door, then back at the mirror. His heart nearly stopped; he couldn't believe his eyes. It had lasted only a split second, but what he'd seen was unmistakable. Obviously, Jessie and the doctor hadn't noticed the mirror, hadn't realized that Jack was watching them even though they were standing behind him.

They'd locked fingers, as if holding hands, then released.

For one chilling moment, Jack couldn't breathe.

The elevator doors opened. Jack held the DOOR OPEN button to allow the others to exit. Dr. Marsh passed without a word, without so much as looking at Jack. Jessie emerged last. Jack took her by the arm and pulled her into an alcove near the bank of pay telephones.

"What the hell did you just do in there?"

She shook free of his grip. "Nothing."

"I was watching in the mirror. I saw you and Marsh hold hands."

"Are you crazy?"

"Apparently. Crazy to have trusted you."

She shook her head, scoffing. "You're a real piece of work, you know that, Swyteck? That's what I couldn't stand when we were dating, you and your stupid jealousy."

"This has nothing to do with jealousy. You just held hands with the doctor who supposedly started this whole problem by misdiagnosing you with ALS. You owe me a damn good explanation, lady."

"We don't owe you anything."

It struck him cold, the way she'd said "we." Jack was suddenly thinking of their conversation on the courthouse steps just minutes earlier, where Jessie had heaped such praise on the kind and considerate doctor. "Now I see why Dr. Marsh performed the diagnostic tests himself. It had nothing to do with his compassion. You never had any symptoms of ALS. You never even had lead poisoning. The tests were fakes, weren't they?"

She just glared and said, "It's like I told you: We don't owe you anything."

"What do you expect me to do? Ignore what I just saw?"

"Yes. If you're smart."

"Is that some kind of threat?"

"Do yourself a favor, okay? Forget you ever knew me. Move on with your life."

Those were the exact words she'd used to dump him some seven years earlier.

She started away, then stopped, as if unable to resist one more shot at him. "I feel sorry for you, Swyteck. I feel sorry for anyone who goes through life just playing by the rules."

As she turned and disappeared into the crowded

lobby, Jack felt a gaping pit in the bottom of his stomach. Ten years a trial lawyer. He'd represented thieves, swindlers, even cold-blooded murderers. He'd never claimed to be the world's smartest man, but never before had he even come close to letting this happen. The realization was sickening.

He'd just been scammed.

# 6
.

Sparky's Tavern was having a two-for-one special. The chalkboard behind the bar said WELL DRINKS ONLY, which in most joints simply meant the liquor wasn't a premium brand, but at Sparky's it meant liquor so rank that the bartender could only look at you and say, "*WELL*, what the hell did you expect?"

Jack ordered a beer.

Sparky's was on U.S. 1 south of Homestead, one of the last watering holes before a landscape that still bore the scars of a direct hit from Hurricane Andrew in 1992 gave way to the splendor of the Florida Keys. It was a converted old gas station with floors so stained from tipped drinks that not even the Environmental Protection Agency could have determined if more flammable liquids had spilled before or after the conversion. The grease-pit was gone but the garage doors were still in place. There was a long wooden bar, a TV permanently tuned to ESPN, and a never-ending stack of quarters on the pool table. Beer was served in cans, and the empties were crushed in true Sparky's style at the old tire vise that still sat on the workbench. It was the kind of dive that Jack would have visited if it were in his own neighborhood, but he made the forty-minute trip for one reason only: The bartender was Theo Knight.

" 'Nother one, Jacko?"

"Nah, I'm fine."

"How do you expect me to run this joint into the ground if you only let me give away one stinking beer?" He cleared away the empty and set up another cold one. "Cheers."

As half-owner of the bar, Theo didn't give away drinks to many customers, but Jack was a special case. Jack was his buddy. Jack had once been his lawyer. It was Jack who'd kept him alive on death row.

Jack's first job out of law school had been a four-year stint with the Freedom Institute, a ragtag group of lawyers who worked only capital cases. It was an exercise in defending the guilty, with one exception: Theo Knight. Not that Theo was a saint. He'd done his share of car thefts, credit card scams, small-time stuff. Early one morning he walked into a little all-night convenience store to find no one tending the cash register. On a dare from a buddy, he helped himself. It turned out that the missing nineteen-year-old clerk had been stabbed and beaten, stuffed in the walk-in freezer, and left to bleed to death. Theo was convicted purely on circumstantial evidence. For four years Jack filed petitions for stays of execution each time the governor—Jack's own father—signed a death warrant. At times the fight seemed futile, but it ended up keeping Theo alive long enough for DNA tests to come into vogue. Science finally eliminated Theo as the possible murderer.

Theo thought of Jack as the guy who'd saved his life.

Jack thought of Theo as the one thing he'd done right in his four years of defending the guilty at the Freedom Institute. It made for an interesting friendship. Best of all, Theo had kept his nose clean since his release from prison, but he could still think like a criminal. He had the kind of insights and street smarts that every good defense lawyer could use. It was exactly the point of view Jack needed to figure out what had gone wrong with Jessie Merrill.

"What are you laughing at?" said Jack.

Theo was a large man, six-foot-five and two-hundred-fifty pounds, and he had a hearty laugh to match. He'd listened without interruption as Jack laid out the whole story, but he couldn't contain himself any longer. "Let me ask you one question."

"What?"

"Was it the big tits or amazing thighs?"

"Come on, I'm married."

"Just what I thought. Both." He laughed even harder.

"Okay. Pile it on. This is what I get for feeling sorry for an ex-girlfriend."

"No, dude. Abuse is what you get for sitting too far away for me to slap you upside the head. Then again, maybe you ain't sitting so far . . ." He reached across the bar and took a swing, but Jack ducked. Theo caught only air and laughed again, which drew a smile from Jack.

"Guess I was pretty stupid, huh?" said Jack.

"Stupid, maybe. But it ain't like you did anything wrong. A lawyer can't get into trouble if he don't know his client is scamming the court."

"How do you know that?"

"Are you forgetting who you're talking to?"

Jack smiled. Theo had been the Clarence Darrow of jailhouse lawyers, a veritable expert on everything from writs of habeas corpus to a prisoner's fundamental right to chew gum. He was of mixed ancestry, primarily Greek and African-American, but somewhere in his lineage was just enough Miccosukee Indian blood to earn him the prison nickname "Chief Brief," a testament to the fact that some of the motions he filed with the court were better than Jack's.

Theo lit a cigarette, took a long drag. "You know, it's not even a hundred percent you were scammed."

"How can you say that?"

"All you know is that your client held hands in the elevator with this Dr. Swamp."

"Not Swamp, you idiot. Dr. Marsh."

"Whatever. That don't make it a scam."

"It was more than just the hand-holding. I flat-out accused her and Dr. Marsh of faking her tests. She didn't deny it."

"I didn't deny it either when the cops asked me if I killed that store clerk. Sometimes, even if you ain't done nothing, you just think you're better off keeping your mouth shut."

"This is totally different. Jessie wasn't just silent. She looked pretty damn smug about it."

"Okay. And from that you say Jessie and this big, rich doc got together and pulled a fast one on a group of Vatican investors."

"Viatical, dumbshit, not Vatican. What do you think, the pope is in on this too?"

"No, and I ain't even so sure this doctor was in on it."

"Why would you even doubt it?"

"Because this cat could lose his license. You gotta

show me more than a good piece of ass to make a doctor do something like this."

As bad as things had looked in the elevator, Theo had hit upon a crucial link in the chain of events. The criminal mind was at work. Jack asked, "What would you want to see?"

"Somethin' pretty strong. Maybe he needs money real bad, like right now."

Jack sipped his beer. "Makes sense. Problem is, I can't even get Jessie and her doctor friend to return my calls."

"I'd offer to give Jessie a good slap, but you know I don't rough up the ladies."

"I don't want you to slap her."

"How about I slap you then?" he said as he took another swing. This one landed. It was a playful slap, but Theo had the huge hands of a prize fighter.

"Ow, damn it. That really hurt."

" 'Course it did. You want me to slap Dr. Swamp, too?"

"No. And for the last time, moron, his name is Marsh."

"I'll get ol' swampy good—pa-pow, one-two, both sides of the head."

"I said no."

"Come on, man. I'll even do him for free. I hate them fucking doctors."

"You hate everyone."

"Except you, Jack, baby." He grabbed Jack's head with both hands and planted a loud kiss on the forehead.

"Lucky me."

"You is lucky. Just leave it to Theo. We'll get the skinny on this doc. You want to know if you got scammed, you just say the word."

Jack lowered his eyes, tugging at the label on his bottle.

Theo said, "I can't hear you, brother."

Jack shook his head and said, "It's not as if I can do anything about it. There's no getting around the fact that everything Jessie told me is protected by the attorney-client privilege. She could have pulled off the biggest fraud in the history of the Miami court system. That doesn't mean her own lawyer can just walk over to the state attorney's office and lay it all out."

"That's a whole 'nother thing."

"What the hell am I thinking, anyway? I'm a criminal defense lawyer. I don't do my reputation any good by ratting on my own clients."

"Listen up. What you do with the information once you get it ain't my department."

"You think I want to get even with her, don't you? That I want to nail my ex-girlfriend for playing me for a fool?"

"All I'm asking is this: Do you want to know for a hundred percent certain if the bitch stuck it to you or not?"

Their eyes locked. Jack knew better than anyone that Theo had ways of getting information that would have impressed the CIA.

"Come on, Swyteck. You didn't drive all the ways over here just to talk to Theo and drink a beer. Do you want to know?"

"It's not about revenge."

"Then why bother?"

He met Theo's stare, and a moment of serious honesty washed over them, the way it used to be when staring through prison glass. "I just need to know."

"That's good enough for me." Theo reached over the

bar and shook Jack's hand about seven different ways, the prison-yard ritual. "Let's get to it, then. We'll have some fun."

"Yeah," said Jack, raising his beer. "A blast."

# 7
·

Theo slammed the V-8 into fifth gear. The car almost seemed to levitate. Jack smiled from the passenger seat. No one could get his thirty-year-old Mustang to hum the way Theo could. Not even Jack.

"When you gonna give me this car?" asked Theo.

"When you gonna buy me a Ferrari?"

"I can get you a sweet deal on a slightly used one. You won't even need a key to start it."

Jack gave him a look, not sure he was kidding. "Some things I don't need to know about you, all right?"

Theo just smiled and downshifted as they turned off the highway and into Coconut Grove. Jack held on, trying not to land in Theo's lap as he dug his ringing cell phone from his pocket. He checked the display and recognized the incoming number. He wasn't in the mood to talk, but this was one call he never refused.

"Hello, *Abuela*."

It was his grandmother, an eighty-two-year-old Cuban

immigrant who, once or twice a week, would drop by his office unannounced to deliver excellent guava-and-cream-cheese pastries or little *tazas* of espresso straight from Little Havana. Her specialty was a moist dessert cake called *tres leches*. Not many people expected a guy named Jack Swyteck to have an *abuela*. It was especially interesting when Anglos would confide in him and say they were moving out of Miami to get away from all the Cubans. Funny, Jack would tell them, but my *abuela* never complained about too many Cubans when she was growing up in Havana.

He listened for nearly a solid minute, then finally cut in. "*Abuela,* for the last time, you did not invent *tres leches*. It's Nicaraguan. We're Cuban. *Cubano: C-U-B-A-N-O. Comprende?* . . . We'll talk about this later, okay? . . . I love you. Bye, *mi vida*."

The car stopped at a traffic light. Jack switched off the phone only to find Theo staring at him. "You and Julia Child going at it again?"

"My grandmother is the laughingstock of Spanish talk radio. She's been phoning in every afternoon to tell the world how she invented *tres leches*."

"*Tres leches?*"

"It's a cake made with three kinds of milk. White frosting on top. Very moist, very sweet."

"I know what it is. It's fucking great. Your grandmother invented that?"

"Hardly."

"Except I hate when they put those maraschino cherries on top. I bet that's not part of the original recipe. Call your *abuela,* let's ask her."

"She did *not* invent it, okay? It's Nicaraguan."

The light turned green. Theo punched the Mustang through the intersection. "You know, I think I read somewhere that maybe *tres leches* isn't from Nicaragua. Some people say it was invented by a Cuban lady in Miami."

"Don't start with me."

"I'm serious. It might even have been in the *Herald*. Long time ago."

"Since when do you read the food section?"

"Try spending four years on death row. You'll read the *TV Guide* in Chinese if they'll give it to you."

Jack massaged his temples, then tucked the phone back into his pocket. "Why do I even try to argue with you?"

After two minutes on Bayshore Drive they made a quick turn toward the bay and crossed the short bridge to Grove Isle condominiums. Grove Isle wasn't quite as chic as it was in its heyday, back when beautiful young women used to crash at poolside to meet rich young men or even richer old men. But it was still an exclusive address in an unbeatable setting. A short walk or bike ride to shops and restaurants in Coconut Grove, balconies with killer views of Biscayne Bay and downtown Miami in the distance.

Sandra Marsh lived alone in the penthouse apartment in Building 3. It was one of the many things she stood to acquire in the impending divorce from her husband of twenty-four years, Dr. Joseph Marsh. It had taken Theo just twenty-four hours to get through to her. It had taken all of thirty seconds on the phone to talk her into a meeting.

All he had to do was mention money and her soon-to-be-ex-husband.

They valeted the car and checked in with the security guard, who found their names on the guest list and directed them to the pool area. It was two-thirty in the afternoon. Palm fronds rustled in the warm breezes off the bay. As promised, Mrs. Marsh was dressed in a red terry-cloth robe and a big Kaminski sun hat, reclining on deck in a chaise lounge that faced the water, recovering from her two-o'clock deep-tissue massage.

"Mrs. Marsh?" said Jack.

She opened her eyes, tilted back her hat, and looked up from beneath the broad brim. She checked her Rolex and said, "My, you boys are prompt. Please, have a seat."

Jack sat on the chaise lounge facing Mrs. Marsh. Theo remained standing, his eye having caught an attractive sunbather in a thong bikini with a rose tattoo on her left buttock. Jack started without him.

"Mrs. Marsh, I'm Jack Swyteck. I was the lawyer for a woman named Jessie Merrill."

"I know you and your case. I have plenty of friends who keep me abreast of my husband's going-ons."

"Then you also know he was a witness."

"I know he was the doctor for that woman."

"Do you know *that woman*?" he asked, pronouncing the words the same way she had.

"What does that have to do with anything? Your friend told me this was about some financial dealings of my husband."

"It could be. But it depends, in part, on the nature of his relationship with Ms. Merrill."

"She was his little slut, if you call that a relationship."

"I do," said Theo.

Jack shot him a look that said, *Get serious.* "How long was that relationship going on?"

"I don't know."

"Did it start before or after she started seeing him as a patient?"

"I didn't find out about it until sometime after. But I can't say it wasn't going on longer."

"Did Jessie have anything to do with the two of you splitting up?"

She stiffened. "These questions are getting way too personal."

"I'm sorry."

"Well, I'm not," said Theo. "Look, lady, here's the bottom line. Mr. Swyteck here has to dance around the issue like a fly on horseshit because he thinks he still owes some loyalty to Jessie Merrill. Well, you and I don't have the same worries, so can we talk straight?"

"That depends on what you want to know."

"Let's say your husband suddenly came into a pile of money—say a million and a half bucks, or some share of it. Isn't that something you'd like to know about?"

"Surely. Our divorce isn't final yet. I'd have my lawyer adjust the property settlement immediately."

"You'd want a cut, naturally."

"I'd want more than a cut. After four kids and twenty-four years of marriage, I'm leaving that bastard broke. He'll be working till he's ninety-five just to pay my bar tab."

Jack and Theo exchanged glances, and she suddenly seemed to realize that perhaps she was giving two perfect strangers too much of what they wanted to hear.

"I think it's time I referred you gentlemen to my lawyer," she said.

"Just a few more questions."

"No, I'm not comfortable with this. I'll tell her to expect your call. She's in the book. Phoebe Martin."

Jack started to say something, but she extended her hand, ending it. Jack shook her hand, and Theo gave her a mock salute.

"Thank you for your time, ma'am."

"You're welcome."

She reclined into her chaise lounge, retreating into silence. Jack and Theo turned and walked across the pool deck toward the valet stand. As soon as they were out of Mrs. Marsh's earshot Jack asked, "What do you think?"

"Hell with tending bar, I'm opening a tattoo parlor," he said as he gathered one more eyeful of the woman with the pink rose on her tanned and firm buttock.

"Be serious," said Jack.

They stopped at the valet stand. Jack handed over his claim ticket, and the kid with the pressed white uniform and monster thighs took off running.

Theo lit a cigarette. "I think you got a middle-aged doctor, a hot new girlfriend with her hand on his balls, and a pissed off wife with two hands on his wallet."

"She's definitely not going to go easy on him."

"The ex gets at least half of everything he has. Probably more."

"Much more," said Jack. "If her lawyer is Phoebe Martin, our doctor friend really might be broke. I'll bet she gets eighty percent of every dime."

"You mean every dime she can find."

"Nothing like a million and a half bucks to keep a new girlfriend happy. Especially when the Wicked Witch of the West doesn't even know about it."

"True, true," said Theo. "Scam those investors and send that money right off to a Swedish bank account."

"You mean Swiss bank account."

"That's what I said. Swiss."

"No, you said Swedish."

"You think I don't know the difference between a bank and a fucking meatball?"

"Okay, forget it. You said Swiss."

Theo let out a cloud of smoke. "Hate them fucking Swiss anyway."

"What's to hate about the Swiss?"

"Cheese with holes in it. What's with that shit, anyway? Stinking thieves selling us all a bunch of fucking air."

"God, you really do hate everyone."

"Except you, Jack, baby." He grinned and pinched Jack's cheek so hard it turned red. The Mustang rumbled up to the valet stand, and Theo jumped ahead of Jack on his way to the driver's side. "Except you!"

Jack rubbed the welt on his face and retreated to the passenger side, smiling as he shook his head. "God help me."

exposing him to the likes of Peggy Lee and Perry Como. Without a doubt, some of the most romantic tunes ever had come straight out of the 1940s, but the lyrics to this particular song she'd chosen were pretty aggravating. Even if your heart *was* "filled with pain," to Jack's ear it still didn't rhyme with "again."

"Jack, what are you doing?"

He glanced into the bowl. His hands were buried in a thick, sweet mixture of flour, sugar, and condensed milk. "Shoot, I forgot the eggs."

"You forgot your brain. You've got *tres leches* up to your elbows."

"I'm just following the recipe. It says beat fifty strokes by hand."

"As opposed to using an electric mixer, Einstein."

He flashed an impish grin. "Oh."

She handed him a wooden spoon and rolled her eyes. "Lawyers. You're so literal."

"Yeah," he said, thinking once more of Jessie's parting words. "Always playing by the rules."

"What's that supposed to mean?"

"Nothing."

"It wasn't nothing."

"I was just kidding around."

"But you weren't smiling. You meant something by that."

"I didn't mean anything by it."

She looked away, shook her head subtly and said quietly, "You think I don't know you?"

"Cindy, let it go, okay? We were having fun here."

She returned to her end of the kitchen counter. Jack could see the regret in her eyes, the way they'd slipped into their usual pattern. Without thinking, he ran a messy hand through his hair, giving himself an earful of sweet goo. Cindy snickered to herself. He chuckled, too, and sharing the moment helped to shake off some of the unwanted tension. As he snagged a paper towel to wipe it off, she came to him, grabbed his *tres leches*–coated forearm, and said, "Don't."

"What?"

"I think I'm ovulating."

"Huh?"

She arched an eyebrow, pointing with her eyes toward the bedroom.

He smiled and said, "Now that's the kind of non sequitur I can live with."

He started to wipe his face clean. "Don't," she said. She gently kissed a gob of the sweet mixture off the corner of his mouth, and the tip of her tongue was suddenly exploring his earful of *tres leches*.

It tickled, and he recoiled—but only slightly. There'd been times when it seemed their marriage was hanging by a thread. But every now and then, out came the old Cindy and, oh, what a thread. "My, you're a veritable box of surprises tonight."

"And you are one lucky boy," she whispered.

He smiled and touched her face. "Don't I know it."

•

Jack watched her as she slept, soothed by the rhythm of her gentle breathing. Even after a hot shower, the faint smell of *tres leches* lingered in the bedroom. Nothing like skipping dinner altogether and heading straight for dessert to send you off to dreamland.

Sex wasn't exactly a strong point of their relationship. In fact, it had been nonexistent when they were first married. What should have been the happiest time of their lives was marred by Cindy's recurring nightmares. The medical doctors had ruled out sexual assault, but probably no one would ever know the details of what her attacker had done or threatened to do. Five years was a long time; five years was yesterday. At times Jack felt as though he could only guess how long ago it was in Cindy's mind. The good news was that she'd finally pushed it far enough away to want to try to start a family. It had taken her all that time to convince herself that the world was not such an awful place that a child should never be brought into it.

Jack laid a hand lightly on her belly, wondering if this one would be the one.

The phone rang. It was down the hall in his home office, a separate phone line from the main number. Jack let it ring five times, and the machine got it. The caller hung up. A minute later the phone rang again. On the fifth ring it went to the machine. Another hang up.

Seconds later it was ringing yet again. It was as if someone had his number on redial and was determined to keep calling until a live person answered. If this kept up, Cindy would certainly wake. He knew she hadn't been sleeping well the last few nights, so he sprang from the bed, wearing only his underwear, and hurried down the dark hall. He caught it on the fourth ring, just before the machine would take it.

"Hello."

"It's me. Jessie."

He suddenly felt more naked than he was. "I've been trying to reach you. You didn't return my calls."

"That's because I didn't want to talk to you."

"Then why are you calling now?"

"Because you pissed me off."

"I pissed *you* off?"

"It's odd, don't you think? I was in a lawsuit for

months, and the viatical investors never once accused me of fraud. They thought the diagnosis was all just a mistake. Suddenly, the case is over, and they've become highly suspicious. They think they were scammed."

"How do you know that?"

"Because they're poking around, asking questions. And I think you have something to do with it."

"I haven't said a word to anyone."

"Liar. You and your investigator were on Grove Isle questioning Dr. Marsh's wife, weren't you?"

Jack couldn't deny it, so he steered clear. "Jessie, we should talk."

"I warned you, don't ask so many questions. You have ticked me off bad this time."

He bit back his anger, but he couldn't swallow all of it. "I'm tired of you acting as if *I'm* the one who did *you* wrong."

"If you blow the lid off this, you are really going to regret it."

"So you admit it was a scam. You did it."

"We did it."

He'd known since the elevator, but her admission still shocked him. "You've pushed it too far this time, Jessie."

"Not just me. All of us. So watch yourself, or I'll not only have you disbarred, I'll have you sitting in the prison cell right next to Dr. Marsh."

"What?"

"The simple truth is, I couldn't have done this without you. You were a key player."

"I didn't have anything to do with this."

"No one's going to buy that. Especially when I tell them the truth—that you were in on the deal all the way."

"I can't believe what you're saying."

"Believe it. Now watch your step—partner."

The line clicked in his ear. She was gone before he could say another word.

# 9.

Jack met Theo for a late dinner. Jack had a burger smothered in cheese and mushrooms. Theo opted for the five-alarm chili. Both were staples on the simple menu at Tobacco Road.

In Jack's eyes, Tobacco Road was *the* place in Miami for late-night jazz and blues, and that wasn't just because his friend Theo was a regular sax player. By South Florida standards, it was steeped in tradition. It was Miami's oldest bar, having obtained the city's very first liquor license in 1912 and surviving Prohibition as a speakeasy. The upstairs, where liquor and roulette wheels were once stashed, was now a showcase for some of the most talented musicians in the area—including Theo. Tonight Theo and his buddies were slated to play at least one obligatory cut from Donald Byrd's *Thank You for . . . F.U.M.L. (Fucking Up My Life)*. It wasn't generally regarded as the talented Mr. Byrd's best work, and Jack was certain that the catchy title alone had put it near the top of Theo's all-time favorite list.

Theo splashed more hot sauce on his chili, wiped the beads of sweat from his brow, and asked, "What we gonna do about Jessie?"

Jack had been ignoring Theo's messages all week. It was clear that he'd viewed the interrogation of the soon-to-be-ex-wife of "Dr. Swamp" as just the beginning of the fun.

Jack said, "To be honest, I haven't had much time to think about it."

"What a crock."

"Unlike you, I work for a living. I've been in trial the last four days. We still got one more day of witnesses, then closing arguments on Friday."

"You gonna win?"

"Only if I can explain a miracle."

Jack took a minute to fill him in. His client was an accused serial stalker, not the kind of case Jack would ordinarily take, but the guy seemed to be getting a raw deal. The government's star witness was a woman who'd claimed to have seen him running from her building, even though he'd spent the last ten years in a wheelchair. The prosecutor claimed he wasn't paralyzed at all, just a fat and lazy pig who liked to buzz around town in a motorized wheelchair. "The Lazy Stalker," the media had dubbed him, and a dozen organizations were speaking out to protect the rights of stalking victims, the physically challenged, and the obese alike. Then came the first day of trial—the day of "the miracle." His wheelchair set off the metal detector at the courthouse entrance, so the idiot stood up and walked around the machine. Jack was left scrambling to salvage the case.

Theo yawned into his fist. "Can we just talk about Jessie Merrill? The rest of your life is way too fucking ridiculous."

"You have such a way about you."

"Least I don't talk shit. You trying to tell me that for the past week you haven't even thought about these Viagra-kill investors?"

Jack chuckled. "You just can't get that word, can you?"

"What?"

" 'Viagra-kill?' We're not talking about a terminal case of erectile dysfunction. It's 'viatical.' "

"What the hell kind of word is that, anyway?"

"Latin. The *viaticum* was the Roman soldier's supplies for battle, which might be the final journey of his life. Two thousand years later, some insurance guru thought it was a catchy way of describing the concept of giving someone with a life-threatening disease the money they need to fight their final battle."

"And I guess some of the soldiers live to fight another day. Like Jessie Merrill."

Jack poured some ketchup on his french fries. "She called me."

"When?"

"The day after we went to see Mrs. Marsh. She admitted it was a scam."

"Hot damn. Now we got her."

"No. We don't *got* anybody. You're not going to like this, but I've decided to let it go."

"What?"

"What's done is done. It's not my place to fix it."

"Aw, come on. Think in these terms: How much did she pay you in legal fees?"

"I gave her the friend's rate. Flat fee, twenty grand."

"There you go, my man. I can get you twenty times that much now."

"I'm sure you could. But that would be extortion, now wouldn't it?"

"I don't care what you call it. You can't just let her get away with this."

"I don't have a choice. I was her lawyer. All I can do at this point is be content with the knowledge that, yes, I was played for a sucker. If I start looking for something more than that, it's going to be trouble."

"Don't tell me you're scared."

"I need to move on with my life." As soon as he'd said it, he realized he'd used Jessie's own words. *Weird.*

Theo leaned closer, elbows on the table. "Did she and that doc threaten you?"

"It's not important."

"It is to me. Let me talk to her. She thinks she can threaten us, I'll straighten her out."

"Don't. The best thing I can do for myself right now is to forget about Jessie Merrill and the whole damn thing."

The deep thump of a bass guitar warbled over the speakers. Theo's band was tuning up for the first set. He pushed his empty bowl of chili aside and said, "You really think she's going to let you?"

"Let me what?"

"Forget her."

"Well, yeah. She's got her money. Got no more use for me."

Theo chuckled.

"What are you laughing at now?" said Jack.

Theo rose, tossed his napkin aside. The bass had broken into a rhythm, the drums and trumpet were joining in. "Hear that?" asked Theo.

"Yeah, so?"

"They're playing your song. Yours and Jessie's." He snapped his fingers to the beat. The song had no lyrics, but he sang out part of the album title anyway: "*Thank You for . . . Fucking Up My Life.*"

Theo was only half-smiling. Jack just looked at him and asked, "What are you talking about?"

"You got this old-girlfriend thing going on. Cuttin' her legal fees, cuttin' her a break. I'm talking about some kind of a strange love-hate thing going on here. *Thank you for . . .*"

"That's bull."

"Sure it is. But something tells me you ain't heard the last of Jessie Merrill. Not by a long shot, Jacko. Call me after your trial. Or after this squirrel comes back again for your nuts. Whichever comes first."

Jack watched from his table, alone, as Theo and the rest of the crowd moved closer to the music.

## 10

"**G**ood night, Luther."

The security guard started. Having worked two jobs for eleven years to support a wife and eight children, Luther was a master at sleeping with his eyes wide open. " 'Night, Mr. Swyteck."

The final day of evidence at trial hadn't done "The Lazy Stalker" any good. Perhaps it was the lingering effects of the Jessie disaster, but an embarrassing loss was the last thing he needed. He'd stayed at the office till almost midnight trying to rustle up a gem of a closing argument that would at least keep the jury out a few hours. The case was still a definite loser, but you do the best you can with the facts you're dealt. That was every good lawyer's mantra. It was what sustained you from one day to the next. That, and a good Chinese restaurant with late-night delivery.

"Good luck tomorrow," said Luther.

"Thanks."

Jack stepped through the revolving door and into the

night. It was warm and muggy for February, even by
Coral Gables standards. The rain had stopped an hour
or so earlier, but Ponce de Leon Boulevard was still glistening wet beneath the fuzzy glow of street lamps. A cat
scurried across the wide, grassy island that separated
eastbound traffic from westbound, except that at this
hour there was no traffic. Storefronts were dark on
both sides of the street. At the corner, the last of the
guests at Christy's steakhouse were piling into a taxi.
The humidity flattened their wine-induced laughter,
making them seem much farther away than they were.
Jack started up the sidewalk to the parking lot.

The car was still wet from the rain. As much as he
loved his Mustang, rainstorms and thirty-year-old con-
vertibles were no match made in heaven. He opened the
door and wiped down the seat. He could have cursed
the dampness that was seeping up through the seat of
his pants, but the beautiful sound of that V-8 made all
well again. He threw it into reverse, then slammed on
the brake. Another car had raced up behind him and
stopped, blocking his passage.

*What the hell?*

The door flew open, and the driver ran out. It was
dark, and before Jack could even guess what was going
on, someone was banging on his passenger-side window.

"Let me in!"

The voice was familiar, but it was still startling to see
Jessie's face practically pressed against the glass. "What
the hell are you doing?"

"Open the damn door!"

He reached across the console, unlocked it. Jessie
jumped in and locked the door. She was completely out
of breath. "I'm so scared. You have to help me."

"Help you?"

"*Look* at me, Jack. Can't you see I'm a wreck?"

She looked even more sleep-deprived than Jack was. Bloodshot eyes, pasty pallor. "That's no reason to ambush me like this. How long have you been waiting for me to come out?"

"I had to do it this way. I can't go anyplace where they might be waiting for me. I haven't been home in three days. If I had just popped by your office, they would have found me for sure."

"They, who? The police?"

"Farthest thing from it. These guys are thugs."

"What guys?"

"The viatical investors."

Jack shut off the engine, as if the noise were keeping him from hearing her straight. "Jessie, those investors aren't thugs. They're businesspeople."

"Hardly. That company that sued me—Viatical Solutions, Inc.—is just a front. The real money . . . I don't know where it comes from. But it's not legit."

"How do you know this?"

"Because they're going to kill me!"

"What?"

"They are going to put a gun to my head and blow my brains out."

"Just slow down."

Her hands were shaking. He could see her eyes widen even in the dim light of the street lamps. "Start at the beginning."

"You know the beginning. We scammed these guys."

"You mean you and Dr. Marsh."

"I mean all of us."

"Hold it right there. I didn't have any part in this."

"Don't act like you didn't know what was going on. You let me scam them."

"Wrong. I was completely shocked when—"

"Just cut the crap, all right? This is so like you, Swyteck. You come along for the ride to add a little excitement to your pathetic little life with Cindy Paige, and then when it all hits the fan, you throw up your hands and leave me twisting in the wind."

"What are you talking about?"

"I'm talking about—"

She stopped in midsentence. Her eyes bulged, and her shoulders began to heave. She jerked violently to the right, flung open the car door, and hung her head over the pavement. The retching noise was insufferable—two solid minutes of painful dry heaves. At last, she expelled something. Her breath came in quick, panicky spurts, and then finally she got her body under control. She closed the door and nearly fell against the passenger seat, exhausted.

Jack looked on, both concerned and amazed. "What are you doing to yourself?"

"I'm so scared. I've been throwing up all day."

"When's the last time you slept?"

"I don't remember. Three days ago, maybe."

"Let me see your eyes."

"No."

Jack held her head still and stared straight into her pupils. "What are you on?"

"Nothing."

"The paranoia alone is a dead giveaway."

"I'm not paranoid. These guys are serious. They stand to gain three million dollars under my life insurance policy just as soon as I'm dead. You've got to help me."

"We can start with the name of a good rehab center."

"I'm not a druggie, damn you."

He still suspected drugs, but that didn't rule out the possibility that someone was really out to get her—particularly since she had indeed scammed them. "If somebody's trying to kill you, then we need to call the police."

"Right. And tell them I scammed these guys out of a million and a half dollars?"

"I can try to swing a deal. If these viatical investors are really the bad operators you say they are, you could get immunity from prosecution if you tell the state attorney just who it is that's trying to kill you."

"I'll be dead by the time you cut a deal. Don't you understand? I have no one else to turn to. You have to do something, Jack!"

"I'm helping you the only way I know how."

"Which is no help at all."

"What do you want from me?"

"Call them. Negotiate."

"You're telling me they're killers. You want me to negotiate with them?"

"You've defended worse scum."

"That doesn't mean I do business with them."

"Can't you see I'm desperate? If we don't come to some kind of terms, they're going to make me *wish* I'd died of Lou Gehrig's disease."

"Then give them their money back."

"No way. It's mine."

"It's yours only because you scammed them."

"I'm not giving it back. And I'm not calling the police, either."

"Then I don't know how to help you."

"Yes, you do. You just want to stick it to me, you bastard."

"I'll do for you what I'd do for any other client. No more, no less."

"Fool me once, shame on you; fool me twice, shame on me. That's what you're thinking."

"I don't know what to think."

"Damn you, Swyteck! You never know what to think. That's why we blew up seven years ago."

He looked away, resisting the impulse to blow her off. A car passed on the street just outside the lot, its tires hissing on the wet pavement. Jessie pushed open the car door and stepped down.

"Where are you going?"

"As if you care."

"Leave your car here. Don't drive in this condition. Let me take you home."

"I told you, I can't go home. Don't you listen, ass-hole?" She slammed the door and started away from the car.

Jack jumped out. "Where can I reach you?"

"None of your business."

"I'm worried about you."

"The hell you are. I'm not going to let you talk me into calling the police just so you can ease your conscience." She fished her keys from her purse, and Jack started after her.

"Don't follow me!"

"Jessie, please."

She whirled and shot an icy glare that stopped him in his tracks. "You had your chance to help me. Now don't pretend to be my friend."

"This isn't just talk. I'm truly worried about you."

"Fuck you, Jack. Be worried for yourself."

She opened her car door and got inside. The door slammed, the engine fired, and she squealed out of the parking lot like a drag racer.

As the orange taillights disappeared into the night,

Jack returned to his car and locked the doors, his mind awhirl. He'd just finished the most bizarre conversation of his life, and four little words had given him the uneasy sensation that it wasn't over yet.

Exactly what had Jessie meant by *"Be worried for yourself"*?

He started his car and pulled out of the lot. He hated to admit it, but Theo's favorite song was playing in his head. *Thank you for . . .*

Cindy was staring into the eyes of a killer. Or at least it exuded a killer's attitude. It was a two-pound Yorkshire terrier that seemed to think it could take on a pack of hungry Rottweilers simply because its ancestors were bred to chase sewer rats. Scores of color photographs were spread across the table before her. A dozen more images lit up the screen on her computer monitor in an assortment of boxes, like the credits for *The Brady Bunch*, all of "Sergeant Yorkie" and his adorable playmate, a four-year-old girl named Natalie.

Cindy's South Miami studio had been going strong for several years, but she did portraits only three days a week. That left her time to do on-site shoots for catalogs and other work. The studio was an old house with lots of charm. A small yard and a white lattice gazebo offered a picturesque setting for outdoor shots. For reasons that were not entirely aesthetic, Cindy preferred outdoor shots when dealing with animals.

A light rap on the door frame broke her concentration. Cindy was alone in her little work area, but not alone in the studio. It had been five years since that psychopath had attacked her, and even though she was in a safe part of town, she didn't stay after dark without company. Tonight, her mother had come by to bring her dinner.

"Are you okay in there, dear?"

"Just working."

A plateful of chicken and roasted vegetables sat untouched on the table, pushed to one side. A white spotlight illuminated the work space before her. It was like a pillar of light in the middle of the room, darkness on the edges. A row of photographs stretched across the table, some of them outside the glow of the halogen lamp. The shots were all from the same frame, but each was a little different, depending on the zoom. In the tightest enlargement the resolution was little better than randomly placed dots. She put the fuzzy ones aside and passed a magnifying glass over the largest, clear image. She was trying to zero in on a mysterious imperfection in the photograph she'd taken of the little girl and her dog.

"You've been holed up in here for hours," her mother said.

Cindy looked up from her work. "This is kind of important."

"So is your health," her mother said as she glanced at the dinner plate. "You haven't eaten anything."

"No one ever died from skipping dinner."

She went to Cindy's side, brushed the hair out of her face. "Something tells me that this isn't the only meal you've missed in the last few days."

"I'm all right."

Her mother tugged her chin gently, forcing Cindy to

look straight at her. It was the kind of no-nonsense, disciplinary approach she'd employed since Cindy's childhood. Evelyn Paige had been a single mother since Cindy was nine years old, and she had the worry lines to prove it. Not that she looked particularly old for her age, but she'd acted old long before her hair had turned silver. It was as if her husband's passing had stolen her youth, or at least made her feel older than she was.

"Look at those eyes. When's the last time you had a good night's sleep?"

"I'm just busy with work."

"That's not what Jack tells me."

"He told you about my dreams?"

"Yes."

Cindy felt slightly betrayed, but she realized Jack was no gossip. It was Jack, after all, who'd stuck with her through the darkest times. He wouldn't have gone to her mother if he wasn't truly concerned about her. "What did he tell you?"

"How you aren't sleeping. The nightmares you're having about Esteban."

"They're not really nightmares."

"Just the kind of dreams that make you afraid to close your eyes at night."

"That's true."

"How long has this been going on?"

"October."

"That long?"

"It's not every night. October was when I had the first one. On the anniversary of . . . you know—Esteban."

"What does Jack say about this?"

"He's supportive. He's always been supportive. I'm trying not to make a big deal out of it. It's just not good for us. Especially not now. We're trying to make a baby."

"So, these dreams. Are they strictly about Esteban?"

Cindy was looking in the general direction of her mother, but she was seeing right past her. "It always starts out like it's supposed to be about him. Someone's outside my window. I can hear the blanket of fallen leaves scuffling each time he takes a step. Big, crispy leaves all over the ground, more like the autumns they get up north than we have in Florida. It's dark, but I can hear them moving. One footstep at a time."

"That's creepy."

"Then I walk to the back door, and it's not Esteban."

"Who is it?"

"Just more leaves swirling in the wind. Then one of them slams against the door, and *bam*, he's suddenly there."

"Esteban?"

"No." She paused, as if reluctant to share. "It's . . . Daddy."

"That's . . . interesting," Evelyn said, as if backing away from the word "creepy" again. "You sure it's your father?"

"Yes."

"Does he come to you as an old man, or does he look like the young man he was when he died?"

"He's kind of ghostly. I just know it's him."

"Do you talk to him?"

"Yes."

"What about?"

"He wants Jack."

Her mother coughed, then cleared her throat. "What do you mean, he wants Jack?"

"He wants Jack to come and play poker with him."

"That's . . ." The word "interesting" seemed to be on the tip of her tongue, but it didn't suffice. "I can see why you're not sleeping. But we all have strange dreams. Once I dreamed I was talking with a man who was supposed to be your father, but he looked like John Wayne. He even called me 'pilgrim.' "

"This is different. It's not that Esteban shows up at my back door looking like Daddy. It's more like one thought drifting into another. It's as if Daddy comes in and takes over the dream, forcing me to stop thinking of Esteban."

"That sounds normal. Don't people always tell you to think happy thoughts when you want to stop scaring yourself?"

"Yeah."

"So, you're lying in bed at night thinking of this man who assaulted you. And your mind drifts to happy thoughts of your father to make you stop."

"That was my take on it, too. But it still frightens me. Especially the way he seems to be asking for Jack."

"What does Jack say about that?"

"I haven't told him that part. Why freak him out?"

"Exactly. And why freak yourself out? Esteban is dead. Whatever he did to you, he can never do it again."

"I know that."

"You can't let him creep into your dreams this way."

"It's not that I let him. I just can't stop him."

"You have to force yourself to stop."

"I can't control my dreams."

"You must."

"Can you control yours?"

"Sometimes. Depending on what I read or think about before I fall asleep."

"But not all the time."

Evelyn seemed ready to argue the point but stopped, as if realizing that she wasn't being honest. "No, I can't always keep them under control."

"No one can. Especially when dreams are trying to tell you something."

"Cindy, don't spook yourself like that. Dreams are a reflection of nothing but your own thoughts. They don't tell you anything you don't already know."

"That's not true. This dream I'm having about Daddy and Esteban is definitely trying to tell me something."

"What?"

"I don't know yet. But I've had the same dream in the past, and every time I have it, something bad happens. It's a warning."

"Don't do this to yourself. It's only a dream, nothing more."

"You don't really believe that."

Her mother just lowered her eyes.

"Before Daddy died," said Cindy, "you had that dream. You knew it was going to happen."

"That's overstating it, sweetheart."

"It's not. You saw his mother carrying a dead baby in her arms. A week later, he was dead."

"How do you know about that?"

"Aunt Margie told me."

Margie was Evelyn's younger sister, the family bigmouth. Evelyn blinked nervously and said, "I didn't see it. I dreamed it."

"And why do you think you dreamed it?"

"Because I was worried about your father, and those worries found their way into my dreams. That's all it was."

Silence fell between them, as if neither of them believed what she'd just said. Cindy said, "I get this from you."

"Get what?"

"The ability to see things in dreams. It's something you passed on to me."

"Is that what you think? You have a gift?"

"No. A curse."

Their eyes locked, not with contempt or anger, more along the lines of mutual empathy. Her mother finally blinked, the first to look away.

"Don't stay here too much longer," she said. "Try to get some sleep tonight."

"I will. As soon as Jack gets home."

Her mother cupped her hand along the side of Cindy's face, then kissed her on the forehead. In silence, she stepped outside the glow of the spotlight and left the room.

Cindy was again alone. Her eyes drifted back toward the photographs before her, the shots she'd taken of a little girl and her dog. She was relieved that her mother hadn't asked any more questions. She wasn't sure how she would have explained what she'd been doing. Lying never worked with her mother, and telling her the truth would only have heightened her worries. The dreams alone were strange enough.

*Imagine if I'd shown her this.*

One last time, Cindy ran the magnifying glass across the enlarged image before her and held it directly over the flaw. An amateur might have been puzzled, but she was looking through a trained eye. In Cindy's mind, there was absolutely no mistaking it. She extended her index finger toward the photograph—slowly and with trepidation, as if putting her hand into the fire. Her fingertip came to rest in the lower right-hand corner.

It was there, in this one photograph out of ninety-six shots she'd taken outside her studio, that a faint shadow had appeared.

A chill ran up her arm and down through her body. She'd examined it from every angle, at varying degrees of magnification. This wasn't a cloud or a tree branch bending in the breeze. The form was definitely human.

"Daddy, please," she whispered. "Just leave me alone."

She tucked the photograph into an envelope and turned out the light.

# 12

.

Jack and Cindy went out for dinner Friday night, a neighborhood restaurant called Blú, which specialized in pizzas from wood-burning ovens. It was a bustling place with a small bar, crowded tables, and smiling waiters whose English was just bad enough to force patrons to talk with their hands like real Italians. The chefs were from Rome and Naples, and they dreamed up their own recipes, everything from basic cheese pizza like you've never tasted to pies with baby artichokes, arugula, and Gorgonzola cheese. It was Jack's version of comfort food, the kind of place he went whenever he lost a trial.

"How bad was it?" asked Cindy.

"Jury was out all of twenty minutes."

"Could have been worse. Your client could have been innocent."

"Why do you assume he was guilty?"

"If an innocent man were sitting in jail right now, you'd be kicking yourself all over town, not stuffing your face with pizza and prosciutto."

"Good point."

"That's the truly great thing about your job. Even when you lose, it's actually a win."

"And sometimes when I win, it's a total loss."

Cindy sipped her wine. "You mean Jessie?"

Jack nodded.

"Let's not talk about her, okay?"

"Sorry." He'd told her about the latest confrontation with Jessie, though Cindy hadn't seemed interested in the details. The message was pretty clear: It was time to put Jessie behind them.

"Do you think I made a mistake by leaving the U.S. attorney's office?"

"Where did that come from?"

"It ties in with this whole Jessie thing."

"I thought we weren't going to talk about her tonight."

"This is about me, not her." He signaled the waiter for another beer, then turned back to Cindy. "I used to think I was good at reading people, whether they were jurors or clients or whoever. Ever since Jessie, I'm not so sure."

"Jessie didn't just lie. She manipulated you. This latest episode proves what a total wack job she is. You said it yourself, you thought she was on drugs."

"Maybe. But what if these investors really are after her?"

"She should go to the police, exactly like you told her."

"She won't."

"Then she isn't really scared. Stop blaming yourself for this woman's problems. You don't owe her anything."

He piled a few more diced tomatoes atop his bruschetta. "Two years ago, I would have seen right through her."

"Two years ago you were an assistant U.S. attorney."

"Exactly. You remember what my old boss said when we all went over to Tobacco Road after my last day?"

"Yeah, he spilled half of his beer in my lap and said, *Drings are on the Thwytecks.*"

"I'm serious. He warned me about this. Guys go into private practice, get a taste of the money, pretty soon they can't tell who's lying and who's telling the truth. Like ships in dry dock. Rusty before they're old."

"You done?"

"With what?"

"The pity party."

"Hmmm. Almost."

"Good. Now here's some really shitty news. Just because the rust on the SS *Swyteck* is premature doesn't mean this ship is getting any younger, bucko. Even your favorite Don Henley songs are finding their way to the all-oldies radio station."

"You really know how to hurt a guy."

"It's what you get for marrying a younger woman."

"Is that all I get?"

She bit off the tip of a breadstick. "We'll see."

The loud twang and quick beat from Henley's "Boys of Summer" clicked in his brain, triggering a nostalgic smile. *I still love you, Don, but man, it sucks the way time marches on.*

They finished their pizzas and skipped the coffee and dessert. The kick in the ass from Cindy had been a good thing for Jack. Behind the jokes and smiles, however, she seemed troubled.

"Jack?"

"Yes."

"Do you think we're doing the right thing trying to have a baby?"

"Sure. We've talked about this. You're not having second thoughts, are you?"

"No. I just want to make sure you're not."

"I want this more than anything."

"Sometimes I'm afraid you want it for the wrong reason."

"What do you mean?"

"Maybe you think we need another reason to stay together."

"Where would you get an idea like that?"

"I don't know. I'm sorry. I shouldn't have said anything."

"No, I'm glad you said it. Because we need to put that out of your head right now. How long have you been worried about this?"

"I'm not really worried. Well, sometimes I am. It's been five years since . . . you know, Esteban. And people still think of me as fragile. Five years, and I'm still having the same conversations. 'Are you doing okay, sweetie? Getting enough sleep? Have the nightmares stopped? Need the name of a good therapist?' "

He lowered his eyes and said, "You talked with your mother, didn't you."

"Yes. Last night."

"I'm sorry I dragged her into this. I was trying to enlist a little family support. That's all."

"I understand. Look, let's just forget this, okay?"

"You sure?"

"Yes. It'll work out."

"Everything gonna be okay with you?"

"Fine."

"You want another Perrier or something?"

She shook her head. "Let's go home."

He reached across the table and took her hand. Their eyes met as she laced her fingers into his.

"What do you say we stop by Whip 'n' Dip, get a pint of chocolate and vanilla swirl to go, climb under the covers, and don't come out till we kill the whole carton?"

"I'd like that."

"Me, too," he said, then signaled the waiter for their bill.

Jack left a pair of twenties on the table, and in just a few minutes they were in their car on Sunset Drive, moving at the speed of pedestrians. The ice cream parlor was up the street beyond the log jam, though the line was clear out the door, typical on a weekend. Even so, they arrived home before ten-thirty. Cindy went straight upstairs to the bedroom. Jack popped into the kitchen in search of two spoons. It was one of Cindy's pet peeves. If you were going to indulge yourself with dessert, it should be on real silver, not those cheap plastic jobbies with edges so sharp that they could practically double as letter openers.

The master bedroom was on the second floor, directly over the kitchen, and Jack could hear Cindy walking above him. The click of her heels on the oak floor gave way to a softer step, and he realized that she'd kicked off her shoes. A trail of barely audible footsteps led to her dressing mirror. Jack smiled to himself, imagining his wife undressing. But it was a sad, nostalgic smile triggered by what seemed like ancient memories of a time when passions ruled, not problems. She'd reach behind her arching back and unzip her cotton sundress. With a little shrug she'd loosen one strap, then the other, letting the garment fall to her ankles. She'd stand before the full-length mirror and judge herself, unable to see that she didn't really need that push-up contraption. It was a show he'd watched countless times, wishing he could just strip away all the emotional baggage and pull up behind her and kiss the back of her neck, unfasten the clasp, and reach inside, one for the delight of each hand.

But there was never any pulling up behind Cindy, no physical intimacy of any sort, unless she initiated it. That was their life since Esteban. Jack didn't blame her for it. Her only crime had been falling in love with the governor's son. Esteban had been his client, not hers. It was Jack who'd drawn the attacker into their world, not Cindy.

And *that* was something for which he could never forgive himself.

Jack started out of the kitchen, then froze at the sight of some broken glass on the floor. He dropped the frozen yogurt on the kitchen counter and ran to the French doors in the family room. One of the rectangular panes had been shattered. Jack didn't touch anything, but he could see that the lock had been turned. Someone had paid them a visit.

"Cindy!"

His heart raced as he grabbed the cordless telephone and ran to the stairway. He was gobbling up two and three steps at a time and was about to call her name again when he heard her scream. "Jack!"

He sprinted down the hallway. Just as he reached the bedroom door, it flew open in his face. Cindy rushed out. They nearly collided at full speed, but he managed to get his arms around her. He saw only terror in her eyes.

"What is it?" he asked.

She grabbed him but never stopped moving, her momentum dragging him back into the hallway. Her voice was filled with panic. "In there!"

"What's in there?"

She pointed inside the master suite, in the general direction of the bathroom. "On the floor."

"Cindy, what is it?"

She fought to catch her breath, on the verge of hyperventilation. "Blood."

"Blood?"

"Yes! My God, Jack. It's—there's so much of it. Back by the tub."

"Call 911."

"Where are you going?"

"Just call."

"Jack, don't go in there!"

He dialed 911 and handed her the phone. "Just stay on the line while I check this out."

He hurried across the room to the dresser and took the gun from the top drawer. He quickly removed the lock and started toward the bathroom. Jack didn't think of himself as a gun person, but one attack against your wife has a way of making you forever mindful of self-defense. Cindy called his name once more, a final plea to keep him from doing something stupid, but she was soon in conversation with the 911 operator.

"My crazy husband is going in there right now," Jack heard her say. But that didn't stop him. Too many weird things had happened in the last two weeks. He wasn't about to let something—or *somebody*—bleed to death in their bathroom while they waited for the cops.

He stood in the bathroom doorway with arms extended and both hands clasped around the gun. He was aiming at nothing but at the ready. "Who's in here?"

He waited but got no answer.

"The police are on their way. Now, who's in here?"

Still no answer. He stepped inside and checked the floor. He saw no blood, but he'd ventured no farther than the first of two sinks—his sink. It wasn't quite far enough inside their bathroom to see into the back area by the big vanity mirror and Roman tub—the place where Cindy had seen the blood.

He took two more steps and froze. He was standing at Cindy's sink. Her medicine cabinet was half-open, and in the angled reflection he saw it: a glistening, crimson line of blood on a floor of white ceramic tile.

His pulse quickened. Jack had seen plenty of blood before, visited many a crime scene. There was nothing like seeing it in your own house. "Do you need help?"

His voice echoed off the tiled walls, as if to assure him that no answer would come. He took two more steps, then a third. His grip tightened on the gun. His steps became half-steps. Weighted with trepidation, he turned the corner. His eyes tracked the bright red line to its source. He faced the Roman tub and gasped.

A bloody hand hung limply over the side—a woman's hand. For an instant Jack felt paralyzed. He swallowed his fear and inched closer. Then he stopped, utterly horrified yet unable to look away.

She was completely unclothed, only blood to cover her nakedness. An empty bottle of liquor rested at her hip. It was literally a bloodbath, her life seeming to have drained from the slit in her left wrist. Red rivulets streaked the basin, the thickest pool of blood having gathered near her feet.

"Jessie," he said, his voice quaking. "Oh . . . my . . . God."

# 13
.

The Swyteck house was an active crime scene. An ambulance and the medical examiner's van were parked side by side on the front lawn, a seeming contradiction between life and death. The driveway was filled with police cars, some with blue lights swirling. Uniformed officers, crime scene investigators, and detectives were coming and going at the direction of the officer posted at the door. The first media van had arrived soon after the police. More had followed, and six of them were parked on the street. Neighbors watched from a safe distance on the sidewalk.

Assistant State Attorney Benno Jancowitz tried not to smile.

Jancowitz was a veteran in the major crimes section, with two dozen murder trials under his belt, and he had the seemingly carved-in-wax worry lines on his face to prove it. The Miami-Dade office kept at least one prosecutor on call to attend crime scenes, but it was no coincidence that Jancowitz was on this particular assignment. A buddy had tipped him off that the body was at Jack Swyteck's house, knowing that it would be of special interest to Jancowitz.

After four years of death-penalty work for the Freedom Institute, Jack was persona non grata at the state attorney's office. In fact, he'd handed Jancowitz his first loss ever in a capital case. Jack's stint as a federal prosecutor had only worsened things. He was assigned to the public-corruption section and put two cops in jail for manufacturing evidence in the prosecution of a murder that was only made to appear gang-related. The assistant state attorney in the case was Benno Jancowitz. He was never accused of any wrongdoing himself, but the controversy had definitely bumped him off the fast track within the state attorney's office.

Jancowitz caught up with the assistant medical examiner just as she was hoisting her evidence into the back of the van.

"Hey there," he said.

"Mr. Jancowitz, how are you, sir?" It was her style to be rather stiff and formal even with people she liked.

"You about finished in there?"

"Almost. Pretty messy scene, I'm afraid."

"I know, I saw."

She removed her hair net and latex gloves. "Was the victim a friend of the Swytecks?"

"No. A client, as I understand it."

"Ah," she said.

He wasn't sure what the "ah" meant. Maybe something along the lines of *All lawyers at some point in the relationship are capable of killing their client.* "How soon before she'll be coming out?"

"*She* won't be coming out. It's a body now."

"That's one of the things I was going to ask. How long has she been an it?"

She laid a hand atop her evidence kit and said, "I should be able to give you a better idea once I get these maggots under the microscope."

"You got maggots?"

"I scraped them from her eyes. Some in her nose, too. Looks like they're hatching, or about to hatch."

"Where does that put the time of death?"

"Twelve hours, give or take. Not everyone puts as much stock in forensic entomology as I do, but I'm a firm believer that the insect pattern that develops on a corpse is about as reliable an indicator of time of death as you'll find. Absent a witness, of course."

"But you need flies to have maggots."

"Right. Flies are drawn to the smell of a dead body within ten minutes. They lay thousands of eggs, usually in the eyes, nose, and mouth. That's why the hatching is so crucial in determining time of death."

"But this body was indoors."

"Well, they don't call them *house* flies for nothing."

"I didn't really notice any flies inside."

"Doesn't mean they aren't there."

"House was all sealed up, too. Air conditioner was on."

"There was that broken window pane in the back, on the French door. Flies could have easily come in through that."

"Yeah. Or the flies that laid the maggots could have found the body outside in the open air. Before it was moved inside."

"That would sound a lot more like homicide than suicide."

"Yes," he said, thinking aloud. "It would, wouldn't it."

•

Cindy was waiting in the car. She and Jack had been backing out of the driveway, on their way to her mother's house, when a detective arrived on the scene. Cindy was eager to get away from the chaos, but the detective promised to keep Jack only a few minutes. A few minutes had turned into half an hour.

She peered through the windshield, her stomach churning at the sight of her house being transformed into a crime scene. Long strands of yellow police tape kept the onlookers at bay, which triggered a wholly incongruous thought in Cindy's mind. Strangely, it reminded her of the day Jack had asked her to move in with him before they were married. He'd tied yellow ribbons to the dresser handles as a way of marking the drawers that would be hers. If only it were possible to go back to simpler times.

A knock on the passenger-side window startled her. To her relief, it was a police officer. Cindy lowered the window.

"Would you like some coffee?" It was a female officer who spoke with a hint of a Jamaican accent. The voice was mature and confident, which made Cindy realize that this cop wasn't as young as she looked.

"No, thank you."

"It's Starbucks. Still hot."

"Thanks, but caffeine is the last thing my nerves need right now."

"I can understand that." She rested the paper cups on the car hood, reached through the open window, and offered her hand. "I'm Officer Wellens. Call me Glenda."

"Nice to meet you," Cindy said as they shook hands.

Glenda glanced casually toward the house and asked, "You know the woman?"

"She was one of my husband's clients."

"Wow."

"Why is that a wow?"

Glenda shrugged and said, "That was just the first thought that popped in my head. Isn't that what's going through your head right now? Like, 'Wow, how did this happen?' "

"My thoughts are more along the lines of, 'Why did this woman kill herself in my house?' "

"I could give you my two cents' worth. 'Course, you're talking to a woman who's seen about a million domestic violence calls."

"What makes you think this has anything to do with domestic violence?"

"Didn't say it did. It's just my point of view, that's all. Gorgeous young woman strips herself naked and slits her wrist in her lawyer's bathtub. All I'm saying is that I'm trained to think a certain way, so certain thoughts go through my head."

"Like what?"

She leaned against the car and struck a neighborly pose, as if talking over the kitchen windowsill. "I look at this situation and say, 'This woman was trying to make a statement.' "

"You mean she left a note?"

"No, honey. Maybe ten percent of the folks who commit suicide actually leave a note. Most of them let the act speak for itself."

"What kind of statement does this make?"

"I warned you about my point of view, now. You really want to hear what I'm thinking?"

"Yes."

Glenda narrowed her eyes, as if she suddenly fancied herself an FBI criminal profiler. "I look at this crime scene, I see a woman who's obviously at the end of her rope, flipping back and forth between fits of anger and bouts of depression. She can't take it no more. She's so wigged out she can't even express herself in words. So she does this. This is her message."

"What's the message?"

"You askin' my opinion?"

"Yes, your opinion."

"Something along the lines of: 'You think this was a fling, sucker? You think I was your little plaything? Well, guess again. I'd rather kill myself in your bathtub than let you and your pretty wife go on living happily ever after as if I never even existed.' "

Cindy looked away. "That's not what this is."

"Or, it could be she didn't want to die."

"What do you mean?"

"If she really just wanted to off herself, she could have crawled in her own bathtub and slit her wrists. But no. She does it in a place where she knows her lover will find her. She's maybe played out this fantasy in her mind a hundred times. Her man comes home, finds her on the brink of death, he rushes her to the emergency room. Her hero rescues her. He waits at her bedside all night long at the hospital, clutching her hand, praying for her to come to. He realizes how she doesn't want to live without him. And he realizes he can't live without her either."

"That's too weird."

"That's the real world, sister. Tragic. Lots of people

end up killing themselves when what they really wanted was someone to find them in the nick of time and save them."

"Everything you're saying is . . . it all assumes that my husband was having an affair."

Glenda raised an eyebrow, as if to say, *Well, duh!*

"That's not the way it is with Jack and me."

"I'm glad to hear that. 'Cause to look at this, I surely would have thought otherwise."

"Jack would never cheat on me."

"Good for you. My boyfriend's the same way."

"Really?"

" 'Course. He knows I'd cut his balls off if he did."

"How romantic."

Glenda laughed, then took another hit of coffee. She scrunched her face, as if confused, but Cindy was already onto the fact that Glenda was much smarter than she let on. "One thing I was wondering about. The house alarm."

"What about it?" asked Cindy.

"I notice you have one. But it didn't go off when that glass on the French door got busted."

"It wasn't on."

"You don't use your alarm?"

"We only set it when we're home."

"How's that?"

"I've had some bad—" She stopped, not wanting to reveal too much of herself and her dreams. "I've had some trouble with prowlers in the past. I'm kind of a 'fraidy cat."

"Aren't we all?"

"I'm worse than most. I have the motion sensors turned up so high, all it takes is a strong puff of wind to trigger the sirens. That used to happen all the time when we weren't home, and the city of Coral Gables ended up socking us with seven hundred bucks in fines for false alarms. Finally Jack said enough. We don't activate the alarm when we're not home. If somebody wants our stuff, we have insurance. The only thing we care about is whether someone is trying to break into our house while we're still inside it."

"Makes sense, I guess."

"At a hundred bucks per false alarm, you'd be surprised how many people use their alarms that way."

"You're right, I see it all the time. But one other thing makes me curious: How do you suppose Jessie knew that you guys don't set your alarm while you're away?"

Cindy thought for a moment, then looked at her and said, "Maybe she thought we had a silent alarm. It could be as you said, she wanted someone to come save her before she died."

Glenda screwed up her face and said, "Nah, doesn't work."

"Why not?"

"Like you said, your husband wasn't having an affair."

Cindy didn't answer.

Glenda finished her coffee. "Then again, maybe we should ask Mr. Swyteck about that. What do you think?"

"I'm not going to tell you how to do your job."

"Fair enough. Nice talkin' to you, Mrs. Swyteck."

"Nice talking to you, too."

She handed Cindy a business card. "I'm sure you're right. I'm sure things are just fine and dandy between you and Mr. Swyteck. But just in case there's something you want to talk out, woman to woman, my home number is on the back. Call me. Anytime."

"Thank you."

"You bet."

They shook hands, and Cindy raised the passenger-side window. She watched from behind tinted glass as Officer Wellens cut through the chaos in the front yard and returned to the scene of the crime.

# 14
.

It was the most unpleasant evening Jack had ever spent on his patio.

Assistant state attorney Benno Jancowitz was bathed in moonlight, seated on the opposite side of the round, cast-aluminum table. Between his chain-smoking and the burning citronella candle, it was olfactory overload. Yet at times Jack could still almost smell Jessie's blood in the air, his mind playing tricks on the senses.

"Just a few more questions, Mr. Swyteck." Smoke poured from his nostrils as he spoke, his eyes glued to his notes, as if the answers to the world's problems were somewhere in that dog-eared notepad. So far he'd spent almost the entire interview combing over the civil trial Jack had won for Jessie.

Finally he looked up and said, "Know anybody who'd want Jessie Merrill dead?"

"I might."

"Who?"

"The viatical investors who I beat at trial."

"What makes you think they'd want to kill her?"

"She told me in those exact words. She thought they were out to kill her."

"Pretty sore losers."

"They apparently thought she'd cheated them."

"Did she? Cheat them, I mean."

Jack paused, not wanting to dive headlong into the matter of a possible scam. "I can't really answer that."

"Why not?"

"Because we're getting into an area protected by the attorney-client privilege."

"What privilege? She's dead."

"The privilege survives her death. You know that."

"If there was foul play, I'm sure your late client would excuse your divulgence of privileged information."

"She might, but her heirs will probably sue me."

"I don't follow you."

"Right now, Jessie's estate has at least a million and a half dollars in it. Hypothetically, let's say I breach the attorney-client privilege and tell you she scammed the investors out of that money. Her estate just lost a million and a half bucks. Her heirs could have my ass in a sling."

"You want to talk off the record?"

"I've said enough. If something happened to Jessie, I want to help punish the people who did it. But there are some things I can't speak freely about. At least not until I've talked to her heirs."

The prosecutor smiled thinly, as if he enjoyed having to pry information loose. "Did Ms. Merrill call the police about this alleged threat on her life?"

"No."

"Did she tell anyone else about it?"

"I don't think so."

"So she was in mortal fear for her life, and the only person she told was her lawyer?"

"Don't taunt me, Benno. I'm trying to help, and I've told you as much as I can."

"If you're implying there's a possible homicide here, it would help for me to understand the motive."

"The investors reached a viatical settlement thinking Jessie would be dead in two years. It turns out they might have to wait around for Willard Scott and Smucker's to wish her a happy hundredth birthday. In and of itself, that's pretty strong motive."

He wrote something in his pad but showed no expression. "Answer me this, please. When's the last time you saw Ms. Merrill?"

"Last night."

"What time?"

"Around midnight."

"Where'd you two meet up?"

"She was waiting for me."

"Where?"

"The parking lot."

"You go anywhere?"

"No. We talked in my car."

He raised an eyebrow, and Jack immediately regretted that answer.

"Interesting," he said. "What did you two talk about?"

"That's when we had the conversation I just told you about. When she told me she thought the investors might kill her."

"Is that when she told you she'd scammed the investors?"

"I didn't say there was a scam. I told you twice already, I can't talk about that."

"Suit yourself."

"I'm not being coy. I may end up telling you everything. Just let me do my job as a lawyer and sort out the privilege issue with her heirs, whoever they might be."

"Take your time. Get your story straight."

"It's not a matter of getting my story straight. It's a thorny legal and ethical issue."

"Right. So, other than this sacred attorney-client relationship that you've chosen to carry into eternity, did you have any other kind of relationship with Ms. Merrill?"

"We dated before I met my wife."

"Interesting."

It was about his fifth "interesting" remark. It was getting annoying.

He glanced at his notes once more and said, "Just a few more questions. Some mop-up stuff. Ever hear her threaten to kill herself?"

"No."

"She ever make any utterances of farewell or final good-byes—like, those bastards won't have me to kick around anymore?"

"No."

"Ever hear her say she can't go on anymore, that life isn't worth living?"

"No."

"Did she have any kind of physical pain that she couldn't deal with?"

"Not that I know of."

"Were you fucking her?"

"Huh?"

He seemed pleased to have set up the question so nicely, having caught Jack off-guard. "You heard me."

"The answer is no."

"Other than those viatical investors you mentioned, can you think of anyone else who'd want her dead?"

"From the looks of things, maybe she wanted herself dead."

He nodded, as if he'd already considered Jack's theory. "Breaks and enters through the French door, grabs a bottle of vodka from the liquor cabinet, goes upstairs, slits her wrist. Which leaves one gaping question: Why would she kill herself in your house?"

"Who knows? Maybe to make some kind of statement."

"Exactly what kind of statement do you think she was trying to make?"

"I can only guess. I was her lawyer. Maybe she didn't like the job I did."

"You'd just won her a million and a half dollars."

"That's a complicated situation. I already told you, I need to sort out some privilege issues before I can talk freely."

"Ah, yes. The scam."

"I never said there was a scam."

The prosecutor's nose was back in his notes. The silence lasted only a minute or two, but it seemed longer. "Lots of nice pictures in your house," he said finally. "I like that black-and-white stuff."

Jack had no idea where he was headed. "Thanks. My wife took them."

"She's good with the camera, is she?"

"She's a professional photographer."

"That what she does for a living?"

"Partly. She's gotten into design work lately. Graphic arts. She's really good on the computer."

"Pretty busy lady, I would imagine."

"It's a full-time commitment."

"And your job? Hell, that's more than a full-time commitment."

"I'm busy, yeah. We're both busy people."

Jancowitz glanced toward the house and then back. "How are things with you and your wife?"

"Couldn't be better." He felt a bit like a liar, but his marriage was no one's business. Jancowitz didn't seem to believe him anyway.

The prosecutor said, "I couldn't help noticing earlier. You seemed pretty eager to get her in the car, off to the sidelines, as soon as the police started showing up here tonight."

"Cindy was attacked by a man five years ago. Turning her house into a crime scene is a pretty upsetting experience for her."

Again, Jancowitz offered that long, slow nod of skepticism.

"What are you trying to say, Benno?"

He gnawed his pencil. "Well, so far we got a gorgeous young woman, who used to be your lover, dead and naked in your bathtub. Blood is dry, body's still not at room temperature, rigor mortis is fading, but the larger muscle groups haven't completely relaxed. Medical examiner will pin it down better, but I'd guess she's been dead no more than twenty-four hours."

"Which means?"

"Which means that the little talk you had in your car last night certainly puts you in contention for the last person to see her alive. And we've already established that you were the first person to see her dead."

"You're ignoring the empty bottle of vodka, the slit wrist. I told you about those viatical investors just to give you the whole picture. It could be just me, but this maybe, kind-of, sort-of, looks a little like suicide, don't you think?"

"One thing I've learned after twenty-two years. Looks can be deceiving."

He gave Jack the kind of penetrating look that prosecutors laid only on suspects. Jack didn't blink. "Sorry. I don't scare easy. Especially when I've done nothing wrong."

Jancowitz closed his notebook, rose slowly, shook Jack's hand, and said, "I just love a challenge. I'll be in touch."

"Anytime."

He crossed the patio and walked back inside the house. Through the bay window Jack saw him stop in the family room to admire a long wall that was lined with Cindy's photographs. He turned, grinned, and gave the thumbs-up, as if he were admiring her work. He seemed pleased to see that Jack had been watching him.

"Twit," Jack said quietly as he returned the phony smile.

Jack waited for him to disappear into the living room, and then he took out his cell phone and dialed.

It was late, but somehow he sensed he was going to need a lawyer. A good one.

# 15

·

Jack had a noon meeting with Rosa Tomayo at his office. It was literally a matter of walking across the hall. Her office suite was on the same floor, same building as his.

Rosa's firm was three times bigger than Jack's, which meant that besides herself she had two much younger partners to help carry the workload. Not that she needed much help. Rosa was a bona fide multitasker, someone who felt hopelessly underutilized if she wasn't doing at least eight different things at once, all with the finesse of a symphonic conductor. Jack had personally engaged her in spirited debates over lunch only to have her later recount conversations she'd simultaneously overheard at nearby tables. That kind of energy and brain power had landed her among Miami's legal elite, though some would say her reputation was equally attributable to the quick wit and enduring good looks she employed with great flair and frequency on television talk shows. She definitely had style. But she wasn't

the typical showboat criminal defense lawyer who pro-
claimed her client's innocence from the hilltops when,
in truth, the government had merely failed to prove
guilt beyond a reasonable doubt. If Jack ever decided to
seek out a partner, Rosa would have been first on his
list.

When he needed representation, Rosa was the obvious choice.

Calling her from the crime scene last night had turned
out to be the right thing to do. Even though he'd walked
hundreds of his own clients through similar situations, the
perils of a lawyer representing himself were endless. Rosa
helped him focus objectively. They'd agreed that, first
thing in the morning, she would meet with the prosecutor
assigned to the case.

At 12:15 Jack began to pace. *Rosa, where are you?*

The wait was only made worse by the barrage of
calls from the media. Jack dodged them all. As a lawyer
he didn't normally shy away from reporters, but in this
case Jack was avoiding any public statements at least
until Rosa confirmed one way or the other if he was a
suspect.

At 12:45, finally, she was back.

"I think it's solved," she said.

Jack chuckled nervously from his seat at the head of
the conference table.

"I'm serious." She was picking over the deli sandwich platter he'd ordered for lunch. She removed the
sliced turkey from between two slices of rye bread,
rolled it up, and nibbled as she spoke. "I honestly think
it's resolved."

"Already?"

"What can I say? I'm damn good."

"Tell me what happened."

She tossed the rolled turkey back on the platter and started on the ham. It was the way Rosa always ate— two bites of this, a bite of that, talking all the while.

"The meeting was just me and Jancowitz. He claims you all but admitted that Jessie scammed the investors."

"I didn't go that far. I was just trying to give him some insight into the motive they might have to kill her."

"Well, the motive cuts two ways. He sees it as *your* motive to kill Jessie."

"How?"

"Self-righteous son of a former governor gets scammed by a client who used to be his girlfriend. His ego can't handle it, or maybe he thinks it will ruin his stellar reputation. He snaps and kills her, then makes it look like suicide."

"That's weak."

"That's what I said. Which is why I don't think it's their real theory."

"Then where are they headed?"

"Same place you'd go if you were still a prosecutor. You and Jessie were having an affair. She threatened to tell your wife unless you played along with her scam. You got tired of the extortion and whacked her."

"When?"

"Good question. I pressed Benno on the time of death. They're not committing to anything, but bugs don't lie. The medical examiner says that the maggot eggs in Jessie's eyes were already starting to hatch. If you work backward on the timeline of forensic entomology, that puts her time of death somewhere about midday."

"Good for me," said Jack. "I was in trial all day and then went straight to dinner with Cindy."

"That's what I told Benno."

"Except the maggots give us something else to think about. Aren't they more prevalent on a body found outdoors than indoors?"

"Not necessarily."

"But you see my point. Is anyone considering that Jessie's body was moved from somewhere outside the house to my bathtub?"

"I'm pretty sure they've ruled it out. With all the blood that ran from her body, her heart had to be pumping when she was in your tub, which means she was alive when she got there."

"Though not necessarily conscious."

"True. But there are other indicators, too. Benno was talking pretty fast, but I think he said something about how the livor mortis pattern on her backside suggests that she died right where she was found."

"When can we find out something definite?"

"We have to be patient. You know how this works. It could be weeks before the medical examiner issues a final report. Until then, all we get is what Benno deigns to share with us."

"Does that mean I'm a suspect or not?"

"I don't think you're high on the list. In my opinion, he just wants to tweak you, embarrass you a little."

"Oh, is that all?" he said, scoffing.

"Better than making your life miserable for the foreseeable future as the target of a homicide investigation. All you have to do is give him a little of what he wants."

"What are you telling me? You and Jancowitz sat around a table all morning negotiating how best to embarrass me?"

She bit off the tip of a pickle spear. "Basically."

"This is crazy."

"Just listen. Here's the deal. We put down in writing the whole conversation you and Jessie had the night before she died. She was afraid for her life, she admitted that she had scammed the viatical investors, they were threatening to kill her. Then we put in your side of the story. She acted like she was on drugs, you told her to go to the police, blah, blah, blah. And most important, we put in bold and all capital letters that you knew absolutely nothing about the scam until after the verdict was rendered."

"You're confident that there will be no repercussions about breaching the attorney-client privilege?"

"A lawyer can breach the privilege to defend himself from possible criminal charges."

"I know that. But nobody's talked about charging me yet."

"There was a dead body in your house. Trust me. They're talking about it."

Jack glanced at the untouched sandwich on his plate, then back at Rosa. "What kind of immunity are they offering?"

"They won't prosecute you on the scam. No promises on the homicide investigation."

"You think that's enough?"

"Let's be real, okay? You're never going to get immunity on a homicide charge. You're the son of a former governor. Prosecutors cut deals with the little guys so they can nail people like you."

"Then why are you so sure that this letter is the right thing to do?"

"First of all, it's the truth. Second, even though you weren't part of Jessie's scam, you should sleep better at night knowing that the prosecutor has agreed not to try to prove you were involved."

"That's something, I guess."

"Especially when you consider that we're not giving them anything they haven't already deduced from your conversation last night. Like I said, they're assuming there was a scam. This just puts it on record that you knew nothing about it."

"So, in your view, we're giving them nothing?"

"Exactly. It serves the same purpose as a press release, only not as tacky. And it may help down the road, too. Worst-case scenario, Jancowitz asks the grand jury to indict you for the murder of Jessie Merrill. Your involvement in her little scam is sure to play some part in your alleged motive. Somehow, he'll have to explain that from day one of the investigation he had a letter sitting in his file in which you unequivocally denied any involvement."

"You know as well as I do that a prosecutor doesn't even have to mention that letter to the grand jury."

"No, but we can make some hay in the press if he doesn't."

"So, why do you really think Jancowitz even wants the letter?"

"My opinion? He doesn't like you, never did. He can't wait to use your own words to show the world how stupid you were with your own client."

Jack cringed.

"Sorry," she said. "But that's the way he's going to play it. Slick defense lawyer gets outslicked."

"The media will have a feast."

"Yes, they will. But today's newspaper is tomorrow's paper-hat."

"Gee, thanks. I feel better already."

She came to him, laid a hand on his shoulder. "Look, my friend. These are salacious facts. Innocent or not, you won't come out of this smelling like a rose."

Jack knew she was right. The hardest part about being a criminal defense lawyer was defending the innocent. Even when they won, they lost something—status, reputation, the unconditional trust of friends and peers.

"I suppose it will all come out in the end anyway," he said. "I might as well lay it all out from the get-go, do what I can to make sure the investigation heads in the right direction."

"That's exactly where I came out. Of course, we're making certain assumptions. One, you didn't kill her, which goes without saying. And two, she was not your lover."

"Definitely not."

"I'm not just talking about getting naked. I don't want to find some string of flirtatious e-mails down the road somewhere."

"There's none of that."

"Then I say we go public with the scam. Jancowitz is happy because it embarrasses you professionally. We're happy because the truth focuses the attention where it belongs, on the viatical investors."

"You don't think that sounds too simple?"

"I'm not saying we write Jancowitz a letter and then sit on our hands. If they start thinking homicide and definitely not suicide, he might still hound you as a suspect. In that case, we need to be ready to hand them something on a silver platter, something so compelling that it almost forces them to focus their investigation on another suspect. Hopefully, the right suspect."

"We've got two pretty solid theories."

Rosa started to pace, as if it helped her think. "One, the viatical investors killed Jessie. They put the body in your house to deflect guilt from them to you. Or two, Jessie feared a horrible death. She was convinced they were going to kill her. So she killed herself, but she did it in a way and in a place that, as you say, makes a statement. She wanted to create havoc in your life because you refused to help her."

"It has to be one of those," said Jack.

"Lucky for us, there's a common thread to both of them: The viatical investors threatened to kill Jessie. We need to find out who's behind that company."

"Jessie didn't give me much to go on. She basically just said the company itself was a front. The real money was a bunch of bad operators."

"You know what I always say. Bad money has a stench. Follow your nose. You up for it?"

"What's my alternative?"

"You can sit back and hope your love letter to Jancowitz does the trick."

He shook his head, not so sure that Jancowitz would be satisfied in merely embarrassing him. He looked at Rosa and said, "I'll take care of the letter. Then it's time to go fishing."

"You have any particular investigator you'd like to use?"

"The official answer to that is no."

She gave him a knowing smile. "You know, it's really too bad Theo is a convicted felon. I'd use him too, if he could get a license."

"That's the beauty of the arrangement. It keeps me from having to pay him."

"Something tells me you'll find a way around that."

Jack nodded, knowing that with all the freebies Theo had given him, someday he'd owe him his car.

Rosa checked her watch. "Gotta run. If you need me, you know where to find me."

Jack walked her from the conference room to the

lobby. They stopped at the double doors. "Rosa. Thank you."

"No problem. You'd do the same for me. But let's hope you never have to."

She was out the door, but Jack answered anyway, for no one's benefit but his own. "Let's hope."

# 16

It was two A.M., and Jack sat alone at the kitchen table wearing the pajamas his mother-in-law had given him for Christmas. They were a grotesque paisley print, the kind of garment that might ordinarily sit in a dresser drawer until old age seized his senses. So long as he and Cindy were in Mrs. Paige's house, however, he figured he'd be the good son-in-law and wear them.

Since "the incident," as they'd come to call it, Cindy and Jack had been staying in her old room in her mother's house in Pinecrest. It was a temporary arrangement until they could find an apartment. Moving back into their house would never be an option, and Jack feared that even a fast-talking realtor would have a tough time selling it. *And over here, Mr. and Mrs. Buyer, is a spacious master bathroom, which the owners have quite tastefully painted a very lovely shade of red to disguise the blood splatter on the walls.*

The light from under the range hood cast a faint glow across the room. Beads of condensation glistened on the glass of water before him. A seriously flawed segment of Jack's brain was forcing him to play the half-empty/half-full guessing game, so he raised the water glass and guzzled.

*There, damn it. Empty.*

Jack's letter had gone off to the state attorney's office that afternoon. It recounted his entire conversation with Jessie the night before her death. He'd labored over the wording for several hours before enlisting Rosa's help to massage the final draft. She was totally sold on the concept. Jack hadn't realized how *un*sold he was until after he'd wasted four hours trying to fall asleep. A written acknowledgment to the state attorney that his own client had scammed him would hardly bolster his standing in the Miami legal community.

"Are you okay?"

He turned and saw Cindy standing behind him. He'd tried not to wake her when he'd crawled out of the little bed they were sharing, but he'd obviously failed.

"Can't sleep," he said.

"Me neither. I thought I'd check the real estate section for rentals once more."

"Good idea."

As she searched through the recycle bin for yesterday's newspaper, she looked up and asked, "Are you still thinking about that letter you wrote to the state attorney?"

"How did you know?"

"Because I know you."

He lowered his eyes. "I feel like the teacher kept me after school to write five hundred times on the blackboard, 'BULLWINKLE IS A DOPE.' "

"You're not stupid. You're the smartest lawyer I know."

"I did a pretty stupid thing."

"You had no choice. Writing that letter is the only way to focus the state attorney's attention where it belongs—on those investors who were threatening your client."

"I didn't mean writing the letter was stupid. I meant letting Jessie fool me in the first place."

She quit searching for the newspaper and lowered herself into the chair beside her husband. The look in her eye told him that he was in for a reality check. "Jessie's doctor was one of the most respected neurologists in Miami. How could you possibly have suspected that a man of his stature would falsify a diagnosis and defraud a group of viatical investors?"

"I deal with clever thieves all the time. I let my sympathy for Jessie get in the way."

"Of course you did. Even *I* felt sorry for that woman. I'm the one who told you, 'Go ahead and take the case, I don't care if she's your old girlfriend.' Remember?"

"It still blows me away."

"Me too. Especially the doctor. The more I think about this, the crazier it seems that Dr. Marsh would jeopardize his whole career that way."

"Money," he said, shaking his head. "I know a few doctors who love it."

"There has to be something more at work. Something that we don't understand."

He could have detailed some of Jessie's other persuasive powers, but that didn't seem like a smart road to travel with his wife. "Let's not worry about him," he said. "How are you doing?"

"Okay."

She'd averted her eyes when answering. He turned her chin gently. "What's wrong?"

"I got my period," she said quietly.

Jack tried not to show disappointment. "It's okay. We'll keep trying."

"We've been trying for eleven months now."

"Has it really been that long?"

"Yes. And I'm still not pregnant."

"Maybe we should try doing it without our wedding rings. That never seems to fail."

She almost smiled, but this was clearly weighing on her. "How worried are you, honey?" he asked.

"Very."

"Maybe it's me," said Jack.

"It's not you."

"How do you know?"

"I just know."

He wasn't sure how she knew, but debating it wasn't going to cheer her up. "There are plenty of things we haven't tried yet."

"I know. And there's always adoption, too. But I'm almost afraid to think about that."

"Why?"

She paused and said, "Because of the relationship you had with your stepmother."

"That's totally different from adoption."

"It's not, at least from a bonding standpoint. You were just a newborn when your mother died. Agnes raised you from infancy."

"The fact that my stepmother and I never bonded has nothing to do with the fact that she was not my biological mother. My father was so desperate to find me a new mother that he married a woman who turned out to be a drunk."

She took his hand, lacing her fingers with his. "How often do you wonder about your real mother?"

"I go in spurts. Times when I'm really curious, other times when I don't think about her at all. Fortunately, I have my *abuela* to tell me all about her."

"Doesn't that concern you, about adoption? The idea of this mysterious person becoming part of our lives?"

"Adoption isn't like that. There's no *abuela* around to tell stories about the biological mother."

"I didn't mean an actual living person. I meant more like the essence of the birth mother."

"That doesn't seem to bother the millions of other couples who adopt."

"I don't think other people are as in touch with that sort of thing as I am."

"What sort of thing?"

"Feeling someone's . . . presence."

Jack knew that she was talking about her father, and he feared that Jessie's death had triggered something. "Is that why you're awake? Were you having that dream about your father again?"

"No."

"Are you sure?"

"Come on, I didn't want to make this conversation about that. I'm sorry."

"Don't be sorry. This was a traumatic event for both of us. If you want to talk to me or someone else or even a counselor, it's okay."

She fell silent, then looked at him and said, "Actually, there's something I've been wanting to show you."

"What?"

"Wait right here."

She rose and followed the dark hall to the spare bedroom that she'd turned into her temporary home office. In a minute she returned to the table and laid a ten-by-twelve photograph before him and said, "I shot a few rolls of film a couple weeks ago. Just a run-of-the-mill outdoor portrait of a little girl and her dog."

Jack studied the photograph, shrugged, and said, "It's a nice picture."

"Look at the lower right-hand corner. See anything?"

He zeroed in. "Like what?"

"Does that not look like a shadow to you? As if someone might have been standing behind me?"

He looked again and said, "I don't see any shadow."

"You don't *see* that?"

"The entire corner is a little darker than the rest of the photograph, but it doesn't look like a person to me. Was someone there with you?"

"No. That's the whole point. It was just me, the girl, and the dog. Yet I had a weird sensation that someone else was there during the shoot."

"Cindy, please," he said with concern.

"No, it's true. Then I went back and took a really good look at the proofs, and I saw this."

"Saw what?"

"This silhouette."

"It's just a dark spot."

"It's a *person*."

"Cindy—"

"Just listen to me. I'm not losing my mind. I thought I was, to be honest. Between my creepy dreams and this shadow in the photograph, I was starting to think— well, I didn't know what to think. But ever since this thing happened with Jessie, it's beginning to make sense to me."

"What's making sense?"

She paused, as if to underscore her words. "Maybe someone's following me."

"What?"

"Jessie told you that some thugs were behind that viatical investment. She said they were going to kill her, didn't she?"

"Yes."

"What if those same thugs think her lawyer helped her pull off the scam? They could be out to get you, too. They could be out to get *us*."

"No one's going to get us."

"Then why is this shadow in my picture?"

"I honestly don't see it."

Her eyes seemed to cloud over. She looked at the photograph, then at Jack. "You really don't see anything?"

He shook his head. "If you want, we can hire another photographer to examine it. See if their professional judgment squares with yours."

"No."

"You sure?"

"Yes. You're right. It's not there."

Jack recoiled, confused by her sudden reversal. "It's not?"

She shook her head. "The first time I examined this proof, I was sure I saw a human shadow. Then I looked at it again tonight and I wasn't so sure. You just confirmed it for me. I'm seeing things that aren't even there." She chuckled mirthlessly and said, "I really must be freaking out."

"What happened to us is enough to push anyone to the edge."

She moved closer, as if telling him to hold her. He took her in his arms and said, "Everything's going to be okay."

"You promise?"

"Everyone has fears. The imagination can run away with you."

"Tell me about it."

"It'll pass. Believe me. We'll be fine."

"I know. Tonight's just been especially tough. The whole day, really."

"What happened?"

"It's just that . . ."

"What?"

"After this horrible thing happened in our own house, I'd managed to convince myself that God had something really good in store for us. That's why it hit me pretty hard today when I found out I wasn't pregnant."

"Good things *are* in store for us. There are so many options we haven't even talked about yet. Fertility drugs, even artificial insemination, if you want."

She smiled weakly.

"What?" he asked.

"An absurd image just flashed into my head. You sitting all by yourself in the back room of some doctor's office, flipping through the pages of a dirty magazine . . ."

"It's not like that at all."

"Oh, really, stud? How do you think they collect their specimen?"

"I dunno. I just always assumed that's why nurses wear rubber gloves."

"Perv," she said as she pushed him away playfully.

He pulled her back into his arms. "Come here, you."

She settled into his embrace, put her head against his shoulder, and said, "A baby. What a thought."

"*Our* baby. Even more amazing."

"You ready for this?"

"Heck, no. You?"

"Of course not."

"Perfect," he said. "Why should we be different from everyone else?"

She flashed a wan smile, her voice seeming to trail off in the distance. "If only we were just a little bit more like everyone else."

Jack wasn't sure how to answer that, so he kept holding her. After a minute or two, she started to rock gently in his arms. It was barely audible, but she was humming the lullaby, "Hush, Little Baby." In his head Jack was following along and enjoying the melody, until she stopped suddenly in midverse. It was a cold and abrupt ending, like hopes and dreams interrupted. He waited for her to continue, but she didn't.

They stayed wrapped in each other's arms, saying not another word, neither of them wanting to be the first to let go.

# 17
.

In the morning Jack went jogging. He pushed it farther than his normal run, following the tree-lined
path along Old Cutler Road all the way to Coco Plum,
an exclusive waterfront community. The leafy canopy
of century-old banyans extended from one side of the
road to the other, a tunnel Miami-style. Salty smells of
the bay rode in on a gentle east wind. Traffic was
sparse, but by the morning rush hour a seemingly endless stream of BMWs, Jaguars, and Mercedes-Benz con-
vertibles would connect this wealthy suburb to the
office towers in downtown Miami. Certain American-
made SUVs were acceptable in this neighborhood, but
only if they were big enough to fill two parking spaces
at The Shops of Bal Harbour and were used primarily
to drive the future Prada-totin', Gucci-lovin' generation
to and from private schools.

Jack was approaching the four-mile mark of his run
and feeling the pull of a restless night. He and Cindy
had gone back to bed around three A.M. Their talk had

put his worries about Jessie and his letter to the state attorney on the back burner, but Jack's thoughts of his mother were percolating to the surface.

The only thing he knew for certain about his mother was that he'd never known her. Everything else had come secondhand from his father and, much later in his life, *Abuela*. Jack's mother was born Ana Maria Fuentes in Havana and grew up in Bejucal, a nearby town. She left Cuba as a teenager in 1961, under a program called *Pedro Pan* (Spanish for "Peter Pan"), a humanitarian effort that was started by an Irish Catholic priest and that enabled thousands of anxious Cuban parents to spirit away their children to America after Castro took over. Ana Maria was eventually linked up with an uncle in Tampa, and *Abuela* had every intention of joining them just as soon as she had the chance. Unfortunately, that chance didn't come for almost forty years, when *Abuela* was finally able to get a visa to visit her dying brother. For Ana Maria, that meant making a new life for herself without her mother. She worked menial jobs to learn English, and moved to Miami, where she met Harry Swyteck, a handsome young college student who happened to be home on summer break. From the old photographs Jack had seen, it was obvious the boy was totally smitten. Jack was born eleven months after they were married. His mother died while he was in the nursery. Doctors weren't as quick to diagnose pre-eclampsia in the 1960s as they are today, or at least they weren't as accountable for their screwups.

It hadn't dawned on Jack until the homestretch of his morning jog, but maybe *that* was the reason he'd jumped into Jessie's case.

He wondered what his mother would think now, her

son duped by a respected doctor and a woman who'd only pretended to be misdiagnosed. He knew too little about her to hazard a guess. His father had remarried before Jack was out of diapers. Agnes, Jack's stepmother, was a good woman with a weakness for gin martinis and an irrational hatred for a woman she feared Jack's father would never stop loving—his first wife, Jack's mother. She went ballistic each time a letter from *Abuela* arrived from Cuba, and many of them Jack never saw, thanks to her. "Dysfunctional" was the politically correct label that experts might have placed on the Swyteck family. Jack tended to think of it as a royal freak show. But he could still laugh about some things. He was a half-Cuban boy raised in a completely Anglo home with virtually no link to Cuban culture. That alone guaranteed him a lifelong parade of comedic moments. People formed certain impressions about the Anglo Jack, only to do a complete one-eighty upon hearing that he was half-Hispanic. Take his Spanish, for example. Jack was proud of his heritage, but it was with some reluctance that he shared his Cuban roots with anyone impressed by the way this presumed gringo named Swyteck could speak Spanish. It was a conversation he'd had at least a thousand times:

"*Wow, Jack, your Spanish is really good.*"
"*My mother was Cuban.*"
"*Wow, Jack, your Spanish really sucks.*"

It was all how you looked at it.

Jack finished the run and showered long before his normal breakfast hour. The commute from his mother-in-law's house was a little farther than his usual drive, but he still arrived before his secretary. Jack stood outside the double-door entrance, fumbling for the master key, as the elevator opened behind him. He glanced over his shoulder, then did a double take.

"Good morning," said Dr. Marsh.

Jack turned but didn't answer. He hadn't seen the doctor since the last elevator ride, when he and Jessie had held hands. Marsh came forward but didn't offer Jack his hand.

"I said good morning, Mr. Swyteck."

"Oh, it's you, Dr. Marsh. I didn't recognize you without your girlfriend."

"I thought we should talk."

Jack gave him a quick once-over and said, "Come in."

He opened the door and flipped on the lights. Dr. Marsh followed him through the small reception area to the main conference room. They sat on opposite sides of the smoked-glass table top.

The doctor was a handsome man who tried way too hard to look younger. Flecks of gray added distinction to his black hair, but it was coated with a thick styling gel that reflected badly in the light. Beneath his seven-hundred-dollar Armani jacket he wore a Miami Heat T-shirt that was given away at last year's NBA playoffs. It was a look that a twenty-nine-year-old tech-stock millionaire on South Beach might get away with, but not a doctor who'd reached the age where he was lucky to still have all of his hair. Purely on a physical level, he didn't strike Jack at all as Jessie's type. For one, Jessie had hated beards, even well-groomed ones. At least that was what she'd told Jack when he'd let his stubble grow for a week while they were still dating. Maybe she'd just hated them on Jack. Or maybe Jack didn't have a clue as to her likes and dislikes.

Jack said, "Before we start, it should be made clear that you're not here as a client or prospective client. Anything we talk about here is not protected by the attorney-client privilege."

"That's fine. I'm confident you won't be repeating this conversation to anyone anyway." He pulled a package of cigarettes from his inside pocket. "Mind if I smoke?"

"Yes."

He smiled a little, as if he liked Jack's combative edge, then put away the cigarettes. "I hear you've been talking to the state attorney's office."

"That's true."

"What are you telling them?"

"The truth."

The doctor paused, as if he needed a moment to recall what was "the truth." It lasted just long enough to let Jack take control of the conversation. "Who told you I was talking to the state attorney?" asked Jack.

"A detective came to see me last night. Him and an assistant state attorney."

"Benno Jancowitz?"

"Name's not important."

"What did you talk about?"

"They told me you'd given them a written statement."

"That's between me and them," said Jack.

"Don't try to get all legal on me. I know what it says. They read it to me."

"Good. Get used to hearing it. It'll be public information by the end of today."

"Don't you want to know why they read it to me?"

"To give you a chance to confirm or deny your role in the scam, I presume."

"You presume wrong."

"Is that so?"

"Yeah. They wanted me to confirm that *you* were part of it."

"I wasn't part of it," Jack said, without so much as blinking.

Dr. Marsh leaned into the table, not quite as smoothly as he might have, as if he'd overrehearsed the cherished line he was about to deliver. "Trust me, Mr. Swyteck. If there was a scam, you were part of it."

"Are you threatening me?"

"I'm appealing to your sense of reason. We're both smart men, but nobody's perfect. Shit, till I saw what that woman could do with a zucchini squash, I was never one to eat my veggies. Jessie Merrill was one tasty dish."

"She was just another client."

"Yeah, and Anna Kournikova is just another tennis player. My point is this. You and I both made mistakes with the same woman. You got a little more crazy than I did, but you're a criminal defense lawyer, so you know people who do that kind of stuff."

"What kind of stuff?"

"Fixing things. You know, getting rid of problems like Jessie Merrill."

"Are you saying—are you *accusing* me of having hired someone to kill her?"

"The detective told me you were in court the day Jessie died. Ironclad alibi. How else could you have done it?"

"That's the whole point. I didn't do anything."

"I heard about you and that friend of yours who went to visit my wife. You know who I'm talking about: Theo Knight, former death-row inmate."

"Theo is not a murderer. And neither am I."

"Come on. I don't give a rat's ass if you had her whacked. Nobody's saying we have to like each other, but we have to be together on this. I can help you on the back end. You just gotta help me on the front end."

"What front end?"

"That's my boy. 'What front end?' I like that. Lost your memory already, have you?"

"What are you talking about?"

"The front end—the scam. There was none, right?"

"No, not right."

"Careful there. With that murder for hire, the back end's the much uglier rap."

Jack felt the sudden urge to kick his teeth in. "Get out of my office."

"You need me."

"Get out."

"If you say there's a scam, I say you're part of it. If you're in on the front end, you're in way deep on the back end."

"You have ten seconds to be outta here."

He stayed put, defiant, but a nervous stroke of his beard told Jack that he was cracking. Finally, he rose, and Jack showed him to the lobby. They stopped at the double glass doors that led to the elevators.

"You sure you won't play ball?" said Marsh.

"Get out before I bat your head across the room."

"Lay a hand on me, counselor, and I'll sue you for assault."

"I'll look forward to it. No better place than a courtroom to beat your ass."

"Yeah," he said with a smirk. "Just like the last time."

"It won't be like the last time."

"Got that right," he said as his expression ran cold. "I won't have to worry about Jessie fucking things up."

He pushed open the door and left. Jack watched

through the beveled-glass window as the doctor entered the open elevator and checked his handsome facade in the chrome finish.

The doors closed, and for the first time since Jessie's death Jack was really beginning to wonder: Just who was the brain behind the scam?

# 18

‎•

When Jack first met Cindy, she was a wimp when it came to drinking. "Tying one on" meant an extra splash of Bailey's Irish Cream in her heaping bowl of Häagen Dazs. She'd been raised in a strict Methodist household. Her mother sang in the church choir and her father, Jack was told, had just one vice, a little nickel-and-dime-poker game on Tuesday evenings. She'd loosened up over the years, but Jack rarely saw her sloshed.

So, when he came home early at five o'clock and found a completely empty bottle of chardonnay on the kitchen table, he knew something was amiss.

"You share that with anyone?" asked Jack.

She shook her head. Her mother wasn't home. She'd been drinking alone.

Time had passed slowly since Jessie's death, and the media had not yet tired of speculating as to the "true nature" of the "tragic relationship" between Jack and his attractive client. It was obviously beginning to take a toll.

"You lied to me," she said.

He looked at her but couldn't speak. It hurt more than being called a murderer. "What are you talking about?"

"She was your lover, wasn't she?"

"Do you mean Jessie?"

"Who else?"

"No." He hurried to the table, sat in the chair beside her. "Who told you that?"

"A couple of investigators were just here."

"What kind of investigators?"

"Homicide."

"You let them in this house? Cindy, you have to stay away from those people."

"Why? So I don't hear the truth?"

He looked into her eyes. She'd been drinking, for sure. But he could see way past that, to the part that really hurt. She'd been crying. "What did they tell you?"

She took a sip from her wine glass, but it was dry. "They said you and Jessie were having an affair."

"Not true."

"I trusted you, Jack. I felt sorry for Jessie, I told you to take her case. How could you do this?"

"I didn't do anything. It's so obvious what they're up to. They lay this cockeyed romance theory on you to get you mad enough to turn against me. They're fishing, that's all."

"You really think she killed herself?"

"I don't know. But whatever happened to her, we weren't lovers."

"Damn you! The woman slit her wrist in our bathtub—*naked*."

"Looks bad, I know."

"Yeah, all over the news for over a week it's been looking bad. There isn't a person in Miami who doesn't think you two were doing it."

"Everyone but the person who mattered. You believed me."

"I *wanted* to believe you. But sooner or later, even I have to face facts."

"The fact is, it didn't happen between me and Jessie. And there isn't a bit of proof that it did."

The anger drained from her voice, and she was suddenly stone-cold serious. "That's the problem, Jack. Now there is proof."

He could almost hear his own heart pounding. "What?"

"The investigators. They left it for me."

"Left what?"

She pushed away from the table, crossed the kitchen, and stopped at the cassette player on the counter. "This," she said as she ejected the tape.

"What's that supposed to be?"

"Seems your friend Jessie—your *client*—taped one of your little episodes in her bedroom."

"That's not possible. There were no episodes."

"Stop lying! It's your voice. It's her voice. And the two of you aren't talking sports."

He was speechless. "This is crazy. We were never together. And even if we had been, why would she record it?"

"Get real. She's a swindler, and you're a married man with an awful lot to lose. She wouldn't be the first woman to slip a tape recorder under the bed."

"I want to hear it."

"Well, I don't. I've heard enough."

She grabbed her purse and dug for the car keys.

"Wait," he said. "Give me a minute to listen to it."

"No." She started for the door.

"Cindy, please."

"I said no."

He stepped between her and the door. "You're not driving anywhere. You just drank a whole bottle of wine."

She glared, then started to tremble. A huge tear streamed down her check. Wiping it away only brought replacements, a flood. Jack went to her, but she backed away.

"Just stay away from me!"

"Cindy, I would never cheat on you."

"What about Gina?"

He froze. Gina Terisi, years earlier. "That was before we were even engaged. You went to Italy on that photo assignment and told me we were through before you left."

"You obviously took it very well."

"No. I was a wreck. That's how it happened with Gina in the first place."

"Were you a wreck this time? Is that how it happened with Jessie?"

"No. It didn't happen with Jessie."

"It's on tape!"

"I think I know what this is. Just let me hear it."

"I'm not going to sit here while you play that thing."

As she tried to pass, he backed against the door. "You're not driving drunk."

"Let me out!" She punched him in the chest, not a boxer's punch but more like beating on a door in frustration. She practically fell against him, partly catharsis, partly the alcohol. He tried to take her in his arms, but she kept fighting for the doorknob.

"I'll go," he said. "Just give me the tape and promise you won't drive anywhere."

Their eyes locked—those beautiful, blue, moist eyes filled with doubt and disappointment. Quickly she went to the cassette player on the counter and threw the tape at him. He caught it.

"Knock yourself out, Jack. Now leave me alone."

He didn't budge, couldn't move his feet. "Cindy, I love—"

"Don't even say it. Just go!"

He hated to leave on that note, but he didn't want to make things worse by trying to explain the tape before hearing it. He lowered his head, opened the door, and went without another word. He was halfway down the steps when the porch light switched off. It seemed that Cindy wanted it that way—Jack walking to his car in total darkness, alone.

# 19

## •

Jack listened to the audiocassette in the car. Immediately, he knew what it was. The bigger question was, Why was she doing this to him?

Jack had one good friend who'd known the old Jessie. Not in the same way Jack had known her, but they used to hang out together back when Jack was dating Jessie. He'd first met Mike Campbell in Hawaii. Jack spent a summer slumming it in Maui before law school, one last blowout before immersing himself in the study of law. Mike had done him one better, having spent his entire senior year as a transfer student at the University of Hawaii before starting law school in Miami. He'd simply packed up his old Porsche at the landlocked University of Illinois, driven to Los Angeles, hopped on a ship, and finished out his undergraduate degree surrounded by palm trees and beautiful women. They were a couple of young immortals, crazy enough to night-dive in the black ocean beneath the fishing boats, living for the rush of adrenaline that came each time they'd spot holes in the nets that sharks had torn through. Mike was always a bit more fearless, which is why he now lived on the water, with a forty-three-foot Tiara open-fisherman docked in his backyard. He'd second-mortgaged his house and risked everything to wage a ten-year battle against the makers of a polybutylene piping that was supposed to replace copper plumbing in homes across the United States. Turned out that even the minimal levels of chlorine in normal drinking water disintegrated the stuff. Darn. It only ended up costing the big boys 1.25 billion dollars. At the time, it was the largest settlement ever in a case that didn't involve personal injuries. Mike walked away with twenty-two million bucks, thank you very much.

The best part was, it was still impossible to hate the guy.

"You and Jessie on tape?" said Mike.

Jack had stopped by his house and caught him tinkering with the stereo system on his boat. They were sharing a couple of beers on deck, Mike leaning against the rail and Jack reclining in the hot seat, as they called it, a bolted-down fishing chair that made Jack want to strap himself in and reel in a monster sailfish. It was well past sunset, but the landscape lighting from the expensive homes on the other side of the canal shimmered on the waterway.

"Yeah. On tape."

"Like, screaming and everything?"

"Mike, you're not helping."

"Every good lawyer needs all the facts."

"The most important fact, buddy, is that this tape is ancient. It was made before I'd even met Cindy Paige."

"So, was it a high-pitched scream, or more of a guttural—"

"Mike, come on."

"Sorry." He swiveled in his chair and grabbed another Bud from the cooler. "So, it's an old tape. Did you even know she had it?"

"Not really."

"What do you mean, not really?"

Jack tipped back his beer, took a long pull. "Jessie was a lot of fun, but she wasn't nearly as promiscuous as people thought. We didn't jump in bed together, by any means. But once we dated awhile, things progressed. And once we got there, things got kind of . . . interesting."

"Interesting?"

"She wanted to make a videotape."

"What?" he said, smiling.

"I wouldn't go for it. But for about a two-month stretch, she brought it up almost every time we got naked. One night we were out dancing, got pretty drunk. About thirty seconds after we get back to her apartment, we're in bed rolling all over each other. She reaches for the remote control on the nightstand, and I think she's switching on the television to throw a little light on the subject. We're about five seconds away from doing it when I realize that there's a tape recorder on the nightstand. She figures that maybe we'll ease into this with just the audio, then maybe I'll warm up to the idea and do a video. I tell her to turn it off, but at this point I don't care if we're live on National Public Radio. That's how it happened."

"You made an X-rated audiocassette?"

"It was awful. It sounded like a couple of drunks going at it in the dark."

"So, you got rid of it?"

"I told her to, but she kept it. It became a little gag

between us. I'd be working late at the office till maybe ten or eleven o'clock. Instead of getting a nagging call to come home, I'd pick up the phone and on the other end of the line would be this tape of Jessie outdoing Meg Ryan in the *When Harry Met Sally* restaurant scene."

"Beats all heck out of clanging the dinner bell."

"It was good for a couple of laughs, and then she dropped it."

"But she kept the tape?"

"Evidently."

"For how many years?"

"Seven, closer to eight. I don't read much into that. She could have just stuffed it in a shoebox somewhere and forgotten about it."

"And the homicide investigators found it."

"Yeah. Or, more likely, Jessie's estate handed it over to them as evidence."

"As evidence of what? That you and Jessie had sex before you and Cindy even met?"

"I guess it never occurred to anyone that the tape might be from another decade."

"How could they not see it?" said Mike. "You ever gone back to one of your old cassettes? They look *old*."

"But a copy doesn't look old. Cindy's looked brand-new. Unless you have the original, it wouldn't be so obvious that the tape is eight years old."

"So, where's the original?"

"I don't know. The police might have it, but that would be really scummy of them to copy an old cassette onto a new reel and pass it off to my wife as a recent affair."

"So, presumably Jessie's estate kept the original, and for some reason they gave the police a copy that makes it look new."

"Or, I suppose, the original could be gone, and the

only thing Jessie left behind was a copy that looks brand-new."

"Why would she do that?"

Jack paused, as if afraid to come across as paranoid. "Because she wanted someone to think that she and I were having a recent affair."

"Ah, I see," he said, smiling. "And which conspiracy theory do you subscribe to on the Kennedy assassination? Would it be the Mafia, the Cubans, or perhaps the cluster of icebergs that got the *Titanic*?"

"Okay, it's a little out there. But whatever went on here, it sure convinced my wife."

Mike leaned forward in his captain's chair, looked at Jack with concern. "How is Cindy doing?"

"So-so. This doesn't help."

"I thought about you two when I saw this on the news. I called you."

"I know. I got the message. So many people called, I just didn't have a chance to return them all."

"I thought about calling Cindy, but I didn't know what kind of shape she'd be in. Bad enough finding a body in your house. But it has to be especially hard on her, after the nightmare she went through with that psycho former client of yours."

Jack looked down at his empty beer bottle. "First him, now Jessie. Guess I need to work on my choice of clients."

"Water through the pipes, as I always say."

"Polybutylene pipes."

Their bottles clicked in toast. "God love 'em," said Mike.

They shared a weak smile, then turned serious. "Tell me the truth," said Jack. "After all these years, why do you think Jessie had that tape?"

"Could be as you said. She packed it away in her closet and forgot it even existed."

"Or?"

"I don't know. You are the son of a former governor. Maybe she thought you'd run for office some day and she could embarrass you."

Jack peeled the label from his beer. "Possible, I suppose."

"Or it could be that she's been listening to that tape over and over again for the last decade, turning away the likes of George Clooney and Brad Pitt, crying her eyes out night after night for Jack Swyteck, world's greatest lover."

"You think?"

"Oh, absolutely."

"Wow. I never would have figured that out on my own. You're a genius."

"I know."

"Seriously," said Jack. "You're a plaintiffs' lawyer."

Mike glanced around his gorgeous boat. "Last time I checked."

"Go back in time eight months. On the face of it, Jessie Merrill had an attractive case. Sympathetic facts, a young and beautiful client."

"I'll give you that."

"She could have gone to a zillion different lawyers. Most of them would have taken the case. Hell, some would have signed on even if she'd told them flat-out in advance that the whole thing was a scam."

"Not me, but some of them, yeah."

"Yet, she picks me. A guy whose practice is ninety-percent criminal. Why?"

Mike didn't answer right away, seeming to measure his words. "Maybe she wanted a really smart lawyer who she knew she could fool."

"Thanks."

"Or, for some bizarre reason, she wanted you back in her life."

"But why? After all these years, why?"

He shrugged and said, "Can't help you there, my friend. You'll have to answer that one yourself."

Jack leaned back in the deck chair, watched the moonlight glistening on the little ripples in the brackish water alongside Mike's boat. "I wish I knew," was all he could say.

Mike tossed his empty into the open cooler. "You need a place to stay tonight?"

He considered it, then said, "No. I can't let this fester."

"What are you going to do?"

"Tell Cindy the truth."

"That won't be easy."

"Cake," Jack said. "The hard part is getting her to believe it."

He grabbed an end of the cooler, and Mike grabbed the other. They climbed from the boat, the empties rattling against the cold ones as they walked toward the patio.

# 20

·

The chain lock was on the door when Jack got to his mother-in-law's house. It opened about six inches and then caught.

"Cindy?" he called out through the narrow opening.

"Go away, Jack." It was her mother's voice, coming from the other room.

"I just want to talk."

"She doesn't want to talk to you."

Part of him wanted to plead directly with Cindy to let him in, but he knew there was no getting through to her as long as her mother was acting as gatekeeper.

"Cindy, it's just as I thought. That tape is old. It was made before I'd even met you."

No one answered.

"Call me, please. I'll leave my cell phone on."

"Better get an extra long–life battery," her mother said.

"Thanks a ton, Evelyn." He closed the door and retreated quietly to his car.

He wasn't sure where to go. He drove around the neighborhood for a few minutes, heading generally in the direction of U.S. 1. He considered going back to Mike's, then changed his mind. Cindy was foremost in his thoughts, but his earlier talk with Mike had helped frame another question that, on reflection, just might tie in with his current marital woes: Exactly what information about Jack had Jessie's estate handed over to the state attorney?

This wasn't a job for Theo. He turned down Ludlam Road and decided to pay a visit to Clara Pierce.

In Florida, the executor of the estate is called a personal representative, and with Clara the term "personal" seemed particularly appropriate. It had been years since Jack had been to Clara's house. They'd first met when Jack was dating Jessie. She was a lawyer and one of Jessie's oldest friends, which was how she ended up drafting Jessie's will and being named the PR. Jessie and Jack had actually double-dated with Clara and her then-husband. David and Jack had stayed friendly through the divorce, though Jack had tried not to take sides. David was a real estate attorney who'd given up his own career to be their son's primary caretaker. He did it all—the bottle feedings, the diapers, the back-and-forth from school, homework, soccer, Little League. He fought for custody when they divorced, and lost. At the time, Jack didn't blame Clara for turning on the tears to convince a judge that a boy needed his mother. Having never known his own mother, Jack was perhaps an easy sell. But it bugged him to no end when she'd packed up the boy's things and shipped him off to boarding school two months after the court awarded her custody. It only confirmed that she hadn't really wanted her son, she just didn't want her husband to have him. The only thing that mattered to Clara was winning.

Clara didn't seem shocked to see Jack. She invited him into the kitchen for coffee.

"Your son still a hotshot center fielder?" Jack asked, baiting her.

"Oh, yeah. He's always been, you know, really centered."

Typical of Clara not to know that her own son was a pitcher, not a center fielder. Even Jack's stepmother would have known the difference, and she thought Mickey Mantle was a mouse that sat over your fireplace.

"Cream and sugar?" she asked.

"Black's good."

She sat on the bar stool on the other side of the counter, facing Jack. She was still dressed in office attire, a basic navy blue business suit and white silk blouse. Clara wasn't big on style. She'd worn her hair the same way for eight years, tight and efficient curls as black as her coffee. She took a sip from her cup and eyed him over the rim, as if to say, *What gives?*

"A couple of homicide investigators came to see Cindy today," said Jack. "They gave her an audiotape of me and Jessie. Know anything about it?"

"Of course. I gave it to them."

"Why?"

"I've inventoried every item of her personal property. That's my job as PR. The police asked me for anything that might shed light on the nature of the relationship between you and Jessie. So I gave them the tape."

"You could have called to give me a heads-up. It's the least I would have done for an old friend."

"You and I were never really friends."

She wasn't being acerbic, just brutally honest. Jack said, "I didn't side with David over you. I was subpoenaed for the custody hearing. I told the truth. David was a good father."

"That has nothing to do with this. Jessie was my friend, and the police are trying to find out how she died. I intend to cooperate, and I'm not going to pick up the phone and call you every time something happens. That's not my job."

"Did you know that the audiotape was made back when Jessie and I were dating?"

"No. It looked brand-new."

"You mean the copy you gave to the state attorney looks brand-new."

"No. I'm talking about the only tape I've ever seen."

"You mean the tape you found among Jessie's possessions looked like new?"

"Yes."

Jack tried not to look too puzzled, but his conversation with Mike about being paranoid was echoing in his brain. *Maybe it was icebergs that got Kennedy.* "Jessie must have copied it onto a new tape and destroyed the original."

"Why would she do that?"

He had a theory, but not one that he wanted to share with Clara. "I'm not sure. You got any ideas?"

"I don't even want to guess what kind of games you and Jessie were playing. I just want to help the police find out what happened to her."

"I didn't kill her."

"I hope that's true. I sincerely mean that."

"Come on, Clara. You don't really believe I'm a killer."

"You're right, I don't. But I didn't believe Jessie

would scam a viatical company out of a million and a half dollars, either."

"She did."

"So you say."

"I saw her and Dr. Marsh holding hands just minutes after the verdict."

"So what? He was happy she won. That doesn't mean the two of them were partners in crime."

"She told me it was a scam, and he practically admitted it too. Right in my office."

"He's a respected, board-certified neurologist."

"Evidently, he's also a thief."

"If he's the thief, then why is it your name instead of his on the joint bank account?"

Jack nearly choked. "What bank account?"

"Grand Bahama Trust Company. The offshore bank where Jessie put the money she got from the viatical investors. She had an account there. Jessie *and you* had an account there."

He blinked several times and said, "There must be some mistake."

"Account number zero-one-oh-three-one. A joint account in the name of Jessie Suzanne Merrill and John Lawrence Swyteck. That is your name, isn't it?"

"Yeah, but—a joint account?"

"Don't get any ideas. If you even try to touch that money, I'll be right in your face. Those funds are staying in her estate."

"Don't worry. I want no part of any money she got in a scam. I'll stipulate that it's not mine."

"Good. I'll get you the papers tomorrow."

"Fine. But I need to get to the bottom of this joint bank account. This is the first I ever heard of it."

"You expect me to believe that?"

"It's true."

"Why would Jessie put your name on an account worth a million and a half dollars and not even tell you?"

"Maybe for the same reason she wanted to make that old audiotape look new again."

She narrowed her eyes, as if he were insulting her intelligence. "Let me give you a little advice. Just admit that you and Jessie were doing the deed. This Clinton-like denial is only going to make people think you killed her."

"They won't think that. No more than you do. You wouldn't have invited me into your house if you thought I was a murderer."

She didn't answer.

Jack said, "If anyone killed Jessie, it was the investors whom she scammed."

"That's a theory."

"It's more than that. The night before she died, Jessie came to me, pleading with me to help her. She was sure these investors were going to kill her."

"I know all that. The detectives showed me the letter you wrote to the state attorney. But your investor theory just doesn't add up for me."

"I don't see why not."

"Simple. If the viatical investors were the killers, they wouldn't have made her death look anything like suicide."

"What makes you say that?"

"I'm the PR of her estate. I've seen her life insurance policy. She bought it twenty-two months ago. It's void if she took her own life less than two years after the effective date. It's a standard suicide exclusion."

His response came slowly, as if weighted by the

implications. "So, if her death is ruled a suicide, the investors lose their three-million-dollar death benefit."

"Bingo. I don't care how bad you say those guys are, they can't be idiots. If they were behind it, Jessie would have been found dead in her car at the bottom of some canal. Her death would have looked like an accident, not suicide."

Jack stared into his empty coffee cup. It suddenly seemed like a gaping black hole, one big enough to swallow him and his whole theory about the investors as killers.

"You okay?" asked Clara.

"Sure. That suicide exclusion is news to me, that's all. I guess that's why the cops are looking at me and not the investors."

"You got that right."

Jack sipped his coffee, then caught Clara's eye. "You seem to know more than you say."

"Could be."

"Is there anything else I should know?"

"Yes."

"What?"

"Don't piss me off. Because if I wanted to hurt you, believe me: I could really hurt you."

Her tone wasn't threatening, but he still felt threatened. She rose, no subtle signal that it was time for him to leave. Jack placed his coffee mug on the counter and said, "Thanks for the caffeine."

"You're welcome."

She walked him to the foyer and opened the front door. He started out, then stopped and said, "I didn't kill Jessie."

"You said that already."

"I didn't have her killed, either."

"Now there's something I hadn't heard yet."

"Now you have."

"Yes. Now I have. Finally."

They said good night, and Jack headed down the steps, the door closing behind him.

## 21

By nine o'clock Jack was on a second plate of *ropa vieja*, a shredded-beef dish with a name that translates to "old clothes." According to his grandmother, the name only described the meat's tattered appearance and had nothing to do with the actual ingredients. Then again, she'd fed him *tasajo* without disclosing that it was horse meat, and she would argue until her dying breath that Cubans do so eat green vegetables, as fried plantains were the tropical equivalent thereof.

Jack had a lot to learn about Cuban cuisine.

The stop at *Abuela*'s was yet another diversion. He'd tried to call Cindy but had gotten nowhere, which was perhaps just as well. Perhaps he needed to take a little time to refine an explanation that, as yet, sounded only slightly better than "Good news, honey, it's been at least a decade since my last sex tape."

"*Más, mi niño?*" Predictably, *Abuela* was asking if he wanted more to eat.

"*No, gracias.*"

She stroked his head and ladled on more rice. He didn't protest. Jack could only imagine what it must have been like to enjoy cooking, more than anything else in the world, and yet have practically nothing in the cupboard for thirty-eight years. *Abuela* had a great kitchen now. The townhouse Jack had rented for her was practically new, and she shared it with a lady friend from church. She'd lived with him and Cindy for a short time. They'd sit around the dinner table every night, Jack speaking bad Spanish and *Abuela* answering in broken English, each of them trying to learn the other's language in record time so that they could communicate freely. But having a place of her own made it easier to get out and enjoy herself.

Hard to believe, but almost three years had passed since Jack's father called to tell him that *Abuela* was flying into Miami International Airport. Jack had nearly dropped the phone. Never had he expected her to come to Miami at her age, even on a humanitarian visa to visit her dying brother. He'd tried many times to visit her in Cuba, and while many Americans did visit relatives there, Jack was never approved for travel. His father's staunch anti-Castro speeches as a state legislator and later as governor had surely played a role in the Cuban government's obstinacy. She'd come over on a temporary visa, but she was on her way to U.S. citizenship and would never go back. Their initial face-to-face meeting evoked a whole range of emotions. For the first time in his life, Jack had a profound sense that his mother had actually existed. She was no longer just an image in a photo album or a string of anecdotes as told by his father. Ana Maria had lived. She'd had a mother who'd loved her and who now loved Jack, gave him big hugs, fed him till he could have exploded—and then served dessert.

"I made flan," she said with a grin.

"Ah, your other invention."

"I only perfected flan. I didn't invent it."

They laughed, and he enjoyed her warm gaze. All his life he'd been told that he resembled his father, a well-intended compliment from people who had never met his mother. *Abuela* saw him differently, as if she were catching a precious glimpse of someone else each time she looked into his eyes. Those were the rare moments in his life when he actually felt Cuban.

She served an enormous portion of the custardlike dessert, spooning on extra caramel sauce. Then she took a seat across from him at the table.

"I was on the radio again today," she said.

Jack let the flan melt in his mouth, then said, "I thought we agreed, no more radio. No more stories about inventing *tres leches*."

She switched completely to Spanish, the only way to recount with proper feeling the entire fabricated story. With a totally straight face, she told him yet again how she'd invented *tres leches* a few years before the Cuban revolution and shared the recipe with no one but her ex–best friend, Maritza, who defected to Miami in the mid-sixties and sold out to a Hialeah restaurant for a mere twenty-five dollars and a month's supply of pork chunks.

*Abuela* was the only bilingual person on the planet who was patient enough to endure his stilted Spanish, so he answered in kind. "Abuela, I love you. But you do realize that people are laughing when you tell that story on the radio, don't you?"

"I didn't tell that story today. I talked about you."

"On Spanish radio?"

"The news people all say terrible things. Someone has to tell the truth."

"You shouldn't do this."

"It's okay. They like having me on their show now. What does it matter if they tease the crazy old lady who says she invented *tres leches*? So long as I get to slip in a few words about my grandson."

"I know you mean well, but I'm serious. You can't do that."

"Why can't I tell the world you are not a murderer?"

"If you start talking publicly about this case, people will want to interview you. Not just reporters. Police and prosecutors, too."

"I can handle them."

"No, you can't." He was serious without being stern. She seemed to get the message.

*"Bueno,"* she said, then switched over to English. "I say nothing to no one."

"It's best that way. Any media contacts need to be approved by my attorney and me. Even Spanish radio."

Her eyes showed concern. Jack pressed her hand into his and said, "It was nice of you to try to help."

She still looked worried. Finally, she asked, "How are you and Cindy?"

"We're . . . okay."

"You tell her you love her?"

"Of course."

"When?"

"All the time."

"When last?"

"Tonight." *Just before she kicked me out of the house*, he thought.

"Is good. Is *muy importante* that you tell your wife how you feel."

"I did."

She cupped her hand, gently patted his cheek. "Maybe you should tell her again."

From the moment Jack had walked into her apartment, he thought he'd managed to keep his problems with Cindy to himself. It amazed him how well *Abuela* had come to know him in the short time she'd been in this country. "Maybe you're right."

He rose to help with the dishes, but she wouldn't allow it. "Go to your wife. Your beautiful wife."

He kissed her on the forehead, thanked her for dinner, and left through the back door.

Jack had a renewed sense of energy as he followed the sidewalk around to the back of the building. He definitely had some smoothing over to do with Cindy. But for the moment it was refreshing to step outside the cynical world and let himself believe, as *Abuela* did, that love conquers all.

His car was parked in a guest space, two buildings away from *Abuela*'s townhouse. He followed the long, S-curved sidewalk through a maze of trees. A rush of wind stirred the waxy ficus leaves overhead. He reached for his car keys, stopped, and glanced over his shoulder. He thought he'd heard footsteps behind him, but no one was in sight. Up ahead, the sidewalk stretched through a stand of larger trees. The old, twisted roots had caused the cement sections to buckle and crack over the years. It was suddenly darker, as the lights along this particular segment of the walkway were blocked by low-hanging limbs.

Again, he heard footsteps. He walked faster, and the clicking of heels behind him seemed to quicken to the same pace. He stepped off the sidewalk and continued through the grass. The sound of footsteps vanished, as if someone were tracing his silent path. He returned to the sidewalk at the top of the S-curve. His heels clicked on concrete, and a few seconds later the clicking resumed behind him.

He was definitely being followed.

Jack stopped and turned. In the darkness beneath the trees, he could see no more than twenty meters. He saw no one, but he sensed someone was there.

"*Abuela*? Is that you?" He knew it wasn't her, but somehow it seemed less paranoid than a nervous "Who's there?"

No one answered.

Jack waited a moment, then reached for his cell phone. Just as he flipped it open, a crushing blow to the center of his back sent him, flailing, face-first to the sidewalk. The phone went flying, and his breath escaped with nearly enough force to take his lungs right along with it. He tried to get up and wobbled onto one knee. A second blow to the same vertebrae knocked him down for at least another eight-count. This time, he was too disoriented to break the fall. His chin smashed against the concrete. The hot, salty taste of blood filled his mouth.

With his cheek to the sidewalk, he counted two pairs of feet. Or was he seeing double?

"What . . . do . . ." He could barely form words, let alone sentences.

His hand exploded in pain as a steel-toed boot smashed his fingers into the sidewalk. He tried to look up, but it was futile. In the darkness, it would have been hard for anyone to make out a face. In Jack's battered state, the attacker was a fuzzy silhouette.

"Consider yourself warned, Swyteck."

The voice startled him. It sounded female. *I'm getting whooped by a woman?*

He laid still, playing possum. The boot extended toward him, gently this time, poking his ribs, as if to see if he was conscious. Somehow, he found the strength to spring to life and grab an ankle, pulling and twisting as hard as he could. His attacker tumbled to the ground, and Jack tumbled with her. His arms flailed as he tried to get hold of another leg, but she was amazingly strong and quick. They rolled several times and slammed into a tree. Jack groaned as his attacker wiggled free. He started toward her, but she threw herself at him, legs whirling like a professional kickboxer. Her boot caught him squarely on the side of the head, and down he went.

He was flat on his belly as someone grabbed him from behind, took a fistful of hair, and yanked his head back.

"One more move, and you bleed like a stuck pig."

Jack went rigid. A cold, steel blade was at his throat. The voice was a man's. He hadn't been seeing double; there were two attackers. "Take it easy," said Jack.

"Silence," he said with a slap to Jack's head. "Like we said, consider yourself warned."

"Warned—of what?"

"Pin Jessie's murder on whoever you want. Just don't pin it on us."

"Who . . . you?"

The man pulled Jack's head back harder. "We don't like to hurt grandmothers, but if you keep putting her on the radio to point fingers where she shouldn't, it's on your head."

He focused long enough to regret he'd ever told *Abuela* about the viatical investors. "She's not part of this."

"Shut up. You don't know who you're fucking with.

Get your grandma off the radio, or there'll be another bloodbath. Understand?"

"You don't—" Jack stopped in midsentence. The blade was pressing harder against his throat.

"Yes or no, Swyteck. Do you understand?"

"Yes."

"Make sure you do," he said, then slammed Jack's head forward into the sidewalk one last time. Jack fought to stay conscious, but he was barely hanging on. He saw nothing, heard nothing, as his world slowly turned darker than night itself, and then all was black.

## 22

Cindy's brain was throbbing. She lifted her head from the pillow, and it weighed a ton. She'd had even more wine after Jack left, putting herself way over her limit. She closed her eyes and let her head sink back into goose down, but it felt like a vise grip pressing at either ear.

She had to move, or, she was certain, she would die.

Her hand slid across the sheet and found the edge of the mattress. She pulled herself up onto her side and checked the digital alarm clock on the nightstand. The numbers were a blur without her contact lenses, and she couldn't reach to pull it closer. There was no telling what time it was.

Just like in her dream. *That awful dream.*

She didn't think she was dreaming. But she didn't feel awake, either. Never in her life had she been hungover like this, not even from those prom-night slush drinks spiked with Southern Comfort. Slowly, her eyes adjusted to the dim lighting. The blinds were shut, but the faint outline of dawn brightened the thin openings between slats. She took a moment, then sat up in bed.

The sound of footsteps thumped in the hallway.

"Mom?"

No one answered, but her voice was weak, stolen by the effects of too much alcohol. Cindy looked around the room. The empty wine bottle was on the bureau, and the mere sight of it was enough to make her sick. She felt a need to run for the bathroom, but, mercifully, the nausea quickly passed. How ironic, she thought, all the school mornings she'd lain in this very room just *pretending* to be sick. She'd hated school as a kid, and, for the longest time, she'd hated this house. She didn't think of it as the house she'd grown up in, at least not entirely. Only after her father was dead had the rest of the surviving family moved there, the widow, two daughters, and three very young boys. Yet it seemed full of memories. Or, at least, at the moment, it was filling her head with memories. Through her mind's eye, she was looking at herself again, the way she could in her dream, except this wasn't a dream— or at least it wasn't *the* dream. The Cindy she saw was nine years old, in their old house, the one before this one, the house in New Hampshire.

•

The leaves rustled outside her bedroom window. As she lay awake staring at the ceiling, the wind plucked the brown and crispy ones from the branches and sent them flying through the night sky. Some were caught in the updraft and swirled high. The others fell to the ground, weaving the endless carpet of dead leaves across their lawn. Tourists came from all over the country to see autumn like this. Cindy loathed it. For a brief two weeks, the green leaves of summer turned themselves into something that no living thing could become without courting disaster, blazing flickers of flame at the end of twisted branches. And then, one by one, the flames were extinguished. It was as if the leaves were being fooled. Tricked into death.

A gust of wind howled outside, and a flock of dead leaves pecked at her window. Cindy pulled the covers over her head. *Stupid fools.*

She heard a noise, a slamming sound. It was as if something had fallen or been knocked over. It had come from downstairs.

"Daddy?"

She was alone with her father in the house for the weekend. Her mother and older sister had traveled to Manchester for a high school soccer tournament. The boys, more than her father could handle, were with their grandmother.

Cindy waited for a response but heard nothing. Only the wind outside her window, the sound of leaves moving. She listened harder, as if with added concentration she could improve her own hearing. Swirling leaves were scary enough, all that pecking on the glass. But it was the crunching sound that really frightened her—the sound of leaves moving outside her bedroom window, one footstep at a time.

"Is that you, Daddy?"

Her body went rigid. There it was. *The crunching sound!*

Someone was walking outside her house, she was sure of it, their feet dragging through the leaves. Just the thought frightened her to the core, brought tears to her eyes. She jumped out of her bed and ran down the hall.

"Daddy, where are you?"

The hallway was black, but Cindy could have found her way blindfolded. She'd run there many nights screaming from nightmares. She pushed open the door to the master bedroom and rushed inside. "Daddy, there's a noise!"

She stood frozen at the foot of the bed. Her eyes had adjusted well enough to the darkness to see that it was empty. In fact, it was still made. No one had slept in it, even though it was long past her bedtime, long past her father's. At least it felt late. The digital clock on the nightstand was stuck on midnight, the green numbers pulsating the way they always did with the power surges on windy nights.

*Am I by myself?*

Cindy ran from the bedroom. Fear propelled her down the stairs faster than she'd ever covered them. Her father had fallen asleep on the couch many times before, and maybe that was where he was. She hurried into the family room. Immediately, her heart sank with despair. He wasn't there.

"Daddy!"

She ran from the family room to the kitchen, then to the living room. She checked the bathrooms and even the large closet in the foyer, doors flying open like so many astonished mouths. He was nowhere. Tears streamed down her face as she returned to the kitchen, and then something caught her eye.

Through the window and across the yard, she could see a light glowing inside the garage. Her father's car was parked in the driveway, so she knew he was home, perhaps busy in the garage with his woodworking. That could have been the noise she'd heard, his scuffling through their leaf-covered yard, the sound of her father carrying things back and forth from the garage.

*After bedtime?*

Part of her wanted to stay put, but the thought of being alone in the big house was too much for a nine-year-old. She let out a shrill scream and exploded out the back door, into a cold autumn night that felt more like winter's first blast. She kept screaming, kept right on running until she passed her father's car and reached the garage at the end of the driveway. With both fists, she pounded on the garage door.

"Daddy, are you in there?" Her little voice was even more fragile against the cold, north wind.

She tried the latch, but it was locked, and she was too small to raise the main door anyway. She ran to the side door and turned the knob. It, too, was locked. On her tiptoes she peered through the window. The light inside was on, but she didn't see any sign of her father. The angle gave her a view only of the front half of the garage.

"Daddy, are you—"

Her words halted as her eyes fixed on the dark patch on the floor. It wasn't really a patch. It moved ever so slightly, back and forth. A spot with a gentle sway. Not a spot. A ghostlike image with arms at its side. Feet that hovered above the ground. A rope around its neck.

And a hunter's cap just like her father's.

She fell backward to the ground, pushed herself away from the garage door, and ran back toward the house. Except she didn't want to go back inside, didn't know where to run. She ran in circles around the big elm tree, crying and screaming, the sound of fallen leaves crunching beneath her feet.

•

A pounding noise jostled her from her memories. She blinked hard, trying to focus. It sounded like the footsteps in the hall she thought she'd heard earlier, but it was louder, like galloping horses. Another round of pounding, and she realized it wasn't footsteps at all.

Someone was knocking at the front door.

Her heart raced. She couldn't even begin to guess who would come calling at this hour, and she didn't want to think about it. She had yet to clear her mind of the memories she'd stirred up. That unforgettable image on the garage floor. The one that looked so much like the dark spot in her photograph of that little girl and her dog. The shadow that had never existed.

Or that had disappeared.

With the third round of knocking, Cindy's feet were on the floor. A voice inside her told her not to answer the door, exactly like her dream. And just like the dream, she found herself ignoring the warning, putting one foot in front of the other as she slowly crossed the bedroom.

A light switched on at the end of the hall. Her mother peeked out of her room and said, "Cindy, what the heck is going on?"

"Don't worry," she said. "I'll get it."

# 23

·

Jack woke to a shrill ringing in his ear. His pillow felt hard as concrete, and then he realized it *was* concrete. His cheek was pressed against the sidewalk, exactly where he'd fallen.

At first, he had no memory of where he was. Dawn was just a sliver of an orange ribbon on the horizon. Jack tried to sit up, but his body ached all over. It was as if he'd been hit by a truck. Finally, he forced himself onto his knees. The ringing in his ear was gone, but he felt nauseous. Probably a concussion. He closed his eyes and tried to stop the spinning. He opened them and strained to focus on something, anything, in the middle distance. Slowly, he began to get his bearings, and the memory of last night came back to him. The footsteps behind him. The blow to his back that sent his cell phone flying across the lawn. His chin banging on the sidewalk.

He touched his jaw. It was definitely sore. His gaze drifted toward the fence, and he spotted a little orange light blinking in the darkness. He squinted, then realized what it was: His cell phone emitted that light whenever he had a message. He tried to stand up, then yielded to the pain. He rolled like a dog and grabbed the phone, then dialed Cindy at her mother's. She answered after just three rings.

"Hi. It's me."

"Jack, where have you been? I've been calling your cell, but you didn't answer."

His head was pounding. "What time is it?"

"Almost five."

"In the morning?"

"Yes, the morning. What's wrong with you? Have you been drinking?"

"No. I got beat up."

"What?"

The simple act of talking made him short of breath. He groaned lightly and said, "Somebody beat the holy crap out of me."

"Are you okay?"

Jack forced a yawn in an effort to loosen his jaw. A sharp pain ran though his head like a railroad spike. "I think I'll be okay." *In about a month*, he thought.

"Who did this to you?" she asked, her voice quaking.

He started to explain, but it hurt too much to talk. "Don't worry. It's going to be okay."

"It's not okay! They just left, and you weren't even here. I had no idea what to do."

He sat bolt upright, concerned. "Who came?"

"The marshals."

"Federal marshals?"

"Yes. They had a search warrant."

"What did they want?"

"Your home computer."

That spike was back in his head. He grimaced and said, "Did you give it to them?"

"Yes, of course. Rosa said I had to."

"You spoke to Rosa?"

"Yes, I couldn't find you. They wanted your office computers, too. Rosa's going ballistic."

"What's the federal government doing in this? Did you ask Rosa?"

"No. But she did say something about the IRS."

Jack was silent. Three little letters no one liked to hear. "You sure that's what she said—IRS?"

"No. She said 'Internal Revenue Service.' "

He took a deep breath, which was a big mistake. All it took was a little extra air in his chest cavity to press against the spine and send him reeling with pain. It was as if he were being kicked in the back all over again.

"Cindy, I'm going to call Rosa now. But as soon as I talk with her, we all need to talk."

"You and I need to talk first. Alone."

Between last night's beating and now the IRS, he'd almost forgotten about the Jessie sex tape. "You're right. We need to talk."

"Sooner rather than later."

"That sounds good to me."

"Okay. Just call me as soon as you finish with Rosa."

"I will."

"Jack?"

"What?"

"What's going on with the IRS?"

"I'm not sure. Listen, I'll get there as soon as I can."

They said good-bye, and Jack switched off the phone. His mouth hurt, partly from having talked too much, mostly from having kissed the sidewalk last night. He spat a little blood into the grass and slowly pushed himself up onto two wobbly feet.

"Wonderful," he said as he tried to straighten his back. "The IRS."

# 24

•

Macon, Georgia, was a good place to die. And that was exactly his plan.

He called himself Fate, the favorite word of Father Aleksandr, the priest in his native Georgian village—the *other* Georgia, the lands beyond the Caucasus Mountains—who'd told him since boyhood that everything happened for a reason. The concept had always overwhelmed him, the very idea that every thought and every deed, every action and every inaction, was part of a bigger plan. The problem was, he didn't know what the plan was, couldn't fathom what it should be. What if he made a decision that somehow managed to screw everything up? He preferred to lay that kind of ultimate responsibility on somebody else, even when doing the very thing he did best.

That made him a peculiar killer indeed.

He was seated behind the wheel of his rented van, parked on the street corner a half-block away from the chosen household. The sun had set several hours earlier

behind an overcast sky. The nearest street lamp was at
the other end of the street, leaving him and his van in
total darkness. Frost from his own breath was beginning to build inside his windshield. No matter how cold
it got, he didn't dare start the engine for fear of drawing
attention to himself. He didn't need the heater anyway.
He had his own source of warmth, a fifth of *slivovitz*, a
potent brandy made from plums. "Peps you up, colors
the cheeks" was a slogan known to millions of Eastern
Europeans. At seventy-percent alcohol, it was also the
ultimate insurance against the inhibitions of conscience.
The Budapest whores knew it well. So had the snipers
in Chechnya, who'd dosed themselves heavily on the
devil's drink before potting away at women and children caught in their crosshairs. On occasion, Fate had
known it to make him braver too, though he drank it
simply because he liked it even more than *chacha*, a
grape brandy popular among Georgians. So long as he
followed his own rules, he enjoyed his work; he didn't
need any vodka to ease his conscience.

He poured another capful of *slivovitz* and then lit it
with his cigarette. The genuine stuff burned a pretty
blue flame. He watched it flicker for a moment, then
tossed the flaming cocktail down the back of his throat.

It was a ritual he'd performed since his teenage years,
when Fate had found his first victim—or, more appro-
priately, when his first victim had found Fate. He and
the other hoodlums in his gang never selected a target.
Victims identified themselves. The boys set the criteria
and waited for someone who fit the bill to come along.
The next guy to walk by wearing sunglasses. The next
woman with brown eyes. The next kid on a bicycle.
Back then, it was just for fun, perhaps an initiation or
other gang-related right of passage. That kind of silli-

ness was behind him. His work now had a purpose. He murdered only for hire.

It was the perfect arrangement for a killer who didn't want his work to upset the larger plan. Victims were preselected, not by him but by someone else. He didn't even have to choose the manner of execution. His victims did. It could be a complete surprise, the sleeping victim never regaining consciousness. Or death could be days, even weeks in the offing, a protracted path of suffering punctuated by sharp, futile screams. The decision-making process was deceptively simple. He'd follow his targets home at night and watch them go inside. If they left the porch light on, death would be quick and painless. Porch light off, not so quick—and definitely not painless. The choice was theirs. They sealed their fate without effort and without even knowing it.

*Everything happens for a reason. Not even the smallest act is meaningless. It all determines one's fate.*

He took another hit of *slivovitz* and turned his eyes toward the front porch. Jody Falder was standing outside her front door. She shifted her weight from one foot to the other, apparently trying to stay warm. A cold wind had kicked up at sunset, transforming a mild afternoon into a dark, cold reminder that the South did indeed have winter. She wore no coat. Obviously, she hadn't anticipated the drastic change in temperature, or maybe she hadn't expected to return home so late.

Peering through night-vision binoculars, he watched her fumble for her house key, unlock the door, and disappear inside. Patiently he waited, his eyes glued to the porch light. Two minutes passed, and it was still burning brightly. He gave her more time, careful not to rush things. He couldn't actually see her moving about inside the house, but it was easy enough to monitor her movement from room to room. Kitchen light on, kitchen light off. Bathroom lit, bathroom dark. Finally, the bedroom light came on and remained lit for several minutes. Then it switched off.

He narrowed his eyes, as if peering into the bedroom window, though he was merely imagining the scene unfolding behind drawn curtains. The unexpected cold front had surely left her bedroom colder than usual. Nipples erect, for sure. She'd shed her clothes quickly, slipped on a nightgown, and jumped beneath the covers. At that point, only a lunatic would jump out of a warm bed, run downstairs, and flip off the porch light. It appeared as though she'd made her decision. Porch light on. Quick and painless.

*Lucky bitch.*

He lowered his binoculars, then did a double take. The porch light had suddenly switched off. A twist of fate. It was apparently controlled by electronic timer. Arguably, it wasn't her decision, but rules were rules. Porch light off: No more quick and painless. A sign of the times. We are all slaves to our gadgets.

*Doesn't that just suck?*

A perverse smile crept to his lips as he slipped on his latex gloves, like the hands of a surgeon. It was a real source of personal pride, the way he managed to inflict all that suffering and still make death look like anything but homicide. He grabbed his bag of tools and pulled a black knit cap over his head, the same cap he'd worn on every job since his first mission as a mercenary soldier, a sneak attack on a rebel camp—six women, three old men, and two teenage boys, the first in a long line of noisy amusements for his knives. This job would be much cleaner and quieter, but the hat was still his lucky charm of sorts.

He moved quickly across the yard and toward the darkened house, yearning for that look on her face when she'd look up into his eyes, unable to move, unable to scream, unable to do much of anything but accept the fact that Fate had found her.

## 25

**"I**'m back," said Rosa as she entered Jack's conference room.

"That was quick," he replied.

There was nothing like the government overplaying its hand to set off a career criminal-defense lawyer, and the morning raid by the IRS had propelled Rosa into orbit. She'd insisted that he go to the emergency room while she marched off to an emergency hearing to block the IRS from accessing his computers. Thankfully, his tests had ruled out serious injury. A mild concussion, at worst. He was discharged with some Tylenol and a sheet of preprinted instructions about things he should avoid over the next few days—loud noises, sudden movements, general stress and aggravation. A trip to Disney World seemed out of the question.

"I still can't believe those sons of bitches took your computer," she said. "You're a criminal defense lawyer, not a hardware store. There's privileged information in there."

"What did the judge say?" asked Jack.

"He wouldn't invalidate the warrant. But I per-suaded him to appoint an independent special master to examine your hard drive."

"So the government won't see anything that's on my computers?"

"Not unless the special master determines that there's something the government should see."

"What exactly are they looking for?"

"I'm glad you asked that question. Because we need to talk."

Jack grimaced. No matter what the context, the words "we need to talk" could never be good. "Okay, sure."

"Basically, the government wants anything that shows money flowing back and forth between you and Jessie Merrill. Particularly, they want to know if you ever accessed that Bahamian account that named you and Jessie as joint account holders."

His head was suddenly hurting again. "Oh, that."

"Is there something you forgot to tell your lawyer, Mr. Swyteck?"

"I just found out about that last night from the PR of Jessie's estate, Clara Pierce."

"She obviously told the IRS, too. But let's go back to what you just said: What do you mean, you just found out about it? Your name's on the account."

"I don't know how it got there."

"Well, think hard. Because I don't want to walk into a courtroom ever again without an explanation for it."

Jack went to the window, shaking his head. "I didn't share this theory with Clara, but I'm pretty certain it ties in with Jessie's threats."

"What threats?"

"I told you before. After I figured out she'd scammed

me, she threatened me. She said if I told anyone about it, she'd make them believe I was part of it from the beginning."

"So she put your name on her bank account?"

"Sure. You know how some of these Caribbean banks are. Most of them never meet their customers. Adding a name is a snap."

"But why would she do it?"

"It makes sense," he said, convincing himself as he spoke. "It was the only way she could give teeth to her threat. If I leaked the scam, I'd take myself down with her. The joint account would make it look as if we were splitting the pie, fifty-fifty."

"Pretty risky on her part. As a joint account holder you could have cleaned out the entire account."

"Not if I didn't know about it. It's an offshore account. No tax statements, no IRS notices to tip me off that it even existed."

"What about bank statements?"

"Mailed to her address, I'm sure. Probably a post office box in Katmandu. Assuming a bank like Grand Bahama Trust Company even issues bank statements."

"So you say this was her little secret?"

"Her secret weapon. Something she'd spring on me if I ever threatened to expose her scam. It makes me look like I was part of it."

"Now that she's dead, it also has a way of making it look as if you killed her."

Jack knew that the conversation was headed in that direction, but her words still hit hard. "The million-and-a-half-dollar motive. With no more Jessie, I'm the sole account holder."

"Murder among coconspirators. That's about the size of it."

"You think that theory flies? That I killed her for the money?"

"Not with me it doesn't."

"Thanks, but you're not the jury. Honestly, what do you think?"

"I think we just take this one step at a time. Right now, we have the IRS breathing down your neck. The ugliest beast in the bureaucratic jungle. So let's talk philosophy."

"By 'philosophy,' I assume, you don't mean the great thinkers—Hegel, Kant, Moe, Larry, Curly."

"I mean my own philosophy on how to deal with the IRS. I put criminal tax investigations in a class by themselves. I want to be completely upfront about this, because not everyone agrees with my views."

"Let's hear it."

"Here's a good example. Let's say you're going to have to testify at an evidentiary hearing, and I'm preparing you beforehand for the prosecutor's cross-examination."

"I know the drill. Answer only the question asked. Don't volunteer information. If a question can be answered with a simple yes or no, answer it that way."

"Exactly." She glanced at Jack's wristwatch and asked, "Do you know what time it is?"

"Rosa, I know that game. I'm only supposed to answer the question asked. So, if you ask me if I know what time it is, the answer is not 'It's ten-fifteen.' The answer is 'Yes, I know what time it is.' That routine is so old, I think I've seen it on *L.A. Law, The West Wing, The Practice*, and, if I'm not mistaken, two or three times on *Law & Order*."

"Leave it to television to give you the wrong answer."

"What?"

"Do you know if your watch is accurate?"

"I set it myself."

"Do you know that it's accurate? To the second?"

"To the exact second, no."

"Let's say you're standing outside Westminster Abbey and staring straight at Big Ben. If somebody asks you if you know what time it is, do you know that Big Ben is accurate?"

"I have no way of knowing that."

"Exactly right. Unless you're Father Time, if someone asks you what time it is, your answer can only be what?"

Jack paused, then said, "I don't know."

"You got it, my friend. And *that* is the way you deal with the IRS."

Jack didn't say anything, though it struck him as a little too cute. There was a knock at the door, and Jack's secretary poked her head into the room. "Jack, you have a call."

"Can you transfer it into here?"

"It's personal."

He assumed that meant Cindy. He excused himself and followed his secretary down the hall to his office.

"It's not Cindy," she said. "It's your old boss."

"Chafetz?"

She nodded. Jerry Chafetz was a section chief at the U.S. attorney's office. He'd been Jack's mentor back when Jack was a federal prosecutor. Maria had been Jack's secretary since his days with the government, so they all knew each other.

"What does he want?" asked Jack.

"Not sure. I told him you were in a meeting, but he was emphatic that I interrupt. And he was even more insistent that I not announce who it was in front of Rosa."

Jack entered his office alone and closed the door. He

stared at the blinking HOLD button for a second, then answered.

"Swyteck, how are you?"

Jack managed a smile. They were old friends, but there was something about working for the government that seemed to put friends on a last-name basis.

"Been better, Chafetz. I have to say, the timing of this call is pretty peculiar, even from an old friend like you."

"Timing's no coincidence. I hope you already know this, but I didn't have anything to do with your computers being seized."

"You're right. You didn't have to say it."

"In fact, no one in Florida was behind it."

Jack's pulse quickened. "This was ordered out of Washington?"

"It's the organized-crime strike force." He'd almost sighed as he said it.

"They think I'm with the mob?"

"I can't tell you what they think."

"Who's the bag boy?"

"Sam Drayton. Pretty big player, but I'm so pissed at him right now I can hardly see straight. This predawn-raid bullshit isn't the way to treat a former prosecutor like you."

"I can fight my own battles," said Jack. "Don't get yourself caught in a bureaucratic crack over this."

"I'm not crossing any lines. All I did was get you a meeting."

"A meeting?"

"Somehow, you fit into Drayton's strategy. I can't tell you how, but I was at least able to convince Drayton that your come-to-Jesus meeting ought to be sooner rather than later. It just isn't right for him to string you along like a common criminal."

"So, does Drayton want to offer me a deal?"

"All I'm saying is that you need to meet with Drayton."

"Fine. Rosa's my lawyer."

"You can't bring a lawyer. You can't even tell her we've talked."

"He wants me to go unrepresented?"

"You're a criminal defense lawyer and a former prosecutor. You'll hardly be outmatched."

"It just isn't reasonable."

"What Drayton has to say can't be said in front of your lawyer or anyone else. It's for your ears only, and this is your one and only chance to hear it. Those are his terms, not mine."

Jack fell silent, concerned. He'd seen the rivalries between the strike force and local prosecutors before. The stench of internal politics was almost bubbling over the phone line. "I appreciate our friendship, but don't be sticking your neck out too far, all right?"

"Don't worry about me. This is all about you." There was an urgency in his voice, an edge that Jack almost didn't recognize. "You don't even have to respond to what Drayton tells you. Just listen. Think of it as free discovery."

Jack glanced out the window at downtown Coral Gables, mulling it over. Experience had taught him that it was best not to overanalyze some opportunities. At some point, you had to trust your friends, go with your gut. "All right. Where?"

"Downtown."

"When?"

"As soon as possible. Drayton's here today only."

"Give me an hour."

"Great. See you then."

"Yeah," said Jack. "Can't wait."

# 26

At eleven-thirty, Jack was at the Federal Building in downtown Miami. It was familiar territory.

Chafetz was the man who'd convinced him to become a federal prosecutor, and he was the reason Jack had stayed with the U.S. attorney's office far longer than originally planned. At the time, Chafetz was in the special investigations section, a trial-intensive team that handled complex cases ranging from child exploitation to gang prosecution. It was hard work, high stakes, and never boring. A perfect fit for Jack. He and Chafetz worked side by side, liked each other's style, liked each other. But nothing lasts forever. Chafetz was promoted to section chief, and Jack moved on to private practice. They tried to stay in touch, but it just wasn't the same after Jack started working the opposite side of the courtroom.

Chafetz led Jack to a conference room near his office. Two men were inside, waiting. From the hallway, Jack could see them through the window on the door.

"I'll take Drayton, you can have the little guy."

Chafetz smiled, then turned serious. "I wish I could prepare you better, but you and I don't need anyone accusing us of exchanging favors on the side. Just remember, whatever happens in there, it isn't my show. It's Drayton's."

"I know what you're saying. It's no secret how Drayton operates."

"You know him?"

"Only by reputation. A conceited tight-ass who thinks anyone who lives outside the 202 area code just fell off the turnip truck."

"Dead on, my friend. Just do me a favor. Don't mention turnips in the meeting, all right?"

"Come on, you know me better than that."

"I'm serious. This wasn't easy to pull off."

Jack wasn't sure how Chafetz had convinced Drayton to lay his cards on the table sooner than he otherwise might have. But things like this didn't happen just because you said "pretty please." He looked him in the eye and said, "Thanks."

"You're welcome."

He opened the door, Jack and he entered, and the introductions followed. First was the portly guy with tortoise-shell glasses, a crew cut, and virtually no personality. The letters "IRS" might just as well have been tattooed across his forehead. At his side was Sam Drayton. Instantly, he struck Jack as a walking fraud. It was well known that his wife was a millionaire, but he still wore the cheap, off-the-rack suits of a government lawyer because that was the image he wanted to cultivate. The wristwatch was a forty-dollar Timex, and the pungent cologne smelled like some homemade concoction of Aqua Velva and a three-dollar jug of berry-

scented massage oil that could have masked the odor of
a moose in a spinning class. Jack would have bet his lib-
erty that Drayton had never paid more than six dollars
on a haircut.

All of that is fine, if that's who you are. But there's
nothing more pretentious than a wealthy lawyer who has
to work at being a regular Joe.

Jack took a seat at one end of the table, opposite
Drayton and his IRS agent. Chafetz excused himself
and reached for the door.

"Hey, Chafetz," said Jack as he flipped him a quarter.

He caught it in midair, puzzled.

Jack said, "My turnip truck is parked out front. Feed
the meter, would you?"

They exchanged glances, the way they used to communicate silently as cocounsel in a courtroom. "Sure
thing," said Chafetz as he left the room, suppressing his
smile.

The others looked at one another, clueless as to the
inside joke. Drayton turned to the business at hand.
"Thanks for coming, Mr. Swyteck."

"I wish I could say it was good to be back."

"We know it's an inconvenience. Especially in light
of what happened to you this morning."

"You mean those thieves who took my computers?"

"No. I mean that bruise on your jaw."

"Seems that someone is really ticked off that I might
blame the viatical investors for Jessie Merrill's death."

"We know. We've read the police report you filled
out in the emergency room."

"Seeing how you're part of the strike force, am I correct in assuming that my little incident may have had
something to do with an element of organized crime?"

"To be honest, we want you to help us pinpoint the exact criminal element involved."

"I wish I could, but I can't. Never got a look at who jumped me last night. And I've already told the state attorney everything I know about the threats against Jessie. Unfortunately, she didn't get very specific."

Drayton said, "We hear from a reliable confidential informant that the beating you took last night came on a direct order from a known underworld operative."

"How does your CI know that?"

Drayton didn't answer, didn't even seem to acknowledge the question. He simply rose and went to the whiteboard, rolling a felt-tipped marker through his fingers as he spoke. "For about eight months now, we've had our eye on Viatical Solutions, Inc., or VS, as we call it."

"I didn't know that."

"From the outside, VS appears to be nothing more than a viatical broker. The deals are structured like a legitimate viatical settlement, with one major difference." Drayton marked a red dollar-sign on the whiteboard, then drew an X through it. "The money from the investors is always dirty."

"VS is laundering money?"

"As if you didn't know." The prosecutor leaned into the table and said, "How did your name end up on an offshore bank account with Jessie Merrill?"

"She obviously put it there. How or why, I can only guess."

"How did the investors pay her the one-point-five million?"

"I don't know. That happened before she hired me."

"Was it in cash or a wire transfer from another offshore bank?"

"I said I don't know."

"Perhaps it was a combination," said Drayton, suggesting an answer. "Was it paid in a lump sum, or in installments from various sources?"

"I can't answer that."

"That's unfortunate. Because if you can't help us, we can't help you."

"Help me what?"

"It's no secret that the state attorney suspects foul play in the death of Jessie Merrill. The way the evidence is playing out, you're pretty high on the list of suspects."

"Plenty of innocent people have found themselves on a prosecutor's list of suspects."

"No question. And if just half the glowing things your old boss says about you are true, then you probably will be exonerated. Eventually. But wouldn't it be nice to speed up that process?"

"I'm listening."

"The quickest way to get off the list of suspects is for you to convince the state attorney that someone else did it. We might be able to help you with that."

"Are you sitting on evidence that Jessie Merrill was murdered?"

"This is a money-laundering investigation. All we can tell you is that the people we're investigating—the people who we believe are in control of Viatical Solutions, Inc.—are certainly capable of murder. Your cooperation with us on the money-laundering investigation may well provide the jump-start you need to prove your innocence on the murder charge."

"What do I have to do?"

"Just answer all our questions about the source of the funds, the structure of the transaction. Who did you meet with? How was the money transferred? From what accounts?"

"I told you, I wasn't there."

"And I keep coming back to the same question. Why is your name on that joint account? Just what secrets were you trying to cloak in the shroud of the attorney-client privilege?"

"I can only say it again: I don't know anything about that."

"Obviously, we don't accept that. You have a pretty stainless reputation, but an argument could still be made that you and your client knowingly entered into a transaction that allowed these investors to launder one and a half million dollars in dirty money."

"There's no reason for anyone to believe that."

"Yes, there is. I don't care how clean you are. A married guy makes a mistake, there's no telling what he might do for his girlfriend to keep her from sending an audiotape of their little escapade to his wife."

Jack's heart sank. *Is there anyone Clara Pierce didn't send that tape to?* "That's an old tape. Jessie and I dated before I was married."

"That's a likely story."

"I didn't have anything to do with that joint bank account."

"We'll see what your computers show."

"If that's why you seized them, you're going to be sorely disappointed."

"Computers are just one angle. Fortunately, we have ways of stimulating your personal memory."

"Is that a threat?"

Drayton resumed his position at the whiteboard. "Simply put, you owe the Internal Revenue Service some serious money."

"What?"

Drayton and the IRS agent were suddenly making goo-goo eyes at each other. "Peter, what's the exact number?"

The bean counter flipped open his notebook. "Our latest calculation is in the neighborhood of three hundred thousand dollars."

"That's ridiculous."

"Hardly," said Drayton as he wrote the number on the board. "You and Jessie Merrill were joint account holders on her one and a half million dollars. It's our position that your half of that account is taxable income for legal services rendered. You owe income tax on seven hundred fifty thousand dollars."

"Sorry to disappoint you, but I've already spoken to the PR of Jessie's estate and disavowed any interest in my alleged half of those funds."

Drayton's eyes brightened. "Thank you for sharing that. Peter, make a note. It seems Mr. Swyteck has made a gift of his seven hundred fifty thousand dollars. So, in addition to income tax on that sum, he now also owes gift tax."

The bean counter scribbled in his pad and said, "That brings the total closer to four hundred thousand."

"You arrogant prick," said Jack. "I dedicated a big chunk of my career to this office. And now this is what I get? Trumped up charges from Washington?"

"Calm down, all right? I didn't want to have to threaten you, and I'm not going so far as to say you killed the woman. But there was something funny going on between you and Jessie Merrill. This is an eight-month investigation that needs your help. Fact is, you need our help too."

"I don't need anyone's help. No juror in his right mind is ever going to believe I'm a murderer. I mean, really. If I wanted Jessie Merrill dead, would I kill her in my own bathtub?"

"Good answer, Mr. Swyteck. Did you think of it before or after you murdered Jessie Merrill?"

He knew that Drayton was just role-playing, stepping into the shoes of a state attorney on cross-examination. Still, it chilled him.

"You done?" said Jack.

"That's all for now."

He rose and started for the door.

"Hope to hear from you," said Drayton. "Soon."

"Hope springs eternal," said Jack. He left the room, steadily gaining speed as he headed down the hall to the elevator.

## 27

A blast of chilly air followed Todd Chastan out of the autopsy room. He wadded his green surgical scrubs into a loose ball and tossed them into the laundry bag in the hallway outside the door. A soiled pair of latex gloves sailed into the trash. His pace was brisk as he headed down the gray-tiled hallway.

Dr. Chastan was an associate medical examiner in Atlanta. The office served all of Fulton County and, on request, certain cases from other counties. Chastan had spent nearly the entire morning exploring the internal cavity of a sixteen-year-old boy who'd botched his first attempted robbery of a convenience store. He'd left a loaded .38 caliber pistol, twenty-eight dollars, and about two pints of blood on the sidewalk outside the shattered plate-glass window. Just a few hours later, his young heart, lungs, esophagus, and trachea were resting on a cold steel tray. The liver, spleen, adrenals, and kidneys would be next, followed by the stomach, pancreas, and intestines. His brain had already been sliced into sections, bagged, and tagged. It was all part of a typical medical-legal autopsy required in the seventy or so homicides the office might see in an average year. Over the same period of time, ten times that number of examined deaths might be classified as "natural."

An urgent message from a medical-legal investigator didn't usually spell "natural."

Dr. Chastan made a quick right at the end of the hall, knocked once, and entered the investigator's office. "You paged me?"

Eddy Johnson looked up from the papers on his desk. "It's about the Falder case."

"Falder?" he said, straining to recall.

"The woman you did yesterday. The one with AIDS."

"Yeah, yeah. Her medical history painted a bleak picture. By all accounts, she was on borrowed time. Full autopsy didn't seem necessary. I did an external and sent some tissue and blood samples to the lab."

"Got the report right here," Johnson said as he pulled a file out from under two empty coffee cups and the sports section.

"Something give you concern?" He smiled impishly, but realized that he was in a medical-legal investigator's office, and answered his own question. "Obviously, something gives you concern."

Johnson was deadpan. "Plate's under the microscope. Have a look-see for yourself."

Chastan maneuvered around the swollen folders on the floor and stepped up to the microscope that was resting on the countertop, right beside *Gray's Anatomy*. He closed one eye, brought the other to the eyepiece, and adjusted the lens. He twisted it to the left and then to the right, but something didn't seem quite right. He stood up, scratched his head, then gave another look. Finally, he faced Johnson and asked, "What the hell is that?"

"It's the blood you drew from Ms. Falder."

He blinked, confused. "It's like nothing I've ever seen before."

"That's why I have the file," he said with a wink. Johnson was known around the office as a strange-case specialist.

"What do you think it is?"

"I couldn't even guess. Some kind of virus, maybe."

"We need to send it off to the Center for Disease Control right away."

"I already did, this morning. But there's more to this case that troubles me."

"Such as?"

"She came here with just over two liters of blood in her body."

"I took only three vials."

"That's my point. Where are the other three and a half liters?"

"I don't know. I looked at the photos. No blood at the scene of her death."

"That's right."

"She couldn't have donated it before she died. AIDS aside, nobody walks around with sixty percent of the blood in their body missing."

"Right again," said Johnson.

"Which means what? Somebody took it?"

He gave the doctor a serious look. "I think you and I are now on the same page."

"She had multiple injection marks all over her body. I didn't think anything of it. She had AIDS. She was getting injections almost every other day."

"Looks like one of those holes was used to siphon out her blood."

"That changes everything. If that much blood was drawn while she was alive, it would have sent her into cardiac arrest."

"Which means the cause of death was anything but natural."

"I need that body back," said Chastan. "We need a full medical-legal autopsy. I can get on it this morning."

"Go to it."

He started for the door, then stopped. "Ed, why do you think someone might have wanted this woman's blood?"

"Don't know. But I have a feeling we'll have a better idea when we hear back from disease control."

"You think someone out there is into collecting blood infected with strange organisms?"

"Collecting. Or harvesting."

With all that he'd seen over the years—dismembered bodies, charred babies—it took a lot to get a reaction from Dr. Chastan. But the thought of someone cultivating disease in human hosts was up there. "This could be one sick son of a bitch."

"You got that right." Johnson switched off the light on the microscope and put the blood plate back in the file. "I'll put homicide on notice."

"Sure," he answered. "The sooner the better."

# 28

•

Jack couldn't get The Beatles' "Tax Man" out of his head. It reminded him of Sam Drayton—an old, annoying song that he didn't like in the least, but it was embedded in his brain.

After the meeting, Jack stopped to collect his thoughts at an open-air café on Miami Avenue. Just down the street from the old federal courthouse, it had been one of his favorite coffee spots during his years as a prosecutor. The smell of *arroz con pollo*, today's lunch special, wafted from the noisy kitchen in back. A guy with no shirt, no shoes, and practically no teeth was selling bags of *limas* from a stolen shopping cart at curbside. A largely Spanish-speaking crowd sipped espresso at the stand-up counter along the sidewalk. Jack found a stool inside and ordered a *café con leche*, a big mug of coffee that was half milk. The woman behind the bar remembered him from his days as a prosecutor. She smiled and worked her old magic, frothing up the milk with the steamer just the way Jack liked it.

*"Muchas gracias,"* he said.

"You're welcome," she replied.

It was the same routine they'd followed for eight years, Jack's wooden Spanish evoking a reply in English. The story of his barely Cuban life.

Jack's meeting had gone even worse than he'd feared, but he tried to shake it off. He needed a contingency plan, but he had other things to deal with, too. Things more important. He needed to talk to Cindy.

He took his cell phone from his pocket, flipped it open, and froze.

*What the hell?*

He hadn't noticed anything unusual at five A.M. when he'd called Cindy. It had been dark then, and he was too incoherent to have noticed. But now it was broad daylight. His head was no longer swirling. It was obvious to him.

The cell phone wasn't his.

He sipped his *café con leche* and took a closer look. The phone looked exactly like his, a black Motorola issued by Sprint. He and Cindy used to have the exact same model, until they'd tired of getting them mixed up. He'd ended up buying Cindy a Nokia that looked completely different. It was just too easy to grab the wrong phone when you were racing out of the house in morning.

Someone, it seemed, had made the same mistake last night.

Jack flipped open the Motorola. He was familiar with all of the functions; they were the same as his own phone. He checked the message center. Nine voice mails were stored in the memory. He hit the PLAY button. *"Message one,"* the recorded voice said. *"Yesterday, eleven-thirty-two A.M."*

The message was in a man's voice. The language was foreign. It sounded like a cross between Boris Yeltsin and Robin Williams in *Moscow on the Hudson*. Jack skipped to the next one. *"Message two, yesterday, ten-twenty-one A.M."* A different voice but the same language.

The messages seemed bizarre now, just minutes after hearing that Viatical Solutions was controlled by some "criminal element" that was involved in money laundering. Until now, he'd had little recollection of his attacker's voice, having been pounded so mercilessly. He couldn't say the messages were in the same voice, but he was at least beginning to recall an accent that he'd been too groggy to discern last night. He skipped through the third and fourth messages, the fifth, and on and on. All nine were in the same language.

Russian.

In his mind's eye, he saw himself walking to his car from his grandmother's townhouse last night. A punishing blow from behind sends his cell phone flying out of his hand. In the ensuing fracas, his attacker's cell phone is yanked from her pocket or belt clip. A final blow to his head, and Jack is out cold, leaving the rest to conjecture—perhaps his attacker searching frantically in the darkness until she finds a phone that looks just like hers.

But it wasn't hers. It was Jack's.

*Ho-lee shit*. He smiled, then chuckled out loud. It was about damn time something had cut his way. *We swapped phones!*

*"Señora,"* he said to the hostess. In his best Spanish, he asked for bread and cream cheese. It was a heart attack in the making, but *Abuela* had sold him on the pleasures of slathering Cuban bread with cream cheese and dunking it into his *café con leche*.

She handed him two long strips on wax paper. "Enjoy."

Jack was dunking at a near-frenzied pace, his mind awhirl. When they'd talked that morning, Cindy had told him that she'd called him on his cell but got no answer. It made sense that his attacker wouldn't have answered before five A.M. But just as soon as someone dialed his number at a decent hour, she *would* answer, and then she'd realize that they'd swapped phones. If she were smart, she'd cancel her cell service and erase the messages.

He dropped his bread and cream cheese, hurried to the pay phone and dialed his office voice mail. He replayed each message onto the recording, then relaxed, suddenly feeling in control. She could cancel away, but Jack would forever have her messages.

*Now what?* he thought as he returned to his seat.

The fact that she hadn't canceled her service and erased the messages told him that she wasn't onto the swap just yet. He could call the cops, but they couldn't trace the phone until she used it. Unless she tried to use it in the same battered and confused state that Jack had found himself in earlier that morning, she'd realize that the phone wasn't hers, and she'd pitch it in the Dumpster, for sure. This might be his last chance to call and open up a dialogue. He grasped his attacker's phone and dialed his own number. It rang twice before connecting.

"Hello."

His heart was in his throat. The voice on the other end of the line was one of the voices he'd heard last night—the woman's. "Good morning. This is Jack Swyteck. Remember me?"

She didn't answer. Jack was feeling pretty smug,

imagining her shooting a confused look at the phone in her hand.

He said, "I think you have something of mine. And if you check the number on this incoming call on your Caller ID, you'll see that I have something of yours."

She took a moment, and Jack was certain she was checking. Finally, she said, "Well, now. Isn't this interesting."

"Yours is especially interesting. The messages in your voice mail, all in Russian. I don't speak the language, but I'm sure the FBI or vice squad downtown would be happy to translate for me."

There was a brief but tense silence on the line. "What do you want?" she asked in a low, serious tone.

"I want to talk to you."

"We're already talking."

"No. Unlike you, I'm not stupid enough to transact business over nonsecure airwaves. I want to meet."

"That would be a mistake."

"Perfect. I'd say it's about time I made one of my own. I'm tired of paying for everyone else's."

"I'm not kidding. A meeting would be a terrible mistake."

"It would be an even bigger mistake if you stood me up. So, listen good. You know where the Metro-Dade Government Center is?"

"The tall building downtown next to the museum."

"Right. At four o'clock go into the lobby. Right in the middle, there's a planter with a bronze plaque in memory of a man named Armando Alejandre. Wait for me there. Or I'm going straight to the FBI, and your phone comes with me."

"How do I know you're not going to have me arrested if I show up?"

"Because I want to find out who's trying to hide what really happened to Jessie Merrill. And if I have you arrested, you're not going to tell me a thing, now are you?"

More silence. Finally, her answer came: "You sure this is what you want?"

"Yes. Oh, and one other thing."

"What?"

"When I was a prosecutor, this was my favorite place to meet reluctant witnesses, snitches, the like. It works very well because at least a dozen security guards are always wandering around. So leave your steel-toed boots at home. If you try anything, you'll never make it out of the building." He hit the END button, put the phone in his pocket, and finished off his coffee.

"You like something more?" asked the woman behind the counter.

"*No, gracias. Todo está perfecto.*" He handed over a five-dollar bill.

"Thank you. Have nice day."

*Have nice day*, he thought, smiling to himself. Once again, bad Spanish begat bad English. *Why do I even try?*

"Thank you, ma'am. It already is a nice day."

# 29

Her work didn't require a visit to the studio that morning, but Cindy went anyway. Jessie's death had rendered her own house unlivable, and her mother's house was feeling none-too-cozy after the raid at sunrise by federal marshals. She was running out of places to hide from the rest of the world. Not even her dreams offered any solace. The studio seemed like her only sanctuary.

Her portrait work was strictly by appointment, but she had nothing scheduled today. She'd driven into South Miami looking forward to a solid eight hours alone, a day to herself. There was always work to do, but she wasn't in the mood for anything challenging. She opted for organizing her office, the perfect mindless task for a woman who wasn't sure if she was married to a cheater.

She started with the mound of mail in her in-box, which was no small assignment. She actually had four in-boxes, each created at a different stage of procrastination. There was "Current," then "Aging," followed by "I'll Get to It on a Rainy Day," and finally, "I'll Build the Ark Before I Sort Through This Crap." She was only a third of way through the "Aging" stack when a knock at the door interrupted her.

She double-checked, and sure enough, the sign in the window said CLOSED. She stayed put, hoping that whoever it was would just go away. But the first knock was followed by a second, then another. She finally got up and was about to say *There's no one here,* but then she recognized the face on the other side of the glass. It was Jack's *abuela*. She unlocked the door and let her inside. The little bell on the door startled the old woman as she entered.

"Ooh. Angel got his wings."

Cindy smiled as she recalled that it was two years ago, Christmas, when *Abuela* had come over from Cuba, and her first lesson in English was the movie *It's a Wonderful Life*—over and over again.

"How are you?" said Cindy as they embraced warmly.

"*Bueno. Y tú?*" she answered in Spanish, though Cindy's ear for the language was even worse than Jack's.

"Fine. Come in, please."

*Abuela* followed her zigzag path through canvas backdrops and lighting equipment, stopping at a small and cramped office area. Cindy cleared the stacks of old photo-proofs from a chair and offered her a seat. She would have offered coffee, but *Abuela* had tasted hers before, and it had just about sent her back to Havana.

"I hope you not too busy," said *Abuela*.

"No, not at all. What brings you here?"

"Well, sorry, but I not here to get picture taken."

"Oh, what a pity."

She smiled, then turned serious. "You know why I here."

Cindy lowered her eyes. "*Abuela,* I love you, but this is between your grandson and me."

"*Claro.* But this just take a minute." She opened her purse and removed a stack of opened envelopes.

"What are those?" asked Cindy.

"Letters. From Jack. He wrote these when I live in Cuba."

"To you?"

"*Sí.* This is before I come to Miami."

"Jack wrote all those?"

"*Sí, sí.* Is how Jack and I got to know each other. Is also how I got to know you."

"Me?"

*Abuela* paused as if to catch her breath, then continued in a voice that quaked. "These letters. They are all about you."

Cindy again checked the size of the stack. Her heart swelled, then ached. "*Abuela,* I can't—"

"*Por favor.* I want you to see. My Jack—our Jack—maybe is no so good at saying things in words. If his mother lived, things would be different. She was loving person. Give love, receive love. But Jack, as *un niño,* no have her love. In his home, love was inside. *Comprendes?*"

"Yes. I think I understand."

"If you are Swyteck, sometimes only when heart is broken can love get out."

"That I do understand."

*Abuela* sifted through the stack of letters in her lap, her hands shaking with emotion. "This is *mi favorito.* Is when he asked you to marry. And this one, too, is very good. About your wedding, with pictures."

"*Abuela*, please. These letters were written for you, not me."

She laid the stack aside, clutching one to her bosom. "I wouldn't ask you to read them. I just want you to know they exist."

"Thank you."

"But there is one you must see. *Es especial*." She fumbled for her reading glasses and dug the letter from the last envelope. "Is the oldest. Very different from others. See the top? Jack wrote the time. Two-thirty A.M. What make a man write a letter at this crazy hour?"

Cindy felt that this should stop, but she couldn't bring herself to say it. She just listened.

*Abuela* read slowly, trying hard to make her English perfect, though her accent was still thick. " 'Dear *Abuela*. It's late, and I'm tired, so I will keep this short and sweet. Do you remember the letter you wrote me last June? It would have been your fiftieth wedding anniversary, and you told me the story of how you and *Abuelo* met. It was a picnic, and a friend introduced you to her older brother. He ended up walking you home. You said you didn't know how you knew it, but by the time you got home you knew he was the one.

" 'I went back and re-read that letter tonight. I don't know why. I just did. That's not true. I do know why. I had a date tonight. Cindy is her name. Cindy Paige. I don't really know her that well, but I have that same feeling you described in your letter. It's weird, *Abuela*. But I think she's the one.' "

*Abuela* looked up, and their eyes met.

Cindy blinked back a tear. "He never told me that story."

"I no can explain that. But I know my grandson pretty

good. The young man who sit at his kitchen table and write this letter at two o'clock in the morning . . . he not really writing to his grandmother. He just being honest with his feelings. This letter is like talking to himself. Or to God."

"Or to his mother," said Cindy, her voice fading.

*Abuela* reached forward and took her hand. "I don't know what he did this time. I don't know if your heart can forgive him. But I do know this. He loves you."

"I know," Cindy whispered.

She handed Cindy a tissue. "Sorry I do this to you."

"It's okay. Maybe it's what I needed."

"Smart girl," she said with a little smile, then rose. "You excuse me now, please. I go home, put on my kicking boots, and give my grandson what *he* needs."

"I might actually pay money to see that."

"Ah, but we both love him, no?"

"Yes," she said, squeezing *Abuela*'s hand. "We do."

Cindy watched as *Abuela* gathered up her letters and put them back in her purse. Then she put her arm around the old woman, thanked her, and walked her to the door.

# 30
.

At four P.M., the main lobby of the Government Center was abuzz with rush hour. Jack headed against the stream of homebound workers. Theo was right along with him. Jack knew better than to face an attacker without a big ugly at his side.

Jack had gone straight to Rosa's office after making the phone call from the café. Immediately, it was decision time. Sam Drayton had confirmed that Viatical Solutions, Inc., was controlled by some element of organized crime. Why not tell the cops that his attacker had dropped a cell phone filled with Russian messages?

*Why not?* That was a question Jack the Client had been asking himself. Jack the Lawyer knew better. So did Rosa. The feds were going after him through the IRS, and that might only be the beginning. The state attorney had him on the short list of suspects for the murder of Jessie Merrill. In that posture, you didn't simply hand over anything to the police. You negotiated. And to negotiate properly, Jack had to know what he was selling. That was especially important here. From the moment he'd made the phone call, Jack had a strong feeling that his attacker wasn't what she appeared to be.

Not even close.

In less than twenty minutes they'd summoned a Russian linguist to translate the recorded messages. In thirty, they had a good criminal mind translating the literal English translations into something the lawyers could understand. Theo was perhaps the more indispensable of the two. Three of the messages dealt with, literally, "taking the ponies for a boat ride," which, Theo figured, was probably code for shipping stolen cars out of the port of Miami. The other six sounded as if the caller had a plumbing problem. A sink needed to be unclogged. Jack didn't need Theo to tell him that a sink was the repository in a money-laundering operation.

Theo checked his watch and asked, "You think she'll show?"

"A *musor* always shows."

"A what?"

"Didn't you listen to anything that Russian translator said?"

"Only the part that was in English."

As the name implied, Government Center was the nerve center of Miami-Dade County. Offices in the thirty-story tower housed various local departments and officials, including the mayor and county commissioners. The bustling lobby area served not only the office tower but also the largest and most crowded stop along the Metrorail. It was a three-story, atrium-style complex with a glass roof that allowed for natural lighting. Flags of all fifty states hung from the exposed metal rafters

overhead. Long escalators carried workers and shoppers
to a two-story mall called Metrofare Shops and Cafés.
At the base of the north escalators was a large planter in
the shape of a half-moon, where bushy green plants
flourished. Between two large palms was a simple bou-
quet of white daisies and carnations in a glass vase.
Above the vase was a bronze plaque that read: "Dedicated to the Memory of Armando Alejandre Jr.,
1950–1996, Metro-Dade employee, volunteer of Brothers to the Rescue. His airplane was downed by the
Cuban Air Force during a routine humanitarian flight
over the straits of Florida."

Seated on the ledge of the planter in front of the
plaque was a young woman wearing dark sunglasses,
even though it wasn't very sunny inside the building.
She was alone.

"That must be her," said Jack.

Theo gave him a thin smile. "Let's go."

As they rode down the escalator, Jack's eyes fixed on
the woman. He'd never gotten a good look at his
attacker, but from the beating he'd taken, he'd built her
up to be at least eight feet tall, three hundred and fifty
pounds. She was more like five-six, with slender-but-
muscular arms, and the nicest set of legs that had ever
kicked the daylights out of him. With her long, dark
hair and olive skin, she looked more Latina than Russian. It surprised him how attractive she was.

"You got beat up by *that*?" said Theo as they glided
into the lobby.

"Just shut up."

"I mean, some guys in my bar would pay money to
get her to—"

"I said shut up."

They wended their way through the crowd and

approached from the side. She caught sight of them about ten feet away and rose to meet them, though she skipped right over the hello.

"Who's your friend?" she asked.

"You get my name when we get yours," said Theo.

A group of pedestrians passed by on their way to the train. She asked, "Is this a good place to talk?"

"Perfect," said Jack. "Nobody stands still long enough to hear what we're saying. And like I said on the phone, plenty of security guards around if you decide to get stupid."

She paused, as if to get comfortable with the setting. Then she looked at Jack and said, "That was a gutsy phone call you made."

"Not really."

"Threatening me after I'd already warned you not to mess around with us? I assure you, *that* was risky."

"I just listened to my instincts."

"Exactly what did your instinct tell you?"

"Maybe I'll let my friend tell you." He looked at Theo and said, "Here's a hypothetical for you. One, a woman attacks me in the dark and threatens me."

"Check," said Theo.

"Two, the feds haul me downtown and tell me they have it on good authority from their confidential informant that the order to rough me up came straight from a mysterious organized-crime figure."

"Double check."

"Three, this same woman has nine messages saved on her voice mail, all in Russian. But she speaks English without a hint of a Russian accent."

"Double check and a half."

"I call her and tell her I want to meet. And she just shows up, apparently not the least bit concerned that fifteen police officers might pounce on her the minute she arrives. Now, you tell me: Who do you think this woman is?"

He looked at Jack, then straight at her. "Either she's really stupid."

"Or?"

"Or *she's* the fucking snitch."

"Or as they're known in the Russian mob, *musor*. Rats. The lowest form of life on earth."

"You're a genius, Jacko."

"I know."

"But if we take this one step further, what she's really afraid of is not that we're going to take her cell phone to the police. She's afraid that someone might find out she's a snitch."

"You think?"

"Absolutely. But maybe we should ask *her*." Theo took a half step closer, gave her his most intimidating look. "What do you say there, gorgeous? Think maybe you wouldn't be so pretty anymore if the wrong person were to find out that you are a *musor*?"

She glared right back at him. It impressed Jack that she didn't seem to back down from Theo the way most people did. *Careful, Theo, or she'll kung-fu your ass, too.*

"Aren't you smug?" she said. "Think you got it all figured out, don't you?"

"Not all of it. Just enough to get you to tell us the rest."

"I can't talk to you."

Theo said, "What a shame. Looks like I'll have to float your name on the street as a snitch."

"And then I'll watch Jack's *abuela* wishing to God she'd never left Cuba."

"Takes real guts to threaten an old woman. Who's next on your list, the Teletubbies?"

"Enough with the threats," said Jack. "Let's just talk."

"I can't tell you anything."

"That won't do," said Jack. "You may think we're just a pain in the ass, but refusing to talk to us won't make us go away. No matter what you do, my only option is to keep on plugging away at this viatical company to figure out who threatened Jessie Merrill and why she ended up dead."

"That's very dangerous."

"My alternative is to stand aside and get tagged with a murder I didn't commit."

"That's a bitch. But there's very little I can tell you."

"See, we're already making progress. We've gone from 'I can't talk to you' to 'there's very little I can tell you.'"

Jack detected a faint smile. She glanced at his swollen jaw and said, "Sorry about the bump."

"No problem."

"Didn't really want to do it."

"I know. Sam Drayton said the order came from high up."

She didn't deny it.

Jack said, "Who gave you the order?"

"You know I can't tell you that."

"Who controls the money behind Viatical Solutions, Inc.?"

"You're going to have to figure that out for yourself."

"Is it the same people who threatened Jessie Merrill?"

"If you're trying to pin a murder on the viatical investors, I couldn't help you if I wanted to."

"Why not?"

"Because you're looking in the wrong place."

"Stop with the threats."

"It's not a threat," she said. "Listen carefully. I'm giving you something here. If you think Jessie Merrill was murdered, you're not going to find her killer by looking where you're looking."

"Where should we be looking?"

She answered in the same matter-of-fact tone. "Somewhere else."

Theo groaned. "Come on. Like you don't know anything?"

"I know plenty. I just don't trust you to deny you heard it from me when someone hangs you upside down and shoves a cattle prod all the way up your ass."

Theo blinked twice, as if the uncomfortable image was taking form in his brain.

Jack gave her an assessing look. "How do you know we're looking in the wrong place?"

"Because I've been working this gig long enough to know the people I'm dealing with. I know what one of their hits looks like."

"Come off it," said Theo. "Not every hit is the same."

"Trust me. If Jessie Merrill had been murdered over her viatical scam, you wouldn't have found her body in the Swytecks' bathtub. You wouldn't have found her body at all. At least not in one piece."

Jack and Theo exchanged glances, as if neither was sure how to argue with that.

She said, "You two have no idea what you're stepping into."

"It's money laundering. I know that much from your phone messages and from talking with Sam Drayton."

"Big-time money laundering. Hundreds of millions of dollars. I tell you this only so you can see that Jessie Merrill and her one and a half million is a speck on the horizon. Now go away, boys. Before you get hurt."

"We can take care of ourselves," said Theo.

She extended her hand and said, "Phone, please."

Jack said, "I kept all the messages on tape."

"And you probably hired someone to dust for fingerprints, too. But I don't care."

"Of course you don't," said Theo. "Why should a snitch care about fingerprints?"

"I still want it back."

Jack removed her phone from his pocket and handed it over. She gave him his, then turned and walked away, no thank-you or good-bye. Jack watched as she moved with the crowd toward the escalators that led to the Metrorail gates.

"What do you think?"

"Two possibilities," said Theo. "Either she's protecting someone. Or someone has her scared shitless."

"Or both."

"You want me to tail her?"

"Nah, thanks. Got someone a little less conspicuous covering that already."

Jack caught one last glimpse of her as she reached the top of the escalator. Then, from afar, he gave his friend Mike Campbell a mock salute as he put aside his newspaper, rose from the bench, and followed her to the train.

# 31

.

Jack skipped dinner. He had a rental house to check out and could only hold his breath. *Abuela* had found it for him.

Jack had planned on staying in a hotel until Cindy took him back, but *Abuela* seemed to think she'd be more inclined to patch things up if he had a place for them to be alone together, away from Cindy's mother. She probably had a point.

The house was in Coconut Grove on Seminole Street, a pleasant surprise. It was small but plenty big for two, built in the forties, with all the charming architectural details that builders in South Florida had seemed to forget after 1960. The lot was huge for such a small house, but there was no grass. The lawn was covered with colorful bromeliads, thousands of green, purple, and striped varieties, all enjoying the shade of twisty old oak trees. An amazing yard with nothing to mow. To heck with the rental. Jack was barely inside and was already thinking of buying.

"You like?" asked *Abuela*.

Jack checked out the pine floors and vaulted ceiling with pecky-cypress beams. "It's fabulous."

"I knew you would like."

A man emerged from the kitchen, *Abuela*'s latest beau. Jack had met him before, the self-proclaimed best dancer in Little Havana. At age eighty-two he still seemed to glide through the living room as he came to greet Jack, smiling widely.

"Jack, how you been?"

He pronounced "been" like "bean," but he insisted on speaking English to Jack, as did most of *Abuela*'s friends, all of whom considered him thoroughly American, at best an honorary Cuban. Jack knew him only as *El Rodeo*, pronounced like "Rodeo Drive" in Beverly Hills, except when Jack was around and everyone referred to him as "The Rodeo," as if Jack were a native Texan and his middle name was Bubba.

"Is beautiful, no?"

"I love it. How much is it?"

*El Rodeo* pulled out a pen and scribbled a phone number on the inside of a gum wrapper. "You call."

"Whose number is this?"

He continued in broken English, and Jack was able to discern that the house was owned by *El Rodeo*'s nephew, who had just relocated to Los Angeles. Jack tried asking for details in Spanish, but again *El Rodeo* insisted that English would be easier. They were doing fine until he started telling Jack more about his nephew, a guy whose name apparently was Chip, which struck Jack as odd for a Latino.

"Chip?"

"*Sí*, chip."

"He's cheap," said *Abuela*.

"Ah, cheap."

"*Sí, sí.* Chip."

*A nice enough guy, this El Rodeo, but if his English is better than my Spanish, I truly am a disgrace to my mother's memory.*

Jack tucked the phone number into his wallet. "I'll call him tonight."

"Call now," said *Abuela.*

"I need to think about it. With everything Cindy and I have been through, I wonder if she'll be afraid to move back in with me unless it's a condo with twenty-four-hour security."

"Don't have fears control life. You and Cindy want children. House is better, no?"

He wasn't thinking that far ahead, but her optimism warmed him. "I should at least see the rest of the house."

"Okay." *Abuela* took *El Rodeo*'s arm and led him out the door. "We give you time to look around more on your own. You decide quick."

Jack hadn't intended to kick them out, but they were out the French doors before he could protest. He drifted toward the kitchen.

The window was open, and he could hear his *abuela* and *El Rodeo* outside on the patio talking about the busloads of tourists that cruised through Little Havana, where *El Rodeo* and his friends played dominoes in the park. It bothered *El Rodeo* to be treated as a spectacle, an ethnic oddity that these tourists only thought they understood. Not even Jack had understood until *Abuela* had moved to Miami. The evening newscasts had a way of conveying the impression that the only thing fueling the Cuban-American passion was hatred—hatred for Castro, hatred for any politician who wasn't staunchly opposed to Castro, hatred of yet another Hollywood star who thought it was cool to shake hands and smoke cigars with the despot who'd murdered their parents, siblings, aunts, and uncles. That emotion was real, to be sure. But there were neighborhoods filled with people like *El Rodeo,* a man who'd quietly tended bar in Miami for the past four decades, a photograph of the restaurant he'd once owned hanging on the wall behind him, the keys from his old house in Havana resting in a jar atop the cash register. He just refused to give up on something he loved, refused to admit he'd never get it back.

Tonight, as Jack wandered through a house that might be his, without a wife for the foreseeable future, he could relate more than ever.

"Hello, Jack."

He turned, startled by the sound of her voice. "Cindy? How'd you—"

"Same way you got here. *Abuela* invited me."

"She has a way."

"She definitely does. We had a nice talk in my studio. She got me to thinking." Her voice quaked, not with anger but emotion. "Maybe I overreacted."

"You believe me, then? That the tape of me and Jessie is B.C.? Before Cindy?"

She gave him a little smile, seeming to appreciate the humor. "Now that I've had time to think about it, yes, I believe you."

"We're going to prove it, if we have to."

"I'm sure you will."

"We hired an audio expert. It could still be tough, since we're working from a copy."

"The police won't give you the original?"

"From what Clara Pierce tells me, there is no original. It was destroyed, which tells me that Jessie went the extra mile to make it look as if she and I were having a recent affair. I think she was getting ready to blackmail me into staying quiet about her viatical scam."

"You don't have to convince me. Once I sobered up, I realized that the tape couldn't have been what it appeared to be. If you two were having an affair, I would have known it. I'm not that blind."

He went to her and held her tightly.

"I'm sorry I doubted you," she said.

"I understand. I mean, the way her body was found in our bathtub—"

"Let's not recount the details, okay? Let's just . . . be happy. Happy we have each other. That's all I want, is to be happy."

"Me, too," he said, still holding her tight.

A squeal of delight emerged from the patio. They turned and saw *Abuela* standing at the French door and peering in through the glass, blowing them kisses.

Jack smiled and mouthed the word *"Gracias."*

"Let's go," Cindy said softly. "It's time to start packing."

"I'm right behind you."

In less than five minutes Jack was in his convertible following Cindy back to Pinecrest. It would take at least a couple of days to arrange for a mover to bring their furniture to the new house, so they would have a few more nights with his mother-in-law. The plan was for Cindy to arrive ten minutes ahead of Jack and break the news that Jack was moving back in until the rental was ready. Apparently, her mother was less convinced of Jack's fidelity than Cindy was. Jack waited in his car in the driveway until Cindy came out to give him the all-clear.

His car phone rang, startling him. After the cellular swap, the car phone was his only wireless number. He answered. It was Mike Campbell.

"How'd you make out?" asked Jack.

"Well, there was a time in my life when it would have bothered me to follow a woman around for almost two hours and not even be noticed, but I guess in this context, that's a success."

"Nice work. Where'd she lead you?"

"Some pretty bad neighborhoods. She likes to mingle with the homeless. Especially if they're junkies."

"Damn. Sounds to me like she knew she was being followed. Took you on a wild goose chase."

"Except that she didn't seem to be wandering around aimlessly. She stopped at two places, and both times it looked to me as though it was her intended destination. As if she had some kind of business there."

"You mean drug business?"

"No. Blood business."

"Blood?"

"Yeah. She visited a couple of mobile blood units. You know, those big RV-looking things where people come in, let a nurse stick them in the arm, and walk out with cash."

"What the hell's that all about?"

"I didn't want to give myself away by asking any questions. I was hoping it would mean something to you."

"No," said Jack. "Not yet."

"The first truck was parked just off Martin Luther King Boulevard and Seventy-ninth Street. The other one was about a mile west. Both had GIFT OF LIFE painted on the side with a phone number underneath. You want it?"

"Yeah," he said, then wrote it down as Mike rattled off the numbers.

"I got a name for you, too. I asked one of donors who came out of the bloodmobile after she left. Said he thinks her name's Katrina. Didn't get a last name."

"That's a good start."

"You want me to follow up?"

"No, thanks. You go back to practicing law."

"Aw, this is so much more fun."

"Sorry. I'll take it from here."

"Let me know if there's anything else I can do."

"Thanks."

Jack noticed Cindy standing on the front porch. She was smiling and waving him inside.

"And Jack?" said Mike.

"Yeah?"

"Be careful with this woman, all right? Anyone who beats up my friend by night and deals with blood by day kind of worries me."

*Me too,* thought Jack. He thanked him once more and said good night.

# 32

.

Yuri Chesnokov was in his favorite getaway on earth, a city of two hundred thousand thieves, swindlers, whores, hit men, gangsters, kidnappers, drug runners, drug addicts, extortionists, smugglers, counterfeiters, terrorists, and well-armed revolutionaries, some with causes, most without. It was the kind of place where you could get anything you wanted, any time of day, any day of the week. You might also get a few things you didn't want, things you wouldn't wish on anyone. It all depended on what you were looking for.

Or who was looking for you.

Ciudad del Este is a festering urban sore in the jungle on the Paraguay side of the Paraná River. It's difficult to get there, unless you really want to get there. Amazingly, people come in droves. More than a hundred landing strips have been cut into the forests and grasslands in the "Tri-border Region," as the area is known. All are in constant use by small airplanes, not a single flight regulated by authorities. The two-lane bridge from the Brazilian border town of Foz do Iguacu brings in thirty thousand visitors a day, serving as the principal passageway for convoys of buses, trucks, and private cars entering from neighboring Brazil and Argentina. It's a daily ritual, shoppers leaving Rio de Janeiro and other cities late at night and arriving the next morning in the midst of the noisy, fume-filled traffic jam that is the center of Ciudad del Este. Most of the scruffy, bazaarlike shopping centers are on Avenida Monseñor Rodriguez, the main drag from which another five thousand shops fan out in all directions for a twenty-block area. Cheap electronic equipment and cigarettes are big sellers, but only to the truly unimaginative buyers. Behind the scenes is where the real money exchanges hands—cash for weapons, sex, sex slaves, pirated software, counterfeit goods, cocaine by the ton, murder for hire, and just about everything else from phony passports to human body parts for medical transplants. Miami and Hong Kong are the only two cities in the world that see a higher volume of cash transactions. In a country that boasts an official GDP of just $9 billion, Ciudad del Este has risen to a $14 billion annual industry of sleaze, Paraguay's cesspool on the Brazilian border.

Yuri walked from his thirty-dollar-a-night room at the Hotel Munich to a Japanese restaurant on Avenida Adrián Jara, the heart of the Asian sector. An ox cart bumped along the street, maneuvering its way past a pothole large enough to swallow it whole. Mud and ruts were typical for February, when temperatures averaged a humid ninety-five degrees and summer rains were at their peak. It was better than the dry season, when red dust seemed to coat everything, though Yuri saw irony in the pervasive red grit that got in your eyes,

your hair, your clothes, as if it were symbolic of the
growing influence of the Russian mob, the Red *Mafiya*.

"*Cerveza, por favor,*" he told the waiter. Nothing like
a cold beer in the middle of a hot summer afternoon,
and the *cerveza* in Paraguay was consistently good.

It was Yuri's sixth trip to the city in the past three
months, all successful. He was seated at his usual table
in the back of the Café Fugaki, angled in the dark corner with a direct line of sight to the entrance. No one
could approach from behind him, and he could see all
who entered. At the moment, he was the only customer;
a heavy downpour outside keeping away even the most
loyal patrons. His beer arrived in short order, and a
minute later two men joined him. Fahid was Yuri's mid-
dleman, and he'd brought his supplier with him.

Fahid greeted him in Russian, but the pleasantries
had exhausted his limited knowledge of the language.
They continued in English, their common tongue. The
third man, the source, introduced himself as Aman. He
had cold, dark eyes—as cold as Yuri's—and a flat scowl
beneath his black mustache. Yuri offered drinks, but
they declined.

"Fahid tells me you have some problem with the
merchandise," Aman said with a heavy Middle Eastern
accent.

Yuri sipped his beer, then licked away the foam mustache. "Big problems, yes."

"You asked for a virus that easily injects into the
bloodstream and is fatal to people with weak immune
systems. That's exactly what we gave you."

"That may be. But West Nile virus is too . . . how do
you say—exotic?"

"We sold it to you for the same price as much
cheaper products."

"The price isn't the issue."

"If you wanted something specific, you should have said so before we filled the order."

"Five orders you filled, not once did I get West Nile virus. The sixth order, everything changes."

"Not a change. It was within your parameters."

Yuri shot an angry look at Fahid. "I was told it was going to be a strand of pneumonia."

Fahid shrugged and said, "That's what I thought it was going to be."

"The end result is all the same," said Aman. "What's the big deal?"

Yuri's voice tightened. "I'll tell you what the big damn deal is. We stuck a woman in Georgia. Now, instead of a routine death of an AIDS victim from any one of the million or more run-of-the-mill viruses that could have killed her, there's going to be a full-blown investigation into how she picked up this weird virus from someplace in western Africa."

"So what? Investigations blow over."

"I asked you to supply me with something AIDS patients die from every day. Not some bizarre virus that in the last twenty years has killed maybe two dozen people in the entire United States."

"But this is expensive product. I give you the best price anywhere."

"I told you, it's not a question of price, asshole."

"Don't call me an asshole."

"Then don't act like one."

"What you want us to do?"

"I want my money back."

"Oh, for sure. Would you like that with or without interest?"

"You think I'm joking?"

Aman leaned into the table. "Mr. Yuri, you are in Ciudad del Este, not Bloomingdale's. There are no refunds."

Yuri reached across the table and grabbed him by the throat. "You move, and I'll crush your windpipe."

Aman's eyes bulged as he gasped for air, but he didn't dare fight with Yuri. Fahid looked on, too afraid to intervene.

"Stay right there, Fahid. I'm aiming straight at your balls."

Fahid glanced down to see a .22-caliber pistol with a long silencer between his knees. Yuri still had his other hand around Aman's throat. The man's face was turning blue.

Fahid said, "Yuri, come on. Can't we work this out?"

"Just give me my money back."

Fahid glanced once more at Yuri's pistol. "I'm sure that won't be a problem."

"I want to hear it from Aman."

"Take your hand off his throat, and he'll tell you."

He didn't let go. "A simple nod will do. What's it going to be, Aman? Do I get my money?"

Saliva dribbled from the corner of Aman's mouth. He grunted, but the response was unintelligible.

Yuri tightened his grip. "Am I going to get my money back or not?"

Beads of sweat ran from Aman's brow as he struggled to breathe through his compressed windpipe.

"I'm waiting," said Yuri.

His eyes rolled back in their sockets, and his lashes fluttered, as if he were on the verge of losing consciousness.

"Let go of him," said Fahid.

"Shut up. You got five seconds, Aman."

Aman stiffened. His nostrils flared and whistled as he sucked desperately for air. He raised his right hand and curled his fingers into a fist. It shook unsteadily for a few seconds, and then he slowly raised the middle finger.

"You son of a bitch!"

Yuri lunged forward, knocking over the table as he pounced on Aman and flipped him onto his belly. With a knee against Aman's tricep for leverage, he jerked back on the forearm. It was like a gunshot, the sound of bone snapping, and Aman let out a horrible scream as his elbow bent in the wrong direction.

It all happened before Fahid could even blink. Yuri flipped Aman over and jammed a gun into his crotch.

"Stay back, Fahid, or your friend gets an instant vasectomy."

Aman was screaming in pain. There were no other patrons in the restaurant, but the waiters caught a quick look at the commotion and didn't stop running until they were across the street, all in keeping with the silent code of survival in Ciudad del Este: Look the other way.

Yuri grabbed Aman's hand and shoved his middle finger into his mouth. "Give it to me!"

Fahid stepped forward, but Yuri pressed the gun deeper into his friend's groin. "Back off, Fahid, or I'll shoot him."

Fahid froze. Yuri crammed the finger farther down Aman's throat, past the second knuckle and all the way to the base. "Bite it! I want that finger!"

Aman pleaded with a whimper, his eyes watering. Yuri answered with a muffled shot from his silenced pistol. It shattered Aman's left foot. His leg jerked, as if jolted by electricity, and even with his finger halfway down his throat he managed to emit a muted scream.

"Bite it off, right now!"

Aman grimaced, but his jaw tightened at Yuri's command.

"Harder. Bite it all the way through!"

Aman's body shook. Blood ran from his mouth as the teeth tore through the skin and tendons.

"Yuri, stop," said Fahid.

"All the way," he told Aman.

"He's going into shock," said Fahid.

Blood was running down both sides of his face, pooling in the ears. His teeth clenched even tighter as the incisors crushed the bone.

"Let me hear it snap!"

Fahid said, "Stop, okay? I'll get you your money. Consider it my debt. Just let him go."

Yuri looked up at Fahid, then down at Aman. Blood covered his cheeks, his foot was a mangled mess, and his left arm resembled a pretzel. Yuri yanked the middle finger from the clutch of Aman's jaws. It was a broken and twisted stick of raw meat, bitten down to the bone.

"You disgust me," said Yuri. As he rose, he gave two quick punches to Aman's busted elbow, eliciting the loudest scream yet. Aman rolled on the floor in agony, as if not sure which of his painful wounds to tend to.

Yuri said, "I want every penny before I leave town. Not just this order. All six orders."

"I'll deliver it to your hotel tonight," said Fahid. "Then we're square, right?"

"We'll never be square. You assholes cost me my biggest contract ever."

"What?"

"Those bastards I lined up from my Miami office.

They cut me off. And it's your fault. You and your fucking West Nile virus."

He turned and stomped on Aman's bloody foot, drawing one last cry of pain.

Fahid said, "Yuri, I'm sorry about this."

"Not half as sorry as those boys who pulled my contract are going to be."

He tucked his gun into the holster hidden beneath his shirt, dropped twenty dollars' worth of Paraguayan *guaranies* on the chair to cover the beer and the smashed table, and walked out of the restaurant, leaving Fahid to tend to his bloodied partner.

## 33

At 8 A.M. Jack was ready to leave for the courthouse. Cindy had gone into the studio two hours earlier, something about morning light being best for an outdoor shoot. He went to the kitchen for a cup of coffee to go. Cindy's mother was at the table reading the paper.

"Have a good one," said Jack.

"Mmm hmm," she said, her eyes never leaving the crossword puzzle.

Jack started out, then stopped. "Evelyn, I just wanted to thank you."

"For what?"

"For letting Cindy and me stay here with you."

She looked up from her newspaper. "You know there's nothing I wouldn't do for my daughter."

If the words hadn't completely conveyed it, the tone made it clear that she wasn't doing it for his sake. "Can we talk for a minute?"

"What about?"

Jack pulled up a chair and sat across the table from

her. "You've been cool toward me ever since this old audiotape surfaced. Cindy has obviously gotten past it. What do I have to do to make things right with you?"

"There's nothing you need to do."

"Nothing I need to do, or nothing I can do?"

"My, that's the kind of question that certainly brings matters to a head, isn't it?"

Jack looked her in the eye and said, "I wasn't unfaithful to your daughter."

"That's between you two."

"Then why are you making me feel as though I've done something wrong?"

"If you feel that way, then maybe you have."

Jack knew that it was probably best to back away from controversy, the way he always had with Evelyn. But this time he couldn't. "Do you wish I had?"

"Had what?"

"Cheated on Cindy."

"What?

"Do you?"

"What kind of ridiculous question is that?"

"One that you're trying not to answer."

"Why would I ever wish that on my own daughter?"

"You still didn't answer, but here's one possibility: so that she'd leave me."

Her voice tightened. "Do you really want to have this conversation?"

"It's time, don't you think?"

She looked away nervously, then lowered her eyes and said, "It's nothing against you, Jack. Honestly, I don't think you're a horrible person."

"Gee, that's the nicest thing you've ever said to me."

"There was a time when I said nothing but nice things about you."

"And then things changed."

"Esteban changed everything," she said.

Five years after the attack, the mere mention of his name still made his skin crawl. "Cindy told me how you feel. That her nightmares will never end so long as she's with me."

"She was attacked by your client."

"That was when I did death penalty work. I don't anymore. Haven't for years."

"The association is still there. Always will be. Cindy needed to make a break from all of that, and she didn't."

"She's happy with the choices she made."

"She's more fragile than you think."

"She's stronger than you think."

"I'm not just talking about Esteban."

"I know what you're talking about, and I'm nothing like her father."

She paused and settled back into her chair, as if suddenly aware that the intensity of the exchange had her leaning into the table. Her voice dropped to a softer but serious tone. "Do you know why my husband committed suicide?"

"I didn't think anyone really knew why."

"Do you know what his death did to our family?"

"I can only imagine."

"I didn't ask you to imagine. I asked if you knew."

"No. I wasn't there."

"Then you don't know Cindy. And you shouldn't pretend to know what's best for her."

The words angered Jack, not only because they hurt, but because it was so evident that she'd felt that way for a very long time. "You were right from the outset, Evelyn. We shouldn't have had this conversation."

"It was so unnecessary, wasn't it?"

"Some things are better left unsaid."

"Yes. Especially when we both know I'm right."

Jack grabbed his mug of coffee and left the house, down the front steps and across the driveway, thankful for a fast car as his squealing tires carried him away from Cindy's mother and her painful truths.

# 34
.

Jack returned from a hard-fought morning in federal court feeling pretty good about himself. A suppression hearing had gone his way, and it was gratifying to know that, despite the personal hassles, he was still able to do impressive work for his clients. Even the guilty ones.

Jack had barely settled into his office when Rosa popped in from across the hall. It was their habit to kibitz after a court hearing, and he was eager to share the details. She beat him to the punch.

"Jessie Merrill named you in her will."

Jack did a double take. "Named me what?"

"A beneficiary."

The words almost didn't register. He hadn't really been focusing on the probate of Jessie's estate as of late. In fact, he'd given it little thought—perhaps too little thought—since he'd spoken with Clara Pierce, the personal representative. "That can't be."

"I just got off the phone with Clara. Apparently she'd rather deal with your lawyer than with you."

"What did she say?"

"There will be a reading of the will today in her office at three-thirty. You're invited, since you're a beneficiary."

"Did she say what I'm getting?"

"No."

"Then it's probably the Charlie Brown special."

"She intimated that it bolsters your motive to murder Jessie. That hardly sounds like a lump of coal."

"You don't think she left me the money, do you?"

Rosa considered it. "It seems incredible. But I'm beginning to think maybe she was at least a little crazy."

"I'll vouch for that."

"I'm saying something a little different. I'm talking about the kind of mental impairment that's medically verifiable."

"Do you know something I don't know?"

She walked to the window and said, "I hear the medical examiner is about to issue a report."

"I hadn't heard."

"Nothing's official yet. But I have it on pretty good authority that higher-than-normal levels of lead were found in tissue taken from her liver and kidneys. You know what that means, Jack?"

He was looking at his lawyer, yet it was as if he could see right through her. "Jessie did have lead poisoning."

"At one time, yes. It was no longer in her bloodstream by the time she died, but traces of it had deposited in her major organs."

Jack was talking fast, his thoughts getting ahead of him. "Okay, she really was sick at the outset. But that doesn't prove that there was no scam. Somebody, somewhere along the line, got the bright idea to take lead poisoning and turn it into a phony case of ALS in order to dupe a group of viatical investors. Maybe it was her idea, maybe it was her doctor's. Maybe it hit them both at the same time while they were lying in bed together."

"I agree with you, but that's not my point."

"What is your point?"

"Lead poisoning has other ramifications, medically speaking. Even personality problems. Paranoia, hallucinations, irritability."

"The kinds of things you'd expect from a suicide candidate."

"Except that this isn't a normal suicide."

"Is there such a thing?"

Rosa took a seat on the edge of the desk, facing Jack. "Let me explain what I mean. So far, we've uncovered what seems to be a string of some pretty peculiar things that Jessie did before she died. She named you as beneficiary in her will. She named you as the co–account holder of her bank account. She used that audiotape to make it look as if you two were recently in the sack together."

"It's pretty clear she was trying to set me up as an accomplice."

"Most likely to keep you from blowing the whistle on her scam."

"Right. As soon as our audio expert finishes her analysis, we can show the state attorney exactly what she was up to."

"With the original missing, it won't be easy to show that the taped love-making session between you and Jessie happened seven or eight years ago."

"Still, any expert worth her salt can verify that the only tapes in existence are copies. The only reason for Jessie to have made a copy and destroyed the original is to create the impression that she and I were having a recent affair."

"That's all true," said Rosa. "But I'm not sure your extortion theory accounts for the full range of emotions behind that audiotape."

"What are you talking about?"

"As you say, we know that she copied the tape from an old original so it would look new. But that begs the question: Why did she keep the original all these years? You can't tell me that she was planning this scam for seven or eight years."

"I explained all this before. That tape became kind of a running gag between us. She probably ended up stuffing it in a shoebox somewhere and forgetting about it. Until recently, when she needed it."

"I'm not convinced that her keeping it all these years was as innocent and meaningless as you think. I've listened to it."

"So have I."

"Maybe you should listen to it again."

"I really don't want to."

"I want you to. Come on." She started out of the office.

"Where we going?"

"The tape. It's in the file."

"I don't need to hear that again," he said, but she was already down the hall. Jack followed. Rosa dug the tape from a locked filing cabinet, then ducked into the conference room. Reluctantly, Jack caught up just as she was putting the audiocassette in the stereo.

"We don't have to listen to all of it. In fact, the only part that piques my interest is at the very end." She hit FAST FORWARD till the tape ended, then rewound briefly.

"Ready?" she asked.

Jack shook his head. "This is embarrassing."

"It's not that bad. This isn't the two of you grunting and groaning. It's the afterglow. Just you and her talking, when she tries to coax you into going from audio to videotape. Listen." She hit PLAY.

The hiss of recorded silence flowed from the sound system, and then Jack heard his own voice.

*"Can you put the damn camera away, please?"*

*"Come on. We did it on audio. Why not try the video?"*

*"Because it's like a one-eyed monster staring at me."*

*"I stare at your one-eyed monster all the time."*

*"Don't point that thing at my—"*

*"Oh, now you're Mr. Modest."*

*"Just turn it off."*

*"Why?"*

*"Why do you think?"*

*"Because you don't like to have it on while we're talking."*

*"No, I just don't like the thing staring at me like that."*

*"So it's okay to have a tape recorder running while you're fucking me. But it's time to put everything away when we talk about how we feel about each other."*

*"That's not it."*

*"Are you afraid to say how you feel about me, Jack?"*

*"No."*

*"Then say it. Say it on tape."*

*"Stop playing games."*

*"You're afraid."*

*"Damn it, Jessie. I just don't want to do this."*

*"You big chicken. Look, I'm not afraid. I can look straight into the camera and tell you exactly how I feel."*

Again the speakers hissed throughout the conference room, a pregnant pause before Jessie's final words on tape.

*"I don't want to live without you, Jack Swyteck. I don't ever want to live without you."*

Rosa hit END, and the tape clicked off. She looked across the room and said, "Well?"

"Well, what? It's lovers' banter. People say that all the time: I don't want to live without you."

"Sure. And probably ninety-nine times out of a hundred it means simply that they'd rather live with you than live without you. But in that rare case, it might have a more literal meaning: If the choice is between death and living without you, then death it is."

"Those words are said in thousands of bedrooms every day. I'd rather die than lose you, blah, blah, blah. It doesn't mean they're going to go off and kill themselves."

"Most of the time, no. But sometimes it does."

"This was almost eight years ago."

"You don't know what happened in Jessie's life after your split. Her life could have been one long string of personal disasters from the day you broke up."

"You're overlooking the fact that she's the one who dumped me."

"Did she? Or did you force her to break it off by refusing to tell her how you felt? You said it yourself, she wanted to get back together with you six months later."

"Stop the pop psychology, okay? This tape, that relationship—it's all old news. And everything you're saying is totally speculative."

"Don't knock it. If you're indicted for murder, this just might be your defense."

"Yeah, right. Old girlfriend carries a torch for over half a decade. Makes me a joint holder of her bank account, leaves me a pot of money in her will, and doctors up an old tape of us making love, all just to give me motive to kill her. It's ridiculous."

"Listen to me. From the very beginning, we talked about how Jessie might have been trying to make a statement by killing herself in your bathtub. Well, maybe the statement she was trying to make is simply this: 'Jack Swyteck killed me.'"

"You're serious about this? You think she killed herself and framed me for doing it?"

"Think about it. The trick only works once, but it could be the perfect frame-up. Kill yourself, but do it in a way that makes it look like someone else did it. If it's done right, it's ironclad. The real killer is beyond suspicion."

Jack took a seat, thinking. Maybe he had overlooked a plausible defense, perhaps even the best defense, all because he feared his wife's reaction to his past with Jessie. "I swear, every time I think I'm getting my arms around this thing, it slips away from me."

"That's good. I'm not saying an indictment's inevitable, but if the worst comes to pass, confusion is the wellspring of reasonable doubt."

"For my own sake, I'd kind of like to know the truth someday."

"Would you?"

"Of course."

"Then maybe you will. Let's just hope it doesn't scare you."

Jack nodded slowly, saying nothing as he watched Rosa remove their copy of the old audiotape.

# 35

Katrina Padron had blood on her hands. It was all in a day's work. The vial had leaked in her hand. One of the idiots at the mobile unit had failed to seal it properly, something that occurred far too often in the shipment of product from the source to the distribution warehouse. Mishaps were inevitable when dealing with untrained workers. What else could she expect? A month earlier the crew had been operating a video rental shop, next month they might be hawking gemstones. For now, it was human blood. Diseased blood. Lots of it.

*Thank God for latex gloves.*

Katrina was in the back of the warehouse, scrubbing her hands with a strong soap and disinfectant, when her assistant emerged from the walk-in refrigerator. He was dressed in a fur-lined winter coat and carrying a box large enough to hold a dozen vials packed in dry ice and wrapped in plastic bubble wrap.

"Where's this one going again?" he asked.

"Sydney, Australia."

He grabbed a pen and an international packing slip. "I saw a travel show about Sydney on the TV a while back. Isn't that where England used to send its worst prisoners?"

"A long time ago."

"So that means everybody down there descended from some guy who was in jail."

"Not everyone."

"Still, prison is prison. You'd think they'd have enough AIDS-infected blood already. What do they need us for?"

Katrina just rolled her eyes. *Morons, I work with. Total morons.*

He sealed up the box with extra tape and attached the shipping label. "All set. One Australian football ready for drop-kick shipment," he said as he went through the pretend motion.

"Don't even think about it."

"What do you think, I'm stupid or something?" He removed his coat, hung it on the hook beside the big refrigerator door, and started for the exit.

"Hey, genius," said Katrina. "Aren't you forgetting something?"

He turned, then groaned at the sight of the unfinished paperwork in her hand. "Aw, come on. I've been in and out of that refrigerator for three hours. Can't you at least do the invoicing for me, babe?"

"Only if you stop calling me babe."

He winked and smiled in a way that was enough to make her nauseous. "You got it, sweets."

She let him and his remarks go. It was easier that way. She wasn't planning on working this job forever, and if she wasted her time trying to get others to do their fair share she'd never get home at night. The paperwork wasn't really all that time-consuming anyway. One genuine invoice for a legitimate purchase and sale of diseased blood, four phony ones to fictitious customers for extremely expensive inventory that never existed. Bio-Research, Inc., had just enough employees, just enough inventory, and just enough sales to look like a real company that supplied real specimens for use in medical research. It was anything but real.

Most amazing of all, the blood business was a huge step up from her first job.

A dozen years earlier she'd come to Miami from Cuba by way of the Czech Republic, having spent four long years in Prague under one of Fidel Castro's most appalling and least known work programs. At age seventeen, she was one of eighty thousand young Cuban men and women sent to Eastern Bloc countries to work for paltry wages. The host countries got cheap labor for jobs that natives didn't want, and Castro got cash. Katrina had been lured across the ocean by the prospect of exploring a country outside her depressed homeland. Once there, she'd ended up seeing little more than the inside of a sweatshop and the two-bedroom apartment she shared with seven roommates. Not even the wages were as promised, which only galvanized her determination never to return home to Cuba. In time, her sole mission devolved into nothing more than getting out of Prague alive.

At times even that had seemed too lofty a goal.

"Katrina?"

She looked up from her paperwork to see her boss standing in the doorway. Vladimir was strictly a front-office guy. He didn't usually spend any time in the warehouse. Especially since they'd gotten into the dirty-blood business.

"Yes, sir?"

He came toward her, stepping carefully around the boxes scattered about the concrete floor. Under his arm was the glossy red folder that held the latest slick marketing brochure for Viatical Solutions, Inc., which told her that he'd come to see her about his other business. The two companies shared office space.

"I just got off the phone with some guy who says you referred him to me."

"Says *I* referred him?"

"Big, deep voice. Sounds like a burly old football player. Says he wants to meet and talk about a huge book of viatical business for us."

"What's his name?"

"Theo. Theo Knight. You know him?"

Katrina instantly recognized the name but forced herself to show no reaction. "I do."

"I told him I'd meet him at the Brown Bear for dinner. He pretty much insisted you come along. Can you join us?"

She put the blood invoices aside, struggling to keep her own blood from boiling. "Sure. I'd love to chat with my ol' pal Theo."

# 36

·

Jack and Rosa reached the Law Offices of Clara Pierce & Associates at precisely 3:29 P.M. The reading of Jessie Merrill's will was scheduled for half-past three, and one extra minute was plenty of time for Jack to sit in enemy territory.

A receptionist led them directly to the main conference room and seated them in chairs of ox-blood leather at the long stone table. From the looks of things, Clara's practice was thriving. Plush carpeting, cherry wainscoting, silk wall coverings. The focal piece of the room was the exquisite conference table. It was cut from creamy-white natural stone, rough and unfinished, one of those expensive excesses that interior decorators talked lawyers into buying and that was completely nonfunctional, unless you were the type of person who liked to try to put pen to paper on the Appian Way.

The receptionist brought coffee and said, "Please be sure to use coasters. The stone is porous and stains quite easily."

"Sure thing," said Jack. *Beautiful, impractical,* and *high maintenance,* he thought. *Jessie would so approve.*

She closed the door on her way out. Jack and Rosa looked at each other, puzzled by the fact that they were alone.

"Are you sure Clara said three-thirty?" asked Jack.

"Positive."

The door opened and Clara Pierce entered the room. A leather dossier was tucked under one arm. "Sorry I'm late," she said as she shook hands without a smile. "But this shouldn't take long. Let's get started."

"Isn't anyone else coming?" asked Jack.

"Nope."

"Are you saying I'm the only heir?"

"I think I'll let Jessie answer that. Her will is as specific as it can be."

Jack didn't fully understand, but Rosa gave him a little squeeze on the elbow, as if to remind him that they had come only to listen.

Clara removed the papers from the dossier and placed them before her. Jack sipped his coffee and absentmindedly set the mug on the table. Clara's eyes widened, as though she were on the verge of cardiac arrest. With a quick snap of the fingers she said, "Jack, please, coaster."

"Oh, sorry."

"This table is straight from Italy. It's the most expensive piece of furniture I've ever purchased, and once it's stained, it's ruined."

"Just lost my head there for a second. Won't happen again."

"Thank you."

"Can you read the will, please?" said Rosa.

"Yes, surely. Let me say at the outset, however, that

it was not my idea to have an official reading of the will. I would have just as soon let you see a copy when I filed it with the probate court. But it was Jessie's specific request that there be a reading."

"No explanation needed, but thank you just the same."

"Very well, then. Here goes. 'I, Jessie Marie Merrill, being of sound mind and body, hereby bequeath . . .' "

*Sound body, indeed,* thought Jack. Perhaps it should have read, "I, Jessie Marie Merrill, being of sound mind and body that's a whole heck of a lot more sound than I've led everyone to believe, including my dumb-schmuck lawyer, Jack Swyteck, without whose unfathomable gullibility I wouldn't have diddly squat to hereby bequeath, bequest, and devise . . ."

Jack listened to every word as Clara continued through the preamble. After a minute or two she paused for a sip of water, carefully returned her glass to a coaster, and then turned to the meat of Jessie's will.

" 'My estate shall be devised as follows,' " said Clara, reading from page two. " 'One. Within six months of my death, all of my worldly possessions, including all stocks, bonds, and illiquid assets, shall be sold and liquidated for cash.

" 'Two. The proceeds of such liquidation shall be held in a trust account to be administered by Clara Pierce, as trustee, in accordance with the terms of the trust agreement attached hereto as Exhibit A.

" 'Three. The sole beneficiary of said trust shall be the minor male child formerly known as Jack Merrill, born on October 11, 1992 at Tampa General Hospital, Tampa, Florida, and released for adoption by his mother, Jessie Marie Merrill, on November 1, 1992.

" 'Four.' "

It was as if Jack's mind had slipped into a three-second delay. He put down his coffee and said, "Excuse me. Did you just say she had a kid?"

Again, Clara snapped her fingers. "Coaster, please."

Jack moved his coffee mug, but he was almost unaware of his motions. "And his name was Jack?"

"Please," said Clara. "Let me get through the whole document, then you can ask questions."

Rosa said, "Actually, we won't have any questions. We're just here to listen, right, Jack?"

He felt his lawyer's heel grinding into his toe. "But Clara just said—"

"I heard what she said. Please, Ms. Pierce, continue. There won't be any further interruptions."

Clara turned the page. " 'The beneficiary's present whereabouts and current identity are unknown as of this writing. Should he not be located within one year from the date of my death, the trust shall be dissolved and my entire estate shall issue to the beneficiary's father, John Lawrence Swyteck.' "

"What?"

"Damn it, Jack. For the last time, use the stinking coaster."

"Jessie never told me she had a kid."

"Quiet, Jack," said Rosa.

"Coaster, *please*," said Clara.

"And she sure as heck never said I was the father."

Rosa grabbed his arm. "Let's go."

"No, I want to hear this."

"Your coffee mug is still on my table."

"Jack, if you can't shut up and listen, then it's my duty as your lawyer to get you out of here."

"No!" he said as he yanked his arm free of Rosa's grasp. His arm continued across the table in a sweeping motion and collided with the coffee cup. Hot, black liquid was instantly airborne. In what seemed like slow motion, Jack leaped from his seat to catch it, but to no avail. Clara's mouth was agape, her eyes the size of silver dollars. The three of them looked on in horror as a huge black puddle gathered in the dead center of her creamy-stone table and then disappeared, soaking into the porous stone, leaving behind an ugly brown stain. The meeting suddenly took on the aura of a funeral.

Her expensive stone table now resembled fossilized dinosaur shit.

"Clara, I am *so* sorry."

"You bastard! You did that on purpose!"

"I swear, it was an accident."

"It's ruined!"

"I'll pay to have it cleaned."

"It can't be cleaned. You destroyed my beautiful table."

"I just don't know how that happened."

"I think we should go now," said Rosa.

Clara was on the verge of tears. "Yes, please. Both of you, get out of here."

"But we haven't heard the whole will," said Jack.

"You've heard the part that matters."

Jack wanted to hear more, as if he might hear *something* that made sense to him. But Clara seemed impervious to whatever plea he might have pitched. She hadn't moved from her seat. Her elbows were on the table—one of them on a coaster—as she held her head in her hands and stared blankly at the big brown stain.

Jack said, "Sorry about—"

"Just leave," she said, not even looking up.

He and Rosa slipped away in silence, showing themselves to the door.

# 37

S livers of late-afternoon sunshine cut through the venetian blinds. It was annoying to the eye, but Assistant State Attorney Benno Jancowitz left things just the way they were. Any time he hammered out a deal with a witness who was willing to turn state's evidence, he didn't like his guests to get too comfortable.

Seated across the table from the prosecutor was Hugo Zamora, three hundred pounds' worth of criminal defense lawyer with a voice that boomed. At his side was a nervous Dr. Marsh. The desktop was clear, save for the one-page proffer of testimony that had been prepared by Zamora. Typed on the proffer were the exact words that the doctor would utter to a grand jury, assuming that the prosecutor would agree to grant him immunity from prosecution.

Jancowitz pretended to read over the proffer one last time, drumming his fingers as his eyes moved from left to right, line by line. Finally, he looked up and said, "I'm not impressed."

"We're certainly open to negotiation," said Zamora. "Perhaps put a finer point on some of the testimony."

"It just doesn't help me."

"I beg to differ. Your case against Mr. Swyteck rests on the assumption that Jack Swyteck and Jessie Merrill were having an affair. I presume your theory is something along the lines of Jessie Merrill was threatening to reveal the affair to Swyteck's wife, so Swyteck killed her."

"I'm not going to comment on my theories."

"Fine. Let's talk evidence. The proof you have of an affair is the audiotape that came from the inventory of property in Ms. Merrill's estate, correct?"

"I'm not going to comment on the nature of the evidence we've gathered."

"You don't have to. We both know that police departments are sieves. I won't name names, but it has come to my attention that your own expert has confirmed that this so-called smoking gun of an audiotape is not an original. There is no original. All you have is a copy, which leaves the door wide open for Swyteck to argue that the missing original was made before he was even married. It doesn't prove anything."

Jancowitz said nothing.

Zamora continued, "Now, Dr. Marsh here is ready, willing, and able to plug this gaping hole in your case. He, of course, denies that he was ever part of this alleged scam that Mr. Swyteck talks about. But he will tell the jury that after his serving as Jessie Merrill's doctor, they became close friends. That on the night Jessie won her trial against the viatical investors, she came by his apartment to thank him personally. That one thing led to another, and they ended up making love."

"I know, I've read the proffer."

"Just play the tape."

"I don't need to play it."

"I've already fast-forwarded to the important part. It's less than twenty seconds."

He thought for a moment, sipping his lukewarm coffee. "How is it that this tape came into existence?"

"It was something that this Jessie apparently liked to do. You already know that from the other tape you have."

"So you're telling me you have a tape of Dr. Marsh and Jessie Merrill actually having sex?"

"Yes. It's not a very good tape. She just set the camera up on a tripod and then the two of them . . . you know, did their thing."

Jancowitz glanced at Marsh, a man older than himself, and said, "Is it really necessary for me to watch this?"

"No. We can kill the video portion. The only thing that matters is what was said."

"I can live with that," said Jancowitz.

Zamora handed him the tape. There was a small television set with built-in VCR player on the credenza. Jancowitz inserted the videotape and dimmed the screen to black, for the sake of his own eyes and Dr. Marsh's modesty. Then he hit PLAY. Jancowitz returned to his seat, then leaned closer to the set.

"I don't hear anything."

"Turn it up," said Zamora.

He increased the volume. A rustling noise followed, some kind of motion. A woman laughed, though it sounded more evil than happy. A man groaned.

"It sounds like bad porn," said Jancowitz.

No one argued. Dr. Marsh sank in his chair.

On tape, the voices grew louder. The heavy breathing took on rhythm, and Jessie's voice gained strength.

*"That's it. Harder."*

All eyes in the room were suddenly fixed on the screen, even though it was black. No one wanted to make eye contact.

*"Harder, baby. That's it. Give it to me. Come on. Come on, that's it, yes, yes! Oh, God—yes, Jack, yes!"*

Zamora gave the signal, and the prosecutor hit STOP. He gave Jancowitz a moment to take in what had just played and said, "You heard it?"

"Yes."

"She clearly said the name Jack."

The prosecutor grimaced and shook his head. "It just doesn't do it. All you've got is a woman crying out another man's name."

"Not just any name. Jack, as in Jack Swyteck."

"That doesn't establish that she and Swyteck were having an affair. At most, it just establishes that she fantasized about Swyteck while she was making love to Dr. Marsh."

"Right now, you have nothing to prove the existence of an affair. This is a lot better than nothing."

"I think there's plenty more to this triangle than you're telling me. If you want immunity from prosecution, you'd better fork it over."

"We're giving you all we have."

"Then there's no deal."

"Fine," said Zamora. "We're outta here."

"Wait," said Dr. Marsh.

Zamora did a double take. "Let's go, Doctor. I said, we're outta here."

"I'm a respected physician in this community, and the stink from this Jessie Merrill situation is tarnishing my good name. I won't allow this to drag out any longer. Now, Mr. Jancowitz, tell me what you want from me."

"I want the truth."

"We're giving you the truth."

"I want the whole truth. Not bits and pieces."

Zamora said, "Then give us immunity. And you get it all."

The prosecutor locked eyes with Zamora, then looked at Dr. Marsh. "I'll give you immunity, but I want two things."

"Name them."

"I want everything the doctor knows about Swyteck and Jessie Merrill."

"Easy."

"And I want your client to sit for a polygraph. I want to know if the doctor had anything to do with the death of Jessie Merrill. If he passes, we got a deal."

"Wait a minute," said Zamora, groaning.

"Done," said Marsh. "Ask away on the murder. But I won't sit for a polygraph on the viatical scam."

"You got something to hide?" asked Jancowitz.

"Not at all. With the complicated relationship I had with Jessie, I'm concerned that you might get false signs of deception, depending on how you worded the scam question. But if you want to ask me straight up if I killed Jessie Merrill, I got no problem with that."

"Fine," said the prosecutor. "Let's do it."

"Hold on, damn it," said Zamora. "My client obviously wants to cooperate, but I'm not going to sit back and let the two of you rush into something as important as a polygraph examination. Right now, Dr. Marsh and I are going to walk out that door, go back to my office, and talk this over."

"I want to get this done," said Marsh.

"I understand. A few more hours isn't going to kill anyone."

"I'll give you twenty-four hours," said Jancowitz. "If I don't hear from you, I'll subpoena Dr. Marsh to appear before a grand jury."

"You'll hear from us," said Zamora.

"You know the deal. Pass the polygraph on the murder and tell all."

Marsh rose and shook the prosecutor's hand. "Like my lawyer said: You'll hear from us."

The prosecutor escorted them to the exit, then watched through the glass door as they walked to the elevator. He returned to his office, tucked the videotape into an envelope, sealed it, then took out his pen and drew a little star on the doctor's witness file.

# 38

The smoke was thick at Fox's. Just the way Jack wanted it.

Fox's Lounge had been at the same location on U.S. 1 forever, and the decor probably hadn't changed since Gerald Ford was president. It was a time warp with dark-paneled walls, booths trimmed with leather so worn that it felt like plastic, and enough secondhand smoke to gag even a tobacco-industry spokesman. Jack didn't care for cigarettes, except when he really needed a drink. Even then he didn't light up. He just basked in the swirling clouds around him and belted back bourbon until his clothes reeked and his eyes turned red.

It seemed like the perfect way to toast the reading of Jessie's will.

"Make it huge," Jack said into his cell phone. He was speaking with Hirni's Florists, arranging for the immediate delivery of the biggest damn floral centerpiece they'd ever constructed—big enough to cover a stain as big as a manhole cover on Clara's priceless stone conference table. While he was at it, he ordered some roses for Cindy. In a perfect world he would have been home, packing for the scheduled moving day, but somehow he didn't envision himself dashing off to a new house with Cindy happily at his side after telling her about Jack Junior. He needed a little counseling, and for that he turned again to his friend Mike. He was uniquely qualified. He'd known Jack since college, he'd known Jessie when she and Jack were dating, and, most important, he knew they weren't twenty-one anymore and had no business getting drunk on anything but premium brands.

"Old Pappy on the rocks," he told the bartender.

"What the heck's Old Pappy?" asked Jack.

"A little treat I discovered at the Sea Island Lodge. Best bourbon you'll ever drink."

Jack was a little surprised that the bartender had it, but Fox's was a pretty reliable place to find obscure brands, especially old brands, and, if the label was to be believed, no one drank Old Pappy unless it was at least twenty years old.

"What do you make of this mess?" asked Jack.

It had taken him five minutes to bring Mike up to speed. It took less than five seconds for Mike to render his verdict.

"She's a nutcase," he said as he selected a jalapeño popper from the plate of hors d'oeuvres. "She always was."

"What does that mean?"

"Nothing with her ever added up. She did everything for shock value, just to see how people would react."

"This is more than shock value."

"I didn't say she wasn't vindictive."

Jack sipped his bourbon. "This was a stroke of

genius on her part. Her objective was to leave everything to a child she'd given up for adoption. Rather than find him herself, she drops the whole thing in my lap. It's up to me to find him."

"Technically, you don't have to look. If no one finds the kid, you inherit a million and a half dollars."

"That's exactly my dilemma."

"Not sure I follow you."

"The money came from a scam. If I find the child, I'll be handing him a million and a half dollars that I know is dirty. But if I choose not to look for him, I'll forever be accused of cheating my own flesh and blood out of an inheritance from his birth mother."

"Accused by whom?"

"Everyone."

"Everyone? Or yourself?"

"What do you mean by that?"

"I'm just trying to think like Jessie. Maybe her objective wasn't simply to get the money in the hands of the child she gave up for adoption. Maybe she was just as interested in making you feel guilty as hell about the whole situation."

"Years of pent-up anger, is that it?"

"It's a long time, but who knows what was going through her head?"

Jack took another long sip. "I think I know."

"You want to share?"

Jack glanced at the mirror behind the bar, speaking to Mike without looking at him. "Jessie couldn't have kids."

"She apparently had one."

"I mean after that one. I saw her whole medical file during our case. She had PID."

"What?"

"Pelvic inflammatory disease. It's an infection that goes up through the uterus to the fallopian tubes. It was cured, but the damage was done. Doctors told her she'd probably never have kids."

"How did she get it?"

"How do you think?"

Mike nodded, as if suddenly it was all coming together. "You and her break up, she finds out she's pregnant. She comes back to you before she's really started to show and tells you she wants to get back together. But you've already met Cindy Paige, so she keeps the baby a secret. Last thing she wants is you coming back to her just because she's pregnant."

Jack filled in the rest, staring through the smoke-filled room. "She gives up the baby for adoption, meets some guy who gives her PID, and just like that, she finds herself in a situation where she's given away the only child she's ever going to bring into this world."

They glanced at one another and then looked away, their eyes drifting aimlessly in the direction of whatever nonsense was playing on the muted television set.

"Hey, Jack," said Mike.

"Yeah?"

"I think I figured out why Jessie came back to stick it to you as her attorney after all these years."

Jack swirled the ice cubes in his glass and said, "Yeah. Me too."

# 39

·

Katrina walked into the Brown Bear around six-thirty with Vladimir at her side. The restaurant was about half-full, and she spotted Theo instantly. They walked right past the sign that said PLEASE WAIT TO BE SEATED and joined Theo in a rear booth.

Katrina made the introductions, and they slid across the leather seats, Katrina and her boss on one side of the booth, across from Theo.

The Brown Bear was in East Hollywood, just off Hallandale Beach Boulevard. It had a huge local following, mostly people of Eastern European descent. The newspaper dispenser just outside the door wasn't the *Miami Herald* or the South Florida *Sun-Sentinel* but *eXile,* a biweekly paper from Moscow. Behind the cash register hung an autographed photo of Joseph Kobzon, favorite pop singer of former Soviet leader Leonid Brezhnev and a household name to generations of Russian music lovers, known best for his soulful renditions of patriotic ballads. The buzz coming from the many crowded tables was more often Russian or Slovak than English or Spanish. Meals were inexpensive and served family-style, gluttonous portions of skewered lamb, chopped liver, and beef Stroganoff. Caviar and vodka cost extra. On weekends, a three-piece band and schmaltzy nightclub singer entertained guests. Reservations were essential—except for guys like Vladimir.

Katrina wondered if Theo had any idea that the Cyrillic letters tattooed onto each of her boss' fingers identified him as a made man among *vory,* a faction of the Russian *Mafiya* so powerful it was almost mythical.

"Katrina tells me you used to work together," said Vladimir.

She shot Theo a subtle glance. Vladimir had quizzed her on the car ride over, and she'd been forced to concoct a story. Revealing the true circumstances under which she and Theo had met would only have exposed herself as a snitch.

"That's right," said Theo, seeming to catch her drift.

Katrina took it from there. "I've come a long way from slogging drinks at Sparky's, haven't I, Theo?"

"You sure have."

"I like that name," said Vladimir. "Sparky's."

"I came up with it myself. The old electric chair in Florida used to be called 'Old Sparky.' When I beat the odds and got off death row, I thought Sparky's was a good name for a bar."

Vladimir smiled approvingly, as if serving time on death row only confirmed that Theo was all right. "Do you own this Sparky's?"

"Half of it. I'm the operations partner. Buddy of mine put up all the money."

"Other people's money," Vladimir said with a thin smile. "We should drink to that." He signaled the waitress, and almost immediately she brought over three rounds of his usual cocktail, one for each of them.

"What's this?" asked Theo.

"Tarzan's Revenge."

"Ice-cold vodka and Japanese sake poured over a raw quail's egg," said Katrina.

"I didn't know Tarzan drank."

She didn't bother explaining that Tarzan was not Johnny Weissmuller but a flamboyant, muscle-bound Russian mobster famous for wild sex orgies on his yacht and a hare-brained scheme to sell a Russian nuclear submarine to the Colombian cartel for underwater drug smuggling.

"Cheers," said Vladimir, and each of them belted one back.

Just as soon as the first round was gone the waitress brought another. Katrina joined in the second and third rounds but passed on the fourth and fifth. She'd seen Vladimir operate before, knew he could outdrink any American, and knew that Tarzan's Revenge was Vladimir's way of loosening tongues and tripping up rats.

"Tell us more about your proposal," said Vladimir.

"Let me start by being upfront with you. I'm not gonna try to hide the fact that I'm a friend of Jack Swyteck."

"You mean the lawyer?"

"You know who I mean."

Vladimir was stone-faced. "You said you had business."

"That's right. And for me, business is business. Swyteck's not part of it. So, it's your choice. You can tell me to shut up and go away, that you don't want shit to do with any friend of Jack Swyteck. Or you can put my friendships aside and act like a businessman, which means both of us make a lot of money."

Vladimir removed a cigar from his inside pocket, unwrapped the cellophane. "Everyone I do business with has friends I can't stand."

"That's what I thought you'd say. You look like a very smart man."

"What are you offering?"

"Viatical settlements."

"How much?"

"The sky's the limit."

Vladimir laughed like a nonbeliever. "I've heard that one before."

"Maybe so. But not from someone who understands your business the way I do."

"You know so much, do you?"

"You got a lot of cash on your hands."

"What makes you think that?"

"It's written all over your face. And your hands," he said as he glanced at the Cyrillic letters on Vladimir's fingers.

Katrina said nothing, but she was starting to reconsider. *Maybe this Theo isn't as dumb as he looks.*

Vladimir said, "A guy could have worse problems."

"But too much cash is still a problem. So I figure it works this way. You got a pot of dirty money."

"I have no dirty money."

"Just for the sake of argument, let's say you got fifty million dirty dollars. Some from drugs, some from prostitution, extortion, illegal gaming, whatever. We can all talk freely here. We're among friends, right, Katrina?"

"Old friends are the best friends," she said.

"Okay," said Vladimir. "Let's say fifty million."

"Let's say I got a hundred guys dying from AIDS who

are willing to sell their life insurance policies to you for five hundred thousand dollars a pop. You do a hundred separate deals, all impossible to trace, and pay out fifty million in cash. My guys name some offshore companies formed by your lawyer as the beneficiary under their life insurance policy. When they die, the life insurance company pays you the death benefit. Clean money."

"How much?"

"Double. You start with fifty million in dirty money. In two years you got a hundred million in clean money straight from the coffers of triple-A-rated insurance companies."

Vladimir glanced at Katrina. Again she said nothing, though it impressed her the way Theo had put so much together. She suspected that Jack had done at least some of the unraveling.

"Sounds intriguing," said Vladimir. "I might be interested under the right circumstances."

"If you had fifty million dirty dollars?"

"No. If you actually had a hundred fags with life insurance in the pipeline."

"A buddy of mine owns nine AIDS hospices. Three in California, four in New York, two in south Florida. All high-end, all wealthy clientele. No one who checks into these places is long for this earth."

"That could be a very useful connection."

"I thought so."

Vladimir's cell phone rang. He checked the number and grimaced. "I gotta take this. Back in a minute."

Katrina waited until he was safely outside the restaurant, then glared at Theo and said, "What in the hell do you think you're doing?"

"Going to the source."

"What for?"

"It's like Jack and me figured. We find out who's laundering all that viatical money, we find Jessie Merrill's killer."

"Do you have any idea who you're dealing with?"

"Yes. Do you?"

"Eventually Vladimir is going to see right through you. You can't bluff these people."

"Why not? You did."

"That's different. I'm working from the inside."

"Give me a little time. I'll be right there beside you."

"Have you lost your mind? You're going to get yourself killed."

"Only if you blow my cover. But you won't do that. Because if you do, I'm taking you down with me."

She was so angry she could have leaped across the table and strangled him. But Vladimir was back, and she quickly forced herself to regain her composure.

He sank back into the booth and snapped his fingers. The waitress brought another round of Tarzan's Revenge.

"To your health," said Vladimir.

He belted back the drink. Katrina did likewise, keeping one angry eye on Theo.

Vladimir put the unlit cigar back in his pocket, as if signaling that it was time to leave. He looked at Theo and said, "I'm afraid I have to go, but before I do, I want to leave you with this story. You ever heard of the money plane?"

"Money plane? I don't think so."

"Delta Flight 30. It used to leave JFK for Moscow at 5:45 P.M. five days a week. Rarely did it leave with less than a hundred million dollars in its cargo belly. Stacks of new hundred dollar bills, all shipped in white canvas bags. Over the years, about 80 billion dollars came into Russia that way. Just one unarmed courier on the flight, no special security measures. And not once did anyone even try to hijack the plane. Why do you think that is?"

"The food sucked?"

"Because anyone who knew about the money also knew that it was being bought by Russian banks. And if you rip off a Russian bank, nine chances out of ten says you're ripping off the Russian *Mafiya*. Nobody has big enough balls or a small enough brain to do that. So that plane just kept right on flying."

"Very interesting."

"You understand what I'm saying?"

"I'm pretty sure I do."

"Give us two days. If you check out, you meet Yuri."

"Sounds good."

Katrina said, "Tell him what happens if he doesn't check out."

"I think he gets the point," said Vladimir.

"I like to be explicit with my friends. He should hear."

Vladimir leaned forward, a wicked sparkle in his eye. "You don't check out, you meet Fate. And he has not a pretty face."

Theo gave an awkward smile. "Funny how you talk about fate as if it's a person."

"That *is* funny," said Vladimir. "Because we all know that Fate is an animal." He laughed loudly, pounding the table with his fist. Then all traces of a smile ran from his face. "Good-bye, Theo."

Theo rose and said, "You know where to reach me, right, Katrina?"

"Don't worry. We won't have trouble finding you."

She watched as he turned and walked away, then headed out the door, not sure if she should be angry or feel sorry for him.

*Theo, my boy, you were safer on death row.*

# 40

Dr. Marsh sat in silence in the plush leather passenger seat of his lawyer's Lexus. They were just a half-block away from Mercy Hospital, an acute-care facility that sat on premier Miami waterfront, the Coconut Grove side of Biscayne Bay. Year after year it was voted "best view from a deathbed" by a local off-beat magazine. Dr. Marsh had missed his morning rounds at the hospital, and they were popping by the parking lot just to pick up his car. But Jessie Merrill was still weighing on his mind.

"Funny thing about that videotape," said Marsh.

Zamora stopped the car at the traffic light. "How so?"

"I don't know if Jessie was sleeping with Swyteck or not. But she definitely wasn't obsessed with him."

Zamora rolled his cigar between his thumb and index finger. "You'd never guess that from the tape. She screamed his name while having sex with you."

"These tapes she did were purely shock value. There's nothing honest about them."

"I'm not following you."

Marsh looked out the window, then back. "This was exactly the kind of thing that bitch liked to do. She'd get me all hot and then say something to spoil the mood and set me off."

"How do you mean?"

"The tapes weren't the least bit erotic for her. It was all about her warped sense of humor. One time, before I'd decided to get a divorce, she had me on the verge of orgasm and then pretended my wife had just walked into the room. That was her favorite tape of all, watching me fly out of the bed butt-naked. Other times she'd just scream out another man's name. She used my seventeen-year-old son's name once, my partner's another time. But her favorite one was Jack. She knew that one really got me."

"Why did that name bother you so much?"

"I don't know."

"Is it possible that you were a little jealous of Jack Swyteck?"

"No."

"Maybe you had reason to be jealous. Maybe when she screamed his name, it wasn't just for effect."

"It was totally for effect. She just wanted to make me crazy."

"Crazy enough to kill her?"

Their eyes locked. "I told you before, I didn't kill her."

"Then the polygraph should be a breeze."

"I think I've changed my mind on that. I don't want to take a polygraph."

"Why not?"

"I swear, I had nothing to do with Jessie's death. I just don't believe in polygraphs. I think liars can beat them, and I think innocent people who get nervous can fail."

Zamora twirled his cigar, thinking. "I have a good examiner. Maybe I can get Jancowitz to agree to use him."

"I really don't want to take one. I don't care who's administering it. Hell, it tests your breathing, your heart rate, your blood pressure. I get so furious whenever anyone asks me about Jessie Merrill, I'm afraid I'll fail even if I tell the truth."

"Then you shouldn't have acted so eager to do it back in Jancowitz's office."

"I was bluffing. I figured the more willing I seemed to take one, the less likely he was to push for it."

"Prosecutors can never get enough. It's going to be hard to get him to back down."

"Maybe if the testimony we offer is so good, he'll do the deal even if we refuse to sit for a polygraph."

Zamora gave his client a look. "How good?"

"We already have a good base. That joint bank account is pretty damning for Swyteck."

"Why *did* she put him on that account?"

"Damned if I know."

"Why weren't you on it?"

"The money was never intended for me. This was something I was doing for her."

"Got to keep the high-maintenance other woman happy, eh?"

"Do you have any idea how hard it is to provide for another woman when your wife of twenty-four years is suing for every penny in divorce?"

"I understand."

"But let's not lose focus here. We got Jessie Merrill naming Swyteck as her co–account holder on the one-point-five million dollars, and we got her on tape screaming out his name. That's a damn good start. The prosecutor says he wants more, so I'll give him more."

"He doesn't just want more."

"I hear you."

"I'm serious," said Zamora. "There is no upside in lying to a grand jury. We need to comb over every word you say. It all has to be true."

"Sure, I love a true story."

"Just so the emphasis is more on 'true,' less on 'story.' "

The doctor flashed a wry smile. "That's what the truth's all about, isn't it?"

"What?"

The traffic light turned green. Zamora steered his car toward the hospital entrance. Dr. Marsh looked out the window at the passing palm trees and said, "It's all just a matter of emphasis."

# 41
.

It was almost midnight as they lay together in Cindy's old bedroom, their last night at Cindy's mother's. A small twenty-five-year-old lamp on the nightstand cast a faint glow across the bedsheets. It was a girl's lamp with a pink-and-white shade. Jack wondered what had gone through Cindy's head as a child, as she'd lain in this very room night after night. He wondered what dreams she'd had. Nothing like the nightmares she had as a grown-up, surely. It pained him to think that perhaps Evelyn was right, that he only added to Cindy's anxieties.

"Are you really okay with this?" he said.

Cindy was on her side, her back to him. He'd told her everything about the will and the child Jessie had given up for adoption. She'd listened without interruption, without much reaction at all.

She sighed and said, "Maybe I'm just getting numb to the world. Nothing shocks me anymore."

"I know I keep saying this, but it's so important:

Everything that happened between me and Jessie was before you and I ever met."

"I understand."

"Don't go numb on me."

Jack was right beside her but still looking at the back of her head. She wouldn't look at him. "What are you going to do about the boy?" she asked.

"I don't know."

"Are you going to try to find him?"

"I might have to."

"Do you want to?"

"It's all so complicated. I don't think I'll know the answer to that question until some of the dust has settled."

Silence fell between them. Cindy reached for the switch on the lamp, then stopped, as if something had just come to mind. "When did Jessie make her will?"

Jack paused, wondering where this was headed. "About a year ago."

"That was before she came to you and asked you to be her lawyer, right?"

"Yeah, it's when she supposedly was diagnosed with ALS."

"Why do you think she did that?"

"Did what?"

"Wrote her will just then."

"It was part of the scam. She had to make it believable that she was diagnosed with a terminal disease, so she ran out and made a will."

"Do you think it's possible that she really did think she was going to die?"

He thought for a second, almost found himself entertaining the possibility. "No. She told me it was a scam."

"Did she tell you it was her scam or Dr. Marsh's scam?"

"It doesn't matter. They were in it together at the end."

"If they were in it together, then why wasn't his name on the joint bank account?"

"Because they were smart. Only the stupidest of coconspirators would put their names together on a joint bank account."

Silence returned. After a few moments, Cindy reached for the light switch, then stopped herself once again. "In your heart, you truly believe that Jessie ended up dead because she scammed those viatical investors, right?"

"One way or the other, yeah. Either they killed her or she killed herself because they were about to get her good."

"Down the road, if you have to prove to someone— to a jury, God forbid—that Jessie scammed the investors, how are you going to do it?"

"I saw her and Dr. Marsh holding hands in the elevator after the verdict. And then she admitted to me that it was a scam."

"So, really, your only proof of a scam is what you claim you saw in the elevator and what you claim she said to you afterward?"

He felt a pang in his stomach. It was the toughest cross-examination he'd ever faced, and he was staring at the back of his wife's head. "I guess that's what it boils down to."

"That's my concern," she said quietly.

"You shouldn't be concerned."

"But maybe you should be."

"Maybe so."

Finally she rolled over, looked him in the eye, and gently touched his hand. "You and Jessie weren't having an affair. You didn't know about the child. You didn't know about the joint bank account in the Bahamas. You didn't know that she'd left you all that money in her will. She turns up dead, naked, in our bathtub, and the only evidence that someone else might have killed her is your own self-serving testimony. You claim that she admitted the whole thing was a scam, even though you, as her lawyer, knew nothing about it until after the trial was over. I would never tell you and Rosa how to do your jobs, but I've gained enough insights from you over the years to know that it's looking harder and harder for you to avoid an indictment."

"Don't you think I realize that?"

"I'm not saying it to make you mad. My only point is that unless there are twelve Cindy Swytecks sitting on the jury, how do you expect them to believe you? How could *anyone* believe you, unless they wanted to believe you?"

He brushed her cheek with the back of his hand, but even though she'd been the one to initiate physical contact a minute earlier, she felt somewhat stiff and unreceptive. "I'm sorry," he said.

"Me too." She rolled over and switched off the lamp. They lay side by side in the darkness. Jack didn't want to end it on that note, but he couldn't conjure up the words to make things better.

"Jack?" she said in the darkness.

"Yes?"

"What does it feel like to kill someone?"

He assumed she meant Esteban, not Jessie. Even so, it wasn't something he liked to talk about, that battle to the death with his wife's attacker five years earlier. "It feels horrible."

"They say it's easier to kill again after you've killed once. Do you think that's true?"

"No."

"Honestly?"

"If you're a normal human being with a conscience, taking a human life under any circumstances is never easy."

"I didn't ask if it was easy. I asked if you thought it was easi*er*."

"I don't think so. Not unless you're miswired in the first place."

She didn't answer right away. It was as if she were evaluating his response. Or perhaps evaluating him.

She reached for the lamp, and with a turn of the switch the room brightened. "Good night, Jack."

"Good night," he said, trying not to think too much of her decision to sleep with the light on. And then there was silence.

## 42

Yuri was chasing flies. They were all over Gulfstream Park. Not the kind that race horses swat-
ted away with their tails. These were flies with money
to wash.

Yuri loved thoroughbred racing, and in Florida's winter
months the name of the game was Gulfstream Park. The
main track was a mile-long oval wrapped around an invit-
ing blue lake that even on blistering-hot days made you feel
cooler just to look at it. Gulfstream was a picturesque
course with over sixty years of racing tradition, host to premier events like the Breeders Cup and Florida Derby. It sat
within fifty miles of at least ten casinos that were more than
happy to take back your winnings, everything from bingo
with the Seminole Indians to blackjack and slot machines
on any number of gaming cruises that left daily from Palm
Beach, Fort Lauderdale, and Miami. This was as good as
gambling got in Florida, and Yuri was in heaven.

But he hated to be ripped off. Especially by his own
flies.

"Pedro, got a minute?"

Pedro was a new guy, early twenties, pretty smart, not nearly as smart as he thought he was. He was standing at the urinal in the men's room beneath the grandstands. Hundreds of losing tickets littered the bare concrete floor at his feet, but at the moment the two men were alone in the restroom.

He looked at Yuri and said, "You talking to me?"

"Yeah. Come here. I got a big winner for you."

Pedro flushed the urinal, zipped up, and smiled. It was his job to buy winning tickets, all with dirty money. It was one of the oldest games in the money-laundering world. Take the dirty proceeds from a drug deal, go buy a ticket from a recent winner at the track, cash it in and, voilà, your money's legit. You had to pay taxes on it, but that was better than having to explain suitcases full of cash to the federal government. Pedro might wash ten thousand dollars a day this way. He was a fly, always hanging around race tracks the way insects of the same name buzzed around a horse's ass.

"I hit the trifecta in the second race," said Yuri. "Twenty-two hundred bucks."

Pedro washed his hands in the basin, speaking to Yuri's reflection in the mirror. "I'll give you two thousand for it."

"You charge commission?"

"Sure. You still come out ahead. You turn that ticket in to the cashier, you end up paying the IRS five, six hundred bucks in income taxes. You sell it to me, you get fast cash for a measly two-hundred-dollar transaction fee."

"I gotta tell you, Pedro. Every time I've done this in the past, it's been at face value. A twenty-two-hundred-dollar purse gets me twenty-two hundred bucks from a fly."

"Must be a long time since you won anything. I been doing it this way for at least two months."

"Is that so?"

"Yeah."

"Business good?"

"Excellent."

"What does your boss say about that?"

"Nothing I can tell you."

"I think he'd be pissed. Because you haven't been telling him about your ten-percent commission, have you?"

"That's between me and him. You want to sell your ticket or not?"

Yuri grabbed him by the back of the neck, smashed Pedro's head into the sink. A crimson rose exploded onto the white basin. Pedro squealed and fell to the ground, his face bloodied, a broken tooth protruding through his upper lip.

"What the . . . hell?" he said, dazed.

Yuri grabbed him by the hair and looked him straight in the eye. "Two months, huh? That's a thousand bucks a day for fifty race days you been skimming. You got two days to cough up a fifty-thousand-dollar present to your boss. Or I'll come find you, and you'll be spitting up more than just your teeth."

The bathroom door opened. Two men walked in, then stopped at the sight of blood on the sink and Pedro on the floor.

Yuri walked past them and, on his way out, said, "It's okay. He slipped."

The door closed behind him, and Yuri walked calmly into the common area beneath the grandstands. A group of dejected losers watched the replay of the third race on the television sets overhead. Winners were lined up at the cashier window. Dreamers were back in line for the next race, wallets open. Yuri bought himself an ice-cream bar and returned to his box seat near the finish line. It was an open-air seat in the shade, with a prime view of the nine-hundred-and-fifty-two-foot straight-away finish from the final turn.

Vladimir was in the seat next to him. "Flies all under control?"

"Totally."

"I think I'll call you the bug zapper."

"You do and I'll squash you like a cockroach."

Horses with shiny brown coats pranced across the track. The big black scoreboard in the infield said it was five minutes until post time.

"I had an interesting meeting last night. A friend of one of my employees from the blood center claims he can hook us up with fifty million dollars in viatical settlements."

"How?"

"He has connections with some AIDS hospices."

"Fucking AIDS. That's how we got into the mess we're in. All those homos were supposed to be dead in two years. Then they get on these drug cocktails, AZT, whatever, and live forever."

"Well, not forever. We both know that a weak immunity system offers a great many opportunities to expedite the process. How'd your meeting in Paraguay go?"

"I set them straight, but it doesn't do us any good."

"What do you mean?"

"Brighton Beach canceled our contract."

The trumpet blared, calling the horses to the gate. "What?"

"No more money. Not fifty million, not fifty cents."

"Why?"

"They didn't give me a reason. I think it's because of all the attention this West Nile virus is getting from the Centers for Disease Control. They're probably getting nervous."

"Why would they be nervous?"

"Because there just aren't that many cases of West Nile virus in the United States. It could start to look pretty fishy when the authorities figure out that half the reported cases in the United States involved AIDS patients who had viatical settlements."

"How many of our targets ended up getting West Nile?"

"One woman in Georgia's dead from it already. Could be a few more to follow."

"You don't know how many?"

"Not off the top of my head. You know how Fate works, his little game. Only the ones who chose a slow, painful death would have gotten stuck with West Nile. The others got something quick and painless. Relatively quick and painless."

"I'm beginning not to trust this Fate. I think I should meet him."

"I can probably arrange that," said Yuri. "Someday."

Vladimir pressed his fingers to the bridge of his nose, as if to stem a migraine. "I don't understand this. This was such a perfect plan."

"It was never perfect. Look at the Jessie Merrill situation. The minute we branch out from AIDS patients who need a little help dying, we get scammed."

"That's a whole 'nother situation."

"Yeah," said Yuri. "Whole 'nother situation."

The bell rang and horses sprang from the gate. Yuri and Vladimir raised their binoculars and watched through the cloud of dust as the sprinting pack of thoroughbreds rounded the first turn.

# 43

.

Saturday was moving day for Jack and Cindy. Theo was supposed to have dropped by at noon to help with the big stuff, but by one o'clock he was looking like a no-show.

Jack was hauling boxes up the front steps of their new rental house when his cell phone rang. He was pretty sure it was Theo, but the caller's voice was drowned out by loud rap music playing in the background. It was one of the few forms of artistic expression that Jack just didn't get. The lyrics, especially. *Junkies in the gutter all better off dead, Blow-Job Betty sure gives good head*—rhymes for the sake of rhymes, as if the next line might as well be *I like to drive barefoot like my Stone Age friend Fred.*

"Can you turn the music down, please?" Jack shouted into the telephone.

The noise cut off, and Theo's one-word response confirmed that it was indeed him on the other end of the line. "Turkey."

"How can you listen to that stuff?"

"Because I like it."

"I understand that you like it. The implicit part of my question is *why* do you like it?"

"And the implicit part of my answer is what the fuck's it to you? Got it?"

"Got it."

"Good."

"So," said Jack. "What's up?"

"What do you mean, what's up? You called me."

"No. I'm quite certain—oh, what does it matter? When you getting your butt over here?"

"Not today, man. Gotta work. I was just calling to tell you about my meeting with the folks from Viatical Solutions."

"What?"

"After our meeting with Katrina the Snitch, we both agreed that the only way to find out who might have killed Jessie Merrill is to find out who the money people are behind the company. So I met with them."

"What do you think you're doing?"

"Just a little digging, that's all."

"Theo, I mean this. I don't want you messing around with these people."

"Too late. I gotta do it, man. You got me off death row. I can't go around owing you forever."

"You don't owe me anything."

The rap music was back on, even louder than before. Theo shouted, "What did you say?"

"I said, you don't owe—"

*Gonna find that motha' an' pump him full a' lead.*

"Sorry, Jacko, can't hear you, man."

Jack tried once more, but the music was gone, and so

was Theo. "Damn it, Theo," he said as he hung up the phone. "Sometimes you help too much."

Jack went back inside the house. The rental furniture was stacked in the middle of the living room, and it was up to him and his own aching back to rearrange things the way Cindy wanted them. "And sometimes you help too little," he said, still thinking of Theo.

"What?" asked Cindy.

"Nothing. Just a little sole-practitioner syndrome."

"Huh?"

"Talking to myself."

She gave him a funny look. "Oooo-kay. How long has *that* been going on?"

"Long enough for me to think it's normal."

"We should get out more." Cindy gave him a little smile, then returned to her unpacking in the kitchen.

The move was actually quite manageable. The old Swyteck residence was still a crime scene, and the prosecutor had released only limited portions of it, which basically meant that Jack and Cindy could take to their new house only those things that the forensic team had determined were irrelevant to their investigation of Jessie's death. They'd been able to take a few things with them to Cindy's mother's. Earlier that day, a police officer had met Jack at their old house and told him exactly what more he could take. It amounted to an additional thirty-seven boxes, a television set, some clothes, a few small appliances, and their stereo, all of which Jack had packed into a U-Haul van and hauled out by his lonesome. Cindy just didn't want to go back there, and the prosecutor had refused to allow more than one person inside the house anyway.

Jack was up to box twenty-two on the unloading end, moving at a fairly good clip. But Cindy was falling

way behind him on the unpacking, still working on the
first wave of boxes they'd brought from her mother's.
Jack flopped on the rented sofa and closed his eyes,
more tired than he'd realized. He was almost asleep
when he heard a shrill cry from Cindy.

"Jack!"

He sat bolt upright, but he was still only half-awake.

"Jack, come here!"

He got his bearings and ran to the kitchen. She was
seated at the counter surrounded by open boxes and
scattered packing material.

"What is it?"

"Look," she said. "Our wedding album."

Photo albums, home videos, and the like were among
the things they'd taken from their house long ago in the
first wave of personal possessions that the prosecutor had
released from the crime scene. Jack glanced over her
shoulder, and the sight sickened him. "What the hell?"

Cindy flipped from the first page to the second, and
then the next. The bride and groom at the altar, Jack
and Cindy getting into the white limousine, the two of
them stuffing cake into each other's mouths. All were in
the same condition: sliced diagonally from the top left
corner to the lower right by a very sharp knife.

"How did this happen?" he asked.

"I don't know. This is the first I noticed it."

"Did you check it before we took it from the
house?"

"No . . . I don't know. I don't remember. I can't
believe she did this," said Cindy, her voice quaking.

"I can."

She looked up and asked, "What should we do?"

"Put it down, gently."

She laid it on the table.

"Don't touch another page," said Jack. "Our wedding album has just become Exhibit A."

"As evidence of what?"

His eyes locked on the slashed photograph before him. He was beginning to think that perhaps Rosa was right, that Jessie had killed herself. Or that at the very least she'd been driven to suicide.

Or that somebody had done an awfully convincing job of making it look like suicide.

"I wish I knew," he said.

# 44
.

The blood business was booming, and Jack wanted a firsthand look. He found the Gift of Life mobile blood unit just a block away from the same street corner that his friend Mike had told him about after tailing Katrina. Mike, however, had only watched from a distance. Jack was there on business.

It was a cool afternoon, which made his disguise easier. He stopped at Goodwill and bought a crummy sweatshirt, a pair of old tennis shoes that didn't match, black pants with a few paint spots around the cuffs, and a knit cap that was frayed around the edges. Then he went home and burned a pile of garbage in the backyard, standing close enough to the cloud of dirty smoke to overpower the smell of mothballs. With his bare hands he dug a little hole in the earth, doggy-style, getting dirt under his nails, soiling his arms up to his biceps. A swig of cheap bourbon gave his breath the right adjustment. Streaks of engine grease on his hands, face, and clothes provided the finishing touches, compliments of the grimy engine block on his old Mustang.

A half-block away from the blood unit, he stopped along the sidewalk and checked his reflection in a storefront window. He genuinely looked homeless.

Not that his disguise needed to be foolproof. He wasn't hiding from Katrina. In fact, he wanted to talk to her, but a visit to her house or the main office of Viatical Solutions, Inc., could have put them both at risk, depending on who might be watching. A phone call wouldn't work, either, since her line might be tapped. Staking out the blood unit, dressed like a homeless guy, seemed like the best alternative. He was pretty sure that the low-level goons who worked with her in the truck had no idea who Jack Swyteck was, and the disguise was enough to fool them.

"Need twenty bucks, buddy?" said the guy outside the unit.

Jack looked around, not sure he was talking to him.

"Yeah, you," the guy said. "Twenty bucks, and all you gotta do is roll up your sleeve. You interested?"

Jack thought for a second, but this was even better than he'd hoped for. Here was a chance to look around inside. "Sure."

"Come on."

Jack followed him toward the unit, stopping just outside the door to let the latest donor pass. It was a woman, probably in her thirties, who looked about seventy. She appeared to be wearing every stitch of clothing she owned, several dirty layers that smelled of life on the streets and dried vomit.

She smiled at the doorman, half of her teeth missing, and then laid her hand on his belt buckle and said, "How's about I collect some of your specimen, honey?"

"Get away from me," he said, wincing.

"Whatsa matter? Your nice little nurse stuck me with her needle. You don't want to stick me with yours?"

"Get lost."

She snarled and said, "Needle dick."

He pushed her to the pavement.

"Hey, go easy on her," said Jack.

"Needle dick!" she shouted.

"You shut your trap, lady," the doorman said.

"Needle dick, needle dick!"

He stepped toward her, fists clenched, but Jack stopped him. "Come on. I ain't got all day."

The man seemed torn, but finally his business mind prevailed. He hurled a few cuss words at the woman and led Jack up the stairs.

The air inside was stale, trapped by windows that probably hadn't opened in years. The staff was minimal, just a phlebotomist, a cashier, and a thick-necked thug seated near the door. Jack presumed he was packing heat. Donors were paid in cash, so a guard with good aim and plenty of ammunition would have been indispensable, even if he was a blockhead, a matching bookend for Jack's escort.

"Got another one for you," the man said.

The phlebotomist put her cheese sandwich aside and said, "Come on over."

Jack took a seat. A rubber strap, gauze packages, several plastic blood bags, and a needle with a syringe were spread across the table.

"You HIV-positive, partner?" asked the phlebotomist.

Jack looked around. The floors looked as if they hadn't been mopped in months, plenty of dried blood spots on grimy, beige tile. The seats and tabletop weren't much cleaner, and the windows were practically opaque with dirt. How this woman could eat in this place was beyond him. He wasn't about to let her poke him with one of her needles.

"Yeah, HIV," said Jack. "As a matter of fact, I got full-blown AIDS."

"Perfect," she said. "Roll up your sleeve."

He tried not to look confused. "You want bad blood?"

"Of course. Now, come on. Show me a vein."

He didn't move fast enough, so she grabbed his wrist and pushed his sleeve up to his elbow. "Hmm. No tracks."

"I shoot between my toes," he said.

"Make a fist."

Jack obliged, keeping an anxious eye on the syringe. "Is that a new needle?"

She chuckled, still searching his arm for the right vein. "Only been used once by a little old lady who likes needle dicks."

"Don't you start," said Needle Dick.

She tied the rubber strap around his elbow like a tourniquet. If he didn't think fast, he was about to share a junkie's needle. "This is fifty bucks, right?" said Jack.

"I told you twenty," the goon said.

"I ain't doing this for no twenty dollars."

"Shut up and be a good boy. Maybe I'll throw in a half-pint of whiskey."

"No. It's fifty or I'm outta here."

The other goon stood up beside his buddy. With the two of them together, it was like trying to blow by a couple of pro-Bowl linebackers. "Sit down and shut up," he told Jack.

Jack was half-sitting, half-standing. Getting stuck

with a dirty needle wasn't an option, but he wasn't quite sure how he was going to get past these two pork chops.

"I said, sit!" the guy shouted.

"What's going on?"

Jack looked past the goons, relieved to see Katrina.

"Just a little matter of money," said Needle Dick. "Junior here thinks his blood's worth fifty bucks."

She took a good look at Jack, and he could see in her eyes that she'd recognized him instantly, even with the old clothes, knit cap on his head, and grease on his face. He wasn't really worried about a confidential informant giving him up and blowing her own cover, but his heart skipped a beat as he waited for her to say something.

"This jerk's blood isn't worth fifty cents. He scammed us on Miami Beach two weeks ago. His veins are clean. Get him out of here."

The men came toward him, each grabbing an arm. They kicked open the door and threw him out. He landed on the pavement right beside the bag lady.

She looked at him with disgust. "You gonna let a needle dick push you around like that?"

Jack picked himself up, checked the scrape on his elbow where he'd hit the pavement. He glanced toward the van, then answered. "It's okay. I'm a hotshot lawyer. I'll sue his ass."

She flashed a toothless grin, said something about him looking more like a senator, and then just kept talking. Jack listened for about a minute, till he realized that she was chatting with herself.

He felt as though he should walk her to a shelter or something, but he had to stay focused. She went one way, and he went the other, continuing a half block north, where he found a bus bench at the corner and waited. Getting inside the mobile unit had been a bonus, but he still hadn't spoken to Katrina, his main objective. He sensed she wouldn't be far behind him. In ten minutes, his hunch proved correct.

"What the hell were you doing in there?" she said as she took a seat on the bench beside him.

"Funny, I was going to ask you the same thing."

"You and your friend Theo have to stay clear and let me do my job."

"Just exactly what is your job?"

"None of your business."

"You're not even going to let me guess?"

She shot him a look, as if not sure what to make of him. "Okay, Swyteck. Show me how smart you are."

"It's interesting the way you set up these mobile units in high-crime areas, places where the average Joe walking off the street might carry around any number of infectious diseases in his bloodstream."

"Hey, if Mohammed won't come to the mountain . . ."

"So, for twenty bucks and a half-pint of cheap booze they'll gladly drain their veins of infected blood. Then what?"

"What do you think?"

"I don't think Drayton would let you work undercover in this operation if you were using bad blood to contaminate the blood supply or some other terrorist activity. So, I figure you must be selling it to someone who actually wants infected blood for legitimate reasons. Like a medical researcher. Am I right?"

She didn't answer.

Jack nodded, figuring he was right. "Good money in that. I think I saw something on the Internet where some diseased blood can fetch as much as ten thousand dollars a liter on the medical research market."

She focused on the bus across the street. "I'm not talking to you."

"Extremely high margins, I'd say. Especially when the company that collects and sells the blood doesn't even try to comply with the multitude of regulations governing the drawing, handling, storage, shipping, and disposal of blood specimens that, because of their diseased state, technically meet the legal definition of medical waste."

"How do you know we don't comply?"

"I didn't come here without doing my homework."

A low-riding Volvo cruised by, music blasting from the boom box in the truck. Saturday night was starting early.

Jack said, "From the looks of things, I'd say your crew is a lot more interested in appearances than profit. Like every good money-laundering operation."

She looked him in the eye and said, "You have no idea how much money there is in blood."

"My guess is that you sell a whole lot more blood than you ever collect."

"You're a very lucky guesser, Swyteck."

"You produce just enough product to make things look legitimate, but it's a limitless supply of inventory. You create as many sales as you want, no one the wiser. Nice money-laundering operation."

"You're learning a lot more than is healthy for you to know."

"Maybe."

"The irony is, this could really be a good business for someone. All these goons on my crew care about is generating phony invoices to legitimize the cash that washes through our company. With a little effort to collect more specimens, the blood research business could be the most profitable money-laundering operation around."

"Except for viatical settlements," said Jack.

She smiled thinly. "Except for viatical settlements."

Jack crossed his legs, picked at the hole in his old tennis shoe. "Of course, now the million-and-a-half-dollar question is: What's the connection between the two businesses?"

"None. It's just another way of laundering money. Like going into video rentals and opening a Chinese restaurant. No connection, really. Just another sink to wash your dirty money in."

"I think differently."

"Is this another one of your guesses?"

"No. This time it's research."

"A sole practitioner who does research? I'm impressed."

"When I took Jessie's case, I subscribed to an on-line news service about the viatical industry. Kept me right up to date on any development in the industry—trends, lawsuits, whatever."

"And they said something about Jessie?"

"They did, but that's not my point. I've been following it more closely since Jessie's death. What really caught my interest was a recent write-up about a case in Georgia."

"Georgia?"

"A thirty-something-year-old woman had AIDS. They found the West Nile virus in her blood. First documented case in Georgia in decades."

"Not a good thing for someone with a weakened immune system."

"No. But it might be a very good thing for her viatical investors."

"You're being way too suspicious. Viatical settlements are pretty common among AIDS patients."

"Yeah, but this one has a twist. Not only did she have this rare virus, but she was missing three liters of blood."

"She bled to death?"

"No. Somebody took it."

Her look was incredulous. "What?"

"You heard me. Somebody drained three liters of diseased blood from her body and sent her into cardiac arrest."

"And triggered payment under a viatical settlement," she said, finishing his thought for him.

"No one's proved step three yet. That's why I'm here."

"What do you want from me?"

"I want to know about step three."

"You're talking about Georgia, a whole different state."

"We're talking about the Russian *Mafiya*. It's a very small world."

"Look, my plate is full working for Sam Drayton and his task force. I don't have the time or the inclination to be playing Sherlock Holmes for you and your wild-ass theories about some woman in Georgia."

"You need to work with me on this."

"I don't need to do anything with you."

"I can help you."  .

"How?"

"I know that my friend Theo's been poking around your operation."

"Poking's a good word for it. Like a finger in my eye."

"I don't know exactly what he's up to, or how much danger he's gotten himself into. But I don't want him doing it."

"And neither do I, damn it. Eight months I've been working undercover. I know this blood and viatical stuff inside out, partly from running this hellhole of an operation, but mostly from risking my neck and snooping after hours. All of it's at risk now, thanks to Theo Knight."

"That's what I was afraid of."

"So what are you proposing?"

"Help me out on this Georgia angle. See if my hunch is correct."

"And what's in it for me?"

"I'll get Theo out of your hair, before my big-hearted buddy with the good intentions gets us all in trouble."

She thought for a moment, then said, "I'm not promising I'm going to find anything."

"Do the best you can."

"You're just going to trust me?"

"Yeah. Money laundering is one thing. But I don't think you'd knowingly be involved with a company that's killing off viatical investors."

She paused, as if sizing him up. Then she pulled a pen from her pocket and took Jack's hand. She inked out a phone number as she spoke. "This is another level of snooping, and snooping is dangerous stuff. If you get any inkling that your friend Theo is going to do anything stupid, I want a heads-up in time to get out alive."

Jack checked the number on the back of his hand. "Is this a secure line?"

"No cell is secure. But it's safer than calling me at home or the office, where I can never be sure who's listening. Just keep it to yourself."

"You're just going to trust me?" he said, using her own words.

"Yeah," she said, responding in kind. "Jessie Merrill is one thing. But I don't think you'd knowingly blow your only shot to find out if this company's killing off other viatical investors."

Their eyes met, and Jack felt that an understanding had been reached. She rose and said, "So, exactly how are you going to keep Theo under control?"

"Don't worry. I can take care of Theo Knight."

"That's good," she said. "Because if you don't, I promise you: Someone else will." She started up the sidewalk, then stopped and said, "By the way. Nice outfit."

Jack struck a model's pose, showing off the Goodwill special. "Thanks."

She smiled a little, then continued on toward the blood unit. Jack had a slight bounce in his step as he crossed the street and headed for the Metrorail station, digging his hands deep into his pockets, keeping Katrina's phone number to himself.

# 45

### .

It rained on Jack and Cindy's first night in their new house. With no shades or curtains on their windows yet, each bolt of lightning bathed the bedroom with an eerie flash of light. Thunder rattled the windows, seeming to roll right across their roof. A steady drip from the ceiling pattered against the wood floor in the hallway. They had a leak.

Cindy rose in the middle of the night and went to the kitchen. The counter was still cluttered with cardboard boxes, some empty, some yet to be unpacked. She had hoped that her old demons wouldn't follow her to her new house, that she might be able to leave the past behind. But no. The nightmares had come with her.

Lightning flashed across the kitchen. Outside, the falling rain clapped against the patio like unending applause. A river of rainwater gushed from a crease in the roof line, splashing just outside the sliding glass door. The run-off pooled at one end of the patio and rushed in torrents toward a big rectangular planter at the lower end.

Cindy watched from the kitchen window. It was as if the water was being sucked into the deep planter, an opening in the earth from which there was no return. The harder the rain fell, the thirstier the hole seemed to get. There seemed to be no end to the flow into that planter, no limit to what that big, black hole in the ground could hold. It was hypnotic, like nothing she'd ever seen before, except once.

The dark, rainy day on which her father had been buried.

•

Nine-year-old Cindy was at her mother's side, dressed in black, the rain dripping from the edge of the big, black umbrella. Her sister, Celeste, was standing on the other side of her mother. Her grandmother was directly behind them, and Cindy could hear her weeping. Her little brothers were too young and stayed home with relatives. It was a small gathering at graveside, just the four of them and a minister.

"Alan Paige was a righteous man," the minister said, his eulogy ringing hollow in the falling rain. "He was a man who lived by the Scripture."

That was true, Cindy knew. Church every Sunday, a reading from the Bible every night. Her father had only one known vice, a little nickel-and-dime poker game every Tuesday night. Some said it was hypocritical, but Cindy thought it only proved him human. Either way, it hadn't stopped him from leading the charge against the teaching of Darwin's theory of evolution at her school, or from grounding Celeste when she dared to bring home a D. H. Lawrence novel from the public library.

"From dust we come and to dust we return. In Jesus' name we pray, Amen."

The minister gave a nod, and Cindy's mother stepped forward. The cold rain was falling harder, until it seemed that a muddy river was pouring into the open grave. Cindy watched as her tearful mother dropped a single red rose into the dark hole in the earth.

She said a short prayer or perhaps a silent good-bye, and then returned to her daughters. Cindy clung to her, but Celeste stepped toward the grave.

"May I say something?" asked Celeste.

It wasn't part of the program, but the minister rolled with it. "Why, of course you may."

Celeste walked around to the other side of the grave, then looked out over the hole toward her mother, sister, and grandmother.

"Hearing my father eulogized as a man who lived by the Scripture was exactly what I expected. He did know his Scripture, I can say that. I think now is the time for me to share with everyone the part of the Scripture that he often read to his daughters. It's from the Book of Genesis, 19:3, a passage I heard so many times, starting before I could even read, that I've committed it to memory. It's the story of Lot and his two daughters."

Cindy glanced at her mother. The expression on her face had quickly changed from grief-stricken to mortified.

Celeste continued, reciting from memory. " 'Lot and his two daughters left Zoar and lived in a cave. One day the older daughter said to the younger, "Let's get our father to drink wine and then lie with him and preserve our family line through our father." That night they got their father to drink wine, and the older daughter went in and lay with him. The next day the older daughter said to the younger, "Let's get him to drink wine again tonight, and you go in and lie with him so we can preserve our family line through our father." So they got their father to drink wine that night also, and the younger daughter went in and lay with him. So both of Lot's daughters became pregnant by their father.' "

Her voice shook as she finished. The minister stood in stunned silence. Cindy's mother lowered her head in shame. From the hole in the earth, raindrops beat like a drum against her father's casket.

"It's a lie!" shouted Cindy.

No one else said a word.

"You are a *liar*, Celeste! That wasn't the way it was!"

Celeste glared at her younger sister and said, "Tell the truth, Cindy."

Cindy's face flushed with anger, her eyes welling with tears. "It's not true. That's not the way our daddy was."

Celeste didn't budge. She looked at the minister, and then her angry glare moved squarely to their mother. "You know it's true," she said, her eyes like lasers.

All the while, the rain kept falling.

•

Lightning flashed across the kitchen. Cindy was bathed in white light, then stood alone in the darkness.

"Cindy, are you okay?"

She turned to face Jack, but she didn't answer.

He came to her and held her in his arms. "What's wrong?" he asked.

She glanced out the window, one last look at the rainwater rushing across the patio toward the gaping hole in the earth. "Nothing new," she said.

"Come back to bed."

She took his hand and followed him back to the bedroom, ignoring another flash of lightning and one last clap of thunder.

# 46
.

At nine o'clock Monday morning, twenty-three grand jurors sat in a windowless room one floor below the main courtroom, waiting for the show to begin. Expectations were high. They'd seen the flock of reporters perched outside the grand jury room.

By law, grand jury proceedings were secret, no one allowed in the room but the jurors and the prosecutor. The constitutional theory was that the grand jury would serve as a check on the prosecutor's power. In reality, the prosecutor almost always got the indictment he wanted.

"Good morning," he said, greeting his captive audience.

Jancowitz was smiling, and it was genuine. This was a murder case with stardom written all over it. A sharp criminal defense lawyer in a scandalous love triangle. The victim his former girlfriend. Lots of grisly and salacious details, many of them corroborated by a highly respected physician. This case could be his break-out case, his ticket to the talk-show circuit, and he'd been waiting long enough.

At 9:35 he had his first witness on the stand, sworn and ready to testify.

"Your name, sir?" said Jancowitz.

"Joseph Marsh."

"What is your occupation?"

"I'm a board-certified neurologist."

With just a few well-rehearsed questions he led Dr. Marsh toward pay dirt, establishing him as Jessie Merrill's physician and, of course, laying out the kind of professional credentials that commanded a certain level of respect and instant credibility.

Then he turned to the evidence.

"I have here what has been previously marked as state's Exhibit 11. It is a letter from Jack Swyteck to me. It was written just days after Ms. Merrill's lifeless and naked body was found in a pool of blood in his home."

The prosecutor paused. The location of the body was a theme in his case, one that he gladly allowed the jurors a little extra time to absorb.

He continued, "In Mr. Swyteck's letter, he explains an alleged scam that his client, Jessie Merrill, perpetrated on the investors of a company known as Viatical Solutions, Inc. Dr. Marsh, please take a moment to review this exhibit."

The witness looked it over and said, "I'm familiar with this."

"In the first paragraph, Mr. Swyteck states that, quote, Jessie Merrill admitted to me that she and Dr. Marsh falsified her diagnosis of amyotrophic lateral sclerosis, or ALS. End quote. Dr. Marsh, what was your diagnosis of Ms. Merrill's condition?"

"Based upon the initial tests I performed, my diagnosis was 'clinically possible ALS.' "

"Did you falsify any of the tests that led to that initial diagnosis?"

"Absolutely not."

"Did you later change that diagnosis?"

"After further testing, I concluded that she had lead poisoning. Her symptoms mimicked those of ALS."

"Does that mean your initial diagnosis was incorrect?"

"Not at all. As I said, based upon the tests I conducted, my diagnosis was *possible* ALS."

"Now, Dr. Marsh, I've already explained to the grand jurors what a viatical settlement is. My question to you is this: Were you aware that, based upon your initial diagnosis, Ms. Merrill attempted to sell her life insurance policy to a group of viatical investors?"

"I was."

"Did you at any time mislead those investors as to the nature of her illness?"

"Never. Their reviewing physician did press me for a more firm opinion. I told him that if I had to make a judgment at that particular moment I would probably bet on ALS, but by definition any bet is a risk. It was no sure thing."

"Was there ever any collusion between you and Ms. Merrill in an effort to defraud the viatical investors?"

"Absolutely not."

"Thank you. I refer you again to state's Exhibit 11. In paragraph two, Mr. Swyteck states, quote, on the night before her death, Jessie met me outside my office in Coral Gables. She appeared to be under the influence of drugs. End quote. Dr. Marsh, in the six months that you acted as treating physician for Jessie Merrill, did you ever see any signs of substance abuse?"

"Never."

"Next sentence. Mr. Swyteck states, quote: Ms. Merrill said to me in no uncertain terms that she was in fear for her life. Specifically, she told me that the viatical investors had discovered that she and Dr. Marsh had perpetrated a fraud against them. Ms. Merrill further stated to me that the viatical investors were thugs, not legitimate businesspeople. According to Ms. Merrill, someone acting on behalf of the viatical investors had warned her that she was going to wish she had died of ALS if she did not return the one-and-a-half-million-dollar viatical settlement to the investors. End quote."

Jancowitz gave the jury a moment to digest all that. Then he looked at Dr. Marsh and said, "Are you aware of any threats Ms. Merrill received from anyone acting on behalf of the viatical investors?"

"No, sir. None whatsoever."

"As her alleged coconspirator in this supposed scam, were *you* ever threatened by anyone acting on behalf of the viatical investors?"

"Never."

"Were you ever threatened by *anyone* in connection with this matter?"

"Yes."

"Who?"

"Jack Swyteck."

"Tell me about that."

"After Jessie was found dead in the Swyteck house, I went to his office."

"How did that go?"

"Not well. It took only a few minutes for him to realize that I suspected he had something to do with Jessie's death."

"What happened?"

"He went ballistic. Told me to get my ass out of his office before he batted my head across the room."

"As best you can recall, what exactly were you talking about before he threatened you?"

"As I recall, we were talking about whether he was having an extramarital affair with Jessie Merrill."

"What prompted that discussion?"

"I asked him about it."

"Why?"

Dr. Marsh turned his swivel chair and faced the jury, just the way the prosecutor had coached him earlier in their prep session. "My wife and I are separated and we will soon be divorced. I was . . . vulnerable, I guess you would say. I felt sorry for Jessie and took a special interest in her case. That developed into a friendship, and by the time her lawsuit was over it had blossomed into romance."

"So, when Mr. Swyteck states in his letter that he saw you and Jessie Merrill holding hands in the elevator just minutes after the verdict, that statement is true?"

"That is *not* true. I went over to congratulate her. Mr. Swyteck twisted things around to try to put a sinister spin on the whole episode. That was one of the reasons I went to his office to confront him."

"Do you know why he made that up?"

"In a general sense, yes. Mr. Swyteck was extremely jealous of the relationship between me and Jessie. It was becoming irrational, to the point where he'd accuse her of things like this alleged scam on the viatical investors. Things that never happened."

"Did you ever ask Mr. Swyteck if he and Ms. Merrill were involved in a romantic relationship?"

"Yes, in the conversation in his office, I asked him."

"What was his response?"

"He denied it and became extremely agitated."

"Is that when he threatened to bat your head across the room?"

"No. It's my recollection that he didn't actually threaten me until I asked him point blank whether he had hired someone to kill Jessie Merrill."

Jancowitz checked his notes at the lectern, making sure that he'd set the stage properly for his big finish. "Just a few more questions, Dr. Marsh. You testified that you are *not* aware of any threats that Jessie Merrill may have received from anyone acting on behalf of the viatical investors."

"That's correct."

"Are you aware of any threats that she received from anyone other than the investors?"

"Yes."

"How did you become aware of those threats?"

"We talked on the telephone after it happened. She told me."

"What was the nature of those threats?"

"She was told that if she said or did anything to tarnish the name and reputation of Jack Swyteck, there would be hell to pay."

"Did she tell you who conveyed that threat to her?"

He leaned closer to the microphone and said, "Yes. A man by the name of Theo Knight."

The prosecutor struggled to contain his excitement. It wasn't the whole story, but it was more than enough at this stage of the game. "Thank you, Dr. Marsh. No further questions at this time."

# 47
## ·

Vladimir had a business meeting at "the club," a generic term that lent the place much more dignity than it deserved. The actual name on the marquee was "Bare-ly Eighteen," a strip joint where any middle-aged man with ten bucks and an aching hard-on could watch recent high school dropouts dance naked on tables. No jail bait, but not a single dancer over the age of nineteen, guaranteed. Of course, if *60 Minutes* ever called, the girls were all honor students in premed who simply liked to dance naked for extra money.

Vladimir knew the truth, which was why he never showed up at the club with less than a pocketful of ecstasy pills, a wildly popular, synthetic club-drug that acted both as a stimulant and a hallucinogen. The distribution pipeline was largely European, so Russian organized crime had found huge profit in it. Each aspirin-sized tablet was manufactured in places like the Netherlands at a cost of two to five cents and then sold primarily in the over-eighteen clubs for twenty-five to forty bucks a pop. A girl—*any* girl, not just a stripper—could go nonstop for eight hours on one pill, dancing, thrusting, craving the caress of strangers. At his cost and with those kinds of results, Vladimir was happy to give it away to his own dancers, especially when he had guests to impress.

He handed the bag of pills to the bouncer at the entrance. "One for each girl," he said, then pointed with a glance toward the double-D blonde on stage showing off her tan lines. She had a pacifier in her mouth, a telltale sign that she was already on ecstasy. The drug sometimes made users bite their own lips and tongue, and a pacifier was a curious but commonly accepted way of preventing that. In a strip club, it had the added bonus of making it look as though she really loved to suck.

"Give her two," said Vladimir.

"Yes, sir." The guy was a brute, and no one but Vladimir was ever a "sir."

Vladimir had with him two men dressed in expensive silk suits. One was big and barrel-chested, with a neck like a former Olympic wrestler's. The other was shorter and overweight with the round, red face of a Russian peasant who'd somehow found money. Vladimir led them through the lounge area, a circuitous route to his usual booth in the back. It gave them a chance to enjoy the scenery before turning to business. The bar was basically a dark, open warehouse with neon figures on the walls and colored spotlights suspended from the ceiling to highlight each dancer. Young, naked flesh was everywhere, surrounded by men who coughed up the cash to gawk, talk, laugh, and shout at women as if they owned them. A numbing sound system drowned out most of the obscenities, blasting the perennial bad-girl anthem, the old Robert Palmer hit "Addicted to Love."

At the snap of his fingers, Vladimir's two hottest dancers hopped off nearby tables and assumed new posts at the brass firehouse pole closer to his booth. Vladimir sat with his back to the stage, facing a mirrored wall of cheap thrills. His guests sat across from him with an unobstructed view of the show. As if the girls cared or would even remember, he introduced his guests. The wrestler's name was Leonid, a Brighton Beach businessman whose business was best left unexplained, though it was pretty common knowledge around the club that Miami was second only to Brighton Beach in terms of number and organization of Russian *Mafiya*. The short guy was Sasha, a banker from Cyprus.

"Where's Cyprus?" asked the Latina girl. She had the habit of running the tip of her tongue across her front teeth, which could have been the ecstasy. Or perhaps her braces had just been removed and she liked the smooth sensation.

"It's an island in the eastern Mediterranean," Sasha said.

"A suburb of Moscow," said Vladimir.

She licked her teeth and kept dancing, having no way of knowing what Vladimir really meant. Cypriot bankers laundered so much money for the Russian mob that the city of Limasol might as well have been a suburb of Moscow.

A topless barmaid with a gold ring through her left nipple brought them a bottle of ice-cold vodka and poured three shots. The bottle was gone in short order, and halfway through the second Vladimir steered the conversation toward business, speaking in Russian.

"You like my club?" he asked.

His guests couldn't take their eyes off the girl in the long, red wig swinging naked on the pole.

Vladimir said, "I have to run this joint seven days a week for an entire month to clean the amount of cash I can wash in a single viatical settlement."

Leonid from Brighton Beach shot him a steely look. "We didn't come here to talk viatical settlements. That's off the table."

"I just don't understand why."

The banker raised his hands, as if refereeing. "Let's not go down that road. The fact is that Brighton Beach was planning to flush ten million dollars a month through viatical settlements for the foreseeable future. That option is no longer attractive. So all we want to know, Vladimir, is this: What alternative are you offering?"

He sipped his vodka. "The blood bank is coming along."

"Ha!" said the wrestler. "What a joke."

"It's not a joke. It's on the verge of taking off."

"Will never work. You can't possibly do enough volume to wash ten million dollars a month."

"How would you know?"

"The best money-laundering operations have some amount of legitimate business. You have two stinking vans. You can't even draw enough blood off the street to fill the handful of orders you get each week."

"We've filled every single order."

"Yeah. And you had to take blood from cadavers to do it."

The banker grimaced. "You took blood from cadavers?"

Vladimir was smoldering.

"Tell him," said the wrestler.

"It's not important."

"Then I'll tell him. We had a woman in Georgia with a two-million-dollar viatical settlement. AIDS patient. Should have been dead three years ago, so the order went out to expedite her expiration. Vladimir farmed out the job to some joker who injected her with a bizarre virus, which is a whole problem by itself. But to make matters worse, he took three liters of blood from her."

"Is that true, Vladimir?"

He belted back the last of his vodka, then poured himself a refill. "Who would have thought they'd notice?"

"Ever heard of an autopsy, you idiot?" said the wrestler.

"It was an honest mistake. Why leave perfectly good AIDS-infected blood in a dead body when you can sell it for good profit?"

"It's that kind of small-time, foolish greed that makes it impossible for us to do business with you people in Miami."

"So this is why Brighton Beach canceled the viatical contract?" said Vladimir.

"Your man shot her up with a virus so rare that the National Center for Disease Control has her blood under the microscope. And then he took three liters of her blood with him. Why not just paint a big red 'M' on your chest that stands for 'murderer'? You're going to get us all caught."

"So you admit it. One mistake in the whole arrangement, and the hot shots in Brighton Beach think they can just walk away from our deal."

"We don't have to explain ourselves to you people.

The decision was made, and it was blessed at a high level. End of story."

"It's not the end of it," Vladimir said as he pounded the table with his fist. "We put a lot of time into this viatical deal. Things are in place. And you just think you can pull the plug, see ya later?"

"We have good reasons."

"None that I've heard."

"I've said all I'm going to say."

"Then fuck you!" said Vladimir as he threw a glass of vodka in his guest's face.

The wrestler lunged across the table. Dancers screamed and ran for it as the banker ducked to the floor. Three huge bouncers were all over the wrestler before he could get a hand on Vladimir.

The wrestler was red-faced, eyes bulging. But the bouncers had both his arms pinned behind his back.

"This is the way you treat your guests?" he said, huffing. "I was *invited* here."

"And now you're invited to leave." Vladimir jerked his head, a signal to his boys. "Throw his ass out."

The wrestler cursed nonstop in Russian and at the top of his lungs as the bouncers put the strong-arm on him and dragged him away.

The banker peered out from under the table.

"You too, Sasha. Beat it."

The little man scurried away like a frightened rabbit.

The barmaid immediately replaced the spilled bottle of vodka. Vladimir refilled his drink, and with a snap of his fingers the dancers resumed their posts at the brass poles, backs arched, breasts out, hair flying. The music had never stopped, and the scuffle was over.

Or maybe it had just begun.

Either way, the girls kept right on dancing.

# 48

##### •

Jack watched the six-o'clock evening news from the couch in his living room. Cindy was right beside him, their fingers interlaced. She was squeezing so hard it almost hurt, and Jack wasn't sure if it was a sign of support or anger.

Rumors of an impending indictment had been flying all afternoon, and in a competitive news market where a story just wasn't a story unless "You heard it here first," the media was all over it.

A silver-haired anchorman looked straight at him as the obligatory graphic of the scales of justice appeared behind him on the screen. "A former girlfriend is dead, and a questionable million-and-a-half-dollar deal is under scrutiny by a Florida grand jury. Jack Swyteck, son of Florida's former governor Harold Swyteck, may be in trouble with the law again."

"Why do they have to do that?" said Cindy.

"They always have." His entire life, any time he'd

gotten into trouble, he was always "Jack Swyteck, son of Harold Swyteck."

Trumpets blared and drums beat, the usual fanfare for the *Action News* opening.

"Good evening," the newsman continued. "We first brought you this exclusive story several weeks ago, when the dead body of thirty-one-year-old Jessie Merrill was found in the home of prominent Miami attorney Jack Swyteck. At first blush her death appeared to be suicide, but now prosecutors aren't so sure. *Action News* reporter Heather Brown is live outside the Metro-Dade Justice Center. Heather, what's the latest?"

The screen flashed to a perfectly put-together young woman standing in a parking lot at dusk. The Justice Center was visible in the distant background, and a half-dozen teenage boys wearing bulky gang clothing, thick gold chains, and backward Nike caps, were gyrating behind her, as if *that* added credibility to her live report. Long strands of black hair slapped at her face like a bullwhip. She'd obviously committed the cardinal rookie mistake of positioning her roving camera crew downwind.

"Steve, sources close to this investigation have told *Action News* that a grand jury has been looking into the death of Jessie Merrill for some time now. Information obtained exclusively by *Action News* indicates that Miami-Dade prosecutor Benno Jancowitz has presented to the grand jury something that one source calls substantial evidence that Ms. Merrill's death was not suicide but homicide. This source went on to tell us that indictments could come down at any time now."

The anchorman jumped in. "Is there any indication who may be charged and what the charges may be?"

"That information has yet to be released. But again,

the operative word here is 'indictments,' plural, not just the indictment of a single suspect. Sources tell us that this could turn into a case of alleged murder-for-hire. Right now, the spotlight is on Jack Swyteck and his former client, Theo Knight. Mr. Knight has a long criminal record and even spent four years on Florida's death row for the murder of a nineteen-year-old convenience store clerk before being released on a legal technicality."

"Technicality?" said Jack, groaning. "The man was innocent."

Cindy gave him a soulful look, as if she fully understood the telling nature of the media's negative spin on Theo's belated vindication. It would probably be the same for Jack. In the court of public opinion, it didn't matter what happened from here on out. The stigma would always be there.

Jack switched stations and caught the tail end of the anchorwoman's report on *Eyewitness News*: "Repeated calls to Mr. Swyteck this afternoon went unanswered, but I understand that *Eyewitness News* reporter Peter Rollings has just managed to catch up with his famous father, former Florida governor Harold Swyteck, on Ajax Mountain in Aspen, Colorado, where he and the former first lady are enjoying a ski vacation."

"What the heck?" said Jack.

The screen flashed to a snow-covered man on the side of a steep mountain. It was a blizzard, nearly white-out conditions. Jack watched his father stumble off the chair lift, practically assaulted by some guy in a ski mask who was chasing him with a microphone.

"Governor! Governor Swyteck!"

Harry Swyteck looked back, obviously confused, one ski in the air in a momentary loss of balance, poles flailing like a broken windmill. He finally caught his balance, and momentum carried him down the slope.

The shivering reporter looked back toward the camera and said, "Well, looks like the former governor won't speak to us, either."

Jack hit the OFF button. "I can't watch this."

The phone rang. For an instant, Jack was sure that his father was calling from deep in some snow bank to ask "What the hell did you do this time, son?" The Caller ID display told him otherwise. Jack hadn't been answering all afternoon, but this time it was Rosa.

"Well, the wolves are out," she said.

"I saw."

"Your old man should take up hot-dog skiing. He must have skidded at least fifty yards on one ski before sailing down that mountain."

"That's not funny."

"None of this is. That's why I called. I want to meet with both you and Theo. Tonight."

"Where?"

"I'm home already, so let's do it here."

"How soon?"

"As soon as you can get your buddy over here. We need to get to Theo before the prosecutor does."

"You don't seriously think that Theo would cut a deal with Jancowitz, do you?"

"You just heard the news as plainly as I did. Theo is targeted as the gunman in a murder-for-hire scheme. It's standard operating procedure for a prosecutor in a case like this: You get the gunman to flip in order to nail the guy who hired him."

"I agree that we should meet, but you need to understand. I didn't hire Theo to do anything. And even if I had, Theo would never testify against me. I'm the guy who got him off death row."

"Let me ask you something, Jack. How many years did Theo spend on death row?"

"Four."

"Now answer me this: You think he wants to go back?"

Jack paused, and he didn't like the direction his thoughts were taking him. "I'll see you in an hour. Theo and I both will be there. Together. I guarantee it."

# 49

Katrina picked at the peas in her microwaved-dinner tray. The evening news had drifted into the weather segment, but she was still pondering the lead story. Two things were clear to her. The indictments were a foregone conclusion. And the timing of the leaks had a funny smell to them. She pushed away from the kitchen table and grabbed her car keys.

It was time to call Sam Drayton.

Rarely did she make a call directly to the lead prosecutor, but this was no time to get caught up in Justice Department bureaucracy. In less than five minutes she reached the 7-Eleven on Bird Road. She jumped out of her car, hurried past the homeless guy sleeping on the curb, and called Drayton from the outside pay phone.

"Moon over Miami," she said into the telephone. It was the code phrase that would immediately convey to him that she was talking of her own free will, not with a mobster's gun to her head.

"What's up, Katrina?"

"Swyteck and his friend Theo are all over the local news tonight. Story has it that they're going to be indicted in a murder-for-hire scheme."

"Is that so?"

"As if you didn't know."

"I'm in Virginia. How would I know?"

The homeless guy had his hand out. Katrina gave him a quarter and waved him away. "Look, if Swyteck and his friend are going to be indicted, that's fine. That's the way the system works. But these leaks aren't fair."

"I can't control what comes out of the state attorney's office."

"Like hell. You asked Jancowitz to leak it, didn't you?"

"Grand-jury investigations are secret by law. That's a pretty serious accusation."

"Two days ago, after Swyteck paid me a visit at the blood unit, I called and told you I needed him and Theo Knight out of my hair. Suddenly it's all over the news that they're about to be indicted in a murder conspiracy. You expect me to believe that a leak like that one is just a coincidence?"

"Totally."

"Stop being cute. Swyteck's bad enough. But do you know what it means to a guy like Theo Knight to have the word on the street that he's a grand-jury target on a murder charge?"

"I told you, I can't control what Jancowitz does."

"Don't you understand? Theo sat across the table from my boss at the Brown Bear and talked viatical business. He made it clear that he's figured out the money-laundering scheme. Vladimir isn't going to let a guy like that just sit around peacefully under the threat of an indictment. He'll put a bullet in his brain before he can cut a deal with the prosecutor and tell everything he knows about the money-laundering operation."

"I can't control what the Russian mob does."

"Is that all you can say, that everything's out of your control?"

"I can't control the things I can't control."

"Then maybe you can't control me, either."

"Watch yourself, Katrina. Don't bite the hand that feeds you."

"You've got nothing on me. I went to the U.S. attorney's office the minute I discovered that my employer might be doing something illegal. I volunteered for this undercover work because I wanted to nail these bastards worse than you did."

"Ah, yes. Katrina the Whistleblower."

"It's true. I was squeaky clean coming in."

"You're not squeaky clean anymore, honey. You turn against me, I'll turn against you. As far as I'm concerned, you've been part of an illegal operation for the past eight months."

"You son of a bitch. You just see this as a cost of doing business, don't you? If someone gets in your way, you just push them aside for good."

"I'm simply trying to preserve the integrity of an eight-month investigation that has cost the U.S. government over a million dollars."

"And a bullet in the back of Theo Knight's head is a small price to pay. Is that it?"

"Listen, lady. We wouldn't be in this mess in the first place if you hadn't fumbled around in the dark and picked up the wrong cell phone."

"Actually, we wouldn't be in this mess if you hadn't told me to beat the holy crap out of Jack Swyteck for treading too close to your blessed investigation."

"I never told you to do that."

"Maybe not in so many words. But I told you that Vladimir was going to make me prove myself somehow, and you said go ahead and do what I had to do. I'll stick to that story until the day I die."

Silence fell over the line, then Drayton finally spoke. "I'm warning you, Katrina. Don't you dare do anything stupid."

"Don't worry. If I do, you'll be the last to know." She hung up the phone and returned to her car.

# 50

•

Jack picked up Theo from Sparky's, and the two of them reached Rosa's house in Coco Plum around eight o'clock. Hers was typical for the neighborhood, a thirteen-thousand-square-foot, multilevel, completely renovated, Mediterranean-style quasi hotel with a pool, a boat, and drop-dead views of the water.

"Nice digs," said Theo as they stepped down from Jack's car.

"Yeah. If you like this sort of overindulgence."

"Spoken like a true have-not."

They climbed thirty-eight steps to the front door but didn't have to knock. Rosa spotted them in the security cameras. She greeted them at the door and then led them to her home office, a term that struck Jack as especially meaningful, as this particular office did seem larger than the average home.

Rosa's former law partner was already inside waiting for them. Jack knew Rick Thompson. They shook hands, and he introduced himself to Theo. Then Rosa explained his presence.

"I invited Rick because it seems appropriate for Theo to have his own lawyer. From what we've heard so far, you two may end up being codefendants on a conspiracy charge."

Rick said, "You never want alleged coconspirators to be represented by one lawyer. It tends to reinforce the idea of a conspiracy."

"I agree with that," said Jack.

"Sounds good to me, too," said Theo. "Except I doubt I can afford my own lawyer."

Rosa said, "No problem. Jack will pay for it."

Jack did a double take, but before he could say anything, Theo slapped him on the back and said, "Thanks, buddy."

"You're welcome," was all he could say.

Jack and Theo seated themselves in the armchairs on one side of the square coffee table in the center of the room. Rick sat on the leather couch. Rosa stood off to the side as her housekeeper brought pitchers of iced tea and water on a silverplated tray. Jack glanced discreetly at his lawyer and caught her taking in a long, meditative eyeful of the framed work of art that hung behind her desk. It was a contemporary piece by the late Cuban-born artist Felix Gonzalez-Torres, a renowned boundary-buster who was best known for ephemeral pieces made of candies or printed paper that visitors could touch or even take home with them. Rosa liked to call her little share of Felix "the stress-buster," as it calmed her just to look at it. Jack wasn't sure if the magic flowed from the innate beauty of the work or from the sheer joy of having acquired it long before the artist died and his work started selling at Christie's for seven figures.

When the housekeeper was gone, Rosa turned to

face her guests. Her expression was noticeably more relaxed, as if Felix the Artist had done his job, but her delivery was still quite serious. "I'm told we could see target letters as early as tomorrow, indictments by the end of the week. Two defendants, one basic charge: Murder for hire."

Theo said, "I heard that on the news two hours ago. You sure you're getting your money's worth here, Jacko?"

"Just listen."

Rosa continued, "It's important for us all to agree that anything we say in this room is privileged. This is one setting in which it's worth stating the obvious. This is all joint defense."

"Of course," said Jack.

"Theo?" asked Rosa.

"Whatever Jack says."

"Wrong answer," said Rick. "Jack's not your lawyer. I am."

"Like I said. Whatever Jack says."

Rick grumbled. "I can't represent someone under those circumstances."

Jack looked at his friend and said, "You have to listen to your own lawyer. Not Rosa, and not even me. Those are the rules."

"If you say so."

"Good," said Rosa. "Now that that's settled, let's talk turkey. Rick, tell Jack and Theo what you found out."

Rick scooted to the edge of his chair, as if sharing a national-security secret. "Dr. Marsh is represented by Hugo Zamora. I know Hugo pretty well, pretty good guy. I called him up and just asked him point-blank, hey, what did your client tell the grand jury?"

"I thought grand-jury testimony was secret," said Theo.

"It is, in the sense that grand jurors and the prosecutor can't divulge it. But a witness can disclose his own testimony, which means that his lawyer can, too."

Jack asked, "What did Hugo tell you?"

"The most important thing has to do with Dr. Marsh's testimony about the threats against Jessie Merrill. Marsh did testify that Jessie was in fact threatened before her death."

"That's fantastic," said Jack. "That corroborates exactly what I've been saying all along. The viatical investors threatened her."

"Not exactly."

"What do you mean?"

"Marsh didn't say that it was the viatical investors who threatened Jessie. He said it was Theo."

"Theo? What kind of crock is that?"

Rick continued. "Marsh claims that Theo met with Jessie the night before she died and told her straight out that if she said or did anything to hurt Jack Swyteck, there would be hell to pay."

Jack popped from his chair, paced across the room angrily. "That is so ridiculous. The man is a pathological liar. The very idea that Theo would go to Jessie and threaten her like that is . . . well, you tell him, Theo. That's crazy."

All eyes were on Theo, who was noticeably silent.

"Theo?"

Finally, he looked Jack in the eye and said, "You remember that night we met in Tobacco Road?"

"Yeah. You were playing the sax that night."

"And you said Jessie Merrill admitted to the scam but told you to back off or she'd tell the world that you were part of it, too. You were all upset because she and her doctor boyfriend were so damn smug.

And so I says maybe we should threaten her right back. Remember?"

"What are you telling me, Theo?"

A pained expression came over his face. "I was just trying to scare her, that's all. Just get her and Swampy to back down and realize they can't push my friend Jack Swyteck around."

Jack felt chills. "So what did you do?"

"That's enough," said Rick.

Theo stopped, startled by the interruption. His lawyer continued, "This discussion is taking a completely different track from what I expected. As Theo's lawyer, I say this meeting's over. Theo, don't say another word."

"Theo, come on, now," said Jack.

"I said that's enough," said Rick. "I don't care if you are his friend. I won't stand for anyone pressuring my client into saying something against his own best interest. You told him to listen to his lawyer, not to you or to Rosa. At least play by your own rules."

"Let them go," said Rosa.

Theo rose and said, "We'll get this straightened out, man. Don't worry."

Jack nodded, but it wasn't very convincing. "We'll talk."

Rick handed Jack a business card and said, "Only if I'm present. Theo has counsel now, and you talk to him through me. Those are the *new* rules."

Jack could only watch in silence as Theo and his new lawyer turned and walked out, together.

# 51

•

Katrina switched on the lights at 8:00 A.M. As usual, she was the first to reach the combined offices of Viatical Solutions and Bio-Research, Inc. That hour to herself before nine o'clock was always the best time to get work done.

And it was the best time to snoop.

She walked by her work station in the back, past the filing cabinets, and down the hall to Vladimir's office. The door was locked, but a little finesse and a duplicate key solved that problem. She was sure she was alone, but it still gave her butterflies to turn the knob and open the door.

Over the past eight months she'd had her share of close calls. Rifling through the files of a money-laundering operation was dangerous work. Sam Drayton was a prick, and she hadn't gone undercover with any illusion that the U.S. government would bail her out of trouble. Truth be told, she'd gotten everything she'd wanted from the feds, which was nothing more than a chance to get inside the Russian mob without risk of going to jail. Katrina had her own agenda, and she was closer than ever to reaching it—at least until Theo Knight had come along. With him sticking his nose where it didn't belong, time was truly of the essence.

She walked carefully around Vladimir's massive desk to the computer on his credenza. It had taken nearly sixteen weeks of casual conversations about his mother's birthday, his dog's name, his old street-number in Moscow, but finally she'd cracked his password.

She typed it once on the blue screen, then again at the prompt: KAMIKAZE.

It stood for "Kamikaze Club," a Moscow bar where Russian mobsters used to gather with their well-dressed mistresses to get smashed on vodka and bet on the fights. Young men were pulled off the streets, thrown into the ring, and ordered to slug it out with their bare hands. Only one would walk out alive. The loser ended up in a landfill, eyes gouged out, jaw torn off. After five impressive victories, Vladimir earned himself a job as a bodyguard for a *vor v zakone,* "thief in law," the highest order of made men in the *Mafiya.*

Katrina logged on to his Internet server and scrolled down the e-mails he'd sent over the last week. She recognized the usual money-laundering contacts, but this morning her focus was on that shipment of blood to Sydney. The buyers had requested a specimen from an AIDS-infected white female, but the only blood in their vault was typical of junkies, filled not just with AIDS but also hepatitis, and any number of parasites and street illnesses that made their blood unsuitable for strict AIDS research. Somehow, Vladimir had come up with three liters of AIDS-infected blood from an otherwise clean source.

Only then did Swyteck's theory about that woman in Georgia seem not so cockeyed.

The fifth e-mail confirmed it. The message was to an investor in Brighton Beach, written in Vladimir's typical bare-bones style, the less said, the better. "Insurer: Northeastern Life and Casualty. Policy Number: 1138–55-A. Benefit: $2,500,000. Decedent: Jody Falder, Macon, Georgia. Maturity date . . ."

The date chilled her. All within a matter of days, Vladimir had fresh, AIDS-infected blood to ship to Sydney, and his viatical investors were in line for a big payday. It hardly seemed coincidental.

Swyteck was right. *This isn't just about money laundering anymore.*

A door slammed, and her heart skipped a beat. It was the main entrance, and she was no longer alone. She switched off the computer, ran to Vladimir's office door, and fumbled for her key.

A man was singing to himself in the kitchen, fixing himself a morning coffee.

*Vladimir!* Her hand was shaking too much to insert the key and lock the door.

"That you, Katrina?" he said, calling from the kitchen.

His voice startled her, but on her fifth frantic attempt at the lock she felt the tumblers fall into place. She thanked God, hurried down the hallway, and forced herself to smile as she entered the kitchen. "Good morning."

"Coffee?" he asked.

"No, thanks. I had some invoicing work to do." She could have kicked herself. He hadn't even expressed any surprise at seeing her, and she was already offering some knee-jerk justification for being in the office a little early.

"Good." He sipped his coffee. It was so strong, the aroma nearly overwhelmed her from across the room. Then he stepped toward her and said, "Let's you and me take a walk."

The words chilled her. She'd known Vladimir to take many a walk with employees and even a few customers. None of them ever came back smiling.

"Sure."

He grabbed his briefcase, took it with him.

*This is it,* she thought. Although she'd never been caught snooping, the scenarios had played out in her mind many times. Never did it turn out well for her. Vladimir didn't take chances with a suspected *musor*.

He led her out the back door, the warehouse entrance. It was a hot, sunny morning, and the smell of baked asphalt-sealant stung her nostrils. They crossed the parking lot and walked side by side beneath the black-olive trees that lined the sidewalk, heading toward the discount gasoline station and the perpetual roar of I-95. Rush-hour traffic clogged all eight lanes on Pembroke Pines Boulevard.

"I've been thinking about your friend Theo."

She caught her breath, relieved to hear that someone else was on his mind. "I figured."

"The three of us talked openly at the Brown Bear."

"Of course. Talk among friends."

"He seemed to have the viatical settlements all figured out."

"He's a pretty smart guy."

"Yuri thinks maybe he's not so smart. He thinks maybe you told him something."

"I told him nothing."

Vladimir stopped. The traffic light changed and a stream of cars and huge tractor trucks raced toward the

I-95 on ramp. "I believe you," he said. "But Yuri has his questions. So there is some repair work that needs to be done there."

"Repair work?"

"Rebuilding of trust."

"Vladimir, I've worked here like a dog for eight months. Guys come and go all the time. But I'm right here at your side, day in and day out."

"I know. That's why I don't want you to look at this as a test of your loyalty. Think of it as an opportunity to prove yourself worthy of advancement."

"What are you asking me to do?"

"Your friend Theo got himself in some serious trouble."

"I know. I saw the news last night."

"So we both know this prosecutor is going to lean hard on him."

"Theo's no *musor*."

"I wish I could believe that. But the good ol' days are gone. No more honor among thieves, the old code of silence. These days, people get caught, they talk. We can't risk Theo cutting a deal and telling that prosecutor what we talked about at the Brown Bear. Hell, I think I even mentioned Yuri and Fate by name."

Katrina knew this was coming. She'd even shared those exact fears with Drayton. "Like I said, what are you asking me to do?"

He lit a cigarette, then flipped his lighter shut. But he just looked at her, saying nothing.

"Please. Theo is my friend. Don't ask me to be part of any setup."

He took a long drag, exhaled. "All the time you've worked here, I've never once so much as seen you hold a gun."

"Never had a need to."

"Seems like a waste. Two years in the U.S. Marines, you must be a decent shot."

"Sure, I can shoot."

He handed her his briefcase. "Take it."

She hesitated, knowing full well what was inside.

He narrowed his eyes and said, "Friend or no, Theo has to go. And the job is yours."

"You . . . you want me to take out my friend?"

"We've all taken out friends. We make new ones."

She couldn't speak.

"Is there a problem?" he asked.

She fought to keep her composure, then took the briefcase and said, "No. None at all."

He put his arm around her, and they started back to the office. "This is a good move for you. An important step. I can feel it."

With each footfall, the briefcase seemed to get heavier in her hand. "I feel it, too," she said.

# 52
·

Katrina was crouched low behind the driver's seat of a Volkswagen Jetta, waiting. The floor mats smelled of spilled beers, and the upholstery bore telltale burn marks of many a dropped joint. She was dressed entirely in black, and with a push of a button the green numbers on her wristwatch glowed in the darkness.

One-fifty A.M., just ten minutes till the end of Theo's bartending shift at Sparky's.

Laughter in the parking lot forced her closer to the floor. A typical ending to another "Ladies' Night," a totally drunk chick and three horny guys offering to drive her home. *Their* home. It was almost enough to make Katrina jump from the car and spring for cab fare, but she didn't dare give herself away.

She had a job to do.

From her very first meeting with Vladimir, she'd decided that if it ever came down to a situation of either her or someone else, someone else would get it. But she'd always thought that the "someone else" would be another mob guy. She hadn't figured on someone like Theo.

A rumbling noise rolled across the parking lot. Katrina could feel the vibration in the floor board. A moment later, diesel fumes were seeping in through the small opening in the passenger side window. She lifted her head just enough to see a huge tractor trailer parked two spaces down. The motor was running, and the fumes kept coming. But the driver was nowhere to be seen. The odor was making her nauseous. She had the sickening sensation that the truck wasn't going anywhere soon, that the driver had simply climbed inside and started the engine to sleep off his liquor in the comfort of an air-conditioned rig.

The fumes thickened, and she could almost taste the soot in her mouth. A dizzying sensation buzzed through her brain. The noise, the odor, the steady vibration—it all had her desperate for a breath of fresh air, but she forced herself to stay put. The very act of telling herself to tough it out and stay alert was eerily reminiscent of her life in Prague, not the beautiful old city as a whole but the noisy textile mill where she'd worked more than a decade earlier.

Back when her name was Elena, not Katrina.

There, in an old factory that still bore the scars of Hitler's bombs, the oldest machines ran on diesel fuel, not electricity. The engines were right outside the windows, and even in the dead of winter, enough fumes seeped in through cracks and crevices to give Katrina and her Cuban coworkers chronic coughs, headaches, and dizzy spells. It was just one more hazard in a fourteen-hour workday, six days a week. Katrina had often pushed herself to the verge of blacking out, but the fear of falling perilously onto one of the giant looms around her kept her on her feet. Safety guards and emergency shut-offs were nonexistent, and the machines were unforgiving. Hers was one of the newer ones, about thirty years old. The one beside her was much older, predating the Second World War and constantly breaking down. Each minute, countless meters of thread fed through the giant moving arms. At that rate, you didn't want to be anywhere near one of those dinosaurs when it popped, and you could only hope to find the energy to duck when a loosened bolt or broken hunk of metal came flying out like shrapnel.

Katrina had prayed for the safety of her coworkers, but she also thanked the Lord that she wasn't the poor soul working one of those man-eaters. Years later, she still felt guilty about that. One nightmare, in particular, still haunted her. Never would she forget what happened on that cold night in January when machine number eight turned against its master, when her name was still Elena.

• 

A loud pop rattled the factory windows, rising above the steady drone of machinery. Instinctively, Elena dived to the floor. One by one, the machines shut down like falling dominoes. A wave of silence fell over the factory, save for the pathetic screams and groans emerging from somewhere behind machine number eight, a tortured soul with a frighteningly familiar voice.

Elena raced across the factory, pushed her way through the small gathering of workers around the accident, and then gasped at the sight. "Beatriz!"

She and her best friend Beatriz had joined Castro's Eastern Bloc work program together, with plans to defect at the first opportunity. Each had pledged never to leave without the other.

Elena went to her, but Beatriz lay motionless on her side, a thick pool of blood encircling her head. She checked the pulse and found none. She tried to roll Beatriz onto her back, then froze. The left side of her face was gone. A sharp hunk of metal protruded from her shattered eye socket.

"My God, Beatriz!"

The ensuing moments were a blur, her own cries of anguish merging with the memory of Beatriz's painful screams. Tears flowed, and words came in incoherent spurts. Beatriz never moved. Kneeling at her side, Elena lowered her head and sobbed, only to be ripped away by a team of men with a stretcher.

"It's too late for that," she heard someone say. But the men rolled the body onto the stretcher anyway, then hurried for the exit.

Elena followed right behind them, through a maze of machinery, passing one stunned worker after another. The doors flew open, and a blast of cold, winter air pelted her face. They put Beatriz in the back of a van, still on the stretcher. Elena tried to get in with her, but the doors slammed in her face. The tires spun on the icy pavement, then finally found traction. Elena stood ankle-deep in dirty snow as the van pulled away.

In her heart she knew that this was the last she'd see of Beatriz.

She couldn't move. It was well below freezing, but she was oblivious to the elements. Half a block away she spotted a police car parked at the curb. It seemed like a sign, Beatriz whisked away in an ambulance right past the police. It was time for someone in a position of authority to see the deplorable conditions they worked under.

On impulse, she ran down the icy sidewalk and knocked on the passenger-side window. The officer rolled down the window and said something she didn't understand.

"Come see," she said, but her command of the language was still very basic. "The factory. Come see."

He gave her a confused look. His reply was completely unintelligible, a dialect she'd never heard before. She'd learned Russian as a schoolgirl in Cuba, but there was surprisingly little crossover to Czech.

"What are you doing, girl?"

She turned and saw her foreman. He was a stocky, muscular man with extraordinarily bad teeth for someone as young as he was.

"Leave me alone. I want him to see what happened."

He said something to the cop that made him laugh. Then he grabbed Elena by the arm and started back toward the factory.

"Let go of me!"

"Are you stupid? The police can't help you."

"Then I'll talk to someone else."

"Yes, I know you will. We're going to see the boss man right now." His grip tightened on her arm till it hurt. He took her down a dark alley that ran alongside the factory. The pavers were frozen over with spilled sludge and dirty run-off from the roofs, and about every third step her feet slipped out from under her. At the end of the alley were two glowing orange dots, which finally revealed themselves as the taillights of a Renault.

Her foreman opened the door, shoved Elena in the back seat, climbed in beside her, and closed the door. The motor was running, and a driver was behind the wheel in the front seat.

"This is her," said the foreman.

"Hello, Elena," the driver said.

It was dark inside, and from the back seat she could see only the back of his head. "Hello."

"I heard there was an accident with your friend. I came as soon as I could."

"What do you care?"

They made eye contact in the rearview mirror, but she could see only his eyes. "Do you think it makes me happy when someone gets hurt in my factory?"

Elena didn't answer, though she was taken aback to realize that she was talking to the owner of the factory.

"Listen to me," he said. "I know it's dangerous in there."

"Then why don't you fix it?"

"Because that's the way it's always been."

"And you can't do anything about it?"

"I can't. But you can."

"Me?"

"You can make things safer, at least for yourself."

"I don't understand."

"It's very simple. This is a big factory. There are many jobs. Some are dangerous. Some are very dangerous. Some are not dangerous at all."

"Seems to me that the women are always getting the most dangerous jobs."

"Not all women. Some get the dangerous jobs, some get the not-so-dangerous jobs. It all depends."

"On what?"

"On which part of your body you want to sacrifice."

"What is that supposed to mean?"

"Machine number eight should be up and running in a day or two. You'll be taking over Beatriz's spot."

"What?"

He shrugged, as if it were none of his doing. "Or I suppose I could tell your foreman to assign it to somebody else. It's up to you."

"What choice are you giving me?"

He turned partly around, as if to look at her, but his face was blocked by the headrest. He spoke in a low serious voice that chilled her. "Everything happens for a reason. No decision is meaningless. We all determine our own fate."

"Like Beatriz?"

"Like you. And like hundreds of other girls much smarter than your friend."

She could have smashed his face in, but an Eastern Bloc prison was no place for an eighteen-year-old girl from Cuba.

"Sleep on it," he said. "But we need your answer."

The foreman opened the door and pulled her out into the alley. A cold wind swept by her, stinging her cheeks. She stood in the darkness and watched as the car backed out of the alley.

She brushed away a tear that had frozen to her eyelash, but she felt only anger.

*You pig,* she thought as the car pulled away. *How dare you hide your evil behind such twisted views of fate.*

•

The lock clicked; a key was in the car door. Katrina cleared her mind of memories and sharpened her focus. The door opened, but the dome light didn't come on. She'd taken care of that in advance to reduce the risk of detection.

Theo climbed inside and shut the door.

She was close enough to smell his cologne, even feel

the heat from his body. Her pulse quickened as she rose on one knee. With a gloved hand, she guided the .22-caliber pistol toward the back of the headrest.

Theo inserted the key.

As the ignition fired she shoved the muzzle of her silencer against the base of his skull. "Don't make a move."

The engine hummed. His body stiffened. "Katrina?"

"Shut up. Don't make this any worse than it already has to be."

# 53

·

Jack went into the office as if it were a normal day. He was following the same advice he'd given countless clients living under the cloud of a grand-jury investigation: If you want to keep your sanity, keep your routine.

He was doing pretty well, until a certain hand-delivery turned his stomach.

It was a letter he'd expected but dreaded. As a prosecutor, he'd sent many of them, and he could have recited the language from memory. *This letter is to inform you that you have been identified as a target of a grand jury investigation. A "target" means that there is substantial evidence to link you to a commission of a crime. Blah, blah, blah. Very truly yours, Benno Jancowitz III.* The only surprise was that Benno Jancowitz was "the Third."

*Who in his right mind would keep that name around for three generations?*

Line one rang, and then line two. Jack reached for

the phone, then reconsidered. The target letter would surely push the media to another level of attack. He let his secretary answer. Screening calls was just one of the many ways in which Maria was worth her weight in gold.

He answered her on the intercom. "How bad is it?"

"I told Channel 7 you weren't here. But line two is Theo Knight's lawyer."

"Thanks. I'll take it." With a push of the button Rick Thompson was on the line. Jack skipped the hello and said, "I presume you're calling about the target letter."

"Not exactly."

"Theo didn't get one?"

"I don't know if he did or not. I can't find him."

"What?"

"We were supposed to meet in my office three hours ago. He didn't show. I was wondering if you might know anything about that." Rick's words were innocent enough, but his tone was accusatory.

"No, I don't know anything about that," said Jack, a little defensive.

"I called him at home, called him at work, tried his cell, and beeped him five times. Not a word back from him."

"That's weird."

"I thought so, too. Which is why I'm calling you. I was serious about what I said last night at Rosa's house. I appreciate Rosa bringing me into this case. But just because she's my friend doesn't mean I'm going to treat you and Theo any differently than another client and codefendant. If I'm Theo's lawyer, I'm looking out for his best interest."

"I don't quibble with that one bit. All I'm saying is

that if you can't reach your client, it's none of my doing."

"Okay. I'm not making any accusations. It just concerns me that all of a sudden he seems to have dropped off the face of the earth."

"That concerns me, too."

"If you hear from him, tell him to call his lawyer."

"Sure."

As he said good-bye and hung up, his gaze settled on the target letter atop his desk. It had been upsetting enough for him, and he could only imagine how it might have hit a guy who'd spent four years on death row for a crime he didn't commit.

Jack faced the window, looked out across the treetops, and found himself wondering: *How big was the "if" in "if you hear from him"?*

Jack turned back to his desk and speed-dialed Rosa. Her secretary put him straight through. It took only a moment to recount the conversation with Theo's lawyer.

Rosa asked, "You don't think he split, do you?"

"Theo? Heck, no. He doesn't run from anything or anybody."

"You really believe that?"

"Absolutely."

"Why?"

"I represented him for four years."

"That was for a crime he didn't commit."

"Are you saying he killed Jessie Merrill?"

"Not necessarily. Just that people naturally draw inferences when the accused makes a run for it."

"Nobody said he's running."

"Then where is he?"

"I don't know."

"You sure?"

He paused, not sure what she was asking. "Do you think I told him to run?"

"Of course not. But maybe Theo thinks you did."

"You're losing me."

"The conversation you had at Tobacco Road is a perfect example. You told him that Jessie Merrill threatened you, and he took it upon himself to go threaten her right back. Maybe this is the same situation. You could have said something that made him come to the conclusion that you'd be better off if he just hit the highway."

"I haven't spoken to Theo since he and Rick Thompson walked out the front door of your house."

"Then maybe his sudden disappearance has nothing to do with you at all. Maybe it's all about what's best for him."

"Theo didn't kill her. He wouldn't. Especially not in my own house."

"Think about it, Jack. What was the first thing you said to me when we talked about Jessie's body in your house?"

He didn't answer right away, though he recalled it well. "I said, if I was going to kill an old girlfriend, would I really do it in my own house?"

"It's a logical defense. You think Theo was smart enough to give it to you?"

"It's not that smart. I said the same thing to Sam Drayton at the U.S. attorney's office. He tore it to shreds, asked me if I thought it up before or after I killed Jessie Merrill."

"Theo's not a prosecutor."

"Theo's not a lot of things, and he's especially not a murderer."

"I hope you're right. But if you're going to look for him, which I know you are, let me ask you this. You call him a friend, but how well do you really know Theo Knight?"

Jack's first reaction was anger. Serving time for a murder he didn't commit had forever put Theo in a hole. But he was no saint, either, and Jack knew that.

"Jack, you still there?"

"Yeah."

"Honestly. How well do you know him?"

"Do we ever really know *anyone*?"

"That's a cop-out."

"Maybe. I'll let you know what I find out." He said good-bye and hung up.

# 54

•

It was almost midnight, and Yuri was ready to make a move.

He and Vladimir had spent the last six hours in their favorite hotel on the Atlantic City boardwalk. The Trump Taj Mahal was renowned for its understated elegance—but only if you were a Russian mobster. To anyone else, it was flash and glitz on steroids. Fifty-one stories, twelve hundred rooms, and restaurant seating for three thousand diners, all complemented by such subtle architectural details as seventy Arabian-style rooftop minarets and no fewer than seven two-ton elephants carved in stone. The chandeliers alone were worth fourteen million dollars, and each of the big ones in the casino glittered with almost a quarter million pieces of crystal. Marble was everywhere—hallways, lobbies, bathrooms, even the shoe-shine stands. Miles of tile work had actually exhausted the entire two-year output of Italy's famous Carrera quarries, Michelangelo's marble of choice for his greatest works of art.

There was even a ten-thousand-dollar-a-night suite that bore Michelangelo's name. Fitting. It was impossible to walk through this place without wondering what Mich would think.

"Let's go," said Yuri.

"What's your hurry?"

"Enough fun and games. It's time we got what we came for."

Vladimir grumbled, but he didn't argue. Blackjack was considered a house game, and for the past two hours he'd conducted himself as the perfect house guest. He was down almost twenty grand at the high-limit table. He gathered up his few remaining chips and stuffed them into the pockets of his silk suit. Then he ordered another drink for the woman seated beside him, a statuesque redhead with globes for breasts and a tear-shaped diamond dripping into her cleavage.

"I'll be back," he said with a wink.

"I'll be waiting."

Yuri grabbed his elbow and started him toward the exit. They were in the Baccarat pit, a special, velvet-roped area in the casino where the stakes were high and drop-dead-gorgeous women sidled up to lonely men with money in their pockets and Viagra in their veins. No one seemed to care that most of the babes were planted by the hotel to encourage foolish wagering.

"You think she's a prostitute?" asked Vladimir.

Yuri rolled his eyes and kept walking, making sure that Vladimir stayed right with him. He made a strategic decision to avoid the temptation of the craps tables by leading him through Scheherazade restaurant. It overlooked the Baccarat pit, making it one of the few five-star restaurants in the world where you could eat lunch and lose your lunch money at the same time.

"These guys aren't the kind of people you keep waiting," said Yuri.

"We're not late."

"Not being late ain't good enough. You get there early and wait. It shows respect."

"Sorry. Didn't know."

They hurried down the long corridor and ducked into one of the tower elevators just past the Kids' Fun Center. An elderly couple tried to get on behind them, but Yuri kept them at bay.

"All full," he said as he pressed the CLOSE DOOR button. He punched forty-four, and the elevator began its ascent, the two of them admiring their reflections in the chrome door. Then Yuri turned and straightened Vladimir's tie.

"Just do what I say from here on out, all right? This meeting is too important to fuck up."

"What should I say?"

"Just answer the questions asked. That's all."

Vladimir rearranged his tie, making it crooked again. "I look okay?"

Yuri gave him a friendly slap on the cheek. "Like a million bucks."

The elevator doors opened and Yuri led the way out. Vladimir seemed almost giddy as they walked briskly down the hallway.

"*Bratsky Krug,*" said Vladimir. "I can't believe it."

"Believe it," said Yuri.

"I laid eyes on one of these guys only once before. I ever tell you that story?"

"Yes." Only a thousand times, the guy who plucked him out of the Kamikaze Club in Moscow, the bare-knuckled fights to the death. *Bratsky Krug* was Russian for "circle of brothers." It was the ruling council of the *vory*, a powerful alliance of Russian mobsters. It didn't have the power or structure of the Italian *Cosa Nostra*, but it had been known to settle inter-gang disputes. Yuri hadn't promised his friend that the council would settle the viatical disagreement between Miami and Brighton Beach. For someone as starstruck as Vladimir, he knew, the prospect of meeting one of these "brothers" was reason enough to make the trip.

The corridor was quiet. Door after door, the whole wing seemed to be asleep. Most of the rooms were under renovation and unoccupied, which was precisely the reason Yuri had chosen the forty-fourth floor for the meeting. He stopped at 4418 and inserted the passkey.

"You don't knock?" said Vladimir.

"You expect them to pay for the room? Like I said, we get here early, they come to us. We're the ones who wait."

He pushed open the door, then stepped aside, allowing Vladimir to enter first. It was dark inside, the entranceway lit only by the sconces in the hallway. Vladimir took a half-dozen steps forward and stopped. Yuri was right behind him. The door closed, and the room went black.

"How about some lights?"

Yuri didn't answer.

"Yuri?"

With a click of a lamp switch on the other side of the room, bright white light assaulted his eyes. Vladimir reached for his gun.

"Don't," said Yuri as he pressed the muzzle of his silencer against the back of Vladimir's head.

Vladimir froze, then chuckled nervously. "What's— what's going on, man?"

Yuri watched the expression on Vladimir's face as a man stepped out from the shadows. It was Leonid, the Brighton Beach mobster whom Vladimir had thrown out of his strip club.

"What the hell are you doing here?" asked Vladimir.

Two more thugs stepped into the light. Instinctively, Vladimir went for his gun again, but Yuri pressed the pistol more firmly into his skull.

"I wouldn't," said Yuri.

Vladimir lowered his arm to his side. All color seemed to drain from his face as the reality of the setup sank in.

"Yuri, what's this all about?"

"Leonid told me about the meeting he and his banker from Cyprus had with you at Bare-ly Eighteen. Seems you were extremely rude."

Vladimir squinted into the spotlight. "They canceled our contract for no good reason. We skimmed a little blood, used a virus they didn't like. What's the big deal? You don't walk out on a deal over little shit like that."

"I hear different. Seems the straw that broke the camel's back was the Jessie Merrill hit."

"We didn't have anything to do with Jessie Merrill's death."

"No," said Yuri. "*I* didn't have anything to do with it. You, I'm not so sure of."

"You were in charge of the hits, Yuri. Not me."

A kick to the left kidney sent Vladimir to his knees. "You keep pushing it on me, don't you? Jessie Merrill was the job of an amateur. You think I'm an amateur?" he said, giving him another kick.

Vladimir doubled over in the spotlight, his face twisted with pain. "No."

"No, what?"

"No, you're not an amateur."

"That's right. You're the only amateur in this bunch, Vladimir. Piece of dirt from the Kamikaze Club."

"I didn't do Jessie Merrill."

Yuri walked beyond the glow of the spotlight, faced Vladimir head-on, and then kicked him once more, this time in the groin. Vladimir cried out and fell face-down.

Yuri said, "You're not thinking the way Brighton Beach thinks. If you didn't hit Jessie Merrill, that means I did."

Vladimir struggled for his breath. "That's not . . . what I'm saying."

"But that's what *they're* saying, asshole. If I don't get the truth out of you, they pin it on me. Isn't that right, Leonid?"

"That's my orders," Leonid said flatly. "If I don't hear a confession out of Vladimir's own mouth, both him and Yuri is in the shithouse."

Vladimir tried to get up, but made it only to one knee. A trickle of blood oozed from the corner of his mouth. "I don't confess to things I don't do."

Yuri grabbed him by the throat and pulled him up, eye-to-eye. "It was a perfect plan. AIDS patients die every day. All we had to do was find the right virus, and we were clear to call home as many viatical settlements as we wanted, no one the wiser. But Jessie Merrill was a healthy broad. You kill her and it's all over the newspapers that she had a viatical settlement."

"I totally agree with you. I would have to be an idiot to kill her."

"A fucking idiot, Vladimir. Because only a fucking idiot would be stupid enough to kill her and then make it look like suicide. The insurance company doesn't pay if she killed herself!"

"I know that. I swear, it wasn't me."

Yuri pressed the gun to the bottom of his chin, aiming straight for the brain.

"It wasn't you or me!" said Vladimir. "If we did it, it would have looked like an accident for sure."

"You're lying!"

"No, I swear. When we found out she scammed us, all I did was scare her. I *didn't* kill her."

"Then who did?"

"I think it's them," Vladimir said, his voice cracking. "Brighton Beach hit her, and now they're blaming us just as an excuse to get out of their deal."

Leonid stepped forward, his eyes bulging as if he were about to explode. "You see what I'm saying, Yuri? It's the same attitude I got at his club. The man's rude."

"I'll handle this." Yuri got right in his face and said, "So, you think Leonid is stupid enough to make Jessie's death look like suicide?"

"I didn't say that."

"I definitely heard you say that. You hear him say that, Leonid?"

"That's the way I heard it. Fucking rude, I tell you."

"If they're so stupid, maybe I should show these boys in Brighton Beach what an accident looks like? What do you think of that, Vladimir?"

Vladimir blinked rapidly, as if on the verge of tears. "Yuri, please. I got kids."

Yuri pushed him to his knees, then stepped away from the spotlight and into the darkness. He grabbed a two-foot pipe from the corner, then returned to Vladimir, tapping the pipe against his palm to the rhythm of each footfall.

Vladimir lowered his head.

Yuri stepped past him. Then he whirled on one foot, swung his arm back toward Vladimir, and slammed the pipe across the bridge of his nose. Vladimir screamed and fell over backward, blood gushing from his smashed nostrils.

"Ouch," said Yuri, mocking him. "Did you see how hard that poor slob's face hit the steering wheel?"

"Must have been going at least thirty miles an hour," said Leonid.

Yuri stepped closer, took a good look at Vladimir's bloodied face. In a blur of a motion he unloaded another hit, this time to Vladimir's jaw. It was a quick one-two, the deep thud of pipe followed by the crisp cracking of bone.

"Looks more like fifty miles an hour to me," said Yuri. Then he looked around the room, the wheels turning in his head. "You know, he wasn't wearing his seat belt, either. Who's got a fucking tire iron?"

"That's enough," said Leonid. "I want him to taste that river water."

"Fine by me," said Yuri.

Leonid gave a quick nod, and on command the two thugs lifted Vladimir from the floor. He was unconscious and bleeding on them, but they didn't seem to mind the occupational hazard. They dragged him across the room to a room-service cart. Vladimir folded in half quite easily, but he was still too big to fit inside the lower food-warming compartment. Yuri walked over with the pipe, wedged it against the cart for leverage, and jerked Vladimir's left shoulder in such a way that his left elbow could touch his right ear.

"Perfect," said Yuri as he closed up the cart with Vladimir inside.

Leonid opened the door, and his men started out with the cart.

"Hey, idiots," said Yuri. "Jackets, please."

They stopped and saw that Vladimir's blood was on their sleeves. They slipped them off and stuffed them into the cart with the body.

"Much better," said Yuri.

They wheeled the cart into the hallway. The door closed, and Vladimir was gone.

Yuri tossed the bloody pipe in the corner. "We square now?"

"I never did hear Vladimir's confession," said Leonid. "I just bashed my partner's face in, and Brighton Beach still wants to hold Jessie Merrill against me?"

"Don't worry. We're fine on that score. I was just thinking that you worked him over pretty good, and he still didn't admit it. He swears all he did is scare her."

"So?"

"So, maybe he didn't hit Jessie Merrill."

"Which means what? Our viatical business is still on?"

"Sorry, Yuri. Too much heat around that. It's over."

"Damn it. Now whose fault is that?"

"Not mine, not yours. Could be nobody's fault."

"It's always *somebody's* fault. Someone needs to take the blame."

Leonid shrugged. "You want to blame someone, blame whoever it was who killed Jessie Merrill."

Yuri smiled thinly, as if it were a revelation. "You're right. That's exactly who's to blame."

"I'm always right. Come on. I'll buy you a drink."

They started toward the door, then Yuri said, "Hey, if you think Vladimir wasn't behind the Merrill hit after all, you want to call back your men?"

He thought for a second. "Nah. I still say he's rude."

"King of the Kamikaze Club. No fucking class."

They shared a little laugh, then Leonid held the door open as Yuri went back and switched off the spotlight.

# 55

·

Cindy hadn't intended an ambush, but it was beginning to feel that way. Ever since Jack had told her that he was a beneficiary under Jessie's will, she'd wanted to talk straight to the lawyer who had drafted it. She feared she might chicken out if she made an appointment, so she showed up at Clara's office unannounced.

"Ms. Pierce is with a client," said the receptionist.

"I'll wait," said Cindy.

"It could be a while."

"No hurry." Cindy took a seat in the lobby beside the big spider plant. It had long, beautiful leaves that seemed a little too perfect in shape and color. *Real,* she wondered, *or a convincing fake?* An amusing thought. From what Jack had told her about Clara, the question could have applied to more than just the potted plants.

She flipped through the entire stack of old magazines before the receptionist finally called and led her down the hall, past the main conference room. Cindy caught a glimpse of a monstrous white-stone table that wasn't at all her taste. It had a nice centerpiece of dried flowers, however.

*Looks like something Jack would order.*

At the corner office, Clara stepped out from behind her desk and shook hands. Cindy had never met her, but the introductions had an uneasy quality that marked any meeting between two people who knew they would never, ever be friends.

"I've heard a lot about you," said Clara.

"Likewise."

She offered Cindy a place at the end of the couch. Cindy seated herself, and Clara sat in the armchair facing her. Clara said, "I wouldn't say I'm shocked to see you, but it is a surprise."

"I'm a little surprised myself."

"Did Jack send you?"

"No. He doesn't even know I'm here."

Clara arched an eyebrow, as if the admission interested her. "Would he be unhappy if he knew?"

"That depends on what you tell me."

"That depends on what you ask."

Cindy scooted forward to the edge of her seat and looked her in the eye. "I want honest answers."

"I won't lie to you. But I do owe a fiduciary obligation to Jessie's estate. If there's something I can't reveal, I'll tell you I can't discuss it. Fair enough?"

"I suppose it's the best I can hope for."

"It is. So, what is it that you'd like to know?"

Cindy took a breath. "I want to know . . ."

Clara waited, but Cindy didn't finish. "Know what?"

"I want to know if my husband has done anything to find the child that Jessie gave up for adoption."

"Has he done anything? You mean you don't know?"

"We don't really talk about it."

"Have you asked him?"

"I told you: We don't discuss it."

"Why not?"

"I'm not here to talk about what goes on between Jack and me. Do you know what Jack has done to find the child?"

"Why would I have that information?"

"You were Jessie's friend. You drafted her will. If I were looking for a child that Jessie had given up for adoption, you're the first person I would talk to. Maybe you'd have some leads. At the very least, you'd know which blind alleys your friend Jessie had followed in her own efforts to find her child."

"I have some insights, yes."

"Have you shared any of that with Jack?"

"No."

"Why not?"

"He hasn't asked for it."

Their eyes locked. "Will you share it with me?"

"Why do you want it?"

"As I understand it, everything Jessie owns goes to Jack if the child isn't located."

"That's correct."

"Then it's important that we find the child. As Jack's wife, the last thing I want is for him to inherit something he doesn't really deserve."

"The last thing you want is for him to inherit something from his old girlfriend."

"Is there some reason I shouldn't feel that way?"

"No. But the very fact that you're here underscores the question: Why *doesn't* Jack feel that way?"

"He does, I'm sure."

"How can you be sure?"

"Because he's my husband."

"Interesting answer."

Cindy narrowed her eyes, confused. "Why is that interesting?"

"Jessie told me about a conversation she and Jack had right before the jury returned its verdict. She asked him why their reunion, if you will, hadn't really blossomed into anything. Jack's answer was like yours. He said, 'Because I'm married.' "

"So?"

Clara shrugged and said, "A nicer explanation might have been something along the lines of because Jack loves you. At the time, I thought Jessie was being a little harsh in her judgment. But now that I've met you, maybe she's right. Maybe Jack is just a poor, lost soul who's playing by the rules."

Cindy struggled not to say what she was thinking. "Are you going to answer my questions about this adopted child or not?"

Clara looked away, as if mulling it over. "I'm not sure I can help you."

"Why not?"

"It's awkward. I don't care to get caught in the middle of whatever's going on between you and your husband."

"The only thing going on is that Jack is too shocked by all of this to do anything about it. Somebody has to step up to the plate and find this child, so we can all put it behind us and move on. That's all I'm here for."

"No. You're here because you don't believe whatever it is your husband is telling you about this child."

"You're reading way too much into this."

"Am I?"

The doubtful expression made Cindy feel small. Finally, Cindy lowered her eyes, rose from the couch, and said, "This was a bad idea. I think I'd better go."

Clara followed her to the door. "Jack always did like kids."

"Excuse me?"

"He and Jessie used to double date with my husband and me. Even way back then, he said he wanted kids. He was so good with my son David."

Cindy blinked, confused.

Clara said, "As I recall, Jack had a pretty rocky relationship with his own father. Guys like that often go the extra mile to keep history from repeating itself. He probably would have made a pretty good dad."

"I'm sure he would."

"Seems ironic, then, doesn't it?"

"What?"

"You never gave Jack a child. Jessie did."

Cindy didn't know how to answer, but it didn't matter. She couldn't speak. She just stood numbly for a moment, ice-cold, waiting for the pain to pass.

"Thanks a lot for your time," she said, then closed the door on her way out.

# 56

.

It was late Friday afternoon, and Jack was at his *abuela*'s when Rosa phoned him on his cell. Expecting bad news, he ducked out of the kitchen and took the call in the living room, out of his grandmother's earshot.

"Indictment is down," said Rosa.

He closed his eyes and slowly opened them, absorbing the blow. "How bad?"

"One count, one defendant."

"Me?"

"No. Theo."

The knot in his stomach twisted. A moment of relief for himself, a deep-felt pain for his friend. "No murder for-hire-scheme, like we thought?"

"Not yet."

"You think it's coming?"

"Could be like we talked about earlier. The prosecutor will use the indictment as leverage against Theo, try to get him to turn against you."

"He could have done that even if he'd indicted both of us."

"He's being cautious, as he should be. You're a respected lawyer, the son of a popular former governor. You can bet that the state attorney herself is insisting that the evidence against you be ironclad."

"Marsh's testimony obviously wasn't enough."

"Or the prosecutor has some reservations about it. I heard a rumor that Marsh refused to take a polygraph."

"That's just great. They're not sure if their star witness is telling the truth, so they can't indict me. But it's fine and dandy to indict Theo."

"Theo's a former death-row inmate. I don't care if he was innocent the last time, the bar's a lot higher for you than for him."

"This really pisses me off."

"Calm down, okay? We don't know what additional evidence they have against Theo. It could be worse than we think."

Jack sighed, realizing she was right.

Rosa said, "Right now we have to focus on making sure they don't convince Theo to flip against you. That would be all the evidence they need to go after you on murder for hire."

"The only way they can do that is to get Theo to lie. That'll never happen."

There was a brief pause, then Rosa shifted gears. "Where are you now?"

"My grandmother's house. I didn't want to be home or at the office when the indictment issued. Just can't deal with the media right now."

"Where's Cindy?"

"With her mom."

"Are you two . . ."

"I don't know what's happening with us."

"Have you heard anything at all from Theo?"

"Not a word."

"Well, his arraignment is set for Monday morning at nine. If we don't hear from him by then, he'll officially be a fugitive."

"I've been trying to find him ever since his lawyer told me he couldn't reach him. I called his friends, talked to his partner, the people he works with. No one seems to know anything."

"Then do more."

"I will. But the indictment isn't going to make it any easier. There's no bail for murder in the first degree. The thought of going back behind bars isn't going to sit well with him."

"You need to find him and convince him that he has no choice. A no-show on Monday only digs a deeper hole for all of us."

Jack started to pace. Through the archway at the end of the hall, he could see his grandmother standing at the kitchen island preparing dinner. Strange, but he suddenly smelled jail food. "I need to get on this. Where can I reach you tonight?"

"I'll be here in my office pretty late. You should come by. Jancowitz is delivering the grand-jury materials to Theo's lawyer tonight, and he promised to share with me. Could be interesting stuff."

"Yeah. Like reading my best friend's obituary."

"We're a long way from that, Jack."

He thanked her, said good-bye, and hung up. He took a few steps toward the kitchen, then stopped. Only one thing seemed worse than telling *Abuela* that an indictment might be around the corner, and that was letting her hear it first on television. He drew a deep breath and entered the kitchen.

"Who called?" she asked.

"Rosa."

She was flattening a mound of dough into a paper-thin sheet, back and forth with a rolling pin. It was for her famous meat-filled pastry shells that were tasty enough to tempt even a life-long vegetarian. "What she tell you?"

"Not good news."

"How not good?"

Jack stood on the opposite side of the island, grabbed a sliver of extraneous dough, and rolled it into a ball as he told her about Theo, and how they might still come after him. He could see the emotion in her eyes, but she kept working the dough faster and faster as the news unfolded. He finished in a minute or two, but the silence lingered much longer. Just the sound of the rolling pin and the slice of the knife on the granite countertop—rolling the dough, flattening it into sheets, slicing it into triangles.

"Careful," said Jack. "You're going to cut yourself."

Her pace only quickened. Another wad of dough, another flattened square, a diagonal slice that turned the square into two triangles.

After the third cut, Jack grabbed her wrist and said, "Do that again."

"*Como?*"

"The slicing motion. Do it again."

She flattened another sheet, put the rolling pin aside. Then she took her knife and sliced diagonally across the sheet of dough.

"You slice from top right to bottom left," he said.

"*Sí.*"

"Not from top left to bottom right."

She tried it. "*Aye, no.* That would be very awkward for me."

"Of course it would be," he said, looking off to the middle distance. "You're left-handed."

"*Toda esta bien?*" she asked. Is everything okay?

"*Perfecto,*" he said as he leaned across the island and planted a kiss on her cheek. "*Gracias, mi vida.* I love you."

"I love you, too. But what this about?"

"It's complicated, sort of. But it's really simple."

"What you talk about?"

"You made it all so simple."

"Me?"

"Yes, you. You're beautiful. I'll explain later. I gotta go."

He grabbed his car keys, ran out the front door, and jumped into his Mustang. The traffic lights were all green on his way to Rosa's office, a minor miracle that he interpreted as a sure sign that he was onto something. He was in a hurry, to be sure, but the need for speed was more a matter of adrenaline than timing. Less than fifteen minutes later he was banging on the entrance doors to Rosa's office suite. She let him in and then backed away, as if fearful that he might ricochet off the walls and knock her flat.

"What's with you?" she asked.

Jack caught his breath and said, "Do you have the grand-jury materials yet?"

"Yeah. Just came."

"I need to see the autopsy photos."

"I'm sure they're in there."

He followed her to her office. The materials were in two boxes atop her desk. Jack sifted through one; Rosa, the other.

"Here they are," said Jack. He removed the photographs from the envelope and spread them across the desktop. The gruesome sight cut his enthusiasm in half. Jessie's lifeless body on a slab evoked chilling memories of the bloody scene in his bathroom.

"What are you looking for?" asked Rosa.

"This." He cleared away the other photographs and laid one on the desktop. It was a close-up of the wound to Jessie's wrist. He examined it carefully and said, "Bingo."

"Bingo what?"

"Jessie's left wrist was slashed, which is exactly what you'd expect from a right-handed person."

"Are you saying Jessie was left-handed?"

"No. She was right-handed."

"Then what's the big revelation?"

"The slash mark runs at the wrong angle."

"What?"

He turned his palm face-up, demonstrating. "Look at my wrist. Let's call the thumb-side the left and the pinky-side the right. A right-handed person would probably slash top left to bottom right, or even straight across, left to right. But top right to bottom left is an awkward movement."

Rosa checked the photograph once more. "It's not a severe angle. But now that you mention it, Jessie's appears to be top right to bottom left."

"Exactly."

"So what does this mean? She didn't kill herself? We sort of knew that all along."

"It means more than that." Jack took the letter opener from her desk, then grabbed Rosa's wrist to make his point more clearly. "I'm right-handed. Let's say I'm facing you and cutting your left wrist, trying to make your death look like a suicide. My natural movement is to cut from top left to bottom right. That leaves a wound at the exact same angle you would leave if you had cut your own wrist. Try it."

She took the letter opener, ran it across her veins. "You're right."

Jack took back the opener and switched hands. "But if I'm a left-handed person, and I cut your left wrist, the cut runs at the opposite angle. From your vantage point, it's top right to bottom left."

She simply nodded, following the logic. "So exactly what are you saying?"

"I'm saying that the only way you end up with a slit at this angle is if a left-handed person is facing his victim just as I'm facing you right now and slashes her left wrist."

Rosa looked at the photo, then at Jack, her expression stone-cold serious. "Know anyone who's left-handed?"

"I think I've got a pretty good idea."

"Who?"

He tapped the blade of the letter opener into the palm of his hand and said, "Someone I've suspected since the day he came to my office, talking about Jessie's death as if it were just a business hassle."

"One Dr. Joseph Marsh?"

"You got it," said Jack.

## 57

Dr. Marsh lived in a Mediterranean-style house near Pennsylvania Avenue, a few blocks west of where the noisy Miami Beach nightlife began. The neighborhood was once a haven for retirees, but with the overall revitalization of South Beach, mountain bikes and Rollerblades had long since replaced the wheelchairs and walkers. It was an eclectic area, lots of artists, musicians, gays, and young people—the perfect relocation spot for a rich, recently divorced doctor in pursuit of hard bodies.

Jack parked on the street and killed the engine. It was a dark night, and the canopy of a sprawling oak tree blocked most of the light from a distant street lamp. Rosa was barely visible in the passenger seat beside him.

"This is the last time I'm going to say this, Jack. I don't think a confrontation with the government's chief witness is a good idea."

"I don't intend to get in his face. I've met him several

times but I've never really focused on whether he's left-handed or right-handed. I just have to see with my own eyes."

"What are you going to do, ask him to grab his glove and have a catch?"

"No, I thought I'd just tell him to slap you upside the head."

"I just want you to be sure about this."

"I am. This thing I figured out with the angle of the slash on Jessie's wrist is only one piece of the puzzle. Even if Marsh is left-handed, that's not the only thing that points to him as the killer. I think she screwed him over."

"How do you mean?"

"Somehow, the entire million and a half dollars that Jessie wormed out of her viatical investors ended up in a bank account that didn't have his name on it. I'm sure that Marsh went along with that arrangement because he wanted to prevent his wife from getting her hands on it in the divorce. But something tells me that when it came time to give the doctor his half of the loot, Jessie gave him the heave-ho—'It's been nice, doc, thanks for helping with the scam, now see ya later.' "

"You realize we're totally shifting gears. The whole defense we've been crafting so far is that Jessie was murdered by the investors she scammed."

"Which is probably why we aren't making any head-way. One thing has always bothered me about that anyway. Why would they kill Jessie and let the doctor live?"

"I don't know."

"And how do you think Dr. Marsh is going to react when I ask him that question?"

"I think he'll say exactly what he said to the grand

jury: *you* killed her. So, please, don't have that kind of talk with him. Just get him to sip coffee or write something down, anything to satisfy yourself that he's left-handed. Don't take it any further than that."

"We'll see how it goes."

"No, I already see where it's going. If all you really wanted to know was whether Marsh is left-handed, you could go ask his wife. You want to get in there, go toe-to-toe, get your friend Theo off the hook, and stem off your own indictment. He got the best of you in that last conversation you had in your office, and now you want to even the score."

"I'm just feeling him out, okay? From what I've seen of Dr. Marsh, he's way too impressed by his own cleverness. If I keep my composure and push the right buttons, I honestly think he's arrogant enough to say something we can use to hang him."

She shook her head, as if she didn't approve. "I see there's no talking you out of this."

"Nope."

"You realize I'm not going with you. The last thing I need to do is be a witness to a conversation that might disqualify me from being your lawyer."

"I agree."

"Good luck."

"Thanks." He stepped down from the car, pushed the door shut, and headed up the walkway. It was a short walk, but it seemed long. The small front lawn was well kept, surrounded by an eight-foot-tall cherry hedge that was trimmed and squared-off neatly to resemble fortress walls. Jack almost checked for a moat. Long rows of colorful impatiens flanked either side of the curved path of stepping stones that led to the front door. The driveway was off to the left, and the doctor's

Mercedes was parked in it. That was promising, almost as good as a sign on the door saying THE DOCTOR IS IN.

Jack climbed one step at a time, three in total, acutely aware of the scratchy sound of his soles on rough concrete. This was technically no sneak attack, but the closer he got to the front door, the less welcome he felt. It wasn't anything he heard or saw. Just vibes.

He drew a breath and knocked on the door.

A full minute passed. Jack heard nothing. He knocked again, a little harder. Then he waited. He checked his watch. Almost ninety seconds. It was a small house. Even from the most remote corner, it couldn't possibly take more than a minute or so to reach the front door. Unless he was showering or sleeping or—

*Who the hell cares if I'm bothering him?* He knocked a third time, a good solid pounding that could easily have preceded the announcement, *Police, open up!*

He waited a full three minutes. No one home. Or at least no one was willing to come to the door. In the back of his mind he could almost see Rosa smiling and saying something along the lines of *Just as well, God's doing us a favor.*

He turned away and climbed down the stairs. Instead of taking the serpentine footpath, he exited by way of the driveway, a more direct route to the street. The silver Mercedes was a ghostly shade of gray in the moonless night. It seemed odd that the car was in the driveway and yet the doctor hadn't answered the door. Jack took two more steps toward the driveway, then froze. He hadn't noticed in the darkness, but on the other side of the big Mercedes was a smaller, black vehicle, almost invisible in the night. It was a Volkswagen Jetta, and in an instant, Jack recognized it.

*Theo?*

He sprinted toward the Jetta, pressed his face to the glass and peered through the dark, tinted windows. Theo's windows were so dark they were illegal, making it impossible to see in. Jack walked around to the windshield, but he saw nothing inside. He tried the doors, but they were locked. He stepped back and nearly bumped into Dr. Marsh's Mercedes. As he turned, something inside caught his eye. The driver-side window wasn't as dark as Theo's, so he could make out the image inside.

His heart was suddenly in his throat.

A man was slumped sideways over the console, his torso stretching from the driver's seat to the passenger side. On impulse, Jack opened the door and pulled him straight up in his seat.

"Dr. Marsh!" he said, as if he could revive him.

The doctor was staring back at him, eyes wide open, but the stare was lifeless. The back of his head was covered with blood.

Jack released his grip, his hands shaking. The body fell face-first against the steering wheel. He backed away, grabbed his cell phone, and dialed 911, his mind racing with one scary thought.

*Theo, where on God's earth are you?*

## 58

Before Dr. Marsh's death hit the late-evening news, Jack was at Theo's townhouse. He'd driven Theo home from his late-night gigs often enough to know that a key was behind the barbecue in the backyard. Technically speaking, he was still trespassing, but a true friend didn't stand on the sidelines at a time like this.

The police arrived at Dr. Marsh's house within minutes of the 911 call. They'd asked plenty of questions about Theo's whereabouts. Jack didn't have any answers, and he quickly realized that it was up to him to go out and get them.

Jack turned the key in the lock, then pushed the door open. He took a step inside, and switched on a light. Almost immediately his heart thumped, as the big cuckoo clock on the kitchen wall began its hourly ritual. In a minute, Jack could breathe again, and he watched the wooden characters continue their little dance around the musical clock. They weren't the typical cuckoo-clock figures. Instead of the little man with the hammer who comes out and strikes the bell, this one had an axe-wielding woodsman who lopped off a chicken's head. Theo had ordered it from some offbeat mail-order catalog and given it to Jack after his successful last-minute request for a stay of execution. Jack gave it back when Theo was finally released from prison. Death row did weird things to your sense of humor.

*But I still like having you around, buddy.*

Jack continued down the hall and headed for the bedroom. In Jack's mind, it wasn't even within the realm of possibility that Theo might have killed the doctor. Jack hadn't exactly spelled it out this way to the police, but even if you believed that Theo was capable of murder, he was way too savvy to pull the trigger and then leave his car parked on the victim's front lawn.

Still, there were two most likely possibilities. Either Theo was on the run or something awful had happened to him. After mulling it over, Jack settled on a surefire way to rule out one of them.

The bedroom door was open, and Jack went inside. A small lamp on the dresser supplied all the light he needed. This wasn't the kind of search that required him to slice open seat cushions, upend the mattress, or even check under the bed. Jack went straight to the closet and slid open the door.

Instantly, he saw what he was looking for. It was in plain view, exactly where Theo kept it. He popped open the black case to reveal a high-polished, brass instrument glistening in the light.

Jack took the saxophone in his hands and held it the way Theo would have. He could almost hear Theo playing, felt himself connecting with his friend. Jack had no idea where Theo was, but this much he knew:

Theo had lived without his music for too long in prison, and he would never do it again. Not by choice.

His heart sank as he considered Theo's fate—as the least scary of possibilities evaporated in Jack's mind.

*No way he ran.*

Carefully, almost lovingly, he placed the sax back on the closet shelf, then headed for the door.

# 59

The Luna Lodge was the kind of seedy motel that could be rented by the week, the day, or the hour. Katrina didn't want to stay a minute longer than necessary, but she wasn't feeling optimistic. She'd sprung for the weekly rate.

She'd chosen a ground-floor room in the back where guests could come and go from their cars with virtually no risk of being spotted. Privacy was what the Luna Lodge was all about, with an extra set of clean sheets coming in at a close second. She could hear the bed squeaking in the room above her. For a solid thirty-five minutes, it sounded like the bedposts pounding on her ceiling. The guy upstairs was Superman, but that wasn't what was keeping her awake. She'd spent hours seated in a lumpy armchair that faced the door, wondering how deep was the mess she'd gotten herself into.

The chain lock was on, the lights were off, the window shades were shut. The room smelled of mold, mildew, and a host of other living organisms that she didn't even try to identify. The sun had set hours earlier, but a laser of moonlight streamed through a small tear at the top of the curtain. Until just then, she hadn't noticed that the big amoeba-shaped stain on the carpet was actually the color of dried blood.

Her eyes were closing, and her mind wandered. Being so close to all this sin evoked a flurry of memories. She suddenly felt cold, though the chill was from within her. It was like a winter night in Prague, the night she'd parted with her pride. She was just nineteen, a mere teenager, locked in a bathroom she shared with seven other roommates in a drafty apartment.

•

A brutal February wind poured through cracks around the small rectangular window. She was sitting on the edge of the sink, a battered metal basin so cold that it burned against the backs of her bare thighs. It was meticulous work, but she did it quickly. Then she pulled up her panties, buttoned her slacks, and put the scissors back in the cabinet.

The fruits of her efforts were in a small plastic bag. She hid it in her pocket so her roommates wouldn't see. Three of them were sharing a couple pieces of bread and a bland broth for dinner as she made her way past them. They didn't ask where she was going, but it wasn't out of indifference. She sensed that they knew, but they'd chosen not to embarrass her. Without a word, she stepped out of the cluttered apartment, then headed down the hall and out the back door of the building.

A black sedan was parked at the curb. The motor was running, as white wisps of exhaust curled upward in the cold air. A sea of footprints in frozen slush covered the sidewalk. The ice crunched beneath her feet as she headed for the car, opened the back door, and climbed inside. She closed the door and handed the bag to the man in the driver's seat. It was the same man she'd met in the alley the night her friend Beatriz had been killed at the factory.

"Here you go," she said.

He held the bag up to the dome light, eyeing it with a disgusting fascination. It was a peculiar fetish among certain Czech men, one that kept many a young Cuban woman in Castro's work program from starving. There was decent money to be had from a bagful of pubic clippings.

"Too short," he said.

"It's only twenty-days' growth. What do you expect?"

"I can't use this."

"Then give me more time between collections. At least six weeks."

"I can't wait that long."

"Then what do you expect me to do?"

He opened the bag, smelled it, and smiled. "I think it's time we expanded our line of merchandise."

"No way."

"Not a good answer."

"I don't care."

"You'd better care."

"I don't. This isn't fair."

"Fair?" he said, chuckling. Then he turned serious. "It's like I always say, honey. Everything happens for a reason. No decision is meaningless. We all determine our own fate."

"If that's what you say, then you're an asshole."

"Yeah. I'll be sure to make a note of that. Meanwhile, you think about the choices you want to make. Think about your fate."

•

A low, throaty groan startled her. It was a man's voice, definitely not the hooker next door. She focused just in time to see Theo's eyes blink open.

"How's your head?" she asked.

He was lying on his back, his body stretched across the mattress like a drying deer skin. Each wrist and ankle was handcuffed to a respective corner of the bed frame. He tried to say something, but with the gag it was unintelligible.

Katrina rose and inspected the big purple knot above his left eyebrow. It was squeezing his eye half shut, and he withdrew at her slightest touch.

"That was a stupid thing to do," she said. "Next time you try to escape, I'll have to shoot you."

His jaw tightened on the gag, but he uttered not a sound.

She returned to her chair and laid her pistol across her lap. "I suppose you're wondering how long I think I can keep you tied up like this."

Short, angry breaths through his nostrils were his only reply.

"The answer is: Long enough for me to figure out what to do. See, if I don't kill you, they're going to kill me. And then they'll come and find you and do the job that I was supposed to do. So it's really in everyone's best interest for you to behave yourself and let me figure this out."

His breathing slowed. He seemed less antagonized.

"Now, I'm sure you'd love to lose that gag in your mouth. And after lying here unconscious for so long, you must be dying to use the bathroom. So nod once if you think you can behave yourself."

He blinked, then nodded.

"Good." She went to him and stopped at the edge of the mattress. Then she aimed the gun directly at his head and said, "You try anything, I'll blow your brains out."

She took the key from her pocket and unlocked the left handcuff. She handed him the ice bucket. "Roll over and pee into this."

Still gagged, he shot her a look that said, *You gotta be kidding.*

"Do it, or hold it."

Begrudgingly, he rolled on one side, unzipped, and did his business. From the sound of things, Katrina was beginning to think she might need a second bucket. Finally it was over. He rolled onto his back, and Katrina locked the handcuff to his wrist.

"Thirsty?" she asked.

He nodded.

"If you scream . . ." She pressed the gun to his forehead, as if to finish the sentence.

She reached behind his neck, loosened the knot, and pulled the gag free. She offered him a cup of water, which he drank eagerly. When he finished, he stretched his mouth open to shake off the effects of the gag, then winced. The mere use of any facial muscles was a painful reminder of the bruise above his eye.

"Damn, girl. Where'd you learn to kick like that?"

"Where'd you get those tattoos?"

He looked confused, then seemed to understand. "You served time?"

"I think of it that way."

"What for?"

"What's it to you?"

"Just curious."

The creaking noise resumed overhead, the steady squeak of the bed in the room above them. Katrina glanced at the ceiling, then shot Theo a look that required no elaboration.

"You were a hooker?" he said.

"No. I refused to be one."

"They put you in jail because you *wouldn't* ho'? I don't get it." The squeaking stopped. Theo lay still for a moment, still staring at the ceiling. "To be honest, I don't get any of this. You're a government informant. If someone is making you do something you don't want to do, just go to the police."

"It's not that simple."

"Just explain to them that things have gotten out of hand. Someone wants you to hit me or they're gonna hit you."

"I can't do that."

"Why not?"

"Because if I go to the police and tell them the fix I'm in, they'll pull me from the assignment."

"Exactly. Problem solved."

"You just don't understand." Her gaze drifted across the room, then settled on the brownish-red spot of dried blood on the carpet. "There's an old Russian proverb," she said vaguely. " 'Revenge is the sweetest form of passion.' "

"What does that have to do with calling the police?"

"If they pull me off the job now, I stifle my own passion."

He looked straight at her, seeming to understand that somewhere behind those troubled brown eyes was an old score to settle.

"I'm good at revenge. Maybe I could help."

"This is something I have to do myself."

He nodded, then gave a little tug that rattled the chains of his handcuffs. "Funny."

"What?"

"When I was fifteen, I used to have this fantasy about being kidnapped by a Latina babe."

"Not exactly living up to the dream, is it?"

"Nope."

"Hate to break this to you, pal. Life never does." She stuffed the gag back in his mouth and cinched up the knot behind his head.

## 60

Jack went from Theo's to Sparky's. It was getting late, but the crowd had found its collective second wind. Loud country music was cranking on the sound system, and a group of Garth Brooks wannabes were twirling their women across the dance floor.

*Theo's gone one night, and the place is already swarming with rednecks.*

Like most dives, Sparky's was the kind of place where liquor flowed freely but everything else came at a price. All day long, theories about Theo's disappearance had been bouncing off the walls. For twenty bucks the barmaid steered Jack in the most promising direction.

"Buy you a drink?" said Jack as he sidled up to the bar.

A skinny guy with weathered skin looked up from his glass and said, "You queer?"

"No, sorry. But I have a couple friends who are, if you're interested."

He popped up from his barstool. "Watch your mouth, jackass."

"Easy, friend. Just a little joke."

"I don't think you're so funny."

Jack took a moment. Usually he tried to befriend people before bullying them into divulging information, but this guy was too much of a jerk to waste time schmoozing.

"You're a truck driver, aren't you?"

"That's right."

"That's your rig parked out back?"

"What's it to you?"

"I hear you sell drugs out of it."

"That's bullshit."

"Don't worry. I'm not a cop."

"I don't sell nothin' to nobody. Just drive my truck, that's all."

"Well, I hear differently. So let me spell this out for you. Theo Knight left this joint around two o'clock this morning. Nobody's seen him since. His partner tells me the cops have been here asking questions. I hear you're the only one around here who seems to have any idea what might have happened to him."

"I didn't tell the cops nothin'."

"I'm sure you didn't. That's because you were out cutting a deal in your truck when you saw what you saw."

He smiled nervously. "You heard that, huh?"

"From a good source. So, you want to tell me what caught your eye? Or should I call my old boss at the U.S. attorney's office and tell him to get a search warrant for your rig?"

The trucker swirled the ice cubes around in his glass, sipped the last few drops of bourbon. "Tough guy, are you?"

"Just a man with a mission."

He checked the door, as if it were some big secret,

then glanced back and said, "Your friend Theo left with some chick."

"Who?"

"A brunette. Black clothes, nice body. Could have been Latina. She was hanging around his car out back in the parking lot, then she got in. He came out about twenty minutes later, and they drove off together. That's all I saw."

"Did they seem friendly together, were they arguing, or what?"

"I didn't see them together. His Jetta has dark-tinted windows, so I couldn't see inside. Like I say, I saw her get in, then a little later he gets in. I don't know if she was smoking a joint in there or what. She waited for him, then they left. That's it."

"Anything else you remember?"

"Yeah. The bumper sticker. It said, I BRAKE FOR PORN STARS. It just kind of stuck in my brain."

Definitely Theo's car, thought Jack. "That's all I need to know. Thanks."

Jack climbed off the barstool and headed out the door to the parking lot, leaving the loud music and stale odors behind him. The moon was almost full, bright enough to cast his shadow across the parking lot. He leaned against his car, thinking, but he didn't have to think long. Brunette, good-looking, nice body. It was just as he'd suspected, and the trucker's story was all the ammunition he needed.

He pulled his phone from his pocket, then stopped, not sure whom to call first. If he notified the cops, Katrina would probably hire herself a lawyer and never talk. He gave it another moment's thought, then went with his gut and dialed the cell-phone number Katrina had given him outside the mobile blood unit.

"What did you do to Theo Knight?" he said when she answered.

There was silence. Jack said, "Don't hang up, Katrina. I'm onto you. Theo's missing, and you left Sparky's with him last night."

"Says who?"

"I have a witness who saw you waiting in the car."

She didn't answer. Jack said, "I'm giving you one chance to tell me what happened to Theo. If you don't, I'm going to the police."

She paused, a long, tense silence that bespoke her angst. Jack said, "What's it going to be?"

"Don't go to the police."

"Why shouldn't I?"

"Because if you do, there's a good chance Theo could end up dead."

"Is that a threat?"

"No."

"Is he alive?"

"Yes."

"Do you know that for a fact?"

"Yes."

"Let me be clear about this. Are you saying you kidnapped him?"

"No. I mean, not really. It's not like I'm asking for a ransom or anything. It's more like he's in hiding, for his own safety."

"Say what?"

"All I can tell you is that I'll do everything I can to keep him safe. But if you butt in, there's a good chance he'll end up dead. And it won't be my fault."

"What's going on?"

"I can't explain now. Just give me twenty-four hours to sort some things out."

"Are you out of your mind?"

"You just have to trust me on this. I'm a confidential informant, I'm not a criminal, remember?"

"I'm not trusting you anymore. I'm going to the police."

"Fine. Go. But after keeping your friend alive on death row for all those years, it seems pretty stupid of you to sign his death warrant now. And that's exactly what you'd be doing if you run to the cops."

Jack gripped the phone, thinking. "I don't like this. After that meeting at the blood unit, I thought we had a working relationship. But I haven't heard a thing from you about that Georgia case, or anything else, for that matter."

There was silence, but finally she answered. "You were right about Georgia."

His heart sank a bit. "They're killing viatical settlors?"

"I checked the computers. That woman in Georgia was one of our clients."

"So if they got Jessie, too, that means Viatical Solutions, Inc., murdered two clients in less than a month."

"It's not for sure. And it's not just Viatical Solutions, Inc., either. We created dozens of viatical corporations, most of them just shells that we activate whenever we need one. When I first started this job, I thought all these companies were just a lot of needless paperwork, but now it makes sense. Every client does business with a different company. The one in Georgia was called Financial Health, Inc."

"Smart," said Jack. "It would look pretty suspicious if any single company showed too good a rate of return."

"I am so close to blowing the lid off this."

"You have to come forward."

"I need more time."

"You can't have it. What if they go out and murder another client next week?"

"I'm not talking a week. Twenty-four hours is all I need. Then Theo will be back safe, and this whole operation will be blown wide open. I promise."

He weighed it in his mind, but he and Theo both needed someone on the inside. Busting her chops over a few hours would only push her out of their camp. "All right. I'll give you twenty-four hours. But I want proof that Theo's alive, before noon."

"Like what?"

The image of Theo's saxophone suddenly flashed in his brain, giving Jack the perfect proof-of-life question. "Ask him for the title of his favorite Donald Byrd album."

"Okay. You'll have it by noon."

"One last thing."

"What?"

"Theo Knight is my friend. If you're playing me for a fool and something happens to him, I'm coming after you. You understand me?"

"More than you know," she said.

Jack switched off the phone and buried it in his pocket.

# 61
.

At 5:30 A.M. the runners were gathering at Cartagena traffic circle. This was a regular Saturday morning ritual in Coral Gables, the predawn gathering of bodies clad in Nike shorts and spandex, ready to head out on a ten- or fifteen-mile run before the rest of the world rose for breakfast. Himself an occasional runner, Jack admired them in a way, but mostly he regarded them as the South Florida version of those crazy Scandinavians who cut holes in the Arctic ice and jumped in for a refreshing dip in mid-January.

Rosa wasn't answering her cell phone, but Jack found her exactly where he'd expected, her leg propped up on the fence as she stretched out her hamstrings.

"What are you doing here, Swyteck?"

"I have to talk to you."

"I have to run. Literally."

Her friends seemed annoyed by the intrusion, each of them checking their ultraprecise wristwatches/heart-monitors/speedometers.

Jack whispered in her ear, "Theo's been kidnapped."

She shot him a look, as if to say, *Are you shittin' me?*

"I'm totally serious," he said.

Rosa told her friends to go on without her, then followed Jack to an isolated spot beneath a banyan tree where they could talk in private. In minutes he brought her completely up to speed, ending with his conversation with Katrina.

"Why didn't you call me last night?"

"I wasn't sure I should call anyone, since I agreed not to call the police."

"So why are you telling me now?"

"Because I haven't been able to sleep. Things are happening so fast, I need another brain to process it all. I don't want to be wrong."

"You were right about one thing. Theo didn't run."

"I knew Theo was no murderer."

"Well, back up a second. Just because he didn't run doesn't mean he didn't kill Jessie Merrill."

He considered her words, appreciating the distinction. "You still think he might have killed her?"

"I don't know."

"Katrina told me on the phone that her company probably killed a woman in Georgia to cash in on a viatical settlement. Seems to me they did the same thing with Jessie."

"Except that Jessie was healthy."

"What difference does that make?"

"Someone with AIDS is expected to die. So it doesn't raise red flags if the viatical company hastens the process. Especially if you go to the trouble of doing ten different clients under ten different company names, which is apparently the way they did it. But Jessie Merrill was a totally different situation. She wasn't sick, wasn't expected to die. Killing her immediately raised red flags. The thugs that Katrina worked for had to be smart enough to have known that."

"We're talking about the Russian *Mafiya*, not Russian scientists. You get these guys pissed enough, all intelligence goes out the window."

"Maybe."

"It's not just a maybe. It's certainly more likely that they did it than Theo."

"Yes, if you look at it strictly from that perspective. But there's other evidence to consider."

"Like what?"

"For example, what does this new information about the viatical companies do to your theory about the angle of the cut?"

"I don't think it affects it one way or another."

"You said it was probably a left-handed person who slit Jessie's wrist."

"So what? I'm sure the Russian *Mafiya* has plenty of left-handed hit men."

"I'm sure they do. But answer me this: Is Theo right-handed or left-handed?"

"Right-handed. Ha! In your face."

"In your dreams."

"What does that mean?"

"This theory you have about the angle of the cut. Don't you find it odd that the medical examiner's report doesn't even make mention of it?"

"No. The angle is subtle, I'll admit. And a left-handed killer doesn't fit the prosecutor's theory of the case, so, of course, the report doesn't mention it."

"That's a little cynical," she said. "Don't you think?"

"Theo sat on death row for a murder he didn't commit. We have a right to be cynical."

"We? *We* have a right? You're not his lawyer any-more, Jack."

"No. I'm his friend."

"Which is why I'm so worried. Just a take step back, play devil's advocate the way any good lawyer would."

"How do you mean?"

"You say the medical examiner doesn't see the same angle on the cut because a left-handed killer doesn't suit the prosecutor's theory of the case. Well, maybe—just maybe—you do see the angle because a *right*-handed killer doesn't fit *your* theory of the case."

"But you saw it, too. I showed you the autopsy photo, and you said you saw the angle."

"Damn it, Jack. *You're* right-handed. Don't you think I wanted to see something that says the killer was left-handed?"

"Are you still wondering if I killed Jessie?"

"No. Not at all. But believe me, the way the evidence is falling out, I'll grab at anything that makes it easier for me to prove you didn't."

"When I showed you the photo of Jessie's wrist, did you see the angle or not?"

"I saw it, but only after you insisted that it was there. I'd feel a whole lot more sure of this theory if the medical examiner had seen it first."

Jack searched for a rebuttal, but nothing came. "Okay," he said calmly. "Okay."

"All I'm saying is that maybe you shouldn't be so sure about this left-handed, right-handed stuff."

"You're saying more than that. You're saying, don't be so sure that Theo isn't the killer."

"Okay. Maybe I am."

"Don't worry. Right now, the only thing I'm sure of

is that I came here hoping that you'd help me sort things out."

"And?"

He walked toward the fence, watched the line of runners streaming down the footpath along the canal. "And now I'm just more confused."

# 62

After a long night with Theo, Katrina went home for supplies. It was early Saturday morning, and she was working on little sleep. She went to the refrigerator and poured herself a little pick-me-up, a mixture of orange and carrot juice. Then she crossed the kitchen and switched to the early-morning local news broadcast. She caught the tail end of the morning's lead story, the indictment of Theo Knight for Jessie's murder. It was the same lead as last night, with slightly more emphasis on the shooting death of Dr. Marsh and the fact that his body was found in his car by Jack Swyteck, right beside an abandoned Volkswagen that belonged to Theo Knight.

Katrina kept one eye on the television screen as the news anchor closed with a comment that Katrina could have scripted: "Neither Theo Knight nor his attorney were available for comment."

She switched off the set. Just what she'd needed, another kick-in-the-head reminder that she had to do something about Theo. Twenty-four hours was all the time she'd bought from Swyteck. She hoped it was enough.

"Good morning, Katrina."

She whirled, so startled that she dropped her juice glass. It shattered at her feet. A man was on the patio outside her kitchen, just on the other side of the sliding screen door. She was about to scream when he said, "It's me, Yuri."

She took a good look. She'd heard plenty about Yuri, but during her eight-month undercover stint, she'd met him only once, briefly, when he'd come to do business with Vladimir.

"You scared me to death."

"Am I not welcome?"

She opened the screen door and said, "To be honest, a knock would have been nice."

He stepped inside. Then he knocked—three times, each one separated by a needlessly long pause. It might have been his idea of a joke, but he wasn't smiling. He didn't look like the kind of guy who smiled much.

He pulled the screen door shut, and the sliding glass door, too. Then he locked it. "You have no reason to be afraid of me. You know that, don't you?"

He gave her a look that made her nervous, but she tried not to show it. "Of course."

His expression didn't change. It was the same cold, assessing look.

Katrina grabbed a paper towel and cleaned up the broken glass and juice on the floor, then tossed the mess in the trash can. Yuri was still watching her every move.

"Can I get you anything?" she asked. "Coffee, juice?"

No response. He pulled a chair away from the kitchen table, turned it around, and straddled it with his arms resting atop the back of it. "Where you been all night?"

"Out."

"Out where?"

"Just out." She folded her arms and leaned against the refrigerator, as if to say it was none of his business.

Again, he was working her over with that penetrating stare, making her feel as if it were her turn to talk even though he'd said nothing.

"You sure you don't want anything to drink?"

"Tell me something, Katrina. How's the dirty-blood business?"

She shrugged, rolling with his sudden change of subject. "Fine."

"You know, we invented the blood bank."

"We?"

"Russians. Most people don't know it, but blood banks never existed until the Soviets started taking blood out of cadavers in the 1930s. This was something I didn't believe until a doctor showed me an old film about it. Soviet doctors figured out that there was a point, after someone died, before rigor mortis, and before the bacteria spread throughout the body, where you could actually take the blood from the dead body and use it."

She said nothing, not sure exactly what point he was trying to make.

"Can you imagine that, Katrina? Taking blood from cadavers?"

With that, she realized where this was headed. It was as if he somehow knew that she'd snooped through Vladimir's computer and discovered the truth about that woman in Georgia who'd turned up dead—short about three liters of AIDS-infected blood.

"Have you ever heard of such a thing?" he asked more pointedly.

"No."

He smiled, but it wasn't a warm smile. "Vladimir always trusted you, you know that?"

"We worked well together."

"I always thought it was because he wanted to get you into bed."

"So did I, until I saw a picture of his daughter. We look a lot alike."

"Lucky you. I, on the other hand, don't care who you look like. And I am far less trusting."

"He told me."

"Of course he did. Vladimir had a habit of sharing things he didn't need to share. That's why he had to leave."

"He's gone?"

"He had some vacation time coming. But that's neither here nor there. What's important is that you and I have to get past this trust issue."

"I thought the Theo Knight hit was supposed to resolve all that."

"It was."

"So, what's left to resolve? You found his car, didn't you?"

"Right where you said it would be. As a matter of fact, I drove it over to Dr. Marsh's house last night."

"What for?"

"Theo had good reason to kill him. Thought I'd do my part to make sure the cops keep racing right down that rabbit hole."

"I saw the news. Dr. Marsh is dead."

"You bet he is. Deader than Theo Knight."

Katrina felt chills. "What's that supposed to mean?"

"Just that I know for certain that Dr. Marsh is dead."

"So is Theo Knight."

"Is he?"

"You think I'd lie about something like this?" she said with a nervous chuckle.

"Probably not. But humor me. Tell me exactly how Theo Knight went down."

"Not much to tell."

"I'm a detail guy. Let's hear 'em."

"I hid in the back seat, waited for him to come out from the bar when his shift ended. Put a gun to his head and told him to drive out west to the warehouse district. Found us a suitable canal. Told him to get out and walk to the edge of the water. And that was it."

"You're leaving out the best part. I want to know exactly how you did it."

"Shot him in the head."

"Silencer?"

"Yes, of course."

"Which side of the head?"

"Back. One shot."

"How close?"

"Less than an inch."

"The end of the barrel touching his skull or not?"

"Uhm, could have been touching. Real close."

He rose and walked across the room, straight toward her. Katrina didn't move, but she felt her body tense up, bracing for something.

He stopped at her side, formed his hand into the shape of a gun, and pressed his finger to the back of her head. "Like this?"

"More or less."

"At that range, the bullet must have exited through his face."

"It did. Right through the forehead."

He stepped away and nodded, but she could tell he didn't believe her. In fact, she felt baited.

"That's strange," he said. "All the hits I've ever done with a .22-caliber, never once has there been an exit wound."

"Is that so?"

"That's the beauty of a .22. That's why it's the preferred weapon of professionals. Doesn't have enough force to pass through the skull twice. It's not like a .38 or a 9-millimeter, in the left side, out the right. A .22 goes in one side and bounces off the inside of the skull, ricochets around until it turns the brain to scrambled eggs."

She fell silent.

"Are you absolutely sure that your little .22-caliber slug came out his forehead, Katrina?"

"Of course I'm sure. Maybe it never happened that way for you, but there's a first time for everything."

"Except the first one doesn't count if there are no witnesses."

"You expected me to off him in public?"

"No. But if I'm ever going to trust you, I expect you to do it in front of me."

"Too late. Theo's dead."

"Then we find another."

"Another?"

"Yeah." His dark eyes brightened, as if this was what he lived for. "There's always another."

# 63

·

Jack returned home at dawn. He tiptoed past the bed, squinting as the first rays of morning sunlight cut across the room. Cindy stirred on the other side of the mattress.

"Where you been?" she asked, yawning.

"All over, checking things out."

"I was worried about you. I tried calling you."

He dug his cell phone from his pocket. The battery was dead. "Sorry. I've been unreachable and didn't even know it."

"Did you find out anything about Theo?"

"I think so. Go back to sleep. I didn't mean to wake you."

He watched her head sink back into the pillow, then lowered himself gently onto the edge of the mattress. The doorbell rang, giving them both a start.

"Now what?" he said, groaning.

"Probably a reporter. Ignore it, please."

"I'd better check it out." He took the long route

through the kitchen, where he dropped his cell phone in the battery charger on the counter. The doorbell rang once more as he reached the foyer and peered through the peep hole. The sight of Katrina on his front porch kicked up his pulse a notch.

"Just a minute," he said, then quickly returned to the bedroom. Cindy was out of bed and pulling on her blue jeans. "Who is it?" she asked.

"Katrina. That government informant Theo and I were dealing with."

"What does she want?"

"I'm not sure," he said as he walked to the dresser. He opened the top drawer, removed the trigger lock from his revolver, and slipped the gun into his pant's waist. He pulled on a long, baggy sweatshirt to hide the bulge.

"Jack, what are you doing?"

"Don't worry, she works for the government as a CI. I'm sure it's fine. But with Theo missing and Dr. Marsh dead, we can't be too careful."

"Jack—"

"Just stay here until I say it's okay to come out. And keep one hand on the telephone. If it sounds like anything is going wrong out there, you dial 911."

"You're scaring me."

"Just stay here. I'll be right back."

He returned to the foyer, took a deep breath. *She's a government informant*, he reminded himself, though as a former prosecutor he knew better than to put much trust in that. At the moment, however, he didn't see a better way to find his friend. With caution, he opened the door.

"Can I come in?" she said.

With a jerk of the head he signaled her inside and let

her pass. Then he locked up behind her and led her into the living room.

She took a seat on the edge of the couch and asked, "Are we alone?"

"Yeah," he lied. "Cindy's at her mother's house."

"Good. Because it's time we talked."

"I'm all for that. But first, Theo. Do you have the answer to my question—the album title?"

"I do." She handed him a small slip of paper.

Jack recognized the handwriting as Theo's, and the answer was exactly what he was looking for: *Thank You for . . . F.U.M.L. (Fucking Up My Life).*

He smiled to himself, then tucked the paper into his pocket. "All right. You just bought yourself a few more hours. But I want to know what's going on."

She took a seat on the leather ottoman, then popped back onto her feet. She seemed wired, and Jack sensed it was nerves, not coffee.

"I'm not sure where to start."

"Why did you take my friend? I want the real reason."

She looked away, then back, as if not sure how to answer even a simple question. "I've been undercover for almost eight months. You know that from our first meeting."

"Our second meeting. At our first, you kickboxed me into the emergency room."

"Good point. Because you understand that it's impossible to play this role without being asked to do things I don't want to do."

"It's every informant's dilemma."

"And I've been fine with it. Until last week. I was given an assignment. Basically, it boiled down to this: Kill Theo or be killed."

Jack went cold. "So you kidnapped him."

"I hid him away. For his own safety."

"You're an informant. Don't you think it would have been smarter just to go to the police?"

"Theo had the same reaction," she said, shaking her head. "But I can't hand this off to the police now. I've invested too much."

"Invested what?"

She was pacing again. "It's no coincidence that I work at Viatical Solutions. I sought this company out, gathered up all the dirt I could, then went to the U.S. attorney and offered to work as an informant."

"And they just went for it?"

"I played it pretty smart. They thought I was a mobster's ex-girlfriend, pissed off and eager to blow the whistle."

"But you weren't."

She shook her head. "I knew I was going to steep myself deep in this company to get the information I needed. The only way to avoid going to jail some day was to turn government informant."

"So what's your real agenda?"

She stopped pacing and looked right at Jack. "There's a guy I've been looking for. He used to own a factory in Prague, which was basically a front for a criminal racket he ran. Drugs, prostitution. It took me a long time, but I finally tracked him to Miami. From everything I've found so far, I'm pretty sure he's working for Viatical Solutions."

"And you want to find him because . . ."

"Because of what he did to me and to a friend of mine named Beatriz. It's personal."

Jack wanted to ask, but she didn't seem inclined to elaborate. "What's his name?"

"I don't know. I'm not even sure what he looks like,

exactly. The closest I ever got to him was looking at the back of his head from the back seat of his car."

"Aren't you worried that he might recognize you first?"

"I looked much different then. Short hair, thirty pounds thinner."

Jack found it hard to imagine her thirty pounds thinner, but it gave some insight into how she must have lived. "How will you know you've got the right guy?"

"I just need a little more time to check things out. Then I'll know."

"Then what?"

"After all this time and effort, I don't intend to shake his hand. But I got a bigger problem right now. As my Russian friends like to say, the house is burning, and the clock is ticking."

"What does that mean?"

She stepped toward the window, peeled back the drapery panel just enough to see across the lawn. Then she faced Jack and said, "I've got a new boss at Viatical Solutions. And something tells me he's looking for the hat trick."

"Hat trick?"

"A little Russian hockey analogy. A hat trick is three goals."

"I know. But I don't understand the context."

"First Jessie. Then Marsh. Now he wants the third son of a bitch who scammed him."

"Are you saying . . ."

"He doesn't believe Theo's dead, so I've got one last chance to prove myself. Which means I have to think fast and figure out what I'm going to do with you."

Jack took a half-step back. "*Do* with me?"

She looked him in the eye and said, "You're my next assignment."

# 64

•

Each breath carried Cindy more deeply into sleep, though it felt like something beyond the realm of sleep, a numbing paralysis that tingled all the way to the tips of her fingers. A simple effort to raise her heavy eyelids was enough to send the room spinning. A burning sensation tinged her nostrils. It wasn't that she couldn't remember what had happened. It had all just happened so fast, the moment she'd stepped into the master bathroom—the blur of motion behind her, the muscular arm around her waist, and the pungent rag that covered her mouth and nose. In a matter of moments, she felt limp. But she was battling it, refusing to be overpowered.

She'd managed to hear most of what Jack and Katrina were saying. The living room was down the hall from her, but sound traveled well in their little two-bedroom house, especially in the stillness of morning. She'd heard enough to know that it was time to dial 911. That was when she'd grabbed the cordless telephone on the nightstand and run into the bathroom. It was suddenly coming clearer to her now. The perfectly round hole that had been cut into the glass door that led to the solarium outside their bathroom. The ambush from behind her. And something else was coming back to her, too.

She seemed to recall that there had been no dial tone. Yes, the phone was dead. That much she definitely recalled, and the fear that flourished in that brief, lucid moment gave her another kick of adrenaline. Part of her knew that she should have been completely unconscious by now, but she wouldn't allow it. Instinct was taking over. It was an almost inexplicable, involuntary, high-gear response to the realization that someone had broken into their house and that Jack was with Katrina, completely unaware. He was in danger and she needed to help. She liked to think it was love that drove her, a kind of love she'd harbored for a long time, as long as she could remember. The feeling was familiar to her, but she was somehow finding it easier to associate that feeling with the distant past than with present events. She tried to resist whatever it was that was pulling her in that direction, fought off the effects of the drug. But she could feel her mind slipping. She found herself retreating to that time and place long ago, where she'd first been tempted to act on her impulse, the God-given instinct to protect a man she loved. Or at least to protect his name.

It had happened when she was nine years old, just two months after her father had committed suicide.

•

A grinding noise emerged from behind the bathroom door, the girls' bathroom on the second floor. Cindy stepped out of her room and listened. It definitely wasn't an electric hair dryer or anything else she'd ever heard coming out of the bathroom. She started down the hall and tried the door knob. The noise stopped.

"Go away!" her sister shouted.

"What are you doing in there?"

"Get out of here!"

The grinding noise was back. Cindy shrugged, then took a bobby pin from her ballerina-style bun and stuck it in the key hole. The lock clicked, and the door popped open.

Celeste grabbed the blender and screamed. "You idiot!"

Cindy was unfazed. She walked in and inspected the mess on the counter. "What are you making?"

"A milkshake. Now will you get out of here, please?"

"Can I have some?"

"No. But if you're going to come in here, at least close the door."

Cindy pushed the door shut, and Celeste locked it. Cindy leaned over the blender and smelled the concoction. "Yuck. It smells like fish."

"Things that are good for you never smell good."

"Is there really fish in there?"

"No, genius. It comes in a bottle."

Cindy checked the label. "Is it really good for you?"

"Yes."

"Then let's pour in some more," she said as she tipped the bottle.

Her sister grabbed it, stopped her. "No. A little is good for you. Too much can kill you."

"Kill you?"

"Yes. Too much is like poison."

"What's in it?"

"Medicine."

"What kind of medicine?"

"None of your business."

"Where'd you get it?"

"One of the high school girls. A senior."

Cindy grabbed the bottle and read the label. "E-R-G-O. What are you taking that for?"

"I said, it's none of your business."

"Tell me or I'll ask Mom."

Celeste shot her an angry look and snatched the bottle back. "I'm taking it because I think I'm pregnant, okay?"

Cindy's mouth fell open. "You were with a boy?"

"No."

"Then how'd you get pregnant?"

Celeste lowered her eyes and said, "I've been having dreams."

"What kind of dreams?"

"About Dad. He comes to me."

Cindy felt her blood begin to boil. "And?"

"At night sometimes, I hear him outside my bedroom window. The leaves crunch every time he makes a step. Then I get up, but I'm not really awake. I can see myself walking down the hall, downstairs. I go to the back door and open it. I see nothing but these swirling leaves in the wind. But then suddenly he's there, and I don't know how, but I'm naked, and he's there, like it used to be, and—"

"Stop it!"

"He pulls me on top of him, and—"

"Celeste, you're a liar!"

"I'm not lying! You were just too young. He would have come for you too, if he hadn't killed himself. He might still come."

"Girls!"

They froze. Their mother was outside the door.

"What's going on in there?"

Celeste went to the door and opened it a crack. "It's okay, Mom."

Cindy listened as her sister and mother talked it out through the slightly opened door. Celeste had turned her back on her sister, and Cindy felt a sudden urge to grab something and hit her over the back of the head, exactly the way she'd felt when Celeste had ruined their father's graveside service with her lies. Cindy could even see it in her mind, Celeste falling to the floor all bloody and unconscious. Celeste and her false accusations. No one had ever spelled it out for her, but Cindy knew it was true: Celeste had driven their own father to suicide, taken him away from her.

Celeste was pleading with their mother, trying to assure her that they weren't up to any mischief and that there was no reason for her to barge in. Cindy grabbed the bottle of ergo and took a good, long look at the label. She wasn't sure what it was, but Celeste had given her all the information she needed. A little was medicine; a lot was poison. She glanced at the "milkshake" on the counter, and a thought came over her.

What might happen if she poured Celeste a little more?

•

"Welcome back," the man said.

Cindy looked up into his cold, dark eyes. Her face was right in front of her, then gone, then back again. It was as if each blink of her eyes lasted several seconds. He put something beneath her nose, and she jerked back violently. Smelling salts, she realized. Slowly, she felt her body coming back to life.

"I need you to stand on your own two feet now," he said as he pulled her up from the bathroom floor.

Her legs wobbled, and she braced her body against his.

"That's it," he said. "You'll be fine in a few minutes. Unless you do something stupid."

Cindy tried to speak, but her mouth couldn't form words. He pried her jaws apart and shoved something long and cold into her mouth until it pressed against the back of her throat. She could taste metal. She could smell the powder from a gun that had been fired many times before. She saw the evil look in his eyes. It felt a lot like a place she'd been before, five years earlier, with a madman named Esteban—a place to which she'd never wanted to return. Her heart pounded, and she was suddenly alert.

"Nothing stupid, you hear me?"

Cindy nodded.

"Okay," he said as he nudged her forward. "Let's go."

# 65
.

"Nobody move," said Yuri, his voice booming across the living room.

Katrina and Jack froze. Yuri had Cindy in front of him with a gun to her head, using her as a human shield. The fear in her eyes was more than Jack could handle.

"Let go of my wife!"

"Shut up!" said Yuri.

"Who are you?" said Jack.

"His name's Yuri," said Katrina. "What do you want?"

"I want you to do as you're told."

"I can't do that."

"So I heard. Did you really think I was foolish enough to send you here alone and not follow you? I heard everything you said."

"Then you're the man. I guess you're just going to have to do Jack Swyteck yourself."

He shoved the gun into Cindy's cheek. "You'll do as you're told. Or I'll kill his wife."

"You're going to kill her anyway."

"Stop," said Jack. "Let her go, Yuri, or whatever your name is. Then you and I can get in your car, and we'll go to a nice quiet place in the woods. You can do whatever it is you need to do with me. Just let Cindy go."

"Oh, aren't you the hero?" he said, scoffing. Then his smile faded. "Down on the floor, Swyteck. Face-first."

Jack didn't move. Yuri tightened his grip on Cindy's throat. Her eyes bulged, and she gasped audibly. "I said, get down!"

Jack lowered himself to the rug.

"Hands behind your head."

Jack locked his fingers as commanded.

"Very good. Now, Katrina. Let's do what we came here to do."

She glared at Yuri, then glanced at Jack on the floor. The room was silent. Slowly, she reached inside her jacket and removed her .22.

" 'Atta girl," said Yuri. "Now move closer. Remember what I told you about the bullet in the brain. I want to see you use that .22 the way it's supposed to be used."

She crossed the living room, then stopped at the edge of the rug. She was close, but not so close that Jack could reach out and grab her ankle.

"Don't do this, Katrina."

"Put a sock in it, Swyteck," said Yuri. "I'm trying to be a nice guy. I'm giving you the privilege of dying with the faint hope that I might actually let your wife live. One more word, and I'm taking that away from you."

A tense silence fell over the room. Katrina could hear the sound of her own breathing.

Yuri narrowed his eyes and said, "Do it, Katrina."

She could feel her palm sweating as she squeezed the handle of her gun and pointed the barrel in Jack's direction.

"That's it," said Yuri.

She had one eye on Jack, the other on Yuri. Her finger caressed the trigger.

"Do it!"

Her hand was shaking, but her thoughts were coming clear. "This doesn't make sense."

"Stop stalling."

"There are so many easier ways to do this."

"This is the way I want to do it. Now pull the trigger!"

"Why? Why are you making *me* do it?"

"Because I can. Now shoot him!"

"Why? Why is it so important to you that *I* do it?"

"Don't you dare disobey me. I know who you are, you little slut. Did you honestly think you could fool me?"

"What?"

"If I can get you to snip the hairs off your pussy and hand them over to me in a plastic bag, surely I can talk you into pulling the trigger. This is what you are. I know what you're made of, and I own you. It's like I used to say, remember? No decision we make is meaningless. We all determine our own fate. Now do as you're told. Kill him!"

It was him, she realized, and the discovery cut to her core. Bits and pieces of information she'd gathered over the last few months had suggested that he was the man she'd been looking for, and now there was no denying it. Something snapped inside her, a fury sparked by the sickening reality of what drove this pervert. It was all about domination and control, from her friend Beatriz who was killed in his factory for refusing to give her body to him, to her own indignity of selling pubic clippings in a bag—and the truly unspeakable things she was forced to do at gunpoint when the clippings just weren't enough. She couldn't be certain that he'd murdered that woman with AIDS in Georgia, but only this creep was low enough to sell the blood of his victims. *We all determine our own fate.*

She wheeled and fired a shot across the room. Muffled by a silencer, it whistled past Yuri and shattered the vase on the wall unit.

Yuri fired back, another muted volley. But this one found its mark. Katrina fell to the ground. A hot, wet explosion erupted beneath her jacket. Her gun fell to the floor, then she fell beside it.

"Cindy!" said Jack.

A final, deadly quiet shot hissed from Yuri's pistol, and Jack went down behind the couch. Katrina tried to raise her head, and managed to get it an inch above the floor. Just enough to see Yuri ducking into the kitchen with his hostage in tow.

## 66

Jack kept moving, rolling from his hiding place behind the couch toward Katrina. Yuri's bullet had torn a hole through a sofa cushion. On his hands and knees he snaked his way past the ottoman and found Katrina on a blood-soaked rug. She was lying on her back, grimacing with pain.

"How bad is it?" she asked.

Jack tugged at her neckline to expose the wound. It was just below the collarbone. "Didn't hit a major organ. Just gotta stop the bleeding."

"Pressure," she said.

He grabbed a pillow from the couch and pressed it to the wound. Out of the corner of his eye he spotted the cordless phone on the cocktail table. He grabbed it and hit TALK. "Dead," he said.

"I'm sure he cut the phone lines."

"Do you have a cell phone?"

"Not on me. You?"

"In the freakin' kitchen. It's in the battery charger."

A voice boomed from the other side of the swinging door. "How's everybody doing out there?"

"Fantastic," said Jack. "You really know how to throw a party."

Katrina grabbed his elbow, shushing him. "Don't answer him. I'll talk. Keep this between me and him."

"It's *not* between you and him. He's got my wife."

Yuri said, "Everybody stays put. If I hear a door open, a window slide, anything that remotely sounds like someone running for help, I put a bullet in this pretty head. And don't even think about using a cell phone."

Katrina replied, "Whatever you say, Yuri." Then she looked at Jack and whispered, "So long as I keep him talking, you'll know where he is. Is there another way into that kitchen, other than through the swinging doors?"

"Off the hallway to the bedrooms."

"Good. That's your entrance. If I keep him talking, he'll be distracted. How good are you with a gun?"

He pulled his Smith & Wesson from under his sweatshirt. "Good enough to have shot you before you shot me."

"I wasn't going to shoot you," she said.

"I know. That's why I didn't pull it."

"Pulling it is one thing. Can you use it?"

"I carried a gun as a prosecutor. I've taken tons of target practice."

"Then we're in business."

"What's the alternative?"

"There is none. If I'm right about this guy, he's Georgian, part of the *Kurganskaya*. Elite hitmen. Even the Italian Mafia uses them. He's not going to let anyone walk out of here alive. So, you up for it or not?"

"Yeah. I'm in."

"Good. You'll have the advantage with the .38. Yuri's shooting a .22. Smaller slugs, a little more erratic from a distance. That's why he only winged me. You're actually better off not getting too close."

"How close do you think I should get?"

"You'll get one shot. That's all. Get close enough to make it count."

Jack felt butterflies in his stomach. "All right. Let's go."

"Hey, Yuri," she shouted. "This is pretty funny, isn't it? After eight months of collecting blood for you, here I am, bleeding to death on the floor."

Jack waited for an answer, but none came. At Katrina's signal, he started his crawl across the living room toward the main hallway.

"It was a good plan, Yuri. I thought it was especially clever the way you set up all those dummy viatical corporations. One for Jessie Merrill in Florida. One for Jody Falder in Georgia. Tell me something, though. Is there another victim for every single one of those companies you created?"

Jack kept moving across the oak floor, elbows and knees. He was trying to stay focused on his mission, play out the attack in his mind. But it was hard to ignore the things Katrina was saying.

"Every last one of them was going to die anyway," said Yuri.

"Except for Jessie Merrill."

"You think I killed her?"

"Seems exactly like the kind of person you'd love to kill. A young and beautiful woman who played you for a fool."

Jack stopped. Katrina's voice was growing weaker in the distance. He was within two meters of the hallway entrance to the kitchen. He waited for Yuri's reply to gauge his distance from the target.

"Fuck you, Katrina."

Short and sweet, but it was enough for Jack to guesstimate that Yuri was on the far side of the kitchen, near the two-way swinging door that led to the dining room.

"Touchy subject for you?" she said.

"Cut the crap, Katrina. I know what you're trying to do."

Silence fell over the entire house. Jack was inches away from making the turn into the kitchen. He grasped his revolver with both hands, drew his body into a crouch. He was at the ready.

"Swyteck!" said Yuri. "Where are you?"

The question sent Jack's heart racing.

"Answer me," said Yuri. "Reveal your position right now."

Jack braced himself against the wall. He had to make a move. Charge in? Roll and shoot? He wasn't sure. He said a five-second prayer.

"I'm going to count to three," said Yuri. "If I don't hear your voice, that's how long your wife has left on this planet. One."

Jack took a deep breath.

"Two. Th—"

Jack dived through the opening and took aim with his .38. In the blur that was his entrance, he caught sight of the swinging door flying open at the other end of the kitchen. Katrina rushed Yuri, screaming wildly to unnerve him, and Cindy screamed back. Yuri fired a shot, but it came just as Cindy was breaking free from his grasp. The bullet sailed wildly across the kitchen and took out the window over the sink. Cindy dived to the floor, and for a split second Yuri was standing in the center of the kitchen without his human shield.

Jack kept rolling to make himself a moving target. Yuri fired again but hit the oven door. Jack returned the fire, his .38 clapping like thunder in comparison to Yuri's silenced projectiles. It happened fast, but it seemed like slow motion. The recoil of the revolver. The shot ringing out. The flash of powder from the end of the barrel. The look on Yuri's face that changed in an instant. In what felt like the very same moment in time, Yuri was staring at Jack through the penetrating eyes of an assassin, and then the eyes were gone. His head snapped back in a blinding crimson blur.

Yuri fell to the floor, a lifeless thud, blood oozing from his shattered eye socket.

Jack was momentarily frozen, until he could comprehend what he'd seen. Then he ran to Cindy. She was crying, crouched in the corner beside the refrigerator. Jack held her. She was shaking in his arms.

"Are you okay?"

Tears ran down her face, but she nodded.

Katrina groaned from the other side of the room. Jack rose and saw her lying on the floor. He rushed to her side. "Hang on, Katrina. I'm going to get help."

"I'll be okay. I think."

"Cindy, my cell phone's in the charger. Call 911. Hurry!"

Jack checked Katrina's wound once more. It was still bleeding, but he sensed there was still time. If they were quick about it.

"Cindy, did you hear me?"

She didn't answer.

He rose and started toward the phone, then froze. Cindy was standing in the center of the kitchen, visibly shaken, yet managing to point Yuri's gun straight at her husband.

"Cindy, what are you doing?"

"I'm sorry," she said, her voice quaking. "This craziness. I can't take it anymore. It's all your fault."

"Cindy, just give me the gun, okay?"

"Stay away from me!"

He stopped in his tracks. She wiped tears from her eyes with the back of her sleeve, but she kept the gun pointed at his chest.

"Have you found your son yet?" she asked.

"What?"

"The son she gave you. She told me all about it herself."

"When?"

"After you discovered that she'd scammed you. She called me."

"For what?"

"She played that audiotape for me. The one of you two in bed."

"You told me that it had come from the detectives."

"It did. But by then I'd already heard it from the source."

Jack winced, confused. She was starting to scare him. "Why did she play you the tape?"

"She wanted to tell me that she'd had your baby. And that you two were together again."

"If she said that, she was lying."

"Was she?"

Jack heard a gurgling noise behind him. Katrina was fading. "Cindy, give me the gun. We can work this out. This woman needs a doctor."

Her voice grew louder, filled with emotion. "I don't care what she needs, damn it! Can't you just take ten seconds of your life and let it be about me?"

"She could die, can't you see that?"

"She's dying, you're dying, we're all dying. I'm sick of this, Jack. I swear, the only time I see love in your eyes is when I wake up from a nightmare in the middle of the night or hear a strange noise outside my window and need you to hold me and tell me everything's going to be okay."

"What are you talking about?"

"You know what I'm talking about. Isn't that what you really love about me?"

"No."

"Liar! You love it that I *need* you. That's all you love. So you and your Jessie Merrill can just burn in hell together. I don't need you anymore."

Jack couldn't speak. He tried to make eye contact, but it was as if she were looking right through him. She was crying, but it didn't seem like tears of sorrow. Just an outpouring of some pent-up emotion he'd never seen before.

"Cindy," he said in a soft, even tone. "What did you do to Jessie?"

Her expression went cold, but she said nothing.

"Cindy, talk to me."

A calmness washed over her. Jack no longer saw tears, and her body seemed to have stopped shaking. He watched the barrel of the gun as it turned away from him.

"That's it. Give me the gun."

It kept moving, first to one side, then up. Farther up. She glanced at Yuri's body on the floor, then spoke in an empty voice. "It's like the man said: We all determine our own fate."

Jack watched in horror as she took aim at her own temple.

"No!" he cried as he lunged toward her. He fell with his full weight against her, taking her down, grabbing for the gun, trying to avert one more senseless tragedy. Somewhere in the tumble he felt her hand jerk forward.

The next thing he heard was the sickening, muffled sound of one final bullet blasting from the silencer.

## 67

Jack had a view of the restrooms from his seat in the hospital waiting room. Cindy's mother was off to his left, several rows of seats separating them. Over the course of two hours, they'd made eye contact once. He'd just happened to look up and caught her shooting death rays in his direction.

A little after eleven o'clock, the doctor came out to see them. "Mr. Swyteck?"

Evelyn jumped from her seat and came between them. "I'm Cindy's mother."

"I'm Dr. Blanco. The good news is your daughter—your wife—is going to be just fine. She dodged a bullet. Literally. It scorched a path right past her ear. Right down to the skull. Still, it's in the superficial category."

Jack asked, "What about Katrina, the woman who came in the same ambulance? How's she?"

"She's in recovery. Lost a lot of blood, but she made it here in time. I'd expect a full recovery. Probably a couple months of rehab on the shoulder."

"Can we talk about my daughter, please?" said Evelyn. "When can she come home?"

"That's a little problematic. With any self-inflicted wound, we don't want to rush these things. Before I make any promises, I want to get a psychiatric evaluation."

"That seems wise," said Jack.

"Psychiatric?" said Evelyn. "She's not a—I mean, she's a bright girl. She's just been under so much stress."

"Stress may be part of it. But let's get a professional to take a look at the whole picture. Then we can make a judgment."

"When can I see her?"

"That's something our psychiatrist should determine. You can wait here, if you like. I'll send someone down from psych just as soon as I can." He offered a polite smile, shook their hands, and was on his way.

Jack returned to his seat. Evelyn started toward hers, then stopped and turned back. She took the seat across from Jack but said nothing. She just stared.

"I'm sorry for all this, Evelyn."

"You should be."

"No need to beat me up. I'll be beating myself up over this for a long time. It's so obvious to me now."

"What's so obvious?"

"Cindy and Jessie. There's no good reason for Jessie's body to have been found in my own house. Unless Cindy killed her."

"Do you honestly believe that Cindy is capable of murder?"

"No. But the little things are starting to add up now. I remember one of the first nights we spent in your house. Cindy was all upset because she found out she wasn't pregnant. We started talking about fertility, and she was so certain that the problem was with her, not me. Neither one of us had been tested. How would she have known it was her, unless Jessie had told her . . ." He stopped himself, suddenly uncomfortable about having this conversation with his mother-in-law.

"Told her that you had already fathered a child?"

"All I'm saying is, I just can't believe it."

"Then don't believe it. Look, Jessie may have died in your house, but Cindy wasn't even home when it happened. She was with me that whole day."

"Nice try, Evelyn. But you're not the first parent to concoct an alibi for her child."

"You listen to me, smart guy. Cindy's not well to begin with. That man Yuri knocked her out with some kind of drug and then put a gun to her head. How coherent would you be after all that? You can't take anything she said this morning at face value."

The elevator doors opened, and a woman stepped out. Jack caught her eye, and she walked toward him. Jack hadn't seen her in a while, but it seemed that the older Cindy and her sister got, the more they looked alike.

"Hello, Celeste," said Jack.

"Thanks for calling me. How's Cindy?"

"She's going to be fine."

Evelyn turned and walked away, saying nothing to her older daughter. If there was ice between her and Jack, she and Celeste were glaciers apart. Jack had never fully understood it, just accepted it as part of a strange family dynamic.

He escorted Celeste to the vending machine, well away from Evelyn, then took a few minutes to explain everything over a cold soda. He glanced toward the intake desk and saw Evelyn talking with another doctor, presumably the psychiatrist.

"Excuse me one second." He quickly crossed the waiting room and introduced himself to the doctor. As Jack had figured, she was from psych.

"As I was telling your mother-in-law, I will probably want to keep Cindy in the hospital at least overnight, mostly for observation."

"That's fine."

"If she does become violent or show some signs that she might injure herself, we may need to sedate or even restrain her. I'm not saying that's going to happen, but to be on the safe side, I'd like your written authorization to do that."

"You really think that's necessary?"

"I'm her mother. I'll sign."

Jack deferred. The doctor handed a pen and clipboard to Evelyn. She looked over the form, then took the pen. Jack watched her sign.

He tried not to show it, but it was as if he'd been hit by lightning.

"There you go," she said.

The doctor thanked her and tucked the executed form under her arm. "I should have an update for you later this evening. I'll phone you."

"Thank you, doctor."

She turned and headed for the elevator. Jack checked his watch and said, "I have to go, too."

"Fine. You're not needed."

"I'd like to stay, but the homicide detectives are already breathing down my neck."

"What's that all about?"

"Something to do with knives. Whoever killed Jessie also slashed up some pictures of me and Cindy from our wedding album. With everything that's happened now, they want to check out our collection of knives, see if the slashes in the wedding photographs came from any we own."

"They think Cindy slashed her own wedding photos?"

"If she killed Jessie out of jealousy, that would fit, wouldn't it?"

Evelyn mulled it over, then shook her head. "Just go, please. Can't you ever bring anyone good news?"

"I'll be sure to work on that." He walked away but took the long route back to the elevators, making a point of passing by Cindy's sister.

"How about a cup of coffee?" he said.

"Sure."

He led her to the elevator and punched the DOWN button. The doors opened, and they got inside. "There's something I have to talk to you about," he said.

"What?"

"Dreams."

She rocked on her heels. "What kind of dreams?"

"For a few months now, Cindy's been having this same nightmare about your father coming to her. And when he leaves, he wants to take me with him. Do you have any idea what that might be all about?"

She didn't answer.

From inside the elevator, he took one last look at his mother-in-law seated on the other side of the waiting room. Then the doors closed, and the car began its descent.

The color had drained from Celeste's face.

"I thought you might," said Jack.

"I guess maybe it's time you learned our dirty little family secret."

"I'm all ears," he said as the elevator doors parted.

# 68

•

Jack waited in the dark with the window shades shut. He was in the TV room, though he hadn't so much as switched on a light bulb, let alone the set. For almost two hours, he sat alone, familiarizing himself with every sound of the empty house. The air conditioner kicking on, then off. The hum of the refrigerator. The Westminster chime of the grandfather clock.

Celeste had given him plenty to think about. She told him how her accusations had torn the family apart. Cindy had so fervently believed that her lies had driven their father to suicide that she'd even told Celeste of her fantasies about poisoning her older sister or causing her other bodily harm. Their mother had also turned against Celeste, but there was one major difference. Cindy had eventually made peace with Celeste and came to believe that the accusations were true.

Their mother had never made peace, and she'd known the truth from the beginning.

The clock chimed. It was quarter past two. Jack

started to rise, then stopped. He heard something. He listened, then settled back into his chair. It was the sound he'd been waiting for. At last, a key turned in the lock on Evelyn's front door.

•

Evelyn hooked her umbrella on the hall tree and switched on the light. It had been raining off and on since lunchtime, and, as usual, the gods had really turned on the faucets the moment she'd decided to sprint from her car to the front door. Even a hurricane, however, would not have kept her from coming home.

She walked down the hall and headed straight for the kitchen. There was an urgency to her step. She'd played it cool for over an hour at the hospital, fighting the impulse to rush home, which would have only raised suspicions. She'd used the time wisely, considering the things Jack had told her, weighing her options. This was no time for knee-jerk reactions, but now her mission was clear. She had to get home and secure one last loose end.

She flipped on the kitchen light. Her eyes fixed on an empty space on the countertop, which puzzled her. Her heart began to race. She canvassed the entire counter, one end to the other, then back again.

*How can it not be here?*

She went to the cabinet, opened it. Bowls, mixer, can opener—everything was in its place, except the one thing she was looking for.

Her hands began to shake. It *had* to be there. She tried the cabinet under the sink, but there was only a dish rack, detergents, and some paper towels. She went down the entire row of cabinets, flinging one door open after another. She found plates, her bread maker, pots and pans. Still, no luck.

A thought came to her, and she raced to the pantry, threw open the door, then gasped.

Jack was standing inside.

"What—" she started to say, then stopped. She saw it. He was holding it, protecting it the way a running back guards a football at the goal line. Only this pigskin was made of butcher block, and it came with an assortment of handles that protruded from the slots on the top. Knife handles. He had her collection of kitchen knives.

"Looking for this, Evelyn?" he asked.

•

Jack stepped out of the pantry. Evelyn slowly backed into the kitchen. He said nothing, waiting for her to speak. She continued stepping backward until she bumped against the sink.

"What are you doing here? I thought you had a meeting with the police."

He stopped at the kitchen table and placed the knives on top of it. "There is no meeting. I lied."

"Wha-a-a-at?" she said, a nervous cackle.

"I made it up."

"Why?"

"It's the strangest thing. I was watching my grandmother slicing sheets of dough the other day. She's left-handed, so she typically cuts from the top right to the bottom left. To make a long story short, it helped me figure out that Jessie Merrill was probably killed by someone who is left-handed. It all has to do with the angle of the slash on her wrist."

"And to think you were ready to convict your wife, and she's right-handed. Shame on you."

"No, shame on you. It didn't occur to me until you and I met with the psychiatrist at the hospital. You so graciously took it upon yourself to sign the forms for Cindy's treatment. And that's when it hit me: *You're* left-handed."

"How dare you!"

He glanced at the cutlery on the table. "Which knife did you use, Evelyn?"

"This is ridiculous. The police have the knife. It was from your own kitchen. It was found floating in the bathtub with Jessie's body, exactly where you'd expect to find it with a suicide."

"I don't mean the knife you used to slash Jessie's wrist. I mean the knife you used to slash up our wedding album."

Her mouth opened, but she didn't speak.

"That's what you were looking for, wasn't it? I bluffed you into thinking that the police were looking for a match between our knives and the slashes in the wedding album. It got you to thinking: Maybe they'll come looking in your house, too."

"You're talking nonsense."

"When Cindy and I moved in with you, we took just a few personal things with us. The wedding album was one of them. Funny, but it wasn't until after we'd spent some time with you that Cindy noticed it had been mutilated. Someone had taken a knife to it."

"Probably that tramp, Jessie."

"Not her. You did it when I decided it was time to move out of your house. Cindy decided to come with me, rather than stay with you."

"You are so wrong."

"Am I? Then I don't suppose you'll mind if I take these knives downtown to have them analyzed. I noticed that one of them has a nice serrated edge. There might even be a few microscopic traces of photo paper on the blade. You'd be amazed by these lab guys and the things they can find."

Her bravado slowly faded. Her eyes filled with contempt. "This is all your fault."

"That's what Cindy said."

"If you'd truly loved her, you would have stepped aside and made it possible for her to move on and start a new life without you, without the nightmares about that deranged client of yours."

"The nightmares aren't about me or Esteban. They're about your husband. I know. I talked to Celeste."

"Celeste," she said, practically spitting out the name. "You two are just alike. But I see through your phony concern. You don't love Cindy. You love rescuing her all over again every two months, six months, a year—however long it takes for her nightmares to start up again. That's your kind of love."

"What do *you* know about love?"

"I've known this much for a very long time: Cindy will never be happy so long as you're in her life."

It was like hearing Cindy's speech all over again, only this time it was coming from the speechwriter. "You fed this to her, didn't you? You convinced her that I'm the source of all her fears."

She flashed an evil smile. "It didn't take much convincing. Especially after Jessie 'fessed up about you and her."

"Jessie was a liar. This was how she got even with me when I refused to help her wiggle out of her scam. Ruin my marriage."

"She did a very convincing job."

"Are you saying you heard her story?"

"I was sitting next to Cindy in the car when she got the call. I heard everything. Cindy didn't want to believe it. But Jessie said she had proof. She wanted to meet at your house to deliver it personally to Cindy."

"The tape?"

"Yes. The tape."

"So you and Cindy went to our house together."

"No. *I* went. Alone."

Jack paused, stunned by the admission. "You were there waiting when Jessie came by?"

"What decent mother wouldn't do that much for her only daughter?"

The reference to her *only* daughter wasn't lost on Jack. "What did you do?"

She walked as she talked, not a nervous pacing, but more like a professor who was enjoying her speech. "I was extremely polite. I just asked her to remove all of her clothes, get in the bathtub, and drink from a quart of vodka until she passed out."

"How did you get her to do that?"

"How do you think?"

"The knife?"

"Hardly." She walked a few more steps, then stopped at the end of the counter. She opened a drawer, then whirled around and pointed a gun at Jack. "With this."

Jack took a step back. "Evelyn, don't."

"What choice have you left me?"

"You won't get away with it."

"Of course I will. I came home, you startled me, I thought you were an intruder. What a tragedy. I shot my own son-in-law."

"This won't solve anything."

"Sure it will. Right now, it's my word against yours."

"Not quite."

She tightened her glare, then blinked nervously, as if sensing that Jack had something to spring.

"I'm afraid your timing is really bad," he said. "You caught me right in the middle of a conference call."

"What?"

He pointed with a nod toward the wall phone beside the refrigerator. The little orange light indicated that the line was open. "You still there, Jerry?"

"I'm here," came a voice over the speaker. It was Jerry Chafetz from the U.S. attorney's office. Jack had dialed him up the moment he'd heard Evelyn put the key in the front door.

"Mike, you there?"

He gave Mike Campbell a moment to reply, then Jack said, "Turn off the MUTE button, buddy."

There was a beep on the line, and Mike said, "Still here."

"You guys didn't hear any of that, did you?"

"Sorry," said Mike. "Couldn't help but listen. Hate to admit it, but I heard everything she said."

"Ditto," said Chafetz.

Jack tried not to smile, but he knew he had to be looking pretty smug. "Tough break, Evelyn. I'm really sorry. Your bad luck."

The gun was still aimed at Jack, but she seemed to have lost her will. Her stare had gone blank, and her hands were unsteady. It was as if she were shrinking right before his eyes.

Jack went to her and snatched away the gun. "You're right, Evelyn. I do love this rescue stuff." He took her by the arm and started for the door. "Even when Cindy isn't around."

# 69

The message on his answering machine was short and matter-of-fact. Cindy wanted to meet for lunch.

It was their first direct communication in six months, since the shoot-out in their house. Cindy had refused to let him visit in the hospital, and after her discharge they'd separated on the advice of her therapist. From that point forward, Jack's only way to contact his wife was through professionals, either her psychiatrist or her lawyer.

The blame game was deadly, but Jack found it easy to count up any number of reasons she might hate him for life. Her mother was a biggie. She'd pleaded guilty to second-degree murder, a plea bargain on a slam-bang case of murder in the first degree that at least allowed her to avoid the death penalty. And of course there was the irresolvable Jessie problem. Cindy was never going to believe that nothing had been going on between them. In truth, it didn't matter anymore.

Jack was through blaming himself.

He waited at a wrought-iron table beneath a broad Cinzano umbrella. It was a humid, sticky afternoon on South Beach, typical of late summer in the tropics. This particular café was one they'd never visited together, and he suspected that was precisely the reason Cindy had chosen it. No memories, no history, no ghosts.

"Hello, Jack," she said as she approached the table.

"Hi." Jack rose and instinctively helped with her chair. She got it herself and sat across from him, no kiss, no handshake.

"Thanks for coming," she said.

"No problem. How have you been?"

"Fine. You?"

"As good as can be expected."

The waiter came. Cindy ordered a sparkling water. Jack ordered another bourbon.

"Pretty early in the day for you, isn't it?" she asked.

"Not necessarily. I haven't slept since I got your message last night, so I'm not really sure what time of day it is."

"Sorry."

"Me, too. About a lot of things."

She looked away, seeming to focus on nothing in particular. A pack of sweaty joggers plodded by on the sidewalk. A loud Latin beat boomed from the back of a passing SUV on Ocean Drive.

"Have you found your son yet?"

Jack coughed into his drink. He'd suspected that might come up, but not right out of the starting blocks. "Uh, no."

"Are you looking?"

"No. No reason to look."

"What about the money? Jessie left the entire million and a half dollars to her son, if you can find him."

"To be honest, I'm not much interested in trying to funnel stolen money to a child who's probably perfectly happy not knowing me or his biological mother."

"But what's the alternative? Give it back to the Russian mob?"

"If I have any say, it'll go to the relatives of people like Jody Falder, and anyone else Yuri and his pack of viatical investors eliminated in order to cash in on their investments."

"That's probably as it should be."

"In due time. But at the moment, Dr. Marsh's widow is trying to prove that half of that loot is hers. She's suing Clara Pierce for fraud and mismanagement of Jessie's estate. I'm content to let those two tear each other to shreds before I take a stand."

"Good for you."

"Yeah. I guess it is."

Cindy squeezed the lemon wedge into her water. A breeze blew in from the Atlantic and sent their napkins sailing. They reached across the table to grab the same one. Their hands touched, their eyes met and held.

"Jack, there's something I want to say."

He released the napkin, broke the contact. "Tell me."

"That day in the house, when I had the gun. I said some things to you."

"You don't have to explain."

"Yes, I do. I said some very harsh things. And I want you to know that part of me will always love you. But those things I said. Some of them . . ."

"Cindy, please."

"It really is the way I feel."

He felt as though he should have been devastated, but he wasn't. "I know that."

"You know?"

"Yes. For years, your mother held such obvious hatred for me. I always wondered, why can't Evelyn put this all behind her, especially since her own daughter has forgiven me for what happened with Esteban? But now I know: You never really did forgive me, either."

"I tried. I wanted to. I've thought about this so much."

"I've been doing a lot of thinking, too. And as much as I loved you at one time . . ."

"You stopped loving me."

"No. It's not that. It's just that it wasn't love that was keeping us together. When you get right down to it, I think you stayed in this marriage because you were too afraid to be alone. Or worse, afraid of spending the rest of your life living with your mother."

"And why did you stay?"

Jack struggled, wondering if some things were better left unsaid.

She answered for him. "You stayed because you felt guilty about what happened with Esteban."

Jack lowered his eyes, but he didn't argue. "Somehow I thought that if we worked long and hard enough, things would get back to where they were. Before Esteban."

"That's fairy tales, Jack. It doesn't usually work that way in real life."

"So where does that leave us?"

"You know, I used to think that people who bailed out on a marriage were just quitters. But that's not true. Sometimes, the so-called quitters are really idealists. They know there's something better out there for them, and they have the courage to go out and look for it."

"You're ready for that?"

"After all these years together, I think the one thing we owe each other is honesty. Since we've been apart, I haven't had a single nightmare."

"What does that tell you?"

"The nightmares will never go away. Not unless . . ."

"Unless I go away," he said.

"I'm not trying to say it's anyone's fault. It's just the way it is. Can you understand that?"

"I more than understand. I agree."

She gave a weak smile, as if relieved to see that he wasn't going to put up a fight. "That's all I wanted to say," she said.

"So, this is it?"

She nodded. "I should go."

She rose, but he didn't.

"Cindy?"

She stopped and looked at him. "Yes?"

"There's one thing I need to know."

"What is it?"

"Did you think something was going on between me and Jessie even before she called and told you there was?"

"What makes you ask that?"

"For months now, I've been trying to put a timeline together in my head. As best I can figure, Jessie came to me and said that the viatical investors found out that she'd scammed them and were out to kill her. Then, after I didn't help her, she called you and said we were having an affair."

"That's right."

"So, I just wonder: How did the viatical investors find out Jessie had scammed them?"

"Someone obviously told them."

"Yeah, but who?"

"Could have been anyone."

"Not really. There aren't that many possibilities. It wasn't me. It wasn't Jessie. It wasn't Dr. Marsh. Just makes me stop and think: Maybe it was someone I confided in."

She showed almost no reaction, just a subtle rise of the left eyebrow. "That's something you may never know," she said, then turned and started away.

He downed his drink and took solace in the knowledge that he had a little something to counterbalance it all. In a way, it was Cindy who'd started the whole Jessie mess.

"Cindy," he called again.

She stopped, this time seeming a little annoyed. "What now?"

"There's something else that's bothering me."

"If you've got something to say, just say it."

"All right, I will. This is going to sound weird, because your mother has confessed and is sitting in jail. But the idea that she killed Jessie doesn't ring completely true to me."

She made a face, incredulous. "What?"

"Maybe it's because I'm a criminal lawyer, but motives are a bit of an obsession for me. Your mother's don't quite add up in my mind. What she wanted more than anything was for you to find the courage to leave me. Killing Jessie wouldn't necessarily have accomplished that. But your finding her passed out naked in our bathtub might."

Cindy didn't answer.

"Is that how you found her, Cindy? After your mother went to our house and forced her to drink so much that she passed out, was Jessie still alive?"

She flinched a little, virtually unnoticeable to anyone

who didn't know her as well as Jack did. But he definitely caught it.

She said, "What about the angle of the cut on her wrist? That was your whole theory, that someone who was left-handed cut her wrist to make it look like suicide."

"That sounded like a neat idea at the time. But the angle wasn't that pronounced. I was having second thoughts about it even before I accused your mother, when Rosa and I talked that morning before Katrina showed up at our house. The medical examiner didn't put any stock in it at all. Your mother wouldn't have spent a day in jail without a confession."

"But there was still an angle, and my mother is left-handed."

"It isn't foolproof. The killer could have been in a hurry. Maybe she was even enraged, filled with jealousy. There's no telling what angle the slash might take in those circumstances."

"Exactly what is it you're trying to say, Jack?"

"It's an idea that's been floating around in my head the last six months. I'm just trying to go back in time, trying to understand the mind-set. For your own good, your mother is desperate for you to find the courage to leave me and start a new life with no nightmares, no reminders of Esteban. She's so desperate that she finally does something that she hopes will utterly shock you. Instead of shocking you into leaving me, she pushes you into a crime of passion. At the end of the day, she takes the rap for Jessie's murder. After all, it was her plan that went awry."

"So who do you think slashed up our wedding photos? Me?"

"No. That was definitely your mother's work. But she was hoping you'd think it was Jessie who'd done it.

Mom's way of making you feel a little less guilty about having killed my old girlfriend."

"Do you really believe my mother would do this for me?"

"You *were* the 'good' daughter, weren't you? The one who protected her husband's fine reputation long after your sister revealed the truth about him."

Her glare was ice-cold.

He looked into her eyes, searching. There was a time when he could have looked straight into her soul, but this time he saw nothing.

Finally, she answered. "Like I said before, Jack. Sometimes in life you just never know."

He stared at her, waiting for some sign of remorse.

"I deserve to know," he said.

"And I at least deserved a husband who played by the rules."

"Funny. Those were the exact words Jessie used to describe our marriage. Playing by the rules."

"How 'bout that."

"Yeah. How 'bout that."

"Good-bye, Jack."

He watched her turn and walk away. He kept a bead on the back of her head as she flowed with the crowd along the sidewalk. She was a half-block away when she disappeared amid the sea of bobbing and weaving pedestrians. He spotted her once more, then lost sight of her. For good.

●

It was Saturday night, and Jack escaped to Tobacco Road. When it came to broken spirits, there was no better salve than a dark club with live music and a bartender who'd never been stumped by a customer's request for a cocktail. The really beautiful thing about the Road was the lack of beauty—no glitz, no palm trees at the door, no neon lights of South Beach. It was just a great bar by the river that catered to everyone from Brickell Avenue bankers to the likes of Theo Knight.

"Hey, Jacko, you came." Theo threw his arms around him, practically wrestled him off his bar stool.

"Of course I came. Why wouldn't I?"

"Oh, I don't know. Possibly because the only thing worse than having no date on a Saturday night is watching your old pal Theo blow on his saxophone and fight off hordes of groupies."

Jack looked around, spotted a woman at a table who looked as though she'd been there since last weekend. "I can live with it."

Theo laughed, then turned serious. "How you been, man?"

"Okay."

"Hey, I hear Benno Jancowitz is leaving the state attorney's office."

"I heard the same thing," said Jack. "Guess he got tired of prosecuting parking tickets."

"That blowhard deserved a demotion. I mean, it's one thing to go after the son of a beloved former governor. But if you're gonna indict an upstanding character like Theo Knight, you better be damn sure you're right."

Jack chuckled, though evidently not hard enough to suit Theo.

"You sure you okay, Jacko?"

"Fine."

He laid a huge hand on Jack's shoulder, as if to console. "Sorry about you and Cindy, man."

"Don't be. It was over for a long time. Now it's just official."

Theo gave a nod, as if promising never to bring it up again, then ordered himself a club soda. "Hey, there's someone I want you to see."

"Please, don't start setting me up already. I just want to have a couple drinks and listen to music. When's your set starting?"

"Five minutes. But I'm serious. I got someone who's dying to talk to you."

He was about to protest, but Theo had already signaled to the other side of the bar. Two women started through the crowd, and at least from a distance it appeared that his friend Theo was doing him quite the favor. One was wearing black leather pants and a fitted red blouse, and Jack wasn't the only man watching her cross the room. The other was equally striking. He was beginning to think that this single life wasn't going to be such a bad thing, until he got a good look at the tall brunette. Not that she wasn't attractive. He was simply taken aback.

"Katrina?"

"Hello, Jack."

Last Jack had heard, Katrina had helped the feds piece together computer records from Viatical Solutions, Inc., and identify more than a dozen *Mafiya*-controlled viatical companies, thereby preventing any further suspicious deaths and expedited payoffs. With both Yuri and Vladimir dead, however, the focus of the overall money-laundering investigation had shifted elsewhere, taking Katrina off the hook. It was evident to Jack that she'd resolved to return to a normal life.

Katrina said, "This is my friend Alicia."

Jack looked at Theo and said, "What's going on here?"

"I just thought you and Katrina should get to know each other better. Especially since, you know, she and I have become such good friends." He put his arm around her, pulled her close. They were suddenly making eyes at one other.

"You mean you two are . . ."

"Does this surprise you?"

"No, no. Not at all. What better way to start a relationship than by putting a gun to a man's head and kidnapping him?"

"She saved my life."

"Technically, yes. But wasn't it a little bit like setting your house on fire and then calling the fire department?"

Katrina's friend said something to her in Spanish. Jack knew it wasn't intended for his WASPy ears, but he understood every word. For effect, he answered her in Spanish. "You're right, Alicia. I'm no Brad Pitt. But once you get to know me, I usually turn out to be slightly smaller than the biggest asshole you've ever met."

Her shock was evident. "Wow. Your Spanish is really good."

"His mother was Cuban," said Theo.

"Wow. Your Spanish really—"

"I know, I know. It sucks."

The way he'd said it, it was clear that he'd been through that routine a thousand times. The reaction was delayed, but finally the four of them shared a little laugh. The ice had broken.

Katrina said, "Can I buy you a drink, Swyteck?"

Jack thought for a minute, then smiled. "What the heck."

Theo's band was tuning up on stage. "My gig's up. Time for me to blow."

"Just a sec," said Jack. "How about playing that Donald Byrd song for me. You know. The one from the album, *Thank you for . . .*"

"Fucking up my life?"

"That's the one."

The threesome laughed, to the exclusion of Katrina's friend. They alone knew that it was the album Jack had requested when Katrina was holding Theo hostage.

"I'll play it," said Theo. "But only if you promise not to make it your theme song."

"Just this one last time, and that'll be it."

"Then what?"

"Who knows?"

"That's such a great thing, isn't it? If you ask me, it's the only way you know you're alive."

"What?"

"The fact that you just never know."

Jack wasn't quite sure what he meant.

"I'm right, ain't I?" Theo said with a wink. Then he grabbed his saxophone and ran to the stage.

Jack still didn't get it, until Theo took center stage and drilled them with the sax, an overly sharp note worthy of Kenny G. He glanced at Katrina, this gorgeous woman with her eyes locked on Theo. At that moment, on some level, it all made incredible sense to him.

He smiled and thought, *You're exactly right, buddy. You just never know.*

Watch for

# LAST TO DIE

## by James Grippando

available in hardcover
from HarperCollins*Publishers*

The rainstorm was blinding, and Sally was way behind schedule. She hadn't intended to be late, fashionably or otherwise. She just wasn't good with directions, and this wasn't exactly her neck of the woods.

Sheets of water pelted the windshield, sounding like marbles bouncing off glass. She adjusted the wipers, but they were already working at full speed. She couldn't remember rain like this in years, not since she and her first husband lost their restaurant to that no-name tropical storm.

Orange taillights flashed ahead. A stream of cars was inching down the highway at the speed of cooling lava. She slowed to somewhere below the school-zone limit, then checked her watch. Eleven-twenty-five.

*Damn.* He'd just have to wait. She'd get there, eventually.

Their meeting had been arranged by telephone. They'd spoken only once, and his instructions were simple enough. Thursday, 11 p.m. Don't be late. She didn't dare reschedule, not even in this weather. This was her man. She was sure of it.

Just ahead, a neon sign blinked erratically, as if shaken by the storm. It was like trying to read an eye chart at the bottom of a lake, and she could only make out part of it: S-P-something-something-K-Y-apostrophe-S.

"Sparky's," she read aloud. This was the place. She steered off the highway and pulled into the flooded parking lot. Under all this water, she could only guess as to the exact location of the parking spot. She killed the engine and checked her face in the rearview mirror. Lightning flashed—a close one. It lit up the inside of her car and unleashed a crack of thunder that sent shivers down her spine. It frightened her, then triggered a bemused smile. How ironic would that have been? After all this planning, to get hit by lightning.

She took a deep breath and exhaled. *No turning back now. Just go for it.*

She jumped down from the car and started her mad dash across the parking lot in the pouring rain. Almost immediately a blast of wind snatched her umbrella from her hand and pitched it somewhere into the next county. Wearing no coat, she covered her head with her hands and just kept running, splashing with each footfall. In a matter of seconds she reached the door, soaked to her undergarments, her wet jeans and white blouse pasted to her body.

A musclebound guy wearing a Gold's Gym T-shirt was standing at the entrance, and he opened the door for her. "Wet T-shirt contest's not till tomorrow, lady."

"You wish," she said, then headed straight to the restroom to see if she could dry off. She looked in the mirror and gasped. Her nipples were staring back at her, right through her bra and wet blouse.

*Good god!*

She punched the hand-dryer, hoping for hot air. Nothing. She tried again, and again, but to no avail. She reached for a paper towel, but the dispenser was empty. Toilet paper would have to do. She went to the stall, found a loose roll atop the tank, and proceeded to dab furiously from head to foot. It was single-ply paper, not terribly absorbent. She went through the entire roll. She exited the stall, took another look at her reflection in the mirror, and gasped even louder this time. Her entire body was covered with shredded remnants of cheap toilet paper.

*You look like a milkweed.*

She started laughing, not sure why. She laughed so hard it almost hurt. Then, with her hands braced on the edge of the sink, she leaned forward and hung her head. She could feel her emotional energy drifting up to that ever-present knot of tension at the base of her skull. Her shoulders started to heave, and the laughter turned to tears. She fought it off and quickly regained her composure.

"You are a total wreck," she said to her reflection.

She brushed off as much of the toilet paper as she could, fixed her makeup, and said the hell with it. Nothing was going to stop this meeting from happening. She took a deep breath for courage and exited into the bar.

The crowd surprised her, not so much its makeup, which was about what she'd expected, but more the simple fact that there was such a big crowd on a nasty night like this. A group of truckers was playing blackjack by the juke box. Leather-clad bikers and their dyed-blond girlfriends had a monopoly on the pool table, as if waiting out the storm. T-shirts, jeans, and flannel shirts seemed to be the dress code for a seat at the bar. These folks were hardcore, and this was clearly a place that depended on its regulars.

"Can I help you, miss?" the bartender asked.

"Not just yet, thanks. I'm looking for someone."

"Yeah? Who?"

Sally hesitated, not exactly sure how to answer that. "Just, uh, sort of a blind date."

"That must be Jimmy," said one of the men at the bar.

The others laughed. Sally smiled awkwardly, the inside joke completely lost on her. The bartender explained, "Jimmy's the umpire in our softball league. They don't come any blinder."

"Ah, I get it," she said. They laughed again at this Jimmy's expense. Sally broke away and continued across the bar before their interest could return to the lost girl in the wet clothes. Her gaze fixed on the third booth from the back, near the broken air-hockey table. A black guy with penetrating eyes and no smile was staring back at her. He was wearing a dark blue shirt with black pants, which made Sally smile to herself. Never before had she laid eyes on him, but his look and those clothes were exactly what he'd described over the telephone. It was him.

She walked toward the booth and said, "I'm Sally."

"I know."

"How'd you—" she started to ask, then stopped. There wasn't a woman in the joint who looked like her.

"Have a seat," he said.

She slid into the booth and sat across from him. "Sorry I'm late. Raining like crazy."

He reached across the table and plucked a shred of toilet paper from her sleeve. "What's it raining now, fake snow?"

"That's toilet paper."

He raised an eyebrow.

"Long story," she said. "It was all over me. Five minutes ago I looked like a milkweed."

"With breasts."

She folded her arms across her chest. "Yes, well. Some things can't be helped."

"You want something to drink?"

"No, thank you."

He swirled the ice cubes around in his half-empty glass. Rum and Coke, she guessed, since that was the special of the night. The Coke looked completely flat, about what she expected from Sparky's.

"I watched you drive up," he said. "Nice car."

"If you like cars."

"I do. From the looks of things, you do, too."

"Not really. My husband did."

"You mean your second husband or your first?"

She shifted uncomfortably. They hadn't discussed her marital status on the telephone. "My second."

"The French one?"

"What did you do, check up on me?"

"I check on all my clients."

"I'm not your client yet."

"You will be. Rarely do the ones who look like you come this far and back down."

"How do you mean, look like me?"

"Young. Rich. Gorgeous. Pissed off."

"You call this gorgeous?"

"I'm assuming this isn't your best look."

"Fair assumption."

"What about the pissed off part. That fair, too?"

"I'm not really pissed off."

"Then what are you?"

"I don't see how my feelings are at all relevant. The only thing that matters is whether you want to do business, Mr.—whatever your name is."

"You can call me Tatum."

"That your name?"

"Nickname."

"Like Tatum O'Neil?"

He grimaced, sucking down his drink. "No, not like fucking Tatum O'Neil. Tatum like Jack Tatum."

"Who's Jack Tatum?"

"Meanest football player that ever lived. Defensive back, Oakland Raiders. He's the guy who popped Darryl Stingley and turned him quadriplegic. They used to call him Assassin. Hell, he liked to call himself Assassin."

"Is that what you call yourself, too? Assassin?"

He leaned into the table, his expression turning very serious. "Isn't that why you're here?"

She was about to answer, but the bartender was suddenly standing beside their booth. He glared at Sally and said, "What you meetin' with this guy for?"

"Excuse me?" she said.

"This piece of dirt sittin' on the other side of the table. What you meetin' with him for?"

She looked at Tatum, then back at the bartender. "That's really none of your business."

"This is my bar. It's definitely my business."

Tatum spoke up. "Theo, just put a cork in it, will you?"

"I want you out of here."

"Ain't finished my drink yet."

"You got five minutes," said Theo. "Then be gone." He turned and walked back to his place behind the bar.

"What's with him?" asked Sally.

"Tight ass. Guy finds some lawyer to get him off death row, thinks he's better'n everyone else."

"You don't think he knows what we're here talking about, do you?"

"Hell no. He probably thinks I'm pimping you."

Her rain-soaked blouse suddenly felt even more clingy. "I guess I brought that on myself."

"Never mind him. Let's cut the crap and get down to it."

"I didn't bring any money."

"Naturally. I didn't give you a price yet."

"How much is it going to be?"

"Depends."

"On what?"

"How complicated the job is."

"What do you need to know?"

"For starters, what exactly do you want? Two broken ribs? A concussion? Stitches? Mess with his face, don't mess with his face? I can put the guy in the hospital for a month, if you want."

"I want more than that."

"More?"

She looked one way, then the other, as if to make sure they were alone. "I want this person dead."

Tatum didn't answer.

She said, "How much for that?"

He burrowed his tongue into his cheek, thinking, as if sizing her up all over again. "That depends, too."

"On what?"

"Well, who's your target?"

She lowered her eyes, then looked straight at him. "You're not going to believe it."

"Try me."

She almost chuckled, then shook it off. "I'm way serious. You are *really* not going to believe it."

•

Her day had finally arrived.

Sally felt a rush of adrenaline as she sat at her kitchen table enjoying her morning coffee. No cream, two packs of artificial sweetener. A toasted plain bagel with no butter or cream cheese, just a side of raspberry preserves that went untouched. A small glass of juice, fresh-squeezed from the pink grapefruit that her gardener had handpicked from the tree in her backyard. It was her usual weekday breakfast, and today was to be no different from any other.

Except that today, she knew, would change everything.

"More coffee, ma'am?" asked Dinah, her live-in domestic.

"No, thank you." She laid her newspaper aside and headed upstairs to the bedroom. The house had two large master suites on the second story. Hers was on the east side, facing the bay, decorated in an airy, British Colonial style that was reminiscent of the Caribbean Islands. His was on the west, a much darker room with wood-beamed ceilings and an African motif. Sally didn't like all the dead animals on the walls, so they used his room only when he wasn't abroad, which was about every other month for their entire eighteen months of marriage. The arrangement had lasted just long enough for her to reach the first financial milestone of an elaborate pre-nuptial agreement. Eighteen months equaled eighteen million dollars, plus the house—big money for Sally, chump change for Jean Luc Trudeau. Lucky for her, she had the foresight to take the eighteen million not in cash but in stock in her husband's company, which promptly went public and—*kaboom!*—she was suddenly worth forty-six million dollars. She could have earned another quarter-million for each additional month, and there were certainly worse men to be married to than Jean Luc. He was rich, successful, reasonably handsome, and plenty generous to his third and much younger wife. But Sally wasn't happy. People said she was never happy. She didn't apologize for that. She had her reasons.

Sally stepped into her dressing room, draped her robe over the back of a chair, and pulled on a pair of sheer panty hose. Naked from the waist up, she stood in silence before the three-angled mirror. Slowly, she raised both arms, her twenty-nine-year-old body seeming to defy the pull of gravity as she turned. In the full-length panel she saw it, still visible after all this time. A two-inch pink scar at the base of the rib cage. She felt it with the tips of her fingers, lightly at first, then touching more firmly, and finally pressing until it hurt, as if she were trying to stop the bleeding all over again. Years later, and it was still there. Cosmetic surgery could have hidden it, but that would only have destroyed her most important daily reminder that she had in fact survived the attack. Sadly, her first marriage had not survived.

Tragically, neither had her daughter.

"Anything to iron today, Miss Sally?"

Instinctively, she covered her breasts at the sound of a voice, but she was alone in the dressing room. Dinah was waiting on the other side of the closed door.

"I don't think so," she answered, pulling on her robe.

As the sound of Dinah's footsteps faded away, Sally opened the door and walked to the bathroom to fix her hair and makeup. She returned to the dressing room to select an outfit, which took longer than usual, as she wanted it to be just right. She settled on a basic blue

Chanel suit with a peach blouse and new Ferragamo shoes, finishing the look with a strand of pearls with matching earrings. Her platinum and diamond wedding band—two rows of stones for a total of four carats—felt like overkill, as always, but she wore it anyway. She thought she'd put it away for good with the divorce, but today it served a purpose.

She stepped back and took one last look in the mirror—a good, long look. For the first time in ages, she allowed herself a trace of a genuine smile.

*This is your day, girl.*

She grabbed her purse and headed downstairs, exiting through the front doors to the porte cochère, where her Mercedes convertible was parked and waiting with the top down. Her hair was secure in a French twist, but she nevertheless donned the Princess Grace look, a white scarf and dark sunglasses. She climbed behind the wheel, started the engine, and followed the brick driveway to the iron gate. It opened automatically, and she exited to the street.

She drove at a leisurely pace through her neighborhood, the warm south Florida sun on her face. It was a glorious day, even by Miami standards. Seventy degrees, relatively low humidity, a cloudless blue sky. Growing up as a girl, she'd always wanted to live in the Venetian Islands. They sat side-by-side in the bay, like giant stepping stones between the mainland and the larger island of Miami Beach proper. Homes on the waterfront were a boater's dream, many with drop-dead views of cruise ships in port and the colorful skyline of downtown Miami beyond. Technically speaking, it was her dream come true to have a nine-thousand-square-foot house in the midst of this urban paradise.

*Be careful what you wish for.*

Sally stopped to pay the toll, then continued across the Venetian Isle causeway. A couple of old Cuban men were fishing on the Miami side of the bridge, right beneath the sign that read "Absolutely No Fishing."

She was just north of downtown Miami, not exactly the safest part of town, but it was an area in transition. In the not-too-distant past, she would have driven miles out of her way to avoid cutting through here.

She crossed Biscayne Boulevard, made a couple of quick turns and stopped at the traffic light. The entrance ramp to the interstate was just ahead, the lone escape route to twelve east-west lanes perched directly above her. She could hear the expressway traffic, the steady drone of countless cars and noisy trucks echoing all around her. She usually timed her approach so that she could breeze through with no red lights, especially at night, but that wasn't always possible. Like clockwork, the homeless guys emerged from their cardboard homes beneath the on-ramp. Armed with dirty rags and plastic squirt bottles filled with dirty water, they seemed determined to clean the world's windshields. There were two of them. One came toward her, and the other went to the SUV in front of her.

The SUV burned rubber and ran the red light, leaving Sally alone at the intersection, just her and the window washers. It was mid-morning, but in the dark shadows it seemed like dusk. Interstate 395 and the ramps that fed into it crisscrossed overhead like concrete ribbons. Sally's window washer took a different strategy than the guy with the SUV, approaching not from the side but the front of the vehicle. She couldn't have run the red light without running over him.

"No thanks," she shouted.

He kept coming, smiling, taking aim with his squirt

bottle. The other washer returned to his home beneath the ramp, apparently having conceded the Mercedes to his competition.

"I said, 'No thanks.' "

He walked all the way up to the front of her car, standing close enough to snap off her hood ornament. Suddenly, the darkness seemed to break. They were surrounded by scattered beams of sunshine, as if the clouds had shifted just enough to allow patches of daylight to break through the crevices in the maze-like expressway overhead. The longest, brightest ray seemed to fix on her big diamond ring. It was sparkling like fireworks. On any other day, she might have discreetly slid her hand from atop the steering wheel and dropped it in her lap. But not today.

The man was still staring at her through the windshield. Then, slowly, he raised his arm and took aim, straight at her face. She waited for the stream of greasy water to hit the glass, but it didn't come. A moment later, she realized that he wasn't holding a squirt bottle.

She froze, her eyes fixed on the black hole at the end of the polished metal barrel. It lasted only a split second, but it was as if she were suddenly floating outside her own body, watching it unfold. In her mind's eye, she could see the flash of powder from the barrel, see the windshield shatter, see her head snapping back, her body slumping forward, and the spray of blood on the leather seats. She could even hear the horn blasting as her face hit the steering wheel and came to rest there. And for the second time in the same day, she saw herself smiling a genuine smile.

With the lonely crack of a revolver that echoed off concrete, her living nightmare was finally over.